OTHER TRANSLATIONS BY RICHARD PEVEAR
AND LARISSA VOLOKHONSKY

FYODOR DOSTOEVSKY
The Adolescent (2003)
The Idiot (2002)
Demons (1994)
Notes from Underground (1993)
Crime and Punishment (1992)
The Brothers Karamazov (1990)

NIKOLAI GOGOL
Dead Souls (1996)
The Collected Tales (1998)

ANTON CHEKHOV
The Complete Short Novels (2005)

LEO TOLSTOY
Anna Karenina (2003)

THE DOUBLE

AND

THE GAMBLER

THE DOUBLE

AND

THE GAMBLER

Fyodor Dostoevsky

Translated from the Russian by
RICHARD PEVEAR AND LARISSA VOLOKHONSKY

With an introduction by
RICHARD PEVEAR

VINTAGE CLASSICS
Vintage Books
A Division of Random House, Inc.
New York

FIRST VINTAGE CLASSICS EDITION, JANUARY 2007

Copyright © 2005 by Richard Pevear and Larissa Volokhonsky

The Library of Congress has cataloged the Everyman's Library edition as follows:
Dostoyevsky, Fyodor, 1821–1881.
[Dvoinik. English]
The double; and, the gambler / Fyodor Dostoyevsky; translated from the Russian
by Richard Pevear and Larissa Volokhonsky; with an introduction by Richard
Pevear.
p. cm.
1. Dostoyevsky, Fyodor, 1821–1881—Translations into English. I. Pevear, Richard,
1943–. II. Volokhonsky, Larissa. III. Dostoyevsky, Fyodor, 1821–1881. Igrok.
English. IV. Title: Gambler. V. Title.
PG 3326.D8 2005
891.73'3—dc22   2005040065

Vintage ISBN: 978-0-375-71901-1

Book design by Barbara de Wilde and Carol Devine Carson

www.vintagebooks.com

Printed in the United States of America
20   19   18   17

FYODOR DOSTOEVSKY

CONTENTS

INTRODUCTION

In my view, all Russians are that way, or are inclined to
be that way. If it's not roulette, it's something else like it.
                                        Mr. Astley in *The Gambler*

Dostoevsky knew the passion for gambling very well; he was
under its sway intermittently for some eight years, from his first
trip abroad in 1863, where he had beginner's luck at roulette
in Wiesbaden, until the spring of 1871, when he was again in
Wiesbaden and lost everything almost at once. At one point
during those years he even gambled away his young wife's
wedding ring. This last time, however, gripped by a sort of
mystical terror, he went running in search of the local Russian
priest, lost his way in the dark, and wound up not in front of
the Orthodox church but in front of a synagogue. There, for
whatever obscure reason, something decisive occurred. "It was
as though I had had cold water poured over me," he wrote to
his wife. "A great thing has been accomplished within me, a
vile fantasy that has *tormented* me for almost ten years has
vanished." And indeed he never gambled again.

For Dostoevsky, roulette was not only a means of getting
rich "suddenly, in two hours, without any work," as Alexei
Ivanovich, the narrator and hero of *The Gambler*, says, but also
"some defiance of fate, some desire to give it a flick, to stick
[his] tongue out at it." What fascinated him and possessed him
was the "poetry" of the game of chance, the look into the
abyss, the ultimate risk, a susceptibility that he saw as part of
the "unseemliness" of the Russian character. But for Dostoevsky, as for his hero, that unseemliness had its positive side
precisely in its impracticality; it was open to passion and to
the unforeseeable. "Perhaps I'm a dignified man," Alexei
Ivanovich says to Polina,

but I don't know how to behave with dignity. Do you understand
that it may be so? All Russians are that way, and you know why?
Because Russians are too richly and multifariously endowed to be
able to find a decent form for themselves very quickly. It's a matter

of form. For the most part, we Russians are so richly endowed that it takes genius for us to find a decent form. Well, but most often there is no genius ...

The problem of giving expression to this richly endowed but as yet unformed Russian character challenged Dostoevsky throughout his creative life. The old tutor Nikolai Semyonovich discusses it at the end of *The Adolescent* (Dostoevsky's penultimate novel, published in 1875), implicitly drawing a comparison with the work of Tolstoy. "Yes, Arkady Makarovich," he writes to the adolescent hero,

you are *a member of an accidental family*, as opposed to our still-recent hereditary types, who had a childhood and youth so different from yours. I confess, I would not wish to be a novelist whose hero comes from an accidental family! Thankless work and lacking in beautiful forms. And these types in any case are still a current matter, and therefore cannot be artistically finished.

Dostoevsky chose to be precisely that unenviable novelist. In 1863, when the idea of *The Gambler* first came to him, he wrote to his friend Nikolai Strakhov: "The subject of the story is ... a certain type of Russian abroad. Note: Russians abroad were a big topic in the newspapers this summer. All this will be reflected in my story. And also in general it will reflect the contemporary moment (as much as possible, of course) of our inner life." Dostoevsky constantly tried to capture that "contemporary moment" or "current matter" which had not yet found expression. That is one of his most distinctive qualities as a writer. Five years later, after months of work on what would eventually become *The Idiot*, he wrote to another friend, the poet Apollon Maikov, about his idea of portraying "*a perfectly beautiful man* ... The idea flashed even earlier in some sort of artistic form, but only *some sort*, and what's needed is the full form. Only my desperate situation forced me to take up this as yet premature thought. I took a risk, as at roulette: 'Maybe it will develop as I write!' " The gambler's defiance of fate, the risk of embarking on the unforeseeable, thus becomes a metaphor for Dostoevsky's own artistic process.

The two short novels brought together here were both gambles, but of very different sorts and separated by a period of twenty years. The first, *The Double*, dates to 1845. Dostoevsky was then twenty-four years old and still intoxicated with the praise that had been showered on his first novel, *Poor Folk*, which had been finished in the spring of that year and shown in manuscript to the foremost critic of the day, Vissarion Belinsky. Thirty-two years later, in the January 1877 issue of his *Diary of a Writer*, Dostoevsky wrote of how Belinsky had summoned him a few days after that. Carried away with admiration, the fiery critic had cried out to him: "This is the mystery of art, this is the truth of art! This is the artist's service to truth! The truth is revealed and proclaimed to you as an artist, it has come as a gift. Value your gift, then, and remain faithful to it, and you will be a great writer!" Dostoevsky had left Belinsky, as he says, "in rapture."

I stopped at the corner of his house, looked at the sky, at the bright day, at the people passing by, and felt with my whole being that a solemn moment had occurred in my life, a break forever, that something altogether new had begun, something I had not anticipated even in my most passionate dreams...I recall that moment with the fullest clarity. And afterwards I could never forget it. It was the most ravishing moment of my whole life. When I was at hard labor, remembering it strengthened me spiritually. Even now I am ecstatic each time I remember it.

Belinsky had urged him to "remain faithful" to his gift. Another writer might have heeded that advice and continued on the successful path of portraying ordinary people in a sentimental manner and, as Konstantin Mochulsky put it, with "a humanistic-philanthropic tendency ('the humblest person is also a man')." Instead, Dostoevsky wrote *The Double*.

Poor Folk was published on January 15, 1846, in the *Petersburg Almanac*, edited by the poet Nikolai Nekrasov, who had originally brought the manuscript to Belinsky. *The Double*, which Dostoevsky had begun during the summer of 1845, was published two weeks later, on January 30, 1846, in the journal *Notes of the Fatherland*. The closeness in time belies the great difference between them. Belinsky was reserved when Dostoevsky read several chapters from *The Double* at a soirée in his apartment, to which a number of well-known critics and writers, among them Ivan Turgenev, were invited. In the February 1846 issue of *Notes of the Fatherland*, along with praise, he allowed himself some criticism of the novel's prolixity. Other critics were harsher, accusing Dostoevsky of paraphrasing or even plagiarizing Nikolai Gogol's "Diary of a Madman" or of making a hodgepodge of Gogol, E. T. A. Hoffmann, and other lesser-known writers. Above all, *The Double* seemed a betrayal of the "realism" to which Belinsky and his followers were devoted, and which they found so satisfyingly embodied in *Poor Folk*. "We certainly were hoodwinked, my friend, with Dostoevsky the genius," Belinsky wrote later to the eminent critic Pavel Annenkov. The striking originality of *The Double* passed them by. But its publication was enough to marginalize Dostoevsky in Russian literature for many years to come, an exacerbation that may have driven him towards radical politics, ending in his arrest in April 1849 and his mock execution eight months later, followed by ten years of hard labor and Siberian exile. This first gamble was an artistic one, and it cost him dearly.

In the evening of the day he handed the manuscript of *Poor Folk* to Nekrasov, Dostoevsky went to visit a former friend. As he recalled in the same January 1877 issue of *Diary of a Writer*: "We spent the whole night talking about *Dead Souls* and reading from it, as we had done I don't remember how many times. That happened then among young people; two or three would get together: 'Well, gentlemen, let's read Gogol!'—and they might sit and read all night." We tend to forget that Gogol's greatest works, "The Overcoat" and the first part of *Dead Souls*, were published only three years before the moment Dostoevsky describes here and still dominated the literary scene. Gogol's fantastic Petersburg, his world of government clerks, offices, and the table of ranks, of nonentities and impostors, is everywhere present in Dostoevsky's early work. In fact, Dostoevsky's dialogue/struggle with Gogol went on throughout his life. But *The Double* is specifically and quite obviously an expansion on "The Diary of a Madman" and "The Nose." It represents not a plagiarism or imitation, but a "rethinking of Gogol," as Mochulsky observed. What did this "rethinking" involve?

In the autumn of 1845, Dostoevsky wrote to his brother Mikhail about *The Double*, not quoting from the novel but describing his work on it in the voice of its hero, the titular councillor Yakov Petrovich Goliadkin:

Yakov Petrovich Goliadkin upholds his character fully. A terrible scoundrel, you can't get at him. He simply doesn't want to go ahead, claiming that he's just not ready yet, and that meanwhile he's his own man now, that he's never mind, maybe also, and why not, how come not; why, he's just like everybody else, only he's like himself, but then just like everybody else! What is it to him! A scoundrel, a terrible scoundrel! Before the middle of November, there's no way he can agree to end his career.

Goliadkin, as Mochulsky noted, "emerges and grows out of the verbal element. The writer had first to assimilate his character's intonations, to speak him through himself, to penetrate the rhythm of his sentences and the peculiarities of his vocabulary, and only then could he see his face. Dostoevsky's characters are born of speech—such is the general law of his creative work." In Gogol, with the one exception of "The Diary of a Madman," the verbal element is the narrator's voice, not the character's. Gogol's characters are entirely objectified, like parts of nature, pure products of the narrator's words about them; they have no consciousness, and that, in fact, is what makes them so remarkable. For Dostoevsky, on the other hand, consciousness is the central issue: the narrator's speech in *The Double* is a projection of and dialogue with Goliadkin's consciousness; we are given no outside position from which to view him. "Even in the earliest 'Gogolian period' of his literary career," Mikhail Bakhtin observed,

Dostoevsky is already depicting not the "poor government clerk" but the *self-consciousness* of the poor clerk... That which was presented in Gogol's field of vision as an aggregate of objective features, coalescing in a firm socio-characterological profile of the hero, is introduced by Dostoevsky into the field of vision of the hero himself and there becomes the object of his agonizing self-awareness.

This was the "small-scale Copernican revolution," in Bakhtin's phrase, that Dostoevsky carried out "when he took what had been a firm and finalizing authorial definition and turned it into an aspect of the hero's self-definition." The failure to grasp the major implications of this shift in artistic visualization probably accounts for the critical incomprehension that greeted *The Double*.

The disintegration, the inner plurality, of isolated consciousness that Dostoevsky first explored through Mr. Goliadkin remained a constant theme of his work. Many years later, he wrote that he had "never given anything more serious to literature" than the idea of *The Double*. Mr. Goliadkin is the precursor of the man from underground, of Velchaninov in *The Eternal Husband*, of Stavrogin in *Demons*, of Versilov in *The Adolescent*, and finally, most tellingly, of Ivan Karamazov. The notion that *The Double* is an exploration of the abnormal and pathological, the description of a man going mad, is mistaken (though Otto Rank, in his *Don Juan, A Study of the Double*, found in it "an unsurpassed clinical exactitude"). Dostoevsky was concerned here, as everywhere, with penetrating into the depths of the *normal* human soul, but by means of an extreme case and a bold device—the "literal" splitting of his hero into two Goliadkins. The attempt to determine whether Mr. Goliadkin Jr. is a flesh-and-blood double or a fantasy provoked by the "persecution mania" of Mr. Goliadkin Sr. runs into a host of difficulties as we follow the various turns of the story. Dostoevsky deliberately leaves the boundary between fantasy and reality undetermined. The whole novel thus becomes an embodiment not only of psychological but of ontological instability.

The Double was the first expression of Dostoevsky's genius, prefiguring his later work in a way not to be found in anything else he wrote in those years or even in the first years after his return from exile in 1860. In a letter to his brother in 1859, he spoke of his plans to rewrite it: "In short, I'm challenging them all to battle, and, finally, if I don't rewrite *The Double* now, when will I rewrite it? Why should I lose an excellent idea, a type of the greatest social importance, which I was the first to discover, of which I was the herald?" But nothing came of it. For the three-volume edition of his collected works published in 1865 by the bookseller F. T. Stellovsky, he simply abridged the text (that is the version translated here) and supplied it with a new subtitle, "A Petersburg Poem." It was only with *Notes from Underground*, published in 1864, that he returned to the "idea" of *The Double*, not to rewrite it but to re-create it with incomparably more human experience and artistic skill.

Notes from Underground opened the way for the five great novels on which Dostoevsky's fame chiefly rests. In their shade, however, lie some smaller works of a rare formal perfection, more concentrated and at times more penetrating than the major novels, works such as *The Eternal Husband*, "The Meek One," and "The Dream of a Ridiculous Man." *The Gambler* belongs to their number.

The chance Dostoevsky took in writing *The Gambler* was not an artistic one; the risk was all too mundane, but the reward was quite unexpected. The deaths of his first wife and of his beloved brother Mikhail in 1864 had left Dostoevsky heavily in debt. Stellovsky, an unscrupulous "literary speculator," in Mochulsky's words, approached him with the offer of a flat fee of two thousand roubles, without royalties, for an edition of his collected works. Dostoevsky refused, but in the end he had no one else to turn to. The terms of Stellovsky's second offer were stiffer than the first. For three thousand roubles he bought the rights to publish a three-volume edition of Dostoevsky's complete works, and demanded in addition to that a new novel, ten printer's sheets in length, to be delivered to him by November 1, 1866. The agreement further stipulated that if the manuscript was not delivered on time, Stellovsky would become the owner not only of Dostoevsky's existing works but of all he would write for the next nine years.

Meanwhile, Dostoevsky also reached an agreement with the publisher Mikhail Katkov for another work he had in mind. He originally conceived it as a novella, but it eventually grew into *Crime and Punishment*. Work on it absorbed him completely. The first two parts appeared in 1866, in the January and February issues of Katkov's journal, *The Russian Messenger*. The critical response was enthusiastic, encouraging Dostoevsky to continue working on it through the spring and summer. In July, realizing that he was in trouble, he decided to divide his working day in two, writing *Crime and Punishment* in the mornings and the novel for Stellovsky in the evenings. But by the end of September he had still not written a line of the other book. "Stellovsky upsets me to the point of torture," he told his old friend Alexander Milyukov, "I even see him in my dreams." Milyukov suggested that he hire a stenographer and made the arrangements himself. On October 4, 1866, a young woman named Anna Grigoryevna Snitkina came to Dostoevsky's door. She was the best stenography student in the first secretarial school in Petersburg. He dropped work on *Crime and Punishment* and began dictating *The Gambler* to her. On October 29, the novel was finished. Anna Grigoryevna brought him the copied-out manuscript the next day for final corrections, and on November 1, Dostoevsky went to deliver it to Stellovsky. The bookseller was not at home, and his assistant refused to accept responsibility for receiving it. At ten o'clock in the evening, he left the manuscript with the district police officer, who gave him a dated receipt for it. To Stellovsky's undoubted dismay, Dostoevsky had won. A week later, he proposed to his stenographer and was accepted.

Dostoevsky first conceived of *The Gambler* as a short story about "Russians abroad." It is, as Joseph Frank rightly points out,

the only work of Dostoevsky's that is "international" in the sense of that word made familiar by, for example, the fiction of Henry James. It is, in other words, a story in which the psychology and conflicts of the characters not only arise from their individual temperaments and personal qualities but also reflect an interiorization of various national values and ways of life.

The Gambler, Frank concludes, is "a spirited but by no means uncritical meditation on the waywardness of the Russian national temperament." That waywardness is dramatized in its contrasts with the French, who are all external form and thus perfect deceivers, and the Germans, who are stolid "savers" and "so honest it's even frightening to go near them." The one Englishman in the novel, Mr. Astley, is a personally noble and virtuous man, but of limited imagination. He is "in sugar," as the narrator observes. The Russian is none of these things, and that is so not only of the narrator-hero, Alexei Ivanovich, but of his employer, the retired General Zagoryansky, of the general's stepdaughter, Polina, and even of the seventy-five-year-old Russian matriarch whom everyone refers to simply as "grandmother"—a superbly comic and contradictory portrait of the old landowning aristocracy.

Dostoevsky had gone abroad in 1863 not only to try his hand at gambling but to join a young woman by the name of Apollinaria (Polina) Suslova, a twenty-year-old writer who had become his mistress and soon became his tormentor. The milieu of Roulettenburg, the name of the heroine, and her "love/hate" relations with Alexei Ivanovich have led commentators to an autobiographical reading of *The Gambler* that is not borne out by the novel itself. There is certainly much of Dostoevsky's personal experience behind it, in the relations of eros and roulette, but the unexpected ending shows us a Polina who has little in common with Suslova, and there is above all the character of the narrator himself, who is far from being a disguised self-portrait of the author.

Alexei Ivanovich is twenty-four years old, of noble birth but no fortune, employed as a tutor in the general's household. He is also an amateur writer, who is struggling to understand himself and what has happened to him by writing it down. The nameless narrator of *Notes from Underground* is also an amateur writer engaged in the same struggle, as is Arkady Dolgoruky, the narrator-hero of *The Adolescent*. The man from underground is forty years old; Arkady Dolgoruky is going on twenty (Alyosha Karamazov, the hero of *The Brothers Karamazov*, is also twenty). We might say, then, that in the development of Dostoevsky's later work, adolescence is the goal, and Alexei Ivanovich is well on his way to it.

But what drew Dostoevsky to these young protagonists? The Russian émigré thinker Vladimir Weidlé suggests an answer in his magisterial inquiry into the destiny of modern art, *Les abeilles d'Aristée* ("The Bees of Aristaeus"). He speaks of the need "to find for the work of literature, and first of all for the novel, a vital ambiance that does not force it into the mechanization of processes and the rapid drying-up of imagination." Hence we see novelists choosing adolescents as heroes,

or at least young people who do not yet have an entirely fixed and stable personality or an exactly circumscribed place in society. These people, who are not yet caught up in their destiny, can change, can choose, can imagine an unlimited future. It is only with such characters that one can succeed in realizing that thing which has become so infrequent in the novel today and which is designated by a familiar but rarely understood word: adventure.

"Adventure is what advenes, that is, what is added on, what comes into the bargain, what you were not expecting, what you could have done without. An adventure novel is an account of events that are not contained in each other." Such is the admirable definition formulated by Jacques Rivière in one of his finest critical essays.

Even if it becomes explicable by what follows, says Weidlé, the true adventure "must always appear to us first of all as free and unexpected." That condition is what gives inner unity to Dostoevsky's world, from the misadventures of Alexei Ivanovich in Roulettenburg to Alyosha Karamazov's vision of the messianic banquet. For Dostoevsky, it is not the finished man, sculpted by the hand of destiny, who embodies the highest human truth, but the unfinished man, who remains open to what can only ever be freely and unexpectedly given.

Richard Pevear

Russian names are composed of first name, patronymic (from the father's first name), and last name. Formal address requires the use of first name and patronymic. Diminutives are commonly used among family and intimate friends; they have two forms, the casual and the endearing (Pyotr becomes Petrushka or Petrusha). Servants are sometimes referred to by a spoken form of their patronymic (Alexeich, instead of Alexeevich).

The following is a list of the principal Russian names in the two short novels brought together here, with a guide to their accentuation.

The Double
Yákov Petróvich Goliádkin (Sr. and Jr.)
Pyótr (Petrúshka, Petrúsha; no patronymic or last name)
Krestyán Ivánovich Rútenspitz
Vladímir Semyónovich (no last name)
Andréi Filíppovich (no last name)
Olsúfy Ivánovich Berendéev
Klára Olsúfyevna Berendéev
Antón Antónovich Sétochkin
Néstor Ignátievich Vakhreméev
Emelyán Gerásimovich (Gerásimych; no last name)
Iván Semyónovich (no last name)
Alexéich (no first name or last name)
Karolina Ivánovna (no last name)

The Gambler
Alexéi Ivánovich (no last name)
General Zagoryánsky (? or Zagoziánsky; no first name or patronymic)
Polína Alexándrovna (Mlle Pauline, Praskóvya; no last name)
Antonída Vassílyevna Tarassévichev (Grandmother, *la baboulinka*)
Potápych (no first or last name)

Approximate Values of Currencies Used in *The Gambler*

4 pfennigs = 1 kreuzer
60 kreuzer = 1 florin or 1 gulden
2 florins or guldens = 1 thaler
10 florins or guldens = 1 friedrich d'or

3 deniers = 1 liard
4 liards = 1 sol, or sou
20 sous = 1 livre
6 livres = 1 écu (silver)
4 écus = 1 louis d'or
1 livre 3 deniers = 1 franc

1 florin or gulden = 2 francs
1.5 florins or guldens = 1 rouble
1 friedrich d'or = 20 francs
1 louis d'or = 24 francs

THE DOUBLE
A Petersburg Poem

CHAPTER I

IT WAS NEARLY eight o'clock in the morning when the titular councillor[1] Yakov Petrovich Goliadkin came to after a long sleep, yawned, stretched, and finally opened his eyes all the way. For some two minutes, however, he lay motionless on his bed, like a man who is not fully certain whether he is awake or still asleep, whether what is happening around him now is a reality or a continuation of the disordered reveries of his sleep. Soon, though, Mr. Goliadkin's senses began to receive their usual everyday impressions more clearly and distinctly. The dirtyish green, sooty, and dusty walls of his little room, his mahogany chest of drawers, the imitation mahogany chairs, the red-painted table, the oilcloth Turkish sofa of a reddish color with little green flowers, and finally his clothes, hastily taken off the night before and thrown in a heap on the sofa, all gazed at him familiarly. Finally, the gray autumn day, dull and dirty, peeked into his room through the dim window so crossly and with such a sour grimace that Mr. Goliadkin could in no way doubt any longer that he was not in some far-off kingdom but in the city of Petersburg, in the capital, on Shestilavochnaya Street, on the fourth floor of a quite large tenement house, in his own apartment. Having made this important discovery, Mr. Goliadkin convulsively closed his eyes, as if regretting his recent dream and wishing to bring it back for a brief moment. But after a moment he leaped out of bed at a single bound, probably hitting finally upon the idea around which his scattered, not yet properly ordered thoughts had been turning. Having leaped out of bed, he ran at once to the small round mirror that stood on the chest of drawers. Though the sleepy, myopic, and rather bald-pated figure reflected in the mirror was precisely of such insignificant quality as to arrest decidedly no one's exclusive attention at first sight, its owner evidently remained perfectly pleased with all he saw in the mirror. "What a thing it would be," Mr. Goliadkin said half-aloud, "what a thing it would be if something was amiss with me today, if, for instance, something went wrong—a stray pimple popped out somehow or some other sort of unpleasantness occurred; however, so far it's not bad; so far everything's going well." Very glad that everything was going well, Mr. Goliadkin put the mirror back in its former place, and, despite the fact that he was barefoot and still wearing the costume in which he was accustomed to go to bed, he rushed to the window and, with great concern, began searching with his eyes for something in the courtyard on which the windows of his apartment gave. Apparently whatever he was searching for in the yard also satisfied him completely; his face lit up with a self-satisfied smile. Then—though not without having first peeked behind the partition into the closet of his valet Petrushka and made sure that Petrushka was not in it— he tiptoed to the desk, unlocked one of the drawers, rummaged about in the hindmost corner of that drawer, finally took out a shabby green wallet from under some old yellow papers and trash, opened it warily, and peeked carefully and with delight into its remotest secret pocket. Probably a wad of green, gray, blue, red, and multicolored bits of paper looked back quite affably and approvingly at Mr. Goliadkin: with a beaming face he placed the opened wallet on the table before him and rubbed his hands energetically as a sign of the greatest pleasure. Finally he took it out, his comforting wad of banknotes, and for the hundredth time—that is, counting only from yesterday—began to re-count them, painstakingly rubbing each leaf between his thumb and index finger. "Seven hundred and fifty roubles in banknotes!" he finished finally in a half-whisper. "Seven hundred and fifty roubles...a significant sum! An agreeable sum," he went on in a voice trembling and slightly faint with pleasure, squeezing the wad in his hands and smiling significantly, "quite an agreeable sum! An agreeable sum for anyone! I'd like to see the man now for whom this sum would be negligible! A man can go far on such a sum..."

"What is this, though?" thought Mr. Goliadkin. "Where is

Petrushka?" Still wearing the same costume, he peeked once more behind the partition. Again Petrushka was not to be found behind the partition; there was only a samovar left on the floor there, angry, excited, and beside itself, constantly threatening to run away, and babbling to Mr. Goliadkin heatedly, quickly, in its abstruse language, lisping and swallowing its R's—probably saying something like, "Take me, good people, I'm perfectly ripe and ready."

"Devil take it!" thought Mr. Goliadkin. "The lazy brute may finally drive one beyond the last limits; where's he lolling about?" In righteous indignation he went to the front hall, which consisted of a small corridor at the end of which was the door to the vestibule, opened that door a crack, and saw his servitor surrounded by a decent-sized crowd of sundry lackeyish, domestic, and accidental riffraff. Petrushka was telling some story, the others were listening. Apparently Mr. Goliadkin liked neither the subject of the conversation nor the conversation itself. He immediately called Petrushka and went back to his room thoroughly displeased, even upset. "This brute is ready to sell a man for a groat, all the more so his master," he thought to himself, "and he did, he surely did, I'm ready to bet he sold me for a penny. Well, so? . . ."

"They've brought the livery, sir."

"Put it on and come here."

Having put on the livery, Petrushka, smiling stupidly, went to his master's room. He could not have been more oddly costumed. He was wearing extremely shabby green lackey's livery with frazzled gold braid, apparently made for someone a whole two feet taller than Petrushka. In his hands he was holding a hat, also with braid and with green feathers, and at his hip he had a lackey's sword in a leather scabbard.

Finally, to complete the picture, Petrushka, following his favorite habit of always going about casually, in home-style, was barefoot now as well. Mr. Goliadkin inspected Petrushka all around and apparently remained pleased. The livery had obviously been rented for some solemn occasion. It was also noticeable that during the inspection Petrushka looked at his master with some strange expectation, and followed his every movement with extraordinary curiosity, which greatly embarrassed Mr. Goliadkin.

"Well, and the carriage?"

"The carriage has come, too."

"For the whole day?"

"For the whole day. Twenty-five, in banknotes."[2]

"And they've brought the boots?"

"And they've brought the boots."

"Blockhead! Can't you say they've brought them, *sir*? Bring them here."

Having expressed his satisfaction that the boots fit well, Mr. Goliadkin asked for tea, a wash and a shave. He shaved rather painstakingly and washed in the same way, hastily sipped some tea, and proceeded to his main, definitive dressing: he put on almost perfectly new trousers; then a shirt front with little bronze buttons, a waistcoat with rather bright and agreeable little flowers; tied a multicolored silk cravat around his neck, and finally pulled on a uniform jacket, also spanking new and painstakingly brushed. While dressing, he glanced lovingly at his boots several times, lifted now one foot, now the other, admired the style, and kept whispering something under his nose, occasionally winking at his thoughts with an expressive little grimace. However, Mr. Goliadkin was extremely distracted that morning, because he let Petrushka's little smiles and grimaces on his account as he helped him dress go almost unnoticed. Finally, having adjusted everything properly, the fully dressed Mr. Goliadkin put his wallet in his pocket, definitively admired Petrushka, who had put on his boots and was thus in full readiness, and, noticing that everything had been done and there was nothing more to wait for, hastily, bustlingly, with little trepidations of the heart, ran down his stairs. A light blue hackney carriage with some coat-of-arms on it rolled up thunderingly to the porch. Petrushka, exchanging winks with the coachman and various idlers, seated his master in the carriage; in an unaccustomed voice and barely holding back his foolish laughter, he shouted: "Gee-up!" and jumped onto the tailboard, and the whole thing, with noise and thunder, jingling and clattering, rolled off towards Nevsky Prospect.[3] The blue carriage had no sooner driven through the gate than Mr. Goliadkin rubbed his hands convulsively and dissolved into quiet, inaudible laughter, like a man of merry character who has managed to play a nice trick and is as glad of it as glad can be. However, immediately following this fit of merriment, the laughter on Mr. Goliadkin's face changed to a strangely preoccupied expression. Though the weather was damp and gray, he lowered both windows of the carriage and began looking concernedly to right and left at passersby, immediately assuming a decent and decorous air as soon as he noticed someone looking at him. At the turn from Liteinaya onto Nevsky, he gave a start from a most unpleasant sensation and, wincing like some poor fellow whose corn has accidentally been stepped on, hastily and even fearfully pressed himself into the darkest corner of the carriage. The thing was that he had met two of his colleagues, two young clerks from the department where he himself worked. The clerks, as it seemed to Mr. Goliadkin, were for their own part also extremely perplexed at meeting their colleague in this fashion; one of them even pointed his finger at Mr. Goliadkin. It even seemed to Mr. Goliadkin that the other called him loudly by name, which, naturally, was quite an improper thing to do in the street. Our hero stayed hidden and did not respond. "Little brats!" he began to reason with himself. "Well, what's so strange? A man in a carriage; a man needs to be in a carriage, so he takes a carriage. Simply trash! I know them—they're simply brats who ought to be whipped! They only play pitch-and-toss on payday and mooch about somewhere, that's what they do. I could tell them all a thing or two, only..." Mr. Goliadkin did not finish and went dead. A brisk pair of pretty Kazan horses, quite familiar to Mr. Goliadkin, hitched to a jaunty droshky, was quickly passing his carriage on the right. The gentleman sitting in the droshky, chancing to see the face of Mr. Goliadkin, who quite imprudently stuck his head out the window of the carriage, was apparently also extremely amazed at such an unexpected encounter and, leaning out as far as he could, began peering with great curiosity and concern into the corner of the carriage, where our hero had hastened to hide. The gentleman in the droshky was Andrei Filippovich, head of an office in the place where Mr. Goliadkin also served in the quality of assistant to his section chief. Mr. Goliadkin, seeing that Andrei Filippovich recognized him perfectly well, was looking at him all eyes, and it was simply impossible to hide from him, blushed to the roots of his hair. "Should I bow or not? Should I respond or not? Should I acknowledge him or not?" our hero thought in indescribable anguish. "Or pretend it's not me but someone else strikingly resembling me, and look as if nothing has happened? Precisely not me, not me, and that's that!" Mr. Goliadkin said, tipping his hat to Andrei Filippovich and not taking his eyes off him. "I . . . I'm all right," he whispered with effort, "I'm quite all right, it's not me at all, Andrei Filippovich, it's not me at all, not me, and that's that." Soon, however, the droshky passed the carriage, and the magnetism of the directorial gaze ceased. However, he still kept blushing, smiling, muttering something to himself . . . "I was a fool not to respond," he thought finally, "I should simply have taken a bold footing and said frankly, but not without nobility, 'Thus and so, Andrei Filippovich, I'm also invited to dinner, and that's that!' " Then, suddenly remembering that he had flunked it, our hero flared up like fire, frowned, and cast a terrible, defiant glance into the front corner of the carriage, a glance intended to incinerate all his enemies to dust at a stroke. Finally, by some sudden inspiration, he pulled the cord tied to the coachman's elbow, stopped the carriage, and told the coachman to turn back to Liteinaya. The thing was that Mr. Goliadkin felt an immediate need, probably for the sake of his own peace of mind, to say something most interesting to his doctor, Krestyan Ivanovich. And though his acquaintance with Krestyan Ivanovich was quite recent— namely, he had visited him only once the previous week, owing to a certain necessity—a doctor, as they say, is the same as a father confessor, to hide would be stupid, and to know the patient was his duty. "Will all this be right, though?" our hero went on, stepping out of the carriage by the entrance to a five-story house on Liteinaya where he had ordered his equipage to stop, "will it all be right? Will it be decent? Will it be appropriate? So what, though," he went on, going up the stairs, trying to catch his breath and restrain the throbbing of his heart, which was in the habit of throbbing on other people's stairs, "so what? It's my own affair, and there's nothing reprehensible in it...It would be stupid to hide. So I'll make believe that I'm all right, and that I was just passing by...He'll see that it must be so."

Reasoning thus, Mr. Goliadkin reached the second floor and stopped in front of apartment number five, on the door of which hung a beautiful brass plaque with the inscription:

KRESTYAN IVANOVICH RUTENSPITZ
DOCTOR OF MEDICINE AND SURGERY

Stopping, our hero hastened to give his physiognomy a decent, casual air, not without a certain courtesy, and prepared to give the bell-pull a tug. Having prepared to give the bell-pull a tug, he immediately and rather appropriately reasoned that tomorrow would be better, and that now, for the time being, there was no great need. But, suddenly hearing someone's footsteps on the stairs, Mr. Goliadkin immediately changed his new resolve and, just by the way, though maintaining a most resolute air, rang at Krestyan Ivanovich's door.

CHAPTER II

Krestyan Ivanovich, doctor of medicine and surgery, quite hale, though already an elderly man, endowed with thick, graying eyebrows and side-whiskers, an expressive, flashing gaze that by itself apparently drove away all illnesses, and, finally, an important decoration, was sitting that morning in his office, in his easy chair, drinking coffee, brought to him with her own hands by his doctoress, smoking a cigar, and from time to time writing prescriptions for his patients. Having prescribed the last vial to a little old man suffering from hemorrhoids and sent the suffering old man off through the side door, Krestyan Ivanovich sat down in expectation of the next visitor. Mr. Goliadkin came in.

Apparently, Krestyan Ivanovich was not in the least expecting, nor did he wish to see, Mr. Goliadkin before him, because he suddenly became confused for a moment, and his face involuntarily acquired a sort of strange, even, one might say, displeased mien. Since Mr. Goliadkin, for his part, almost always became somehow inappropriately crestfallen and lost at those moments when he happened to abord someone for the sake of his own little affairs, so now, too, not having prepared a first phrase, which was a real stumbling block for him on such occasions, he became considerably embarrassed, murmured something—however, it seems to have been an apology—and, not knowing what to do next, took a chair and sat down. But, recollecting that he had sat down without being invited, he at once felt his impropriety and hastened to correct his error in ignorance of society and good tone by immediately getting up from the seat he had occupied without being invited. Then, thinking better of it and dimly noting that he had done two stupid things at once, he ventured, without the least delay, upon a third, that is, he tried to excuse himself, murmured something, smiled, blushed, became embarrassed, fell into an expressive silence, and finally sat down definitively and did not get up anymore, but only provided himself, just in case, with that same defiant gaze, which possessed the extraordinary power of mentally incinerating and grinding to dust all of Mr. Goliadkin's enemies. Moreover, this gaze fully expressed Mr. Goliadkin's independence, that is, it stated clearly that Mr. Goliadkin was quite all right, that he was his own man, like everybody else, and that, in any case, he kept to his own backyard. Krestyan Ivanovich coughed, grunted, apparently as a sign of his approval and agreement to all that, and fixed his inspectorial, questioning gaze on Mr. Goliadkin.

"Krestyan Ivanovich," Mr. Goliadkin began with a smile, "I have come to trouble you for a second time, and now for a second time I venture to ask your indulgence . . ." Mr. Goliadkin was obviously struggling for words.

"Hm . . . yes!" uttered Krestyan Ivanovich, letting out a stream of smoke from his mouth and placing the cigar on the desk, "but you must keep to your prescriptions; I did explain to you that your treatment should consist in a change of habits . . . Well, diversions; well, and you should visit friends and acquaintances, and along with that be no enemy of the bottle; likewise keep merry company."

Mr. Goliadkin, still smiling, hastened to observe that it seemed to him that he was like everybody else, that he was his own man, that his diversions were like everybody else's . . . that he could, of course, go to the theater, for, like everybody else, he also had means, that he worked during the day, but in the evening was at home, that he was quite all right; he even observed just then, in passing, that, as it seemed to him, he was no worse than others, that he lived at home, in his own apartment, and, finally, that he had Petrushka. Here Mr. Goliadkin faltered.

"Hm, no, that's not the right order, and it's not at all what I wanted to ask you. I'm generally interested to know whether you are a great lover of merry company, whether you spend your time merrily . . . Well, I mean, do you continue now in a melancholy or a merry way of life?"

"Krestyan Ivanovich, I . . ."

"Hm . . . I'm saying," the doctor interrupted, "that you need to reorganize your whole life radically and in some sense break your character." (Krestyan Ivanovich strongly emphasized the word "break" and paused for a moment with a very significant air.) "Not to shun the merry life; to frequent the theater and the club, and in any case be no enemy of the bottle. Staying at home is no good . . . staying at home is impossible for you."

"I, Krestyan Ivanovich, love quiet," said Mr. Goliadkin, casting a significant glance at Krestyan Ivanovich and obviously seeking for words to express his thought more happily. "There's only me and Petrushka in the apartment, Krestyan Ivanovich . . . I mean to say, my manservant, Krestyan Ivanovich. I mean to say, Krestyan Ivanovich, that I go my own way, a particular way. I'm my own particular man and, as it seems to me, I don't depend on anybody. I also go for walks, Krestyan Ivanovich."

"What? . . . Yes! Well, nowadays, going for a walk is nothing pleasurable; the climate's quite poor."

"Yes, sir, Krestyan Ivanovich. Though I'm a peaceable man, Krestyan Ivanovich, as I believe I've had the honor of explaining to you, my way goes separately, Krestyan Ivanovich. The path of life is broad . . . I mean . . . I mean to say, Krestyan Ivanovich, that . . . Excuse me, Krestyan Ivanovich, I'm no master of fine speaking."

"Hm . . . you were saying . . ."

"I was saying that you must excuse me, Krestyan Ivanovich, for the fact that I, as it seems to me, am no master of fine speaking," Mr. Goliadkin said in a half-offended tone, slightly confused and thrown off. "In this respect, Krestyan Ivanovich, I am not like others," he added with some special smile, "and I am unable to speak at length; I never studied how to beautify my style. Instead, Krestyan Ivanovich, I act; I act instead, Krestyan Ivanovich."

"Hm . . . How is it . . . that you act?" Krestyan Ivanovich rejoined. After which, silence ensued for a moment. The doctor gave Mr. Goliadkin a strange, mistrustful look. Mr. Goliadkin, in his turn, also gave the doctor a rather mistrustful sidelong glance.

"I, Krestyan Ivanovich," Mr. Goliadkin began to go on in the same tone as before, slightly annoyed and perplexed by Krestyan Ivanovich's extreme persistence, "I, Krestyan Ivanovich, love tranquillity, not worldly noise. With them there, I say, in great society, Krestyan Ivanovich, one must know how to polish the parquet with one's boots…" (Here Mr. Goliadkin scraped the floor slightly with his foot.) "That's what's called for there, sir, and quips are also called for… knowing how to put together a perfumed compliment, sir… that's what's called for there. And I never studied that, Krestyan Ivanovich—I never studied all those clever things; I had no time. I'm a simple, unsophisticated man, and there's no external brilliance in me. In that sense, Krestyan Ivanovich, I lay down my arms; I drop them, if I may put it that way." Mr. Goliadkin said all this, to be sure, with such an air as to let it be known that our hero did not at all regret laying down his arms in this sense and never having studied clever things, but even quite the contrary. Krestyan Ivanovich, listening to him, looked down with quite an unpleasant scowl on his face, as if anticipating something beforehand. Mr. Goliadkin's tirade was followed by a rather long and significant silence.

"It seems you've diverged slightly from the subject," Krestyan Ivanovich said at last in a low voice. "I confess, I'm completely unable to understand you."

"I'm no master of fine speaking, Krestyan Ivanovich; I've already had the honor of informing you, Krestyan Ivanovich, that I'm no master of fine speaking," said Mr. Goliadkin, this time in a sharp and resolute tone.

"Hm…"

"Krestyan Ivanovich!" Mr. Goliadkin began again in a low but meaningful voice, partly of a solemn sort, and pausing at every point. "Krestyan Ivanovich! on coming in here, I began with apologies. I now repeat the former and again beg your indulgence for a time. I, Krestyan Ivanovich, have nothing to conceal from you. I am a little man, you know that yourself;

but, to my good fortune, I do not regret that I am a little man. Even the contrary, Krestyan Ivanovich; and, to tell all, I am even proud that I am not a great man, but a little one. Not an intriguer—and I am proud of that as well. I act not on the sly, but openly, without cunning, and though I could do harm in my turn, could very well, and I even know to whom and how to do it, Krestyan Ivanovich, I do not want to besmirch myself, and in that sense I wash my hands. In that sense, I say, I wash them, Krestyan Ivanovich!" Mr. Goliadkin fell expressively silent for a moment; he had spoken with meek animation.

"I walk, Krestyan Ivanovich," our hero began to go on, "straight ahead, openly, and without twisting paths, because I despise them and leave them to others. I do not try to humiliate those who have gone one better than you and I...that is, I mean to say them and I, Krestyan Ivanovich, I didn't mean to say you. I dislike half-utterances; petty duplicity is not in favor with me; I scorn slander and gossip. I put on a mask only for masked balls, and do not go around in it before people every day. I will only ask you, Krestyan Ivanovich, how would you go about taking revenge on your enemy, your worst enemy— someone you consider as such?" Mr. Goliadkin concluded, casting a defiant glance at Krestyan Ivanovich.

Though Mr. Goliadkin had spoken it all with the utmost distinctness, clarity, and assurance, weighing his words and calculating their surest effect, nevertheless it was with uneasiness, with great uneasiness, with extreme uneasiness, that he now looked at Krestyan Ivanovich. Now he became all eyes, and timidly, with vexing, anxious impatience, awaited Krestyan Ivanovich's response. But, to the amazement and total shock of Mr. Goliadkin, Krestyan Ivanovich muttered something to himself under his nose; then he moved his chair to the desk and rather dryly, though courteously, announced to him that his time was precious, that he somehow did not quite understand, or something of the sort; that, though he was ready to be of any possible service, as far as he could, he would leave aside all the rest, which did not concern him. Here he took a pen, drew a piece of paper towards him, cut a piece from it for a doctor's form, and announced that he would at once prescribe what was proper.

"No, sir, not proper, Krestyan Ivanovich! No, sir, that is by no means proper!" said Mr. Goliadkin, getting up from his place and seizing Krestyan Ivanovich by the right hand. "That, Krestyan Ivanovich, is by no means needed here..."

But while Mr. Goliadkin was saying all this, a strange transformation was taking place in him. His gray eyes gleamed somehow strangely, his lips trembled, all the muscles, all the features of his face began to move, to twitch. He was shaking all over. Having followed his first impulse and stopped Krestyan Ivanovich's hand, Mr. Goliadkin now stood motionless, as if not trusting himself and awaiting the inspiration for further actions.

Then a rather strange scene took place.

Slightly perplexed, Krestyan Ivanovich sat momentarily as if rooted to his chair and, feeling at a loss, stared all eyes at Mr. Goliadkin, who was staring at him in the same way. Finally Krestyan Ivanovich stood up, holding on slightly to the lapel of Mr. Goliadkin's uniform jacket. For a few seconds the two men stood thus, motionless and not taking their eyes off each other. Then, however, in an extraordinarily strange way, Mr. Goliadkin's second movement resolved itself. His lips trembled, his chin quivered, and our hero quite unexpectedly burst into tears. Sobbing, wagging his head, and beating himself on the breast with his right hand, and with his left also seizing the lapel of Krestyan Ivanovich's lounging jacket, he wanted to speak and immediately explain something, but was unable to say a word. Krestyan Ivanovich finally recovered from his astonishment.

"Come, calm yourself, sit down!" he said finally, trying to sit Mr. Goliadkin in an armchair.

"I have enemies, Krestyan Ivanovich, I have enemies; I have wicked enemies who have sworn to destroy me..." Mr. Goliadkin replied timorously and in a whisper.

"Come, come, what's this about enemies! There's no need to mention enemies, absolutely no need! Sit down, sit down," Krestyan Ivanovich went on, definitively sitting Mr. Goliadkin in the armchair.

Mr. Goliadkin finally sat down, not taking his eyes from Krestyan Ivanovich. Krestyan Ivanovich, looking extremely displeased, began to pace up and down his office. A long silence ensued.

"I'm grateful to you, Krestyan Ivanovich, quite grateful and quite sensible of all you've now done for me. To my dying day I will not forget your kindness, Krestyan Ivanovich," Mr. Goliadkin said finally, getting up from his chair with an offended look.

"Come, come, I tell you, enough!" Krestyan Ivanovich responded rather sternly to Mr. Goliadkin's outburst, sitting him down again. "Well, what is it? Tell me, what's this unpleasantness you have there," Krestyan Ivanovich went on, "and what enemies are you talking about? What is it with you there?"

"No, Krestyan Ivanovich, we'd better drop that now," replied Mr. Goliadkin, lowering his eyes to the ground, "better set it all aside for a time ... for another time, Krestyan Ivanovich, for a more opportune time, when everything is disclosed, and the mask falls from certain faces, and certain things are laid bare. And meanwhile, naturally, after what has occurred with us ... you yourself will agree, Krestyan Ivanovich ... Allow me to bid you good morning, Krestyan Ivanovich," said Mr. Goliadkin, this time resolutely and seriously getting up from his place and seizing his hat.

"Ah, well ... as you wish ... hm ..." (A moment of silence ensued.) "I, for my part, you know, whatever I can ... and I sincerely wish you well."

"I understand you, Krestyan Ivanovich, I understand; I understand you completely now ... In any case, excuse me for having troubled you, Krestyan Ivanovich."

"Hm ... No, that's not what I wanted to say. However, as you wish. Continue the medications as before ..."

"I will continue the medications, as you say, Krestyan Ivanovich, I will, and I'll get them from the same apothecary. Nowadays, Krestyan Ivanovich, even being an apothecary has become an important thing ..."

"Oh? In what sense do you mean to say?"

"In a perfectly ordinary sense, Krestyan Ivanovich. I mean to say, that's how the world goes nowadays..."

"Hm..."

"And that every little brat, not only from the apothecary, turns up his nose before a decent person now."

"Hm...And how do you understand that?"

"I'm speaking, Krestyan Ivanovich, about a certain person... about our mutual acquaintance, Krestyan Ivanovich, say, for instance, about Vladimir Semyonovich..."

"Ah!..."

"Yes, Krestyan Ivanovich; and I know some people, Krestyan Ivanovich, who do not hold so much to the general opinion as not to tell the truth sometimes."

"Ah!...How is that?"

"It's just so, sir. That, however, is a side issue; they sometimes know how to offer a cock with a sock."

"What? Offer what?"

"A cock with a sock, Krestyan Ivanovich; it's a Russian saying. They sometimes know how to congratulate a person opportunely, for example—there are such people, Krestyan Ivanovich."

"Congratulate?"

"Yes, sir, congratulate, as a close acquaintance of mine did the other day..."

"A close acquaintance of yours...ah! how's that?" said Krestyan Ivanovich, looking attentively at Mr Goliadkin.

"Yes, sir, a close acquaintance of mine congratulated another, also quite a close acquaintance, and moreover an intimate, or, as they say, the sweetest of friends, on his promotion, on receiving the rank of assessor.[4] It just came out by itself. 'I am,' he said, that is, 'most feelingly glad of the chance to offer you, Vladimir Semyonovich, my congratulations, my *sincere* congratulations, on your promotion. And my gladness is the greater in that, nowadays, as all the world knows, there are no more little grannies telling fortunes.'" Here Mr. Goliadkin nodded slyly and, narrowing his eyes, looked at Krestyan Ivanovich ...

"Hm...So he said that..."

"He did, Krestyan Ivanovich, he said it and immediately

looked at Andrei Filippovich, the uncle of our little treasure, Vladimir Semyonovich. But what is it to me, Krestyan Ivanovich, that he was made an assessor? What is it to me? And he wants to get married, when the milk, if I may be permitted to say so, is not yet dry on his lips. And so I told him. That is, I mean, Vladimir Semyonovich! I've told you everything now; allow me to leave."

"Hm..."

"Yes, Krestyan Ivanovich, allow me, I say, to leave now. And here, to kill two birds with one stone—once I've cut the lad down with the little grannies, I turn to Klara Olsufyevna (this was two days ago at Olsufy Ivanovich's), and she had just finished singing a heartfelt romance—that is, I say, 'You have been pleased to sing a most heartfelt romance, only you have not been listened to with a pure heart.' And I clearly hint by that, you understand, Krestyan Ivanovich, I clearly hint by that, that what was being sought was not her, but something further..."

"Ah! And what about him?"

"He bit the lemon, Krestyan Ivanovich, as the saying goes."

"Hm..."

"Yes, sir, Krestyan Ivanovich. And I also say to the old man— that is, Olsufy Ivanovich, I say, I know how much I owe you, I fully appreciate your benefactions, which you have showered upon me almost from my childhood. But open your eyes, Olsufy Ivanovich, I say. Look around. I myself am conducting the affair candidly and openly, Olsufy Ivanovich."

"Ah, so that's how!"

"Yes, Krestyan Ivanovich. That's how it..."

"And what about him?"

"What about him, Krestyan Ivanovich! He mumbles—this and that, and I know you, and his excellency's a benevolent man—and on he goes, and smooches it around... But so what? He's gone pretty dotty, as they say, from old age."

"Ah! so that's how it is now!"

"Yes, Krestyan Ivanovich. And yet we're all like that! an old codger! staring into the grave, at his last gasp, as they say, but then there's some women's gossip, and there he is listening; no doing without him..."

"Gossip, you say?"

"Yes, Krestyan Ivanovich, they've made up some gossip. And our bear and his nephew, our little treasure, have mixed their hands in it; they've banded together with the old women and cooked up the business. What do you think? How have they contrived to kill a man?..."

"To kill a man?"

"Yes, Krestyan Ivanovich, to kill a man, to kill a man morally. They've spread...I'm still talking about my close acquaintance..."

Krestyan Ivanovich nodded his head.

"They've spread a rumor about him...I confess to you, I'm even ashamed to say it, Krestyan Ivanovich..."

"Hm..."

"They've spread a rumor that he has already signed an agreement to marry, that he's already engaged elsewhere...And to whom do you think, Krestyan Ivanovich?"

"Really?"

"To a cookshop owner, an indecent German woman, from whom he buys his dinners; instead of paying his debts he's offering her his hand."

"That's what they say?"

"Would you believe it, Krestyan Ivanovich? A German woman, a mean, vile, shameless German woman, Karolina Ivanovna, if you know..."

"I confess, for my part..."

"I understand you, Krestyan Ivanovich, I do, and for my part I feel that..."

"Tell me, please, where are you living now?"

"Where am I living now, Krestyan Ivanovich?"

"Yes...I want...before, it seems, you were living..."

"I was, Krestyan Ivanovich, I was, I was living before. How could I not have been!" replied Mr. Goliadkin, accompanying his words with a little laugh and slightly confusing Krestyan Ivanovich with his reply.

"No, you haven't taken it the right way; I wanted for my part..."

"I also wanted, Krestyan Ivanovich, for my part, I also wanted," Mr. Goliadkin continued, laughing. "However, Krestyan Ivanovich, I've sat too long with you. I hope you will now permit me... to bid you good morning..."

"Hm..."

"Yes, Krestyan Ivanovich, I understand you; I fully understand you now," said our hero, posturing slightly before Krestyan Ivanovich. "And so, permit me to bid you good morning..."

Here our hero scraped with his foot and walked out of the room, leaving Krestyan Ivanovich in extreme astonishment. Going down the doctor's stairs, he smiled and rubbed his hands joyfully. On the porch, breathing the fresh air and feeling himself free, he was even actually ready to acknowledge himself the happiest of mortals and then go straight to the department—when his carriage suddenly clattered up to the entrance; he looked and remembered everything. Petrushka was already opening the doors. Some strange and extremely unpleasant sensation gripped the whole of Mr. Goliadkin. He seemed to blush for a moment. Something pricked him. He was just about to place his foot on the step of the carriage when he suddenly turned and looked at Krestyan Ivanovich's windows. That was it! Krestyan Ivanovich was standing at the window, stroking his side-whiskers with his right hand and looking at our hero with great curiosity.

"That doctor is stupid," thought Mr. Goliadkin, hiding himself in the carriage, "extremely stupid. Maybe he treats his patients well, but all the same... he's stupid as a log." Mr. Goliadkin settled himself, Petrushka shouted "Gee-up!"—and the carriage again went rolling down to Nevsky Prospect.

CHAPTER III

M R. GOLIADKIN SPENT that whole morning in an awful bustle. On reaching Nevsky Prospect, our hero ordered the carriage to stop at the Gostiniy Dvor.⁵ Jumping out of his carriage, he ran in under the arcade, accompanied by Petrushka, and went straight to a silver- and goldsmith's shop. One could see merely by the look of Mr. Goliadkin that he was all aflutter and had an awful heap of things to do. Having agreed on a price of fifteen hundred in banknotes for a full dinner and tea service, and bargained his way into a whimsically shaped cigar box and a full silver shaving kit for the same price, having inquired, finally, about the price of certain other little objects, useful and agreeable in their way, Mr. Goliadkin ended by promising to stop by for his purchases without fail the next day or even send for them that same day, took the number of the shop, listened attentively to the merchant, who was fussing about a little deposit, and promised to give him a little deposit in due time. After which he hastily took leave of the bewildered merchant and went down the arcade pursued by a whole flock of salesclerks, constantly looking back at Petrushka, and painstakingly searching for some other shop. On the way he dashed into a moneychanger's shop and broke all his big notes into smaller ones, and though he lost in the exchange, he broke them all the same, and his wallet grew significantly fatter, which apparently afforded him great pleasure. Finally, he stopped at a store selling various ladies' fabrics. Again negotiating purchases for a significant sum, Mr. Goliadkin, here as well, promised the merchant to stop by without fail, took the number of the shop, and, to the question about a little deposit, again repeated that there would be a little deposit in due time. Then he visited several other shops; in all of them he bargained, asked the price of various objects, sometimes argued for a long time with the merchants, left the shop and came back three times—in short, manifested an extraordinary activity. From the Gostiniy Dvor, our hero went to a well-known furniture store, where he arranged a deal on furniture for six rooms, admired a fashionable and very whimsical lady's toilet table in the latest taste and, having assured the merchant that he would send for it all without fail, left the store, as was his custom, with the promise of a little deposit, then went elsewhere and bargained for other things. In short, there was apparently no end to his bustling. Finally, it seems, Mr. Goliadkin himself began to grow quite bored with it all. He even, and God knows by what chance, began, out of the blue, to suffer pangs of conscience. Not for anything would he now have agreed to meet, for example, Andrei Filippovich, or even Krestyan Ivanovich. Finally, the town clock struck three in the afternoon. When Mr. Goliadkin definitively settled in his carriage, of all the purchases he had made that morning, there actually turned out to be only one pair of gloves and a flask of scent for a rouble and a half in banknotes. Since it was still early for Mr. Goliadkin, he ordered his coachman to stop at a famous restaurant on Nevsky Prospect, of which he had previously only heard, got out of the carriage, and ran to have a bite to eat, to rest, and while away some time.

Having nibbled as a man nibbles when he is looking forward to a sumptuous dinner party, that is, taken a little something to appease his tapeworm, as they say, and drunk a little glass of vodka, Mr. Goliadkin settled into an armchair and, modestly glancing around, peacefully affixed himself to a skinny government newspaper. After reading a couple of lines, he got up, looked in the mirror, straightened and smoothed himself out; then he went over to the window to see if his carriage was there...then sat down again and took the newspaper. It was noticeable that our hero was in extreme agitation. Having glanced at his watch and seen that it was only a quarter past four, and that consequently there was still quite a while to wait, and at the same time considering it improper just to sit like that, Mr. Goliadkin ordered hot chocolate, for which, however,

he felt no great desire at the present moment. Having drunk
the hot chocolate and noticed that the time had advanced a
little, he went to pay. Suddenly someone tapped him on the
shoulder.

He turned and saw his two colleagues before him, the same
ones he had met that morning on Liteinaya—still quite young
fellows in both age and rank. Our hero was neither here nor
there with them, neither friends nor outright enemies. Naturally, decency was observed on both sides; but there was no
further closeness, and there could not be. Meeting them at the
present moment was extremely unpleasant for Mr. Goliadkin.
He winced slightly and was momentarily confused.

"Yakov Petrovich, Yakov Petrovich!" the two registrars[6]
chirped, "you here? On what..."

"Ah! It's you, gentlemen!" Mr. Goliadkin interrupted hastily,
slightly embarrassed and scandalized by the clerks' astonishment and at the same time by the intimacy of their manners,
but anyhow acting the casual and fine fellow willy-nilly. "So
you've deserted, gentlemen, heh, heh, heh!..." Here, so as not
to demean himself and yet to condescend to the chancellery
youth, with whom he always kept himself within due limits,
he tried to pat one young man on the shoulder; but on this
occasion Mr. Goliadkin's popularism did not succeed, and
instead of a decently intimate gesture, something quite different
came out.

"Well, so our bear is sitting there?..."

"Who's that, Yakov Petrovich?"

"Well, the bear there, as if you didn't know who is called the
bear?..." Mr. Goliadkin laughed and turned to the cashier to
take his change. "I'm speaking of Andrei Filippovich, gentlemen," he went on, having finished with the cashier and this
time turning to the clerks with a quite serious air. The two
registrars exchanged meaningful winks.

"He's still sitting there, and he asked about you, Yakov
Petrovich," one of them replied.

"Sitting, ah! In that case let him sit, gentlemen. And he asked
about me, eh?"

"He did, Yakov Petrovich. But what is it with you, all scented, all pomaded, such a dandy?..."

"Yes, gentlemen, so it is! Enough, now..." Mr. Goliadkin responded, looking to one side and with a strained smile. Seeing Mr. Goliadkin's smile, the clerks burst out laughing. Mr. Goliadkin pursed his lips slightly.

"I'll tell you, gentlemen, in a friendly way," our hero said after some silence, as if ("So be it, then!") deciding to reveal something to the clerks, "you all know me, gentlemen, but so far you know me from only one side. No one is to blame in this case, and, I confess, it's partly my own fault."

Mr. Goliadkin compressed his lips and looked meaningfully at the clerks. The clerks again exchanged winks.

"Till now, gentlemen, you have not known me. To explain myself here and now would not be entirely appropriate. I'll tell you only a thing or two in passing and by the way. There are people, gentlemen, who dislike roundabout paths and mask themselves only for masked balls. There are people who do not see the direct destiny of man in the dexterous skill of polishing the parquet with their boots. There are also people, gentlemen, who will not say they are happy and have a full life, when, for instance, their trousers fit well. Finally, there are people who do not like to leap and fidget in vain, to flirt and fawn, and, above all, to poke their noses where they are not asked...I, gentlemen, have told you nearly all; permit me now to withdraw..."

Mr. Goliadkin stopped. Since the gentlemen registrars were now fully satisfied, they both suddenly rocked with extremely impolite laughter. Mr. Goliadkin flared up.

"Laugh, gentlemen, laugh meanwhile! You'll live and you'll see," he said with a feeling of injured dignity, taking his hat and retreating towards the door.

"But I'll say more, gentlemen," he added, addressing the gentlemen registrars one last time, "I'll say more—the two of you are here face-to-face with me. These, gentlemen, are my rules: if I don't succeed, I keep trying; if I do succeed, I keep quiet; and in any case I don't undermine anyone. I'm not an intriguer, and I'm proud of it. I wouldn't make a good diplomat.

They also say, gentlemen, that the bird flies to the fowler. That's true, and I'm ready to agree: but who is the fowler here, and who is the bird? That's still a question, gentlemen!"

Mr. Goliadkin fell eloquently silent and with a most significant mien, that is, raising his eyebrows and compressing his lips to the utmost, bowed and went out, leaving the gentlemen clerks in extreme astonishment.

"Where to, sir?" Petrushka asked quite sternly, probably sick by then of dragging about in the cold. "Where to, sir?" he asked Mr. Goliadkin, meeting his terrible, all-annihilating gaze, with which our hero had already provided himself twice that day, and to which he now resorted for a third time, going down the steps.

"To the Izmailovsky Bridge."

"To the Izmailovsky Bridge! Gee-up!"

"Their dinner won't begin before five or even at five," thought Mr. Goliadkin, "isn't it too early now? However, I can come early; it's a family dinner after all. I can just come *sans façon*,* as they say among respectable people. Why can't I come *sans façon*? Our bear also said it would all be *sans façon*, and therefore I, too . . ." So thought Mr. Goliadkin; but meanwhile his agitation increased more and more. It was noticeable that he was preparing himself for something quite troublesome, to say the least; he whispered to himself, gesticulated with his right hand, kept glancing out the carriage windows, so that, looking now at Mr. Goliadkin, no one would really have said that he was preparing to dine well, simply, and in his own family circle— *sans façon*, as they say among respectable people. Finally, just at the Izmailovsky Bridge, Mr. Goliadkin pointed to a house; the carriage drove noisily through the gate and stopped by the entrance to the right wing. Noticing a female figure in a second-floor window, Mr. Goliadkin blew her a kiss. However, he did not know what he was doing himself, because at that moment he was decidedly neither dead nor alive. He got out of the carriage pale, bewildered; he went up to the porch, took off his hat, straightened his clothes mechanically, and, though feeling a slight trembling in his knees, started up the stairs.

*Without ceremony.

"Olsufy Ivanovich?" he asked the man who opened the door for him.

"At home, sir, that is, no, sir, he is not at home!"

"How's that? What are you saying, my dear? I—I have come to dinner, brother. Don't you know me?"

"How could I not, sir! I was told not to receive you, sir."

"You...you, brother...you must be mistaken. It's me. I've been invited, brother; I've come to dinner," said Mr. Goliadkin, throwing off his overcoat and showing an obvious intention of going in.

"Sorry, sir, but you can't, sir. I've been ordered not to receive you, sir, I've been told to refuse you. That's what!"

Mr. Goliadkin turned pale. Just then the inside door opened and Gerasimych, Olsufy Ivanovich's old valet, came out.

"See here, Emelyan Gerasimovich, he wants to come in, and I..."

"And you're a fool, Alexeich. Go in and send the scoundrel Semyonych here. You can't, sir," he said politely yet resolutely, turning to Mr. Goliadkin. "Quite impossible, sir. They ask to be excused, but they cannot receive you, sir."

"That's what they told you, that they cannot receive me?" Mr. Goliadkin asked hesitantly. "Pardon me, Gerasimych. Why is it quite impossible?"

"Quite impossible, sir. I've announced you, sir; they said they ask to be excused. Meaning they cannot receive you, sir."

"But why? how come? how..."

"Sorry, sorry!..."

"Though how can it be so? It's not possible! Announce me... How can it be so? I've come to dinner..."

"Sorry, sorry!..."

"Ah, well, anyhow, that's a different matter—they ask to be excused. Pardon me, though, Gerasimych, but how can it be so, Gerasimych?"

"Sorry, sorry!" Gerasimych protested, moving Mr. Goliadkin aside quite resolutely with his arm and giving wide way to two gentlemen who at that moment were entering the front hall.

The entering gentlemen were Andrei Filippovich and his

nephew, Vladimir Semyonovich. They both looked at Mr. Goliadkin in perplexity. Andrei Filippovich was about to say something, but Mr. Goliadkin had already made up his mind; he was already leaving Olsufy Ivanovich's front hall, lowering his eyes, blushing, smiling, with a totally lost physiognomy.

"I'll come later, Gerasimych; I'll explain; I hope all this will not be slow to clarify itself in due time," he said in the doorway and partly on the stairs.

"Yakov Petrovich, Yakov Petrovich!..." came the voice of Andrei Filippovich, who followed after Mr. Goliadkin.

Mr. Goliadkin was already on the first-floor landing. He turned quickly to Andrei Filippovich.

"What can I do for you, Andrei Filippovich?" he said in a rather resolute tone.

"What is the matter with you, Yakov Petrovich? How on earth...?"

"Never mind, Andrei Filippovich. I'm here on my own. It is my private life, Andrei Filippovich."

"What is this, sir?"

"I say, Andrei Filippovich, that it is my private life and, as far as I can see, it is impossible to find anything reprehensible here with regard to my official relations."

"What! With regard to your official...What, my dear sir, is the matter with you?"

"Nothing, Andrei Filippovich, absolutely nothing; a pert young lady, nothing more..."

"What?...What?!" Andrei Filippovich was at a loss from amazement. Mr. Goliadkin, who thus far, talking with Andrei Filippovich from downstairs, had been looking at him as if he was about to jump right into his eyes—seeing that the head of the department was slightly bewildered, almost unwittingly took a step forward. Andrei Filippovich drew back. Mr. Goliadkin climbed one step, then another. Andrei Filippovich looked around uneasily. Mr. Goliadkin suddenly went quickly up the stairs. Still more quickly Andrei Filippovich jumped back into the room and slammed the door behind him. Mr. Goliadkin was left alone. It went dark in his eyes. He was totally thrown off and now stood in some sort of muddled reflection, as though recalling some circumstance, also extremely muddled, that had happened quite recently. "Ah, ah!" he whispered, grinning from the strain. Meanwhile from the stairs below came the sound of voices and footsteps, probably of new guests invited by Olsufy Ivanovich. Mr. Goliadkin partly recovered himself, hastily turned up his raccoon collar, covered himself with it as much as he could, and, hobbling, mincing, hurrying, and stumbling, began to go down the stairs. He felt some sort of faintness and numbness inside him. His confusion was so strong that, on going out to the porch, he did not wait for the carriage but went straight to it himself across the muddy courtyard. Reaching his carriage and preparing to put himself into it, Mr. Goliadkin mentally displayed a wish to fall through the earth or even hide in a mouse hole together with his carriage. It seemed to him that whatever there was in Olsufy Ivanovich's house was now looking directly at him from all the windows. He knew he would surely die right there on the spot if he turned around.

"What are you laughing at, blockhead?" he said in a rapid patter to Petrushka, who readied himself to help him into the carriage.

"What have I got to laugh at? It's nothing to me. Where to now?"

"Home now, get going..."

"Home!" shouted Petrushka, climbing onto the tailboard.

"What a crow's gullet!"[7] thought Mr. Goliadkin. Meanwhile the carriage had already driven far beyond the Izmailovsky Bridge. Suddenly our hero pulled the string with all his might and shouted to his coachman to turn back immediately. The coachman turned the horses, and two minutes later they drove into Olsufy Ivanovich's courtyard again. "No need, fool, no need! Go back!" cried Mr. Goliadkin, and it was as if the coachman expected this order: without protesting or stopping by the porch, he drove around the whole courtyard and out to the street once more.

Mr. Goliadkin did not go home but, having passed the Semyonovsky Bridge, gave orders to turn down a lane and stop by a tavern of rather modest appearance. Getting out of the carriage, our hero paid the driver and in this way finally rid himself of his equipage, ordered Petrushka to go home and wait for his return, while he himself went into the tavern, took a separate room, and ordered dinner. He felt quite poorly, and his head was in total disarray and chaos. For a long time he paced the room in agitation; finally he sat down on a chair, his forehead propped in his hands, and began trying with all his might to consider and resolve certain things relating to his present situation ...

CHAPTER IV

THE DAY, THE BIRTHDAY festivity of Klara Olsufyevna, the only-begotten daughter of State Councillor Berendeev,[8] once Mr. Goliadkin's benefactor—the day, marked by a splendid, magnificent dinner party, a dinner party such as had not been seen for a long time within the walls of officials' apartments by the Izmailovsky Bridge and roundabouts—a dinner more like some sort of Balshazzar's feast than a dinner—which had something Babylonian in it with regard to splendor, luxury, and decorum, with Clicquot champagne, with oysters and fruit from Eliseevs' and Miliutin's shops, with various fatted calves and the official table of ranks[9]—this festive day, marked by such a festive dinner, concluded with a splendid ball, a small, intimate, family ball, but splendid all the same with regard to taste, good breeding, and decorum. Of course, I agree completely, such balls do take place, but rarely. Such balls, more like family rejoicings than balls, can be given only in such houses as, for example, the house of State Councillor Berendeev. I say more: I even doubt that all state councillors can give such balls. Oh, if I were a poet!—to be sure, at least such a poet as Homer or Pushkin;[10] you can't butt into it with less talent—I would unfailingly portray for you with bright colors and sweeping brushstrokes, O readers! all of that highly festive day. Nay, I would begin my poem with the dinner, I would especially emphasize that amazing and at the same time solemn moment when the first toasting cup was raised in honor of the queen of the feast. I would portray for you, first, these guests immersed in reverent silence and expectation, more like Demosthenean eloquence[11] than silence. I would then portray for you Andrei Filippovich, even having a certain right to primacy as the eldest of the guests, adorned with gray hairs and with orders befitting those gray hairs, rising from his place and raising above his

head the toasting cup of sparkling wine—wine brought purposely from a far kingdom to be drunk at such moments, a wine
more like the nectar of the gods than wine. I would portray for
you the guests and the happy parents of the queen of the feast,
who also raised their glasses after Andrei Filippovich and
turned on him their eyes filled with expectation. I would portray
for you how this oft-mentioned Andrei Filippovich, having first
let drop a tear into his glass, uttered a felicitation and a wish,
pronounced the toast, and drank to the health . . . But, I confess,
I fully confess, I could never portray all the solemnity of that
moment when the queen of the feast herself, Klara Olsufyevna,
reddening like a rose in spring with the flush of bliss and
modesty, from the fullness of her feelings fell into the arms of
her tender mother, how the tender mother waxed tearful, and
how the father himself thereupon wept, the venerable old man
and state councillor Olsufy Ivanovich, who had lost the use of
his legs from longtime service, and whom destiny had rewarded
for his zeal with a bit of capital, a house, country estates, and
a beautiful daughter—wept like a child, and said through his
tears that his excellency was a beneficent man. And I could
never, yes, precisely never, portray for you the general enthusiasm of hearts that inevitably followed this moment—an
enthusiasm clearly manifested even in the behavior of one
youthful registrar (at that moment more like a state councillor
than a registrar), who also waxed tearful as he listened to Andrei
Filippovich. In his turn, Andrei Filippovich was at this solemn
moment quite unlike a collegiate councillor[12] and the head of an
office in a certain department—no, he seemed to be something
else . . . I do not know precisely what, but not a collegiate councillor. He was loftier! Finally . . . oh, why do I not possess the
secret of a lofty, powerful style, a solemn style, so as to portray
all these beautiful and instructive moments of human life,
arranged as if on purpose to prove how virtue sometimes
triumphs over ill intention, freethinking, vice, and envy! I shall
say nothing, but silently—which will be better than any eloquence—point out to you that fortunate youth, who was
approaching his twenty-sixth spring, Vladimir Semyonovich,

Andrei Filippovich's nephew, who in his turn got up from his place, in his turn is pronouncing a toast, and towards whom are directed the tearful eyes of the parents of the queen of the feast, the proud eyes of Andrei Filippovich, the modest eyes of the queen of the feast herself, the admiring eyes of the guests, and even the decently envious eyes of some of the brilliant youth's young colleagues. I will say nothing, though I cannot help observing that everything in this youth—who was more like an old man than a youth, speaking in a sense advantageous to him—everything, from his blossoming cheeks to the rank of assessor he bore, everything in this solemn moment was all but proclaiming: see to what a high degree good behavior can bring a man! I will not describe how, finally, Anton Antonovich Setochkin,[13] a section chief in a certain department, a colleague of Andrei Filippovich's and once of Olsufy Ivanovich's, and at the same time an old friend of the house and Klara Olsufyevna's godfather, a little old man with snow-white hair, offering a toast in his turn, crowed like a rooster and recited merry verses; how, with such a decent forgetting of decency, if it is possible to put it so, he made the whole company laugh to tears, and how Klara Olsufyevna herself, on her parents' orders, gave him a kiss for being so merry and amiable. I will only say that the guests, who after such a dinner must, naturally, have felt themselves as family and brothers to each other, finally got up from the table; then how the oldsters and solid men, after spending a short time in friendly conversation and even certain, to be sure quite decent and polite, confidences, decorously proceeded to the other room and, not to lose precious time, having divided themselves into parties, with a sense of their own dignity sat down at tables covered with green baize; how the ladies, seating themselves in the drawing room, all suddenly became extraordinarily amiable and began talking about various matters; how, finally, the highly esteemed host himself, who had lost the use of his legs from true and faithful service and had been rewarded for it with all the abovementioned things, began to walk about on crutches among his guests, supported by Vladimir Semyonovich and Klara Olsufyevna, and how, also

suddenly becoming extraordinarily obliging, he decided to
improvise a modest little ball, despite the expense; how, to that
end, an efficient youth (the one who at dinner had been more
like a state councillor than a youth) was dispatched for musicians; how the musicians then arrived, a whole eleven of them
in number; and how, finally, at exactly half-past eight, the inviting strains of a French quadrille and various other dances rang
out...Needless to say, my pen is too weak, sluggish, and dull
for a proper portrayal of the ball improvised by the extraordinarily obliging gray-haired host. And how, may I ask, can I, the
humble narrator of the adventures of Mr. Goliadkin—highly
curious adventures in their way, however—how can I portray
this extraordinary and decorous mixture of beauty, brilliance,
decency, gaiety, amiable solidity and solid amiability, friskiness,
joy, all the games and laughter of all these official ladies, more
like fairies than ladies—speaking in a sense advantageous to
them—with their lily-and-rose shoulders and faces, their airy
waists, and their friskily playful, homeopathic (speaking in high
style) little feet? How, finally, shall I portray their brilliant
official partners, merry and respectable, youthful and sedate,
joyful and decently nebulous, those smoking a pipe during the
intervals between dances in a remote little green room and those
not smoking in the intervals—partners who, from first to last,
were all bearers of a decent rank and name—partners deeply
imbued with a sense of elegance and of their own dignity;
partners who for the most part spoke French with the ladies,
and if they spoke Russian, expressed themselves in the highest
tone, in compliments and profound phrases—partners who
perhaps only in the smoking room allowed themselves a few
amiable departures from language of the highest tone, a few
phrases of a friendly and polite brevity, such as, for example:
"Thus and so, Petka, you cut some nice capers during the polka"
or "Thus and so, Vasya, you really nailed down your little lady
the way you wanted!" For all this, as I have already had the
honor of explaining to you above, O readers! my pen is inad-
equate, and therefore I keep silent. Better let us turn to Mr.
Goliadkin, the real, the only hero of our quite truthful story.

The thing is that he now finds himself in a quite strange, to say the least, position. He, ladies and gentlemen, is also here, that is, not at the ball, but almost at the ball; never mind him, ladies and gentlemen; he is his own man, but at this moment he is standing on a path that is not entirely straight; he is now standing—it is even strange to say it—he is now standing in the hallway to the back stairs of Olsufy Ivanovich's apartment. But never mind that he is standing there; he is all right. He is standing, ladies and gentlemen, in a little corner, huddled in a place not so much warm as dark, hidden partly by an enormous wardrobe and some old screens, among all sorts of litter, trash, and junk, hiding for a time and meanwhile only observing the general course of events in the capacity of an external onlooker. He, ladies and gentlemen, is only observing now; he may also go in, ladies and gentlemen . . . why not go in? He has only to take a step, and he will go in, and go in rather adroitly. Only just now—while standing, incidentally, for the third hour in the cold, between the wardrobe and the screens, amidst all sorts of trash, litter, and junk—he quoted, in his own justification, a phrase from the French minister Villèle,[14] of blessed memory, that "everything will come in its turn, if you have the gumption to wait." This phrase Mr. Goliadkin had read once in a completely unrelated book, but now he called it up quite opportunely in his memory. First, the phrase suited his present situation very well, and second, what will not occur to a man who has been waiting for the happy outcome of his circumstances for almost a whole three hours in a hallway, in the dark and cold? Having quite opportunely quoted the phrase of the former French minister Villèle, as has been said, Mr. Goliadkin at once, no one knows why, also recalled the former Turkish vizier Marzimiris, as well as the beautiful Margravine Louise, whose story he had also read once in a book.[15] Then it came to his memory that the Jesuits even made it a rule to consider all means appropriate, so long as the end is achieved. Having encouraged himself somewhat with this historical point, Mr. Goliadkin said to himself, well, so what about the Jesuits? The Jesuits, all to a man, were the greatest fools, that he himself would go them one better, that if only the pantry (that is, the room whose door gave directly onto the hallway and the back stairs, where Mr. Goliadkin now was) stayed empty at least for a moment, then, in spite of all Jesuits, he would up and go straight from the pantry to the morning room, then to the room where they were now playing cards, and then straight into the ballroom where they were now dancing the polka. And he would go in, he would go in without fail, he would go in despite all, he would slip in, just that, and no one would notice; and once there, he would know what to do. That is the position, ladies and gentlemen, in which we now find the hero of our perfectly truthful story, though, incidentally, it is hard to explain precisely what was happening to him at that moment. The thing was that he had managed to get as far as the hallway and the stairs for the simple reason that, say, why should he not get there, anybody could get there; but he did not dare to penetrate further, did not dare to do it openly...not because he lacked daring, but just so, because he did not want to, because he would have preferred to do it on the quiet. Here he is, ladies and gentlemen, waiting now for this quiet, and he has been waiting exactly two and a half hours for it. Why should he not wait? Villèle himself waited. "What has Villèle got to do with it?" thought Mr. Goliadkin. "Why Villèle? What if I now sort of...up and penetrate?...Eh, you bit player!" said Mr. Goliadkin, pinching his frozen cheek with his frozen hand. "What a little fool, what a Goliadka—that's what your name is!..."[16] However, this endearment towards his own person at the present moment was just by the way, in passing, with no visible purpose. He now made as if to set out and move forward; the moment had come; the pantry was empty, and there was no one in it; Mr. Goliadkin saw all this through a little window; two steps brought him to the door, and he was already opening it. "To go or not? Well, to go or not? I'll go...why shouldn't I go? The brave man makes his way everywhere!" Having encouraged himself in this way, our hero suddenly and quite unexpectedly retreated behind the screens. "No," he thought, "what if somebody comes in? There, somebody has; why was

I gaping when nobody was there? I should have upped and penetrated!...No, there's no penetrating, when a man has such a character! What a mean tendency! I got frightened like a chicken. Getting frightened is what we do, so there! Mucking things up is what we always do: don't even ask us about it. So I stand here like a block of wood, and that's that! At home I'd be having a nice cup of tea now...How pleasant it would be to have a nice cup. If I get home late, Petrushka may grumble. Why don't I go home? Devil take it all! I'm going, and that's that!" Having thus resolved his situation, Mr. Goliadkin quickly moved forward, as if someone had touched a spring inside him; in two steps he was in the pantry, he threw off his overcoat, removed his hat, hastily shoved it all into a corner, straightened and smoothed himself out; then...then he moved to the morning room, from there he flitted to yet another room, slipping almost unnoticed among the passionately engrossed gamblers; then...then...here Mr. Goliadkin forgot everything that was going on around him and directly, like a bolt from the blue, appeared in the ballroom.

As luck would have it, there was no dancing at that moment. The ladies were strolling about the ballroom in picturesque groups. The men clustered in little circles or darted about the room engaging the ladies. Mr. Goliadkin did not notice any of it. He saw only Klara Olsufyevna; beside her Andrei Filippovich, then Vladimir Semyonovich, and another two or three officers, and another two or three young men, also quite interesting, giving or having already realized, as could be judged at first glance, certain hopes...He saw some others. Or no, he no longer saw anyone, no longer looked at anyone...but, moved by the same spring that had caused him to pop uninvited into someone else's ball, he stepped forward, then further forward, and further forward; ran into some councillor in passing, trod on his foot; incidentally stepped on one venerable old lady's dress and tore it slightly, shoved a man with a tray, shoved somebody else, and, not noticing any of it, or rather, noticing it, but just so, in passing, without looking at anyone, making his way further and further forward, he suddenly ended up in front of Klara Olsufyevna herself. Doubtless, without batting an eye, he would have sunk through the earth at that moment with the greatest pleasure; but what's done cannot be undone ... cannot possibly be undone. What was he to do? "If I don't succeed, I keep quiet; if I do succeed, I keep trying." Mr. Goliadkin, to be sure, "was not an intriguer and was no master at polishing the parquet with his boots ..." It just happened that way. Besides, the Jesuits somehow got mixed up in it all ... However, Mr. Goliadkin could not be bothered with them! Everything that walked, noised, talked, laughed, suddenly, as if by some sign, became hushed and gradually crowded around Mr. Goliadkin. Mr. Goliadkin, however, seemed to hear nothing, to see nothing, he could not look ... not for anything would he look; he lowered his eyes to the ground and just stood like that, having given himself in passing, however, his word of honor to shoot himself somehow that same night. Having given himself this word of honor, Mr. Goliadkin said to himself mentally: "Here goes!" and, to his own greatest amazement, quite unexpectedly began suddenly to speak.

Mr. Goliadkin began with congratulations and appropriate wishes. The congratulations went well; but our hero faltered at the wishes. He had the feeling that if he faltered, everything would go to the devil at once. And so it happened—he faltered and got stuck ... got stuck and blushed; blushed and became flustered; became flustered and raised his eyes; raised his eyes and looked around; looked around and—and went dead ... Everything stood, everything was silent, everything waited; a little further away there was whispering, a little closer—laughter. Mr. Goliadkin cast a humble, lost glance at Andrei Filippovich. Andrei Filippovich responded to Mr. Goliadkin with such a look that, if our hero had not already been fully, completely destroyed, he would certainly have been destroyed a second time—if only that were possible. The silence continued.

"This has more to do with my domestic circumstances and my private life, Andrei Filippovich," the half-dead Mr. Goliadkin said in a barely audible voice, "this is not an official event, Andrei Filippovich ..."

"Shame on you, sir, shame on you!" Andrei Filippovich spoke in a half-whisper, with a look of inexpressible indignation—spoke, took Klara Olsufyevna by the arm, and turned away from Mr. Goliadkin.

"I have nothing to be ashamed of, Andrei Filippovich," replied Mr. Goliadkin in the same half-whisper, looking around with his unhappy glance, at a loss, and trying on account of it to find some middle ground in the perplexed crowd, and his own social position.

"Well, never mind, well, never mind, ladies and gentlemen! Well, what is it? Well, it could happen to anyone," whispered Mr. Goliadkin, moving slightly from his place and trying to get out of the crowd surrounding him. They made way for him. Our hero somehow passed between the two rows of curious and perplexed observers. He was driven by fate. Mr. Goliadkin felt it himself, that it was fate he was driven by. Of course, he would have paid dearly for the possibility of now being, without any breach of etiquette, at his former station in the hallway, by the back stairs; but since that was decidedly impossible, he began trying to slip away somewhere into a corner and stand there just like that—modestly, decently, separately, disturbing nobody, drawing no exceptional attention to himself, but at the same time gaining the good graces of the guests and the host. However, Mr. Goliadkin felt as if something was undermining him, as if he was tottering, falling. Finally he made his way to a little corner and stood in it like a stranger, a rather indifferent observer, leaning with his hands on the backs of two chairs, thus taking them into his full possession, and trying his best to glance cheerfully at Olsufy Ivanovich's guests who were grouped near him. Closest to him stood some officer, a tall and handsome fellow, before whom Mr. Goliadkin felt himself a regular little bug.

"These two chairs, Lieutenant, are reserved: one for Klara Olsufyevna and the other for Princess Chevchekhanov, who is dancing here; I am now holding them for them, Lieutenant," Mr. Goliadkin said breathlessly, turning an imploring gaze on the lieutenant. The lieutenant, silently and with a devastating smile, turned away. Having misfired in one place, our hero attempted to try his luck somewhere else and turned directly to an important councillor with a significant decoration on his neck. But the councillor measured him with such a cold gaze that Mr. Goliadkin felt clearly that he had suddenly been showered with a whole bucket of cold water. Mr. Goliadkin quieted down. He decided that it was better to keep silent, not to speak, to show that he was just so, that he was also like everyone else, and that his position, as it seemed to him, was also proper at the very least. To that end, he fixed his gaze on the cuffs of his uniform coat, then raised his eyes and rested them on a gentleman of highly respectable appearance. "This gentleman is wearing a wig," thought Mr. Goliadkin, "and if he takes the wig off, there will be a bare head, as bare as the palm of my hand." Having made such an important discovery, Mr. Goliadkin remembered, too, about the Arab emirs who, if they took from their head the green turban they wear as a token of their relation to the prophet Mohammed, would leave nothing but a bare, hairless head. Then, probably by a particular collision of ideas about the Turks in his head, Mr. Goliadkin went on to Turkish slippers, and here incidentally recalled that Andrei Filippovich wore shoes that were more like slippers than shoes. It was noticeable that Mr. Goliadkin now felt partly at home in his situation. "Now, if that chandelier," flitted through Mr. Goliadkin's head, "if that chandelier tore loose and fell on this company, I would rush at once to save Klara Olsufyevna. Having saved her, I would tell her: 'Don't worry, miss; it's nothing, and I am your savior.' Then..." Here Mr. Goliadkin turned his gaze to the side, looking for Klara Olsufyevna, and saw Gerasimych, Olsufy Ivanovich's old valet. Gerasimych, with a most solicitous and officially solemn air, was making his way straight towards him. Mr. Goliadkin shuddered and winced from some unaccountable and at the same time most disagreeable feeling. He looked around mechanically; it occurred to him to slip away from trouble somehow, underhandedly, sideways, quietly, just to up and—efface himself, that is, to make as though he could not care less, as though it had nothing to do with him. However, before our hero managed to resolve on anything, Gerasimych was standing before him.

"You see, Gerasimych," said our hero, addressing Gerasimych with a little smile, "you ought to give orders. You see that candle there in the candelabra, Gerasimych—it's about to fall; so, you know, order it to be straightened; really, it's about to fall, Gerasimych..."

"The candle, sir? No, sir, the candle's standing straight, sir; but there's somebody asking for you out there, sir."

"Who is asking for me, Gerasimych?"

"I really don't know exactly who, sir. A man from thereabouts, sir. 'Is Yakov Petrovich Goliadkin here?' he says. 'Then call him out,' he says, 'on very necessary and urgent business ...'—that's what, sir."

"No, Gerasimych, you're mistaken; you're mistaken about that, Gerasimych."

"Doubtful, sir..."

"No, Gerasimych, it's not doubtful; there's nothing doubtful about it, Gerasimych. Nobody's asking for me, Gerasimych, there's nobody to ask for me, and I'm quite at home here, that is, where I belong, Gerasimych."

Mr. Goliadkin caught his breath and looked around. So it was! Everything that was in the room, everything, was straining its eyes and ears at him in some sort of solemn expectation. The men crowded nearer and listened. Further away the ladies exchanged alarmed whispers. The host himself appeared at a by no means great distance from Mr. Goliadkin, and though by the looks of him it was impossible to observe that he, in his turn, was also taking a direct and immediate interest in Mr. Goliadkin's circumstances, because it was all done on a delicate footing, nevertheless it all gave the hero of our story the clear feeling that the decisive moment had come for him. Mr. Goliadkin saw clearly that the time had come for a bold stroke, the time for the disgracing of his enemies. Mr. Goliadkin was agitated. Mr. Goliadkin felt a sort of inspiration, and in a trembling, solemn voice began again, addressing the waiting Gerasimych:

"No, my friend, nobody's calling me. You're mistaken. I'll say more: you were also mistaken earlier today when you assured me . . . made so bold as to assure me, I say" (Mr. Goliadkin raised his voice), "that Olsufy Ivanovich, my benefactor from time immemorial, who in a certain sense has taken the place of a father for me, would close his door to me at a moment of familial and festive joy for his parental heart." (Mr. Goliadkin looked around self-contentedly, but with deep feeling. Tears welled up in his eyes.) "I repeat, my friend," our hero concluded, "you were mistaken, you were cruelly, unforgivably mistaken . . ."

It was a solemn moment. Mr. Goliadkin felt that the effect was most certain. Mr. Goliadkin stood modestly looking down and waiting for Olsufy Ivanovich's embrace. Agitation and perplexity could be noticed among the guests; even the un-flinching and awesome Gerasimych faltered at the word "Doubtful, sir" . . . when suddenly out of the blue the merciless orchestra struck up a polka. All was lost, all was blown to the winds. Mr. Goliadkin shuddered, Gerasimych drew back, everything that was in the room billowed up like the sea, and Vladimir Semyonovich was already flying in the lead couple with Klara Olsufyevna, and the handsome lieutenant with Princess Chevchekhanov. Onlookers crowded around with curiosity and delight to watch them dancing the polka—a new, interesting, fashionable dance that had turned everyone's head. Mr. Goliadkin was forgotten for a while. But suddenly everything roused, stirred, bustled; the music stopped . . . a strange incident had occurred. Wearied by the dancing, Klara Olsuf-yevna, barely able to breathe from exhaustion, her cheeks aflame and her breast heaving deeply, finally fell strengthless into an armchair. All hearts strained towards the lovely enchantress, everyone hastened to be the first to greet her and thank her for the pleasure she had given—suddenly Mr. Goliadkin appeared before her. Mr. Goliadkin was pale, extremely upset; he also seemed somehow strengthless, he could barely move. He smiled for some reason, he reached out his hand imploringly. In her amazement, Klara Olsufyevna had no time to draw her hand back and mechanically stood up at Mr. Goliadkin's invitation.

Mr. Goliadkin swayed forward, first one time, then another, then raised his foot, then somehow shuffled, then somehow stamped, then stumbled...he also wanted to dance with Klara Olsufyevna. Klara Olsufyevna cried out; everyone rushed to free her hand from the hand of Mr. Goliadkin, and all at once our hero was shoved nearly ten paces away by the crowd. Around him a little circle also grouped itself. Shrieking and crying came from two old women whom Mr. Goliadkin had nearly knocked down in his retreat. The commotion was terrible; everything questioned, everything cried out, everything argued. The orchestra fell silent. Our hero turned around within his little circle and mechanically, partly smiling, muttered something to himself, that, say, "why not," and, say, "the polka, as it seemed to him at least, was a new and highly interesting dance, made to humor the ladies...but if it came to that, then he was perhaps ready to agree." But it seemed no one was asking for Mr. Goliadkin's agreement. Our hero felt someone's hand suddenly fall on his arm, another hand rested lightly on his back, and with a special solicitousness he was directed somewhere to the side. Finally he noticed that he was heading straight for the door. Mr. Goliadkin wanted to say something, to do something...But no, he no longer wanted anything. He merely laughed it off mechanically. Finally he felt that an overcoat was being put on him, that a hat was being pulled over his eyes; he finally felt himself in the hallway, in the dark and cold, and finally on the stairs. Finally, he stumbled, it seemed to him that he was falling into an abyss; he was about to cry out—and suddenly found himself in the yard. Fresh air breathed on him, he paused for a minute; at that same moment the sounds reached him of the orchestra striking up anew. Mr. Goliadkin suddenly remembered everything; it seemed that all his sagging strength came back to him. He tore from the spot where he had been standing till then as if rooted, and rushed headlong away, anywhere, into the air, into freedom, wherever his legs would carry him ...

CHAPTER V

IN ALL THE PETERSBURG towers that displayed and struck the hour, it struck midnight exactly as Mr. Goliadkin, beside himself, ran out to the embankment of the Fontanka just next to the Izmailovsky Bridge, fleeing from his enemies, from persecutions, from the shower of flicks hanging over him, from the cries of alarmed old women, from ladies' ah's and oh's, and from the destructive gazes of Andrei Filippovich. Mr. Goliadkin was destroyed—fully destroyed, in the full sense of the word, and if at the present moment he retained the ability to run, it was solely by some sort of miracle, a miracle in which he himself, finally, refused to believe. It was a terrible November night—wet, foggy, rainy, snowy, fraught with fluxes, colds, agues, anginas, fevers of all possible sorts and kinds, in short, with all the gifts of a Petersburg November. The wind howled in the deserted streets, heaving the black water of the Fontanka higher than the mooring rings and perkily brushing up against the skinny streetlamps of the embankment, which in their turn seconded its howling with a thin, shrill creaking, which made up an endless, squeaking, rattling concert, quite familiar to every inhabitant of Petersburg. Rain and snow fell at once. Streams of rainwater, broken up by the wind, sprayed almost horizontally, as if from a fire hose, and pricked and lashed at the wretched Mr. Goliadkin's face like thousands of pins and needles. Amid the night's silence, broken only by the distant rumble of carriages, the howling of the wind, and the creaking of the streetlamps, the splashing and burbling water pouring down from all the roofs, porches, gutters, and eaves onto the granite pavement of the sidewalks had a dismal sound. There was not a soul either near or far, nor did it seem there could be at such an hour and in such weather. Thus only Mr. Goliadkin, alone with his despair, trotted just then along the sidewalk of the Fontanka with his usual small and quick step, hurrying to reach as soon as possible his Shestilavochnaya Street, his fourth floor, his own apartment.

Though the snow, the rain, and all that does not even have a name when blizzard and blackness break loose under the November sky of Petersburg, at one blow suddenly attacked Mr. Goliadkin, destroyed by his misfortunes even without that, granting him not the slightest mercy or respite, chilling him to the bone, gluing his eyes shut, blowing from all sides, knocking him off his path and out of his last wits, though it all poured at once onto Mr. Goliadkin, as if purposely cooperating and agreeing with all his enemies to make a fine day and evening and night of it for him—despite all that, Mr. Goliadkin remained almost insensible to this ultimate proof of fate's persecution: so strongly had he been shaken and shocked by all that had happened to him a few minutes earlier at State Councillor Berendeev's! If some stranger, some disinterested observer, had merely glanced from the side now at Mr. Goliadkin's dreary course, even he would have been pervaded at once by all the terrible horror of his misfortunes and would surely have said that Mr. Goliadkin looked as if he wanted to hide somewhere from himself, as if he wanted to escape somewhere from himself. Yes, it really was so! We will say more: Mr. Goliadkin now wanted not only to escape from himself, but to annihilate himself completely, to be no more, to turn to dust. In the present moments he paid heed to nothing around him, understood nothing that was going on around him, and looked as if indeed neither the unpleasantness of the foul night, nor the long way, the rain, the snow, the wind, nor all this harsh weather existed for him. A galosh that came off the boot on Mr. Goliadkin's right foot simply stayed there in the mud and snow on the Fontanka sidewalk, and Mr. Goliadkin neither thought of going back for it nor noticed its loss. He was so bewildered that several times, suddenly, in spite of everything around him, totally pervaded by the idea of his recent terrible fall, he would stop motionless, like a post, in the middle of the sidewalk; at those moments he died, vanished; then suddenly he would tear himself

furiously from the spot and run, run without looking back, as
if escaping from someone's pursuit, from some still more terrible
calamity...Indeed, his situation was terrible!...Finally, at the
end of his strength, Mr. Goliadkin stopped, leaned on the rail
of the embankment in the position of a man who suddenly,
quite unexpectedly, has a nose bleed, and began gazing intently
at the muddy black water of the Fontanka. It is not known
precisely how much time he spent in this occupation. It is known
only that at that moment Mr. Goliadkin reached such despair,
was so broken, so tormented, so exhausted and sagging in what
remained of his spirit, which was weak to begin with, that he
forgot everything—the Izmailovsky Bridge, and Shestilavochnaya Street, and his present...But what of it, in fact? It was all
the same to him: the thing was done, finished, the decision was
signed and sealed; what was it to him?...Suddenly...suddenly
he shuddered all over and involuntarily jumped aside a couple
of steps. In inexplicable alarm, he began to look around; but
there was no one there, nothing special had happened—and
yet...and yet it seemed to him that just then, that minute,
someone had been standing there next to him, also leaning his
elbows on the rail of the embankment, and—wondrous thing!—
had even said something to him, said something rapidly,
abruptly, not quite clearly, but about something quite close to
him, of concern to him. "Did I imagine it, or what?" said Mr.
Goliadkin, looking around once more. "But what am I doing
standing here?...Eh, eh!" he concluded, shaking his head, and
meanwhile, with an uneasy, anguished feeling, even with fear,
he began peering into the dim, moist distance, straining his
vision with all his might, and trying with all his might to
penetrate with his nearsighted gaze into the wet milieu spread
before him. However, there was nothing new, nothing special
struck Mr. Goliadkin's eye. It seemed that everything was in
order, as it ought to be—that is, the snow poured down still
heavier, bigger, and thicker; nothing could be seen beyond a
distance of twenty paces; the streetlamps creaked ever more
piercingly, and the wind seemed to drone its melancholy song
still more plaintively and pitifully, like an importunate beggar

pleading for a copper to feed himself. "Eh, eh! what's the matter with me?" Mr. Goliadkin repeated, starting on his way again, and still looking around a little. And yet some new sensation echoed in Mr. Goliadkin's whole being: not really anguish, not really fear . . . a feverish trembling ran through his veins. It was an unbearably unpleasant moment! "Well, never mind," he said to encourage himself, "never mind; maybe it's nothing at all, and no stain on anyone's honor. Maybe it had to be so," he went on, not understanding what he was saying himself, "maybe it will all work out for the better in time, and there won't be any claims to make, and everything will be justified." Speaking thus, and relieving himself with words, Mr. Goliadkin shook himself slightly, shaking off the snowflakes that covered in a thick crust his hat, his collar, his overcoat, his tie, his boots, and every-thing—but he was still unable to push away, to shake off the strange feeling, the strange, dark anguish. Somewhere in the distance a cannon shot rang out. "What weather," thought our hero. "Listen, mightn't there be a flood?"[17] The water must have risen very high." Mr. Goliadkin had only just said or thought this, when he saw before him a passerby coming in the opposite direction, like him, probably, also out late by some chance. It seemed to be a trifling, chance matter; but, no one knows why, Mr. Goliadkin became confused, and even frightened, slightly at a loss. Not that he feared he was a bad man, but just so, maybe . . . "And who knows about this late-night walker," flashed in Mr. Goliadkin's head, "maybe he's one, too, maybe he's the chief thing here, and not out walking for nothing, but with a purpose, crossing my path and brushing against me." Maybe, however, Mr. Goliadkin did not think precisely that, but only felt momentarily something similar and highly disagreeable. However, there was no time for thinking and feeling; the passerby was two steps away. Mr. Goliadkin hastened at once, as was his wont, to assume a completely special air, an air which showed clearly that he, Goliadkin, was his own man, that he was all right, that the way was wide enough for everybody, and that he, Goliadkin, was not offending anybody. Suddenly he stopped as if rooted, as if struck by lightning, and then quickly

turned to look at the man who had just walked past him—
turned as if something had pulled him from behind, as if the
wind had whirled his weathervane. The passerby was quickly
vanishing into the snowy blizzard. He, too, was walking hastily,
he, too, like Mr. Goliadkin, was dressed and wrapped from
head to foot and, just like him, pattered and minced down the
sidewalk of the Fontanka with scurrying little steps, trotting
slightly. "What...what is this?" whispered Mr. Goliadkin,
smiling mistrustfully—though he shuddered all over. A chill ran
down his spine. Meanwhile the passerby had vanished completely, even his footsteps were no longer heard, and Mr.
Goliadkin still stood and looked after him. Finally, though, he
began to recover his senses. "But what is this," he thought with
vexation, "have I really gone out of my mind, or what?"—turned
and went on his way, hurrying, and quickening his pace more
and more, and trying rather not to think about anything at all.
He even finally closed his eyes for that purpose. Suddenly,
through the howling of the wind and the noise of the storm,
there again came to his ears the noise of someone's footsteps
quite close by. He gave a start and opened his eyes. Before him
again, some twenty paces away, was the black shape of a little
man quickly approaching him. This man was hurrying, flurry-
ing, scurrying; the distance was quickly diminishing. Mr.
Goliadkin could even thoroughly examine his new late-night
comrade—examined him and cried out in astonishment and
terror; his legs gave way under him. This was that same walker
he knew, the one whom he had let pass by some ten minutes
earlier and who now had suddenly, quite unexpectedly, appeared
before him again. But this was not the only wonder that struck
Mr. Goliadkin—and Mr. Goliadkin was so struck that he
stopped, cried out, was about to say something—and started
after the stranger, even shouted something to him, probably
wishing to stop him the sooner. The stranger actually stopped
some ten paces from Mr. Goliadkin, and so that the light of
a nearby streetlamp fell full on his whole figure—stopped,
turned to Mr. Goliadkin, and, with an impatiently preoccupied
air, waited for what he would say. "Excuse me, perhaps I'm

mistaken," our hero said in a trembling voice. The stranger said nothing, turned in vexation, and quickly went on his way, as if hurrying to make up the two seconds lost on Mr. Goliadkin. As for Mr. Goliadkin, he trembled in every muscle, his knees gave way, grew weak, and he sank with a moan onto a hitching post. However, there actually was a cause for such bewilderment. The thing was that this stranger now seemed somehow familiar to him. That would still be nothing. But he recognized, he now almost fully recognized this man. He had seen him often, this man, even used to see him quite recently; but where was it? was it not just yesterday? However, once again this was not the main thing, that Mr. Goliadkin had seen him often; and there was almost nothing special about this man—no one's special attention would have been drawn to this man at first sight. He was just a man like everybody else, a decent one, to be sure, like all decent people, and maybe had some merits, even rather significant ones—in short, he was his own man. Mr. Goliadkin did not even nurse any hatred, or hostility, or even the slightest animosity for this man, even the contrary, it would seem—yet (and the greatest force lay in this circumstance), yet he would not have wanted to meet him for all the treasures in the world and especially to meet him as he had now, for instance. We will say more: Mr. Goliadkin knew this man perfectly well; he even knew what he was called, knew what the man's last name was; yet not for anything, and again not for all the treasures in the world, would he have wanted to name him, to agree to recognize, say, that he was called such-and-such, that such-and-such was his patronymic, and such-and-such his last name. Whether Mr. Goliadkin's quandary lasted a long or a short time, whether he sat for precisely a long time on the hitching post, I cannot say, but only that finally, having recovered a little, he suddenly broke into a run without looking back, for all the strength that was in him; his breath kept failing; he stumbled twice, nearly fell—on this occasion Mr. Goliadkin's other boot became orphaned, also abandoned by its galosh. Finally, Mr. Goliadkin slowed his pace a little, so as to catch his breath, hurriedly looked around, and saw that he had already run, without noticing it, the whole of his way along the Fontanka, crossed the Anichkov Bridge, gone partway down Nevsky, and was now standing at the corner of Liteinaya. Mr. Goliadkin turned onto Liteinaya. His position at that moment was like the position of a man standing over a frightful precipice, when the earth breaks away under him, is rocking, shifting, sways for a last time, and falls, drawing him into the abyss, and meanwhile the unfortunate man has neither the strength nor the firmness of spirit to jump back, to take his eyes from the yawning chasm; the abyss draws him, and he finally leaps into it himself, himself hastening the moment of his own perdition. Mr. Goliadkin knew, felt, and was completely certain that some further bad thing was bound to befall him on the way, that some further trouble would break over him, that, for instance, he would meet his stranger again; but—strange thing—he even wished for that meeting, considered it inevitable, and asked only for it all to be over, for his situation to be resolved at least somehow, only soon. And meanwhile he went on running, running, as if moved by some outside force, for he felt some sort of weakening and numbness in his whole being; he was unable to think about anything, though his ideas kept catching at everything like thorns. Some forsaken little dog, all wet and shivering, tagged after Mr. Goliadkin and also ran along sideways next to him, hurriedly, tail and ears drooping, from time to time glancing at him timidly and intelligently. Some remote, long-forgotten idea—the remembrance of circumstances that had occurred long ago—now came to his head, knocked like a little hammer in his head, vexed him, would not leave him alone. "Eh, this nasty little dog!" whispered Mr. Goliadkin, not understanding himself. Finally, he saw his stranger at the corner of Italianskaya Street. Only now the stranger was going not in the opposite but in the same direction as himself, and was also running, a few steps ahead. Finally, they reached Shestilavochnaya. Mr. Goliadkin was breathless. The stranger stopped right in front of the house where Mr. Goliadkin lived. The bell rang and at almost the same time the iron bolt rasped. The gate opened, the stranger stooped, flashed, and vanished. At almost the same instant, Mr. Goliadkin arrived and shot arrowlike through the gate. Not heeding the caretaker's grumbling, breathless, he ran into the courtyard and at once saw his interesting companion, whom he had lost for a moment. The stranger flashed at the entrance to the stairway that led to Mr. Goliadkin's apartment. Mr. Goliadkin rushed after him. The stairway was dark, damp, and dirty. At each turning, a mass of all sorts of household rubbish was heaped up, so that a stranger, an unaccustomed man, coming to that stairway at a dark time, would be forced to travel it for half an hour, risking a broken leg, and cursing both the stairway and his acquaintances who lived in so uncomfortable a place. But Mr. Goliadkin's companion was like an acquaintance, a familiar; he ran up lightly, without difficulty, and with a perfect knowledge of the locale. Mr. Goliadkin almost caught up with him completely; the skirt of the stranger's overcoat even struck him on the nose once or twice. His heart was sinking. The mysterious man stopped right in front of the door to Mr. Goliadkin's apartment, knocked, and (which, however, would have surprised Mr. Goliadkin at another time) Petrushka, as if he had been waiting and had not gone to bed, opened the door at once and walked after the entering man with a candle in his hand. Beside himself, the hero of our narrative also ran into his lodgings; not taking off his overcoat and hat, he went down the little corridor and, as if thunderstruck, stopped on the threshold of his room. All of Mr. Goliadkin's forebodings had come perfectly true. All that he had feared and anticipated had now become reality. His breath broke off, his head spun. The stranger sat before him, also in his overcoat and hat, on his own bed, smiling slightly, narrowing his eyes a little, nodding to him amicably. Mr. Goliadkin wanted to cry out but could not—to protest in some way, but had no strength. His hair stood on end, and he slumped down where he was, insensible from horror. With good reason, however. Mr. Goliadkin had perfectly well recognized his night companion. His night companion was none other than himself—Mr. Goliadkin himself, another Mr. Goliadkin, but perfectly the same as himself—in short, what is known as his double in all respects.

CHAPTER VI

THE NEXT MORNING, at exactly eight o'clock, Mr. Goliadkin came to in his bed. Straight away all the extraordinary things of yesterday and all that incredible, wild night, with its almost impossible adventures, at once, suddenly, in all their terrifying fullness, appeared to his imagination and memory. Such fierce, infernal malice from his enemies, and especially the last proof of that malice, froze Mr. Goliadkin's heart. But at the same time it was all so strange, incomprehensible, wild, it seemed so impossible, that it was actually hard to give credence to the whole thing; even Mr. Goliadkin himself would have been prepared to recognize it all as unfeasible raving, a momentarily disturbed imagination, a darkening of the mind, if, luckily for him, he had not known from bitter life's experience how far malice can sometimes drive a man, how far an enemy's fierceness can sometimes go in avenging his honor and ambition. Besides, Mr. Goliadkin's racked limbs, his dazed head, his aching back, and a malignant cold witnessed to and insisted on all the probability of last night's promenade, and partly to all the rest that had occurred during that promenade. And, finally, Mr. Goliadkin had already long known that they were preparing something there, that they had someone else there. But—what then? Having thought well, Mr. Goliadkin decided to say nothing, to submit, and not to protest about this matter for the time being. "Maybe they just think to frighten me a little, and when they see that I don't mind, don't protest, and am perfectly humble, that I endure with humility, they'll give it up, give it up themselves, even be the first to give it up."

Such were the thoughts in Mr. Goliadkin's head when, stretching in his bed and spreading his racked limbs, he waited this time for Petrushka's usual appearance in his room. He waited for a quarter of an hour; he heard the lazybones

Petrushka pottering with the samovar behind the partition, and yet he simply could not bring himself to call him. We will say more: Mr. Goliadkin was now even slightly afraid of a face-to-face meeting with Petrushka. "God knows," he thought, "God knows how that knave looks at this whole thing now. He says nothing, but he keeps his own counsel." Finally the door creaked, and Petrushka appeared with a tray in his hands. Mr. Goliadkin timidly gave him a sidelong glance, waiting impatiently for what would happen, waiting to see if he would finally say something concerning a certain circumstance. But Petrushka said nothing; on the contrary, he was somehow more silent, stern, and cross than usual, looking askance at everything from under his eyebrows; generally it was evident that he was extremely displeased with something; he did not look at his master even once, which, be it said in passing, slightly piqued Mr. Goliadkin; he put everything he had brought with him on the table, turned, and silently went behind his partition. "He knows, he knows, he knows everything, the lout!" Mr. Goliadkin muttered, sitting down to his tea. However, our hero asked his man precisely nothing, though Petrushka later came into his room several times for various needs. Mr. Goliadkin was in a most alarmed state of mind. He also felt eerie about going to the department. He had a strong presentiment that precisely there something was not right. "Suppose you go there," he thought, "and run into something or other? Wouldn't it be better to be patient now? Wouldn't it be better to wait now? Let them be as they like there; but today I'd rather wait here, gather my strength, recover, reflect better about the whole thing, and then seize the moment, drop on them out of the blue, and act as if nothing happened." Pondering in this way, Mr. Goliadkin smoked pipe after pipe; time flew; it was already nearly half-past nine. "So it's already half-past nine," thought Mr. Goliadkin, "it's even late to show up. Besides, I'm sick, of course I'm sick, certainly I'm sick; who'll say I'm not? What do I care! So they send to verify it, so let the errand boy come; what indeed do I care? I've got a backache, a cough, a cold; and, finally, I can't go, I simply can't go in such weather; I may fall ill, and then even die for all I know; there's such peculiar mortality nowadays..." With such reasonings, Mr. Goliadkin finally set his conscience fully at ease and justified himself beforehand in view of the dressing-down he expected from Andrei Filippovich for being remiss at work. Generally, in all such circumstances, our hero was extremely fond of justifying himself in his own eyes by various irrefutable reasons and thus setting his conscience fully at ease. And so, having now set his conscience fully at ease, he took his pipe, filled it, and, having just begun to draw on it properly, jumped up quickly from the sofa, threw the pipe aside, briskly washed, shaved, smoothed his hair, pulled on his uniform and all the rest, seized some papers, and flew off to the department.

Mr. Goliadkin entered his section timidly, in trembling expectation of something quite unpleasant—an unconscious expectation, obscure, but at the same time disagreeable; he sat down timidly in his usual place beside the chief clerk, Anton Antonovich Setochkin. Not looking at anything, not distracted by anything, he tried to grasp the contents of the papers that lay before him. He resolved and promised himself to keep as far away as possible from anything provoking, from anything that might seriously compromise him—that is, from immodest questions, from somebody or other's jokes and improper allusions regarding all the circumstances of the previous evening; he even resolved to refrain from the usual civilities with his colleagues, such as inquiries about health and so on. But it was also obvious that to remain that way would not do, was not possible. Anxiety and ignorance about something that closely concerned him always tormented him more than the thing itself. And that was why, despite his promise to himself not to enter into anything, whatever might happen, and to keep away from everything, whatever it might be, Mr. Goliadkin occasionally raised his head on the sly, ever so quietly, and stealthily glanced sidelong to right, to left, peeking into the physiognomies of his colleagues and trying to conclude from them whether there was anything new and particular that concerned him and was being concealed from him for some unseemly purposes. He assumed

that there was an inevitable connection between all his circumstances yesterday and everything that surrounded him now.
Finally, in his anguish, he began to wish only that it be resolved
quickly, even God knows how, even in some disaster—who
cared! It was here that fate caught Mr. Goliadkin: he had barely
managed to wish it, when his doubts were suddenly resolved,
albeit in a most strange and unexpected fashion.

The door to the other room suddenly creaked quietly and
timidly, as if to introduce the entering person as quite insignificant, and someone's figure—quite familiar, however, to Mr.
Goliadkin—appeared bashfully before that same desk at which
our hero was installed. Our hero did not raise his head—no, he
glimpsed this figure only in passing, with the slightest glance,
but he already knew everything, understood everything to the
smallest detail. He burned with shame and buried his victorious
head in the papers, with exactly the same purpose as an ostrich
pursued by a hunter buries its head in the hot sand. The newcomer bowed to Andrei Filippovich, and after that a formally
benign voice was heard, the sort with which superiors in all
official places speak to new subordinates. "Sit down here," said
Andrei Filippovich, pointing the novice to Anton Antonovich's
desk, "here, opposite Mr. Goliadkin, and we'll find something
for you to do at once." Andrei Filippovich concluded by making
the newcomer a quick, properly admonishing gesture, and then
immediately immersed himself in the essence of various papers,
a whole pile of which lay before him.

Mr. Goliadkin finally raised his eyes, and if he did not faint,
it was solely because he had anticipated the whole thing in
advance, because he had been forewarned of it all in advance,
having divined the newcomer in his soul. Mr. Goliadkin's first
move was to look around quickly, to see whether there was
any whispering, whether any office joke was being cooked up,
whether anyone's face was distorted with surprise, whether,
finally, anyone fell under the desk from fright. But, to Mr.
Goliadkin's greatest surprise, no one showed anything of the
sort. The behavior of Mr. Goliadkin's gentleman comrades and
colleagues astounded him. It seemed beyond common sense.

Mr. Goliadkin was even frightened by such extraordinary silence. The essence of the thing spoke for itself: it was strange, outrageous, wild. There was cause for a stir. All this, to be sure, only flashed through Mr. Goliadkin's head. He himself was roasting on a slow fire. There was cause for that, however. The one now sitting opposite Mr. Goliadkin was Mr. Goliadkin's horror, he was Mr. Goliadkin's shame, he was Mr. Goliadkin's nightmare from yesterday, in short, he was Mr. Goliadkin himself—not the Mr. Goliadkin who was now sitting in a chair with a gaping mouth and a pen frozen in his hand; not the one who served as assistant to his chief clerk; not the one who likes to efface himself and bury himself in the crowd; not the one, finally, whose gait clearly says: "Don't touch me, and I won't touch you," or "Don't touch me, since I don't touch you"—no, it was a different Mr. Goliadkin, completely different, but at the same time completely identical to the first—of the same height, of the same mold, dressed the same way, with the same bald spot—in short, nothing, decidedly nothing, had been overlooked for a complete likeness, so that if they had been taken and placed next to each other, no one, decidedly no one, would have undertaken to determine precisely which was the real Goliadkin and which was the counterfeit, which was the old and which the new, which was the original and which the copy.

Our hero, if the comparison is possible, was now in the position of a man at whom some mischiefmaker was poking fun, aiming a burning-glass at him on the sly, as a joke. "What is this, a dream or not," he thought, "a reality or a continuation of yesterday? How can it be? By what right is it all being done? Who has allowed such a clerk, who gave the right for it? Am I asleep, am I dreaming?" Mr. Goliadkin tried to pinch himself, he even tried to get himself to pinch someone else... No, it was not a dream, and that was that. Mr. Goliadkin felt that sweat was pouring down him in streams, that something unprecedented, something unheard-of, was happening to him, which therefore, to complete the misfortune, was also indecent, for Mr. Goliadkin understood and felt all the disadvantage of being the first example of such a lampoonish thing. He even began, finally, to doubt his own existence, and though he had been prepared for anything beforehand, and had wished himself that his doubts would be resolved at least in some way, the very essence of the circumstance, of course, suited the unexpectedness. Anguish oppressed and tormented him. At times he was completely bereft of sense and memory. Recovering after such moments, he noticed that he was mechanically and unconsciously moving his pen over the paper. Not trusting himself, he began to check all he had written—and understood nothing. Finally, the other Mr. Goliadkin, who till then had been sitting decorously and peaceably, got up and disappeared through the door of another section on some errand. Mr. Goliadkin looked around—all right, everything was quiet; only the scratching of pens was heard, the rustle of turning pages, and talking in the corners furthest from Andrei Filippovich's seat. Mr. Goliadkin glanced at Anton Antonovich, and since, in all probability, our hero's physiognomy fully corresponded to his present and was in harmony with the whole sense of the matter, and consequently was highly remarkable in a certain respect, the kindly Anton Antonovich, laying aside his pen, inquired with extraordinary solicitousness after Mr. Goliadkin's health.

"I thank God, Anton Antonovich," Mr. Goliadkin said, faltering, "I'm perfectly well, Anton Antonovich; I'm all right now, Anton Antonovich," he added hesitantly, still not quite trusting the oft-mentioned Anton Antonovich.

"Ah! And I fancied you were unwell; however, no wonder if you were! These days, especially, there are all sorts of infections. You know..."

"Yes, Anton Antonovich, I know, such infections exist... I didn't mean that, Anton Antonovich," Mr. Goliadkin went on, peering intently at Anton Antonovich. "You see, Anton Antonovich, I don't even know how to make you, that is, I mean to say, from which side to approach this matter."

"What, sir? I...you know...I confess to you, I don't understand you very well; you...you know, you should explain more thoroughly in what respect you are in difficulties here," said

Anton Antonovich, who was in some small difficulty himself, seeing that tears had even welled up in Mr. Goliadkin's eyes.

"I really...here, Anton Antonovich...a clerk here, Anton Antonovich."

"Well, sir! I still don't understand."

"I mean to say, Anton Antonovich, that there is a newly hired clerk here."

"Yes, sir, there is—your namesake."

"What?" cried Mr. Goliadkin.

"I'm saying he's your namesake; also Goliadkin. Mightn't he be your brother?"

"No, sir, Anton Antonovich, I..."

"Hm! you don't say. And it seemed to me that he must be a close relative of yours. You know, there's this certain sort of familial resemblance."

Mr. Goliadkin was stupefied with amazement, and for a time he was robbed of speech. To treat such an outrageous, unheard-of thing so lightly, a thing indeed rare of its kind, a thing that would astonish even the most disinterested observer, to speak of a family resemblance when here it was like looking in a mirror!

"You know, this is what I advise you, Yakov Petrovich," Anton Antonovich went on. "You should go to the doctor and ask his advice. You know, you somehow *look* quite unwell. Your eyes especially...you know, there's some special expression in them."

"No, Anton Antonovich, of course I feel...that is, I want to ask you, how about this clerk?"

"Well, sir?"

"That is, haven't you noticed something particular about him, Anton Antonovich...something all too conspicuous?"

"That is?"

"That is, I mean to say, Anton Antonovich, a striking resemblance to someone, for example, that is, to me, for example. You spoke just now, Anton Antonovich, of family resemblance, you made a passing remark...You know, sometimes there are twins like that, that is, exactly like two drops of water, so there's no telling them apart. Well, that's what I mean, sir."

"Yes, sir," said Anton Antonovich, having pondered a little and as if struck by this circumstance for the first time, "yes, that's right, sir! The resemblance is indeed striking, and you're not mistaken in judging that the one could actually be taken for the other," he went on, opening his eyes wider and wider. "And you know, Yakov Petrovich, it's even a wondrous resemblance, fantastic, as they sometimes say, that is, he's exactly like you...Have you noticed, Yakov Petrovich? I even wanted to ask you for an explanation myself; yes, I confess, I didn't pay proper attention to it at first. A wonder, a real wonder! And you know, Yakov Petrovich, you're not from local folk, I'd say?"

"No, sir."

"Neither is he. Maybe he's from the same place as you. If I may venture to ask, where did your mother live for the most part?"

"You said...you said, Anton Antonovich, that he's not from local folk?"

"Right, sir, he's not from these parts. And, indeed, how wondrous that is," continued the loquacious Anton Antonovich, for whom a chat about something was a real feast, "it is actually capable of arousing curiosity; one passes it by so often, brushes against it, shoves it, without noticing it. However, don't be embarrassed. It happens. This, you know—here's what I'll tell you, that the same thing happened to my aunt on my mother's side; she also saw herself double before she died..."

"No, sir, I—excuse me for interrupting you, Anton Antonovich—I, Anton Antonovich, would like to know how this clerk, that is, on what grounds is he here?"

"In place of the deceased Semyon Ivanovich, in his vacant place; a vacancy opened up, so they replaced him. Now, really, the thing is that this dear deceased Semyon Ivanovich, they say, left three children—each one smaller than the next. The widow fell at his excellency's feet. They say, however, that she's got something hidden away; there's a bit of money there, but she's hidden it away..."

"No, Anton Antonovich, sir, I'm still talking about this circumstance."

"That is? Well, yes! but why does it interest you so? I tell you, don't be embarrassed. It's all a bit temporary. What, then? it's not your concern; the Lord God Himself arranged it this way, such was His will, and it's sinful to murmur against it. His wisdom can be seen in it. And you, Yakov Petrovich, as far as I understand, are not at all to blame. There are all sorts of wonders in the world! Mother Nature is generous; and you won't be asked to answer for it, you will not answer for it. Take, for example, incidentally speaking, you've heard, I hope, how those, what do you call them, yes, Siamese twins, are joined at the back, so they live, and eat, and sleep together; they say they bring in a lot of money."

"Excuse me, Anton Antonovich..."

"I understand you, I understand! Yes! well, and so?—never mind! I speak from my utmost understanding, there's nothing to be embarrassed about. What of it? He's a clerk like any other, and seems to be an efficient man. He says he's Goliadkin; not from these parts, he says, a titular councillor. Had a personal talk with his excellency."

"Well, and how was it, sir?"

"All right, sir. They say he gave sufficient explanations, presented reasons; he said thus and so, Your Excellency, I have no fortune, but I wish to serve, and especially under your flattering leadership... well, and everything one ought to say, you know, he put it aptly. Must be a clever man. Well, naturally, he came with a recommendation; no doing without that..."

"Well, but who from, sir?...that is, I mean to say, precisely who mixed his hand in this shameful business?"

"Yes, sir. A good recommendation, they say; his excellency, they say, had a laugh with Andrei Filippovich."

"A laugh with Andrei Filippovich?"

"Yes, sir. He just smiled and said it was good, and that for his part he was not against it, as long as he served loyally..."

"Well, go on, sir. You've revived me a bit, Anton Antonovich; I beg you, go on, sir."

"Excuse me, I again said something that you... Well, yes, sir; well, and never mind, sir; it's an uncomplicated matter; I tell you, don't be embarrassed, and there's nothing dubious to be found in it..."

"No, sir. I, that is, want to ask you, Anton Antonovich, whether his excellency added nothing more...concerning me, for example?"

"How's that, sir? Right, sir! Well, no, nothing; you can be perfectly at ease. You know, of course, to be sure, it's a very striking circumstance and at first...yet I, for example, almost didn't notice at first. I really don't know why I didn't notice until you reminded me. However, you can be perfectly at ease. He said nothing at all, nothing in particular," added the kindly Anton Antonovich, getting up from his chair.

"So, then, sir, I, Anton Antonovich..."

"Ah, you must forgive me, sir. I've been babbling about trifles, and here's an important, urgent matter. I must make inquiries."

"Anton Antonovich!" the politely summoning voice of Andrei Filippovich rang out, "his excellency is asking for you."

"At once, at once, Andrei Filippovich, I'll come at once, sir." And Anton Antonovich, taking a small pile of papers in his hands, flew first to Andrei Filippovich and then to his excellency's office.

"What's this?" Mr. Goliadkin thought to himself. "So this is the sort of game we've got here! This is the sort of wind we've got blowing now...Not bad; it means things have taken a most agreeable turn," our hero said to himself, rubbing his hands and not feeling the chair under him from joy. "So our affair is quite an ordinary affair. So it ends in trifles, resolves itself into nothing. In fact, nobody thinks anything, and they don't peep, the robbers, they sit and keep busy; nice, very nice! I love a good man, love and am always ready to respect...However, if you think about it, this Anton Antonovich...I'm afraid to trust him: he's much too gray-haired and pretty shaky with old age. However, the nicest and greatest thing is that his excellency said nothing and let it pass: that's good! I approve! Only what's Andrei Filippovich doing mixing into it with his laughter? What is it to him? The old stitch! He's always in my way, always trying to run across a man's path like a black cat, always thwarting and spiting him; spiting and thwarting him..."

Mr. Goliadkin looked around again, and again hope revived him. However, he still felt embarrassed by some remote thought, some bad thought. It even occurred to him to somehow sidle up to the clerks, to run ahead harelike, even (somehow as they were leaving after work or approaching them as if on business) in the midst of conversation, and to hint that, say, gentlemen, thus and so, there's this striking resemblance, a strange circumstance, a lampoonish comedy—that is, to make fun of it all and in this way to sound the depths of the danger. Because still waters do run deep, our hero concluded mentally. However, Mr. Goliadkin only thought it; but he caught himself in time. He realized that it would be going too far. "That's your nature!" he said to himself, slapping himself lightly on the forehead. "You immediately start playing, rejoicing! A truthful soul! No, Yakov Petrovich, you and I had better wait and be patient!" Nevertheless, and as we have already mentioned, Mr. Goliadkin was reborn in full hope, as if resurrected from the dead. "Never mind," he thought, "it's as if five hundred pounds had fallen off my chest! There's a circumstance for you! And the coffer had no trick to it. Krylov's right, Krylov's right[18] ... he's a dab, a stitch, that Krylov, and a great fable writer! And as for that one, let him work, let him work all he likes, as long as he doesn't interfere with anybody or touch anybody; let him work—I agree and I approbate!"

But meanwhile the hours passed, flew by, and before he noticed it struck four o'clock. The office closed; Andrei Filippovich took his hat, and, as usual, everyone followed his example. Mr. Goliadkin lingered a little, as long as necessary, and purposely went out after everyone else, last, when everyone had already wandered off their different ways. Going outside, he felt as if he was in paradise, so that he even had a desire to stroll along Nevsky, though it meant a detour. "That's fate for you!" said our hero. "An unexpected turnabout of the whole affair. And the weather has cleared, and there's frost, and sleighriding. And frost suits the Russian man, the Russian man

gets along nicely with frost! I love the Russian man. And there's
snow, a first dust of snow, as a hunter would say. Oh, to be
tracking a hare in the first dust of snow! Ahh! Well, never
mind!"

Thus Mr. Goliadkin expressed his delight, and yet something
kept tickling in his head—anguish or not, but at times his heart
was so wrenched that Mr. Goliadkin did not know how to comfort himself. "However, let's wait till daytime and then rejoice.
What is all this, however? Well, let's reason and see. Well, go on
and reason, my young friend, go on and reason. Well, he's a man
the same as you, first of all, exactly the same. Well, what of it?
If that's what he is, why should I weep? What is it to me?
I stand apart, I whistle to myself, that's all. So it goes, that's
all! Let him work! Well, it's a wonder and a strange thing,
they say, these Siamese twins... Well, who needs them, these
Siamese? Suppose they are twins, but great people have also
looked strange sometimes. It's even known from history that
the famous Suvorov crowed like a rooster[19] ... Well, for him it
was all politics; and great generals... yes, however, what about
generals? I'm my own man, that's all, I don't care about anybody,
and in my innocence I despise the enemy. I'm not an intriguer,
and I'm proud of it. I'm pure, straightforward, neat, agreeable,
unresentful..."

Suddenly Mr. Goliadkin fell silent, stopped short, and
trembled like a leaf, and even closed his eyes for a moment.
Hoping, however, that the object of his fear was simply an
illusion, he finally opened his eyes and glanced timidly to the
right. No, it was not an illusion!... Beside him trotted his
morning acquaintance, smiling, peeking into his eyes, and
apparently waiting for a chance to start a conversation. The
conversation, however, would not get started. The two men
went some fifty steps like that. All Mr. Goliadkin's effort went
into wrapping himself more tightly, burying himself in his overcoat, and pulling the hat down over his eyes as far as possible.
To complete the injury, even his friend's overcoat and hat were
exactly as if they had just been taken from Mr. Goliadkin's
shoulders.

"My dear sir," our hero finally said, trying to speak almost in a whisper and not looking at his friend, "it seems we're going different ways ... I'm even sure of it," he said after some silence. "Finally, I'm sure you've understood me perfectly," he added rather sternly in conclusion.

"I should like," Mr. Goliadkin's friend said finally, "I should like ... you will probably magnanimously forgive me ... I don't know whom to turn to here ... my circumstances—I hope you will forgive my boldness—it even seemed to me that, moved to compassion, you concerned yourself with me this morning. For my part, I felt drawn to you from the first glance, I ..." Here Mr. Goliadkin mentally wished his new colleague would fall through the earth. "If I dared hope that you, Yakov Petrovich, would be so indulgent as to listen ..."

"We—here we—we ... we'd better go to my place," replied Mr. Goliadkin. "We'll cross to the other side of Nevsky now, it will be more convenient for us there, and then take the side street ... we'd better take the side street."

"Very well, sir. Why not take the side street, sir," Mr. Goliadkin's humble companion said timidly, as if hinting by the tone of his reply that it was not for him to choose and that, in his position, he was ready to be satisfied with a side street. As for Mr. Goliadkin, he did not understand at all what was happening to him. He did not believe himself. He still could not recover from his amazement.

CHAPTER VII

H E RECOVERED A LITTLE on the stairs, by the entrance to his apartment. "Ah, what a mutton-head I am!" he mentally denounced himself. "Where am I bringing him? Putting my own head into the noose. What will Petrushka think, seeing us together? What will this blackguard venture to think now? and he's suspicious . . ." But it was too late for regrets; Mr. Goliadkin knocked, the door opened, and Petrushka began taking the overcoats from his master and the guest. Mr. Goliadkin looked in passing, just cast a fleeting glance at Petrushka, trying to penetrate his physiognomy and guess his thoughts. But, to his greatest surprise, he saw that it did not occur to his servant to be surprised and even, on the contrary, that it was as if he had been expecting something like that. Of course, now, too, he looked wolfish, squinted sideways, as if he was getting ready to eat somebody. "They all seem bewitched today," thought our hero, "some demon must have been running around! There certainly must be something special with all these folk today. Devil take it, what a torment!" Thinking and pondering in this way, Mr. Goliadkin led the guest to his room and humbly begged him to sit down. The guest was evidently extremely disconcerted, very timid, followed obediently all the movements of his host, caught his glances, and from them, it seemed, tried to guess his thoughts. Something humiliated, downtrodden, and intimidated showed in all his gestures, so that, if the comparison be permitted, he rather resembled at the moment a man who, having no clothes of his own, had put on someone else's: the sleeves pull up, the waist is almost at the neck, he straightens his scanty waistcoat every minute, or shuffles sideways and gives way, first tries to hide somewhere, then peeks into everyone's eyes and tries to hear whether they may be saying something about his circumstances, or laughing at him, or are ashamed of him—and the man blushes, and is at a loss, and his vanity suffers... Mr. Goliadkin placed his hat on the windowsill; a careless movement knocked it to the floor. The guest straight away rushed to pick it up, brushed off all the dust, carefully put it back in its former place, and put his own on the floor by the chair on the edge of which he humbly placed himself. This small circumstance partly opened Mr. Goliadkin's eyes; he realized that he was greatly needed, and therefore no longer troubled himself with how to begin with his guest, leaving it all, as was only fitting, to the man himself. The guest, for his part, also began nothing, being either timid or slightly ashamed, or else waiting, out of politeness, for the host to begin—no one knows, it was difficult to figure it out. At that moment Petrushka came in, stopped in the doorway, and fixed his eyes in a direction completely opposite to that in which the guest and his master were located.

"Shall I bring two portions of dinner?" he asked casually and in a husky voice.

"I, I don't know... you—yes, bring two portions, brother."

Petrushka left. Mr. Goliadkin looked at his guest. The guest blushed to his ears. Mr. Goliadkin was a kind man and therefore, in the kindness of his heart, at once put together a theory:

"A poor man," he thought, "and he's only been one day on the job; he has probably suffered in his time; maybe these decent clothes are his only belongings, and he has nothing to eat on. Look how downtrodden he is! Well, never mind; it's partly even better..."

"Excuse me for..." Mr. Goliadkin began, "however, will you allow me to know your name?"

"Ya... Ya... Yakov Petrovich," his guest almost whispered, as if guilty and ashamed, as if asking forgiveness for also being called Yakov Petrovich.

"Yakov Petrovich!" our hero repeated, unable to conceal his embarrassment.

"Yes, sir, exactly right... Your namesake, sir," Mr. Goliadkin's humble guest replied, venturing to smile and say something of a jocular sort. But he sank back at once, assuming the gravest air, slightly embarrassed, however, noticing that his host was beyond joking just then.

"You...allow me to ask, by what chance do I have the honor..."

"Knowing your magnanimity and your virtues," his guest interrupted promptly, but in a timid voice, rising slightly from his chair, "I have ventured to turn to you and ask for your... acquaintance and patronage..." his guest concluded, obviously finding his expressions with difficulty and trying to choose words that were not too obsequious and humiliating, so as not to compromise himself in respect to his pride, nor too bold, smacking of indecent equality. In general, it could be said that Mr. Goliadkin's guest behaved like a noble beggar in a patched tailcoat and with a noble passport in his pocket, not yet properly practiced in holding out his hand.

"You embarrass me," replied Mr. Goliadkin, looking around at himself, his walls, his guest. "Is there anything I can...that is, I mean to say, precisely in what respect can I be of service to you?"

"I, Yakov Petrovich, felt drawn to you from the first glance and, be so magnanimous as to forgive me, I venture to place my hopes in you—my hopes, Yakov Petrovich. I...I am a forlorn man here, Yakov Petrovich, a poor man, I've suffered greatly, Yakov Petrovich, and I'm still new here. Having learned that you, with all the ordinary, innate qualities of your beautiful soul, are also my namesake..."

Mr. Goliadkin winced.

"... my namesake, and originating from the same parts as me, I decided to turn to you and explain to you my difficult situation."

"Very well, sir, very well; really, I don't know what to tell you," Mr. Goliadkin replied in an embarrassed voice. "After dinner we'll have a talk..."

The guest bowed; dinner was brought. Petrushka set the table, and guest and host together began to satiate themselves. Dinner did not take long; both men were hurrying—the host, because he was not quite himself and, besides, was embarrassed

about the bad dinner—embarrassed partly because he wanted
to feed his guest well, and partly because he wanted to show
that he did not live like a beggar. The guest, for his part, was
extremely embarrassed and extremely abashed. Having taken
the bread once and eaten his slice, he was now afraid to reach
for a second slice; he was ashamed to take the better pieces, and
insisted every moment that he was not at all hungry, that the
dinner was excellent, and that he, for his part, was completely
satisfied, and would be sensible of it to his dying day. When
the eating was over, Mr. Goliadkin lit his pipe, offered another,
kept for friends, to his guest, the two sat down facing each
other, and the guest began recounting his adventures.

Mr. Goliadkin Jr.'s account went on for three or four hours.
The story of his adventures was, however, made up of the most
empty, the most puny, if one may say that, of circumstances.
It was a matter of working somewhere in a provincial government office, of some prosecutors and chairmen, of some bureau-
cratic intrigues, of the depraved soul of one of the chief clerks,
of an inspector, of a sudden change of superiors, of Mr.
Goliadkin-the-second suffering quite blamelessly; of his elderly
aunt, Pelageya Semyonovna; of how, owing to various intrigues
of his enemies, he lost his post and came on foot to Petersburg;
of how he languished and suffered grief here in Petersburg, how
he sought work fruitlessly for a long time, spent all his money,
ate up all his food, lived almost in the street, ate stale bread,
washing it down with his tears, slept on a bare floor, and,
finally how one good man undertook to solicit for him and
magnanimously set him up in a new job. Mr. Goliadkin's guest
wept as he told it all, and wiped his tears with a blue checked
handkerchief that greatly resembled oilcloth. He concluded by
opening himself completely to Mr. Goliadkin and confessing
that, for the time being, he not only did not have enough to
live on and set himself up decently, but could not even outfit
himself properly, and that he had borrowed a uniform from
someone for a short time.

Mr. Goliadkin was moved to tenderness, was genuinely
touched. However, and even despite the fact that his guest's

story was of the emptiest sort, every word of this story lay on his heart like heavenly manna. The thing was that Mr. Goliadkin was forgetting his last doubts, he unbound his heart for freedom and joy, and finally bestowed on himself the title of fool. It was all so natural! And what cause was there to lament, to raise such an alarm? Well, there is, there actually is this one ticklish circumstance—but there's no harm in that: it can't besmirch a man, stain his ambition, and ruin his career, if it's not the man's fault, if nature itself has mixed into it. Besides, the guest asked for protection, the guest wept, the guest blamed fate, he seemed so artless, without malice or cunning, pathetic, insignificant, and, it seemed, was now ashamed himself, though perhaps in another connection, of the strange likeness of his own and his host's face. He behaved himself with the utmost propriety: all he was looking to do was to please his host, and he looked the way a man looks who is tormented by remorse and feels himself guilty before another man. If the talk, for instance, got on to some doubtful point, the guest at once agreed with Mr. Goliadkin's opinion. If, somehow by mistake, he expressed an opinion that went counter to Mr. Goliadkin's and then noticed that he had gone astray, he at once corrected his speech, explained himself, and made it known immediately that he understood it all just as his host did, his thoughts were the same as his, and he looked at it all with exactly the same eyes as he. In short, the guest made every possible effort to "seek after" Mr. Goliadkin, so that Mr. Goliadkin decided finally that his guest must be a highly obliging man in all respects. Meanwhile, tea was served; it was past eight o'clock. Mr. Goliadkin felt himself in excellent spirits, became cheerful, playful, let himself go a little, and finally launched into a most lively and entertaining conversation with his guest. Mr. Goliadkin, when in a jolly mood, occasionally enjoyed telling some interesting story. So it was now: he told his guest a great deal about the capital, its amusements and beauties, the theater, the clubs, Briullov's painting;[20] about two Englishmen who came on purpose from England to Petersburg in order to look at the fence of the Summer Garden, and then left at once; about the

office, about Olsufy Ivanovich and Andrei Filippovich; about
the fact that Russia was hourly moving towards perfection, and
that here

The art of letters flourisheth today;[21]

about a little anecdote he had read recently in the *Northern
Bee*,[22] and that in India there was a boa snake of extraordinary
strength; finally, about Baron Brambeus,[23] and so on, and so
forth. In short, Mr. Goliadkin was fully content, first, because
he was perfectly at ease; second, because he not only was not
afraid of his enemies, but was now even ready to challenge them
all to a most decisive battle; third, because he, in his own person,
was offering patronage and, finally, was doing a good deed. In
his soul, however, he acknowledged that he was not yet entirely
happy at that moment, that there was one little worm still
sitting in him—a very little one, however—and gnawing at his
heart even now. He was greatly tormented by the recollection
of the previous evening at Olsufy Ivanovich's. He would have
given much now if one thing or another of what had happened
yesterday had not happened. "However, it's all nothing!" our
hero finally concluded, and he firmly resolved in his heart to
behave well in the future and not fall into such blunders. Since
Mr. Goliadkin had now let himself go completely and had
suddenly become almost perfectly happy, he even decided to
enjoy life. Petrushka brought rum and they put together a
punch. Guest and host each drained a glass, then another. The
guest turned out to be still more obliging and, for his part,
showed more than one proof of his straightforwardness and
happy character, was greatly concerned with Mr. Goliadkin's
good pleasure, seemed to find joy only in his joy, and looked
upon him as his sole and true benefactor. Having taken a pen
and a sheet of paper, he asked Mr. Goliadkin not to look at
what he was going to write, and then, when he had finished,
himself showed his host all he had written. It turned out to be
a quatrain, rather sentimentally written—in a beautiful style and
handwriting, however, and evidently composed by the obliging
guest himself. The verses were the following:

> Though me thou mayest well forget,
> I shall ne'er forget thee.
> Anything can happen in this life,
> But, thou, do not forget me!

With tears in his eyes, Mr. Goliadkin embraced his guest and, finally waxing totally sentimental, initiated his guest into some of his secrets and mysteries, laying great stress in his speech on Andrei Filippovich and Klara Olsufyevna. "Well, so you and I will become close, Yakov Petrovich," our hero said to his guest, "you and I, Yakov Petrovich, will live like fish in water, like two brothers; we, my friend, will be clever, we'll be clever together; for our part, we'll conduct an intrigue to spite them ... to spite them we'll conduct an intrigue. And don't trust a one of them. I know you, Yakov Petrovich, and understand your character; you'll just up and tell all, you truthful soul! Keep away from all of them, brother." The guest agreed completely, thanked Mr. Goliadkin, and finally also waxed tearful. "You know, Yasha," Mr. Goliadkin went on in a trembling, weakened voice, "you settle with me for a time, or even for good. We'll become close. What is it to you, brother—eh? And don't be embarrassed and don't grumble that there's such a strange circumstance between us now: grumbling's a sin, brother; it's nature! Mother Nature's generous, that's what, brother Yasha! It's from love for you, from brotherly love for you, that I speak. And you and I are going to be clever, Yasha, for our part we'll undermine them and put their noses out of joint." The punch finally went as far as three and four glasses each, and then Mr. Goliadkin began to experience two sensations: one, that he was extraordinarily happy, the other—that he was no longer able to stand on his feet. The guest, naturally, was invited to spend the night. A bed was somehow put together out of two rows of chairs. Mr. Goliadkin Jr. announced that under a friendly roof even the floor was soft to sleep on, that he for his part would sleep wherever need be, with humility and gratitude; that he was now in paradise, and that, finally, he had suffered many misfortunes and woes in his life, had seen everything, had endured everything, and—who knows the future?—might endure still more. Mr. Goliadkin Sr. protested against that and began to demonstrate that one should place all hope in God. The guest fully agreed and said that, to be sure, there was no one like God. Here Mr. Goliadkin Sr. observed that the Turks were right in certain respects to invoke the name of God even in their sleep. Then, not agreeing, however, with some scholars in some of the aspersions they cast at the Turkish prophet Mohammed, and recognizing him as a great politician in his way, Mr. Goliadkin went on to a very interesting description of an Algerian barbershop, which he had read about in the miscellaneous section of some book. Guest and host laughed much at the simple-heartedness of the Turks; however, they could not help granting due astonishment to the fanaticism aroused in them by opium . . . The guest finally began to undress, and Mr. Goliadkin stepped behind the partition, partly out of the kindness of his heart, so as not to embarrass the man, who had already suffered without that, in case he might not have decent underclothes, and partly to assure himself as far as possible about Petrushka, to test him, cheer him up if he could, and show kindness to the man, so that everyone would be happy and no spilled salt would be left on the table. It should be noted that Petrushka still troubled Mr. Goliadkin a little.

"You go to bed now, Pyotr," Mr. Goliadkin said meekly, entering his servant's compartment, "you go to bed now, and wake me tomorrow at eight o'clock. Understand, Petrusha?"

Mr. Goliadkin spoke extraordinarily softly and gently. But Petrushka was silent. He was pottering about near his bed at the time and did not even turn to his master, which he should have done, however, if only out of respect for him.

"Did you hear me, Pyotr?" Mr. Goliadkin continued. "You go to bed now, Petrusha, and wake me tomorrow at eight o'clock; understand?"

"So I know already, so drop it!" Petrushka muttered under his nose.

"Well, there, Petrusha; I'm just saying it so you'll feel calm and happy. We're all happy now, so you, too, should be calm and happy. And now I wish you good night. Sleep, Petrusha, sleep; we all must work... You know, brother, don't go thinking anything..."

Mr. Goliadkin was about to begin, but stopped. "Won't it be too much?" he thought. "Haven't I overshot the mark? It's always that way; I fill to overflowing." Our hero left Petrushka's very displeased with himself. Besides, he was slightly hurt by Petrushka's rudeness and unyieldingness. "I make advances to the rogue, the master does the rogue that honor, and he doesn't feel it," thought Mr. Goliadkin. "However, that's the mean tendency of all his kind!" Swaying a bit, he returned to his room and, seeing that his guest was already lying down, sat on his bed for a moment. "But confess, Yasha," he began in a whisper and wagging his head, "you scoundrel, aren't you guilty before me? You know, my namesake, you sort of..." he went on, making advances rather familiarly to his guest. Finally, taking leave of him amicably, Mr. Goliadkin went to bed. The guest meanwhile began to snore. Mr. Goliadkin, in his turn, began to stretch out in bed, and meanwhile, chuckling, whispered to himself: "And you're drunk tonight, Yakov Petrovich, my dear heart, what a scoundrel you are, eh, what a Goliadka—that's what your name is!! Well, why are you so glad? You'll be weeping tomorrow, you're such a sniveler: what am I to do with you?!" Here a rather strange sensation echoed through Mr. Goliadkin's whole being, something like doubt or regret. "I really let myself go," he thought, "there's a buzzing in my head now, and I'm drunk; and you couldn't help yourself, you're such a big fool! poured out three buckets of drivel and still wanted to be clever, you scoundrel. Of course, forgiving and forgetting an offense is the foremost virtue, but all the same things are bad, that's what!" Here Mr. Goliadkin got up, took a candle, and went on tiptoe to look at his sleeping guest. For a long time he stood over him deep in thought. "An unpleasant picture! a lampoon, the sheerest lampoon, that's the end of it!"

Finally, Mr. Goliadkin lay down. In his head there was a buzzing, a crackling, a ringing. He began to sink into oblivion... tried to think about something, to remember something highly interesting, to resolve something highly important, some ticklish matter—but could not. Sleep flew down upon his victorious head, and he dropped off as people usually do who, without being accustomed to it, suddenly avail themselves of five glasses of punch at some friendly soirée.

CHAPTER VIII

As usual, Mr. Goliadkin woke up the next day at eight o'clock; on waking up, he at once recalled all that had happened yesterday evening, recalled it and winced. "Eh, I got playful yesterday like some kind of fool!" he thought, getting out of bed and looking at his guest's bed. But what was his surprise when not only the guest but even the bed on which the guest had slept was not in the room! "What is this?" Mr. Goliadkin all but cried out. "What can this possibly be? What does this new circumstance mean?" While Mr. Goliadkin, in perplexity, stared open-mouthed at the now empty place, the door creaked, and Petrushka came in with the tea tray. "But where, where?" our hero uttered in a barely audible voice, pointing his finger at the place reserved yesterday for the guest. Petrushka at first made no reply, did not even look at his master, but shifted his eyes to the right corner, so that Mr. Goliadkin was also forced to look into the right corner. However, after some silence, Petrushka replied in a husky and rude voice that "the master wasn't home."

"You fool, I'm your master, Petrushka," Mr. Goliadkin said in a faltering voice and stared all eyes at his servant.

Petrushka did not respond, but gave Mr. Goliadkin such a look that Mr. Goliadkin blushed to the ears—a look of some sort of insulting reproach, similar to outright abuse. Mr. Goliadkin dropped his arms, as they say. Finally, Petrushka announced that the *other* had left about an hour and a half ago and had not wanted to wait. Of course, the answer was probable and plausible; it was evident that Petrushka was not lying, that his insulting look and the word *other* he had used were merely the consequence of the abominable circumstance known to all, but even so he understood, though vaguely, that something was wrong here and that fate was preparing some further treat for

him, a not entirely pleasant one. "Very well, we'll see," he
thought to himself, "we'll see, we'll crack all this in due
time... Ah, Lord God!" he moaned in conclusion, in a totally
different voice, "why did I invite him, to what end did I do all
that? I'm truly putting my own head into their thievish noose,
I'm tying the noose myself. Oh, head, head! you can't help
yourself, you spill everything like some little brat, some office
clerk, like some rankless trash, a rag, some rotten old shred,
gossip that you are, old woman that you are!... Saints alive!
And the rogue wrote a little ditty and declared his love for me!
How can I, sort of... How can I show the rogue decently to
the door, if he comes back? To be sure, there are many different
turns and ways. Thus and so, I'll say, given my limited
resources... Or frighten him somehow, say, that taking this and
that into consideration, I'm forced to inform you... say, we'll
have to go halves for room and board, and pay the money in
advance. Hm! no, devil take it, no! That would besmirch me.
It's not entirely delicate! Maybe I could do it this way: try to
get Petrushka into it, so that Petrushka irks him somehow,
treats him somehow negligently, is rude to him, and get rid of
him that way? Sic them on each other... No, devil take it, no!
It's dangerous, and again, if you look at it from that point of
view—well, yes, quite wrong! Completely wrong! Well, but
what if he doesn't come? Will that also be bad? I spilled out a
lot to him yesterday!... Ah, bad, bad! Ah, things are in such a
bad way with us! Oh, my head, my cursed head! nothing gets
sawed into you as it should, no sense gets nailed into you! And
what if he comes and refuses? The Lord grant he does come!
I'd be extremely glad if he came; I'd give a lot if he came..."
So reasoned Mr. Goliadkin, gulping down his tea and constantly
looking at the wall clock. "It's now a quarter to nine; time to
go. But what's going to happen; what's going to happen here?
I wish I knew precisely what in particular is hidden here—the
goal, the direction, the various hitches. It would be good to find
out precisely what all these folk are aiming at and what their
first step will be..." Mr. Goliadkin could no longer bear it,
abandoned his half-smoked pipe, got dressed, and set off to

work, wishing to catch the danger, if possible, and verify everything by his personal presence. And there was a danger: he knew himself that there was a danger. "But we'll...crack it open," Mr. Goliadkin was saying, taking off his overcoat and galoshes in the front hall, "now we're going to penetrate all these matters." Having decided to act in such fashion, our hero put himself to rights, assuming a decent and official air, and was just about to penetrate into the next room, when suddenly, just in the doorway, he ran into yesterday's acquaintance, friend, and comrade. Mr. Goliadkin Jr. seemed not to notice Mr. Goliadkin Sr., though they met almost nose-to-nose. Mr. Goliadkin Jr. seemed to be busy, hurrying somewhere, out of breath; he looked so official, so businesslike, that it seemed anyone could have read directly in his face: "Sent on a special mission..."

"Ah, it's you, Yakov Petrovich!" our hero said, seizing yesterday's guest by the arm.

"Later, later, excuse me, you can tell me later," cried Mr. Goliadkin Jr., rushing ahead.

"Though, if you please, it seems you wanted, Yakov Petrovich, sort of..."

"What, sir? Explain quickly, sir." Here Mr. Goliadkin's guest from yesterday stopped as if with effort and reluctantly, and placed his ear directly to Mr. Goliadkin's nose.

"I'll tell you, Yakov Petrovich, that I am astonished at this reception...a reception which, obviously, I could in no way have expected."

"There is a certain form for everything, sir. Report to his excellency's secretary and then address yourself, as is proper, to the office manager. Do you have a petition?..."

"I hardly know you, Yakov Petrovich! You simply amaze me, Yakov Petrovich! Surely you don't recognize me, or else you're joking, owing to your innately merry character."

"Ah, it's you!" said Mr. Goliadkin Jr., as if he had just made out Mr. Goliadkin Sr. "So it's you? Well, what, did you have a good night's sleep?" Here Mr. Goliadkin Jr., smiling slightly—smiling officially and formally, not at all as he ought to have done (because in any case he owed Mr. Goliadkin Sr. a debt of gratitude), and so, smiling officially and formally, he added that he for his part was extremely glad that Mr. Goliadkin had had a good sleep; then he inclined slightly, minced slightly in place, glanced to the right, to the left, then dropped his eyes to the floor, aimed himself at the side door, and, rapidly whispering that he was on a special mission, darted into the next room. There was not a trace of him left.

"Well, that's something!..." our hero whispered, dumbstruck for a moment. "That's really something! There's a circumstance for you!..." Here Mr. Goliadkin felt that for some reason he was covered with gooseflesh. "However," he went on to himself, making his way to his section, "however, I've long been talking about this circumstance; I've long had a presentiment that he was on a special mission—just yesterday I said the man was certainly being employed on some special mission..."

"Did you finish yesterday's document, Yakov Petrovich?" asked Anton Antonovich Setochkin as Mr. Goliadkin sat down next to him. "Do you have it here?"

"It's here," Mr. Goliadkin whispered with a somewhat lost look, gazing at his chief.

"A good thing, sir. I say it because Andrei Filippovich has already asked for it twice. His excellency is likely to request it at any moment..."

"No, sir, it's finished..."

"Well, very good, sir."

"I believe, Anton Antonovich, that I have always fulfilled my duties properly, and I am zealous in the matters entrusted to me by my superiors, sir, and apply myself to them diligently."

"Yes, sir. Well, sir, but what do you mean to say by that?"

"Nothing, Anton Antonovich. I only wanted to explain, Anton Antonovich, that I...that is, I wanted to convey, that sometimes disloyalty and jealousy do not spare any person, seeking their repulsive daily food, sir..."

"Excuse me, I don't quite understand you. That is, to which person are you alluding now?"

"That is, I only meant to say, Anton Antonovich, that I

follow a straight path, and I scorn to take a roundabout path, that I am not an intriguer and, if I may be permitted to say so, I can be justly proud of it ..."

"Yes, sir. That is all so, sir, and to the utmost of my understanding I render full justice to your reasoning; but also allow me, Yakov Petrovich, to observe to you that personal references are not entirely permissible in good society; that behind my back, for instance, I'm prepared to put up with it—because who isn't denounced behind his back!—but to my face, as you will, but I, for instance, my good sir, will not allow insolent things to be said. I, my good sir, have grown gray in government service and will not allow insolent things to be said to me in my old age ..."

"No, sir, I, Anton Antonovich, sir, you—you see, Anton Antonovich—it seems, Anton Antonovich, that you did not quite catch my meaning, sir. But, mercy me, Anton Antonovich, for my part I can only take it as as an honor, sir ..."

"And we also ask to be excused, sir. We were taught in the old way, sir. And your way, the new way, it's too late for us to learn. Up to now, it seems, my understanding has sufficed me in serving the fatherland. As you know yourself, my good sir, I have been decorated for twenty-five years of irreproachable service ..."

"I am sensible, Anton Antonovich, for my part, I am perfectly sensible of all that, sir. But I'm not talking about that, sir, I'm talking about masks, Anton Antonovich ..."

"About masks, sir?"

"That is, again you ... I fear that here, too, you will apprehend the meaning from the other side, that is, the meaning of my speech, as you said yourself, Anton Antonovich. I am only developing a theme, that is, I am introducing the idea that people who wear masks are no longer a rarity, sir, and that it is now hard to recognize the man behind the mask, sir ..."

"Well, sir, you know, it's not really so hard, sir. Sometimes it's even quite easy, sir, sometimes there's no need to look far, sir."

"No, sir, you know, Anton Antonovich, I'm talking, sir, I'm talking about myself, that I, for example, put on a mask only when there's a need for it, that is, uniquely for carnivals or merry gatherings, speaking in a direct sense, but I don't mask myself before people every day, speaking in another more hidden sense, sir. That is what I meant to say, Anton Antonovich."

"Well, all right, for the time being let's leave all that; besides, I have no time, sir," said Anton Antonovich, getting up from his place and gathering some papers for a report to his excellency. "Your affair, I suppose, will not be slow to clarify itself in due time. You will see for yourself whom you are to fault and whom to blame, but for now I humbly beg you to spare me any further personal explanations and discussions harmful to the service..."

"No, sir, Anton Antonovich," Mr. Goliadkin, grown slightly pale, began to say in the wake of the retreating Anton Antonovich, "I, Anton Antonovich, sort of, didn't even think it, sir. What's going on?" our hero went on to himself, left alone. "What winds are blowing here, and what's the meaning of this new hitch?" Just as our disconcerted and half-crushed hero was preparing to resolve this new question, there came a noise from the next room, and some businesslike movement manifested itself, the door opened, and Andrei Filippovich, who just previously had absented himself on business to his excellency's office, appeared in the doorway, breathless, and called Mr. Goliadkin. Knowing what it was about, and not wishing to keep Andrei Filippovich waiting, Mr. Goliadkin jumped up from his seat and, as was proper, immediately began bustling away for all he was worth, preparing and giving a final primping to the requested notebook, and preparing himself to set off, in the wake of the notebook and Andrei Filippovich, for his excellency's office. Suddenly, and almost from under the arm of Andrei Filippovich, who just then was standing right in the doorway, Mr. Goliadkin Jr. darted into the room, bustling, breathless, worn out from work, with an important and decidedly official look, and went rolling straight up to Mr. Goliadkin Sr., who least of all expected an assault like that ...

"The papers, Yakov Petrovich, the papers ... His excellency kindly asks whether you have them ready," Mr. Goliadkin Sr.'s friend chirped in a rapid half-whisper. "Andrei Filippovich is waiting for you..."

"I know that without you," Mr. Goliadkin said, also in a rapid half-whisper.

"No, Yakov Petrovich, I don't mean that; not that at all, Yakov Petrovich; I sympathize, Yakov Petrovich, and am moved to heartfelt concern."

"From which I humbly beg you to deliver me. Allow me, allow me, sir..."

"You will, of course, wrap them in a cover, Yakov Petrovich, and slip in a bookmark at page three—allow me, Yakov Petrovich..."

"No, allow me, finally..."

"And there's a little ink blot here, Yakov Petrovich, have you noticed the ink blot?..."

At this point Andrei Filippovich called Mr. Goliadkin a second time.

"Just a moment, Andrei Filippovich; I'll just fix it a little, there...My dear sir, do you understand the Russian language?"

"It would be best to remove it with a knife, Yakov Petrovich, you'd better rely on me; you'd better not touch it yourself, Yakov Petrovich, but rely on me—I'll just use a penknife on it..."

Andrei Filippovich called Mr. Goliadkin for the third time.

"For pity's sake, where's the blot? There doesn't seem to be any blot here."

"A huge little blot, and here it is! Allow me, I saw it here; allow me...only allow me, Yakov Petrovich, I'll use a penknife here, I'm concerned, Yakov Petrovich, and with my penknife, in all sincerity...like so, and there's an end to it..."

Here, and quite unexpectedly, Mr. Goliadkin Jr., suddenly, for no reason at all, overcoming Mr. Goliadkin Sr. in the momentary struggle that had arisen between them, and in any case totally against his will, took possession of the paper requested by his superiors, and, instead of scraping it with a penknife in all sincerity, as he had perfidiously assured Mr. Goliadkin Sr., quickly rolled it up, put it under his arm, in two bounds reached Andrei Filippovich, who had not noticed any of his antics, and flew with him to the director's office. Mr. Goliadkin Sr. remained as if rooted to the spot, holding the penknife in his hand and as if preparing to scrape something with it . . .

Our hero had not yet quite understood his new circumstance. He had not yet come to his senses. He felt the blow, but thought it was just by chance. In terrible, indescribable anguish, he finally tore from his place and rushed straight to the director's office, praying to heaven on the way, however, that it would all somehow work out for the best and be just by chance, nothing serious . . . In the last room before the director's office, he ran head-on into his namesake and Andrei Filippovich. The two were already on their way back: Mr. Goliadkin stepped aside. Andrei Filippovich was smiling and talking cheerfully. Mr. Goliadkin Sr.'s namesake was also smiling, fawning, mincing at a respectable distance from Andrei Filippovich, and whispering something into his ear with a delighted look, to which Andrei Filippovich nodded in a most benevolent fashion. All at once our hero understood the whole state of affairs. The thing was that his work (as he learned afterwards) had almost exceeded his excellency's expectations and had actually arrived duly on time. His excellency was extremely pleased. It was even reported that his excellency had said thank you to Mr. Goliadkin Jr., a firm thank you; he had said he would remember it when the occasion arose and would never forget . . . Naturally, the first thing for Mr. Goliadkin to do was protest, protest with all his might, to the utmost possibility. Almost forgetting himself and pale as death, he rushed to Andrei Filippovich. But Andrei Filippovich, hearing that Mr. Goliadkin's business was a private matter, refused to listen, observing resolutely that he did not have a free moment even for his own needs.

The dryness of his tone and the sharpness of the refusal struck Mr. Goliadkin. "I'd better get at it somehow from another side . . . I'd better go to Anton Antonovich." To Mr. Goliadkin's misfortune, Anton Antonovich, too, turned out to be unavailable: he was also busy with something somewhere. "It was not without purpose that he asked to be spared any explanations

and discussions!" our hero thought. "That's what he was aiming
at—the old stitch! In that case I'll simply be so bold as to
entreat his excellency."

Still pale and feeling his whole head in a complete muddle,
greatly perplexed about what precisely he must venture upon,
Mr. Goliadkin sat down on a chair. "It would be much better
if all this was just by chance," he kept thinking to himself.
"Actually, such a shady business is even quite improbable. First
of all, it's nonsense; and second, it could never happen. I've
probably imagined it somehow, or something else took place,
and not what actually happened; or I must have gone
myself...and somehow took myself for someone else...in
short, it's a completely impossible thing."

No sooner had Mr. Goliadkin decided that it was a completely
impossible thing than Mr. Goliadkin Jr. suddenly flew into the
room with papers in both hands and under his arm. Having said
some necessary word or two in passing to Andrei Filippovich,
exchanged remarks with this one and that, exchanged courtesies
with this one and that, exchanged familiarities with this one
and that, Mr. Goliadkin Jr., evidently having no spare time to
waste uselessly, seemed about to leave the room, but, luckily for
Mr. Goliadkin Sr., he stopped right in the doorway and began
to talk in passing with two or three young clerks who happened
to be there. Mr. Goliadkin Sr. rushed straight for him. As soon
as Mr. Goliadkin Jr. spotted Mr. Goliadkin Sr.'s maneuver, he
at once began looking around with great uneasiness to see if he
could quickly slip away somewhere. But our hero was already
holding yesterday's guest by the sleeve. The clerks who surrounded the two titular councillors stepped back and waited
with curiosity for what would happen. The old titular councillor
was well aware that good opinion was not on his side now,
he was well aware that there was an intrigue against him: the
more necessary it was for him now to stand up for himself. The
moment was decisive.

"Well, sir?" said Mr. Goliadkin Jr., looking rather insolently
at Mr. Goliadkin Sr.

Mr. Goliadkin Sr. was barely breathing.

"I do not know, my dear sir," he began, "in what way I can explain to you the strangeness of your behavior with me."

"Well, sir. Go on, sir." Here Mr. Goliadkin Jr. looked around and winked at the surrounding clerks, as if giving them to know that the comedy would begin precisely now.

"The insolence and shamelessness of your conduct with me, my dear sir, in the present case expose you still more . . . than all my words. Hope for nothing from your game: it is rather poor . . ."

"Well, Yakov Petrovich, tell me now, did you have a good night's sleep?" replied Goliadkin Jr., looking Mr. Goliadkin Sr. straight in the eye.

"You forget yourself, my dear sir," said the titular councillor, totally at a loss and barely feeling the floor under his feet, "I hope you will change your tone . . ."

"Sweetheart!!" said Mr. Goliadkin Jr., contriving a rather indecent grimace for Mr. Goliadkin Sr. and suddenly, quite unexpectedly, in the guise of a caress, seized his rather plump right cheek with two fingers. Our hero flared up like fire . . . As soon as Mr. Goliadkin Sr.'s friend noticed that his adversary, trembling all over, numb with fury, red as a lobster, and, finally, driven to the ultimate limits, might even venture a formal attack, he immediately, and in the most shameless way, forestalled him in his turn. Having patted him a couple of times more on the cheek, having tickled him a couple of times more, having toyed with him in this way for another few seconds, to the great amusement of the surrounding young men, while he stood motionless and mad with rage, Mr. Goliadkin Jr., with revolting shamelessness, finally flicked Mr. Goliadkin Sr. on his taut little paunch and, with a most venomous and far-insinuating smile, said to him: "You're a prankster, brother Yakov Petrovich, a prankster! You and I are going to be clever, Yakov Petrovich, very clever!" Then, and before our hero had time to recover in the slightest from this last attack, Mr. Goliadkin Jr. suddenly (first delivering a little smile to the surrounding spectators) assumed a most occupied, most busy, most official air, lowered his eyes to the ground, shriveled, shrank, and, saying quickly,

"On a special mission," kicked up his short leg, and darted into the next room. Our hero could not believe his eyes and was still unable to recover himself ...

Finally he did recover. Realizing instantly that he was lost, annihilated in a certain sense, that he had besmirched himself and begrimed his reputation, that he had been laughed at and spat upon in the presence of strangers, that he had been treacherously insulted by the man whom he had regarded still yesterday as the first and most reliable of his friends, that he had finally flunked it for all he was worth—Mr. Goliadkin rushed in pursuit of his enemy. In the present moment he no longer wanted to think about the witnesses of his abuse. "They're all in collusion with each other," he said to himself, "supporting each other and setting each other against me." However, having gone ten steps, our hero saw clearly that all pursuit was vain and useless, and therefore turned back. "You won't get away," he thought, "you'll get trumped in due time, the sheep's tears will be revisited on the wolf." With fierce coolness and the most energetic resolve, Mr. Goliadkin reached his chair and sat down on it. "You won't get away!" he said again. Now the matter had gone beyond any passive defense: it smacked of decision, of offense, and anyone who had seen Mr. Goliadkin at the moment when, flushed and barely controlling his agitation, he stabbed his pen into the inkstand and fiercely sent it scrawling over the paper, could have told beforehand that the matter would not just pass by, and would not end in some old-wife-ish way. He laid up a certain decision in the depths of his soul, and in the depths of his heart he vowed to fulfill it. In truth, he did not yet know very well how he would act, that is, better to say, he did not know at all; but never mind, it made no difference! "And one doesn't get ahead in our age by imposture and shamelessness, my dear sir. Imposture and shamelessness, my dear sir, do not lead to any good, but end in the noose. Grishka Otrepyev[24] alone got ahead by imposture, my good sir, having deceived the blind people, and that not for long." In spite of this last circumstance, Mr. Goliadkin resolved to wait until the mask fell from certain faces and something or other was laid bare. To that end it was necessary, first, that the office hours end as soon as possible, and until then our hero decided not to undertake anything. Later, when the office hours ended, he would take a certain measure. And then, having taken this measure, he would know how to act, how to lay out the whole future plan of his action, to smash the horn of pride and crush the serpent gnawing the dust in contemptible impotence.[25] Mr. Goliadkin could not allow himself to be dirtied like an old rag for wiping muddy boots. He could not agree to that, especially in the present case. If it had not been for the last disgrace, our hero might have decided to restrain his wrath, he might have decided to keep quiet, to submit and not protest too stubbornly; thus, he might have argued, stood his ground a little, proved that he was within his rights, then yielded a little, then he might have yielded a little more, then agreed completely, then, and especially once the other side had solemnly recognized that he was within his rights, then he might even have made peace, even waxed a little tenderhearted, and—who can tell?—a new friendship might even have been born, a firm, warm friendship, broader still than yesterday's friendship, so that this friendship might finally have outshone the unpleasantness of the rather unseemly resemblance of the two persons, so that both titular councillors would have been extremely happy and would have lived on, finally, to be a hundred years old, and so on. Let's finally say it all: Mr. Goliadkin was even beginning to regret a little that he had stood up for himself and for his rights and had at once gotten into trouble for it. "If he were to give in," thought Mr. Goliadkin, "to say he was joking—I'd forgive him, I'd forgive him even more, if only he'd acknowledge it aloud. But I will not allow anyone to dirty me like an old rag. I haven't allowed better people to dirty me like an old rag, much less will I permit this depraved man to try it. I'm not an old rag, I, good sir, am not an old rag!" In short, our hero made up his mind. "It's your own fault, my good sir!" He made up his mind to protest and to protest with all his might to the utmost possibility. Such a man he was! He would in no way agree to permit himself to be insulted, much less would he allow himself to be dirtied like an old rag, and, finally, allow it to this totally depraved man. We won't argue, however, we won't argue. Maybe if someone had wanted, if someone, for example, had so absolutely wanted to turn Mr. Goliadkin into an old rag, he could have done so, could have done so without resistance and with impunity (Mr. Goliadkin sometimes felt it himself), and the result would have been an old rag, and not Goliadkin—just a mean, dirty old rag, but this would not be a simple rag, this would be a rag with ambition, this would be a rag with animation and feelings— unrequited ambition and unrequited feelings, hidden deep within the dirty folds of this rag, but feelings all the same ...

The hours dragged on incredibly long; finally it struck four. A little later everyone got up and, following the superior, headed each for his own home. Mr. Goliadkin mingled with the crowd; his eye was vigilant and never lost sight of the one he needed. Finally our hero saw his friend run up to the office caretakers, who were handing out overcoats, and, as was his mean wont, fidget around them while waiting for his. The moment was decisive. Somehow Mr. Goliadkin squeezed through the crowd and, not wishing to lag behind, also began fussing about his overcoat. But the overcoat went first to Mr. Goliadkin's acquaintance and friend, because here, too, he managed in his own way to sidle up, fawn, whisper, and toady.

Having thrown on his overcoat, Mr. Goliadkin Jr. gave Mr. Goliadkin Sr. an ironic glance, thus acting openly and insolently to spite him, then looked around with his usual impudence, did some final mincing—probably in order to leave a favorable impression—around the clerks, said a word to one, whispered something to another, smooched deferentially with a third, addressed a smile to a fourth, shook hands with a fifth, and darted cheerfully down the stairs. Mr. Goliadkin Sr. started after him and, to his indescribable satisfaction, caught up with him on the last step and seized him by the collar of his overcoat. Mr. Goliadkin Jr. seemed slightly startled and looked around with a lost air.

"How am I to understand you?" he whispered finally, in a weak voice, to Mr. Goliadkin.

"My dear sir, if only you are a noble person, I hope you will remember our friendly relations of yesterday," said our hero.

"Ah, yes. So, then? Did you have a good night's sleep, sir?"

Rage momentarily deprived Mr. Goliadkin Sr. of speech.

"I did, sir ... But allow me to tell you, my dear sir, that your game is extremely convoluted ..."

"Who says so? It's my enemies who say so," the man who called himself Mr. Goliadkin answered sharply and, while saying it, unexpectedly freed himself from the weak grip of the real Mr. Goliadkin. Having freed himself, he rushed away from the steps, looked around, saw a cabby, ran up to him, got into the droshky, and in an instant vanished from Mr. Goliadkin's sight. Desperate, abandoned by everyone, the titular councillor looked around, but there was no other cab. He tried to run, but his legs gave way under him. With an overturned physiognomy, with a gaping mouth, annihilated, shrunken, he leaned strengthlessly against a lamppost, and remained that way for several minutes in the middle of the sidewalk. It seemed that all was lost for Mr. Goliadkin ...

CHAPTER IX

EVERYTHING, EVIDENTLY, and even nature itself, was up in arms against Mr. Goliadkin; but he was still on his feet and not vanquished; this he felt, that he was not vanquished. He was ready to fight. He rubbed his hands with such feeling and such energy, when he recovered from his initial amazement, that from Mr. Goliadkin's look alone it could have been concluded that he would not yield. However, the danger was right under his nose, it was obvious; Mr. Goliadkin felt that, too; but how was he to handle this danger? That was the question. For a moment the thought even flashed in Mr. Goliadkin's head: "What, say, if I just drop it all, what if I simply give it up? Well, what then? Well, nothing. I'll be on my own, as if it's not me," thought Mr. Goliadkin, "I'll let it all pass; it's not me, that's all; and he'll also be on his own, perhaps he'll give it up, too; he'll fuss, the rogue, he'll fuss, fidget a bit, and then give it up. There we have it! I'll succeed by humility. And where's the danger? well, what sort of danger? I wish somebody would point out to me the danger here. A paltry affair! an ordinary affair!..." Here Mr. Goliadkin stopped short. The words died on his tongue; he even swore at himself for this thought; even caught himself at once in baseness, in cowardice for this thought; though his affair still did not budge from the spot. He felt that resolving upon something at the present moment was an urgent necessity for him; he even felt that he would give a lot to whoever told him what precisely he must resolve upon. Well, but how was he to guess it? However, there was no time for guessing. In any case, so as not to lose time, he hired a cab and flew home. "So? how do you feel now?" he asked himself. "How do you feel now, if you please, Yakov Petrovich? What are you going to do? What are you going to do now, scoundrel that you are, rogue that you are! You've driven yourself to the utmost, and now you weep, and now you whimper!" So Mr. Goliadkin taunted himself, bobbing up and down in his cabby's jolty vehicle. To taunt himself and thus aggravate his wounds at the present moment was some sort of deep pleasure for Mr. Goliadkin, even almost a sensual one. "Well, if some magician were to come now," he thought, "or it happened somehow in an official way, and they said, 'Give us a finger from your right hand, Goliadkin, and we're quits; there'll be no other Goliadkin, and you'll be happy, only there'll be no finger'—I'd give up the finger, I'd certainly give it up, give it up without wincing. Devil take it all!" the desperate titular councillor finally cried out. "Well, what's it all for? Well, as if all this had to be; unfailingly this, precisely this, as if it could not possibly have been something else! And everything was fine at first, everyone was pleased and happy; but no, this had to happen! However, words won't do anything. I must act."

And so, having almost resolved on something, Mr. Goliadkin, entering his apartment, seized his pipe without a moment's delay and, sucking at it with all his might, scattering puffs of smoke right and left, began rushing up and down the room in great agitation. Meanwhile Petrushka began to set the table. Finally, Mr. Goliadkin became fully resolved, suddenly abandoned his pipe, threw on his overcoat, said he would not be dining at home, and rushed out of the apartment. On the stairs, Petrushka, out of breath, caught up with him, holding his forgotten hat in his hands. Mr. Goliadkin took the hat, wanted in passing to justify himself a little in Petrushka's eyes, so that Petrushka would not think anything special—say, that there's this circumstance, that I forgot my hat, and so on—but since Petrushka refused even to look and went away at once, Mr. Goliadkin, without further explanations, put on his hat, rushed down the stairs and, muttering that all might still turn out for the best and that the affair would be settled somehow, though, incidentally, he felt a chill even all the way to his heels, went outside, hired a cab, and flew off to Andrei Filippovich's. "However, wouldn't it be better tomorrow?" thought Mr. Goliadkin, taking hold of the bell-pull at the door of Andrei

Filippovich's apartment. "And what am I going to say that's so special? There's nothing special here. It's such a puny affair, yes, finally, it is in fact a puny, a paltry, that is, almost a paltry affair . . . there it is, there's the whole thing, this circumstance . . ." Suddenly Mr. Goliadkin pulled the bell; the bell rang, someone's steps were heard inside . . . Here Mr. Goliadkin even cursed himself, partly for his hastiness and boldness. The recent unpleasantnesses, which Mr. Goliadkin had nearly forgotten about on account of his affairs, and the confrontation with Andrei Filippovich, emerged at once in his memory. But it was too late to flee: the door opened. Fortunately for Mr. Goliadkin, the answer he received was that Andrei Filippovich had not come home from work and was not dining at home. "I know where he's dining; he's dining near the Izmailovsky Bridge," our hero thought and felt terribly glad. To the servant's question, "How shall I announce you?" he said, "Very well, my friend," then "Later, my friend," and ran down the stairs even with a certain briskness. Going outside, he decided to dismiss the carriage and paid the cabby. And when the cabby asked for a little extra, saying, "I waited a long time, sir, and didn't spare my trotter for Your Honor," he added five kopecks extra and even quite willingly; then he himself went on foot.

"The affair, in truth, is such," thought Mr. Goliadkin, "that it cannot possibly be left like this; though, if you reason that way, if you reason sensibly, why should I really fuss over it? Well, no, however, I'll keep talking about it, why should I fuss? why should I wear myself out, thrash about, suffer, kill myself? First of all, the deed is done, there's no going back . . . no going back! Let's reason this way: a man appears, a man appears with a satisfactory recommendation, say, a capable clerk, of good behavior, only he's poor and has suffered various unpleasantnesses—all those bad scrapes—well, but poverty's no vice; which means, I'm outside it. Well, in fact, what is this nonsense? Well, it so happens, it's so arranged, nature itself has so arranged it that a man resembles another man like two drops of water, that he's a perfect copy of another man: should he not be taken into the department because of that?! If fate, if fate alone, if blind fortune alone is to blame here—should he be dirtied like an old rag, should he not be allowed to work...where will there be any justice after that? He's a poor man, lost, intimidated; there's heartache here, there's compassion here telling us to show him kindness! Yes, indeed, they'd be fine superiors if they reasoned the way I do, dunderhead that I am! What a noddle I've got! Enough stupidity for ten sometimes! No, no! they did well, and should be thanked for sheltering the poor wretch...Well, so, suppose, for example, that we're twins, that we were born like that, twin brothers, and that's all—that's the way it is! Well, what of it? Well, it's nothing! It's possible to get all the clerks accustomed to it...and some stranger, coming into our offices, would surely find nothing indecent or insulting in this circumstance. There's even something touching here; that here, say, there's such a thought: that, say, God's design created two perfect likenesses, and our beneficent superiors, seeing God's design, gave shelter to both twins. Of course," Mr. Goliadkin went on, catching his breath and lowering his voice slightly, "of course...of course, it would be better if none of these touching things existed, and there were also no twins...Devil take it all! Who needed it? And what was this need that was so special and would suffer no postponement?! Lord God! A nice kettle of fish the devil's cooked up! See, though, what a character he has, what a playful, nasty temper—what a scoundrel he is, what a fidget, a smoocher, a lickspittle, what a Goliadkin! For all I know, he may behave badly and besmirch my name, the blackguard. And now I have to look at him and take care of him! What a punishment! However, what then? well, who cares! Well, he's a scoundrel—well, let him be a scoundrel, but the other will be honest. Well, so he'll be a scoundrel, but I'll be honest—and they'll say, that Goliadkin's a scoundrel, don't look at him, and don't confuse him with the other one; but this one's honest, virtuous, meek, unresentful, highly reliable at work, and deserves to be promoted—so there! Well, all right...but what if sort of...But what if they sort of...mix us up! You can expect anything from him! Ah, Lord God!...And he'll supplant a man, supplant him, the scoundrel—he'll supplant a man like an old rag and never consider that a man is not an old rag. Ah, Lord God! What a misfortune!..."

Reasoning and lamenting in this way, Mr. Goliadkin ran on without noticing the way and almost without knowing where. He came to himself on Nevsky Prospect and only because he happened to run into some passerby so adroitly and heartily that the sparks flew. Mr. Goliadkin mumbled an apology without raising his head, and only when the passerby, having growled something none too flattering, had gone on for a considerable distance, did he raise his nose and look to see where he was and how. Looking around and noticing that he was precisely by the restaurant where he had whiled away the time in preparation for the dinner party at Olsufy Ivanovich's, our hero suddenly felt a pinching and tweaking in the stomach, remembered that he had had no dinner, nor was there any prospect of a dinner party, and therefore, not to lose precious time, he ran up the steps to the restaurant, to snatch something quickly and hurry on if possible without lingering. And though the restaurant was a bit expensive, that small circumstance did not deter Mr. Goliadkin this time; nor was there any question now of being deterred by such trifles. In the brightly lit room, near the counter, on which lay a miscellaneous heap of all that decent people use for snacks, stood a rather dense crowd of guests. The counterman barely had time to pour, serve, take and give back money. Mr. Goliadkin waited his turn and, having waited, modestly reached out for a little fish pie. Having gone into a corner, turned his back on those present and eaten it with appetite, he returned to the counterman, put the plate down, and, knowing the price, took out a silver ten-kopeck piece and placed the coin on the counter, trying to catch the counterman's eye so as to point out to him that, say, "there's this coin lying here; one little fish pie" and so on.

"That'll be one rouble and ten kopecks," the counterman said through his teeth.

Mr. Goliadkin was properly astounded.

"Are you speaking to me?...I...it seems I took one little pie."

"You took eleven," the counterman objected with assurance.

"You...as it seems to me...you seem to be mistaken... Truly, it seems I took one little pie."

"I was counting; you took eleven. When you take, you have to pay; we don't give anything for free."

Mr. Goliadkin was dumbstruck. "What is this, is some kind of witchcraft being worked on me?" he thought. Meanwhile the counterman was waiting for Mr. Goliadkin's decision; Mr. Goliadkin was surrounded; Mr. Goliadkin had already gone to his pocket to take out a silver rouble, to pay immediately, to be out of harm's way. "Well, if it's eleven, it's eleven," he thought, turning red as a lobster, "well, what of it if eleven little pies got eaten? Well, a man's hungry, so he eats eleven little pies; well, let him eat and enjoy it; well, there's nothing to wonder at and nothing to laugh at..." Suddenly something as if pricked Mr. Goliadkin; he raised his eyes and—at once understood the riddle, understood all the witchcraft; at once all the difficulties were resolved...In the doorway to the next room, almost directly behind the counterman's back and facing Mr. Goliadkin, in the doorway which, incidentally, till then our hero had taken for a mirror, stood a little fellow—stood he, stood Mr. Goliadkin himself—not the old Mr. Goliadkin, not the hero of our story, but the other Mr. Goliadkin, the new Mr. Goliadkin. The other Mr. Goliadkin was evidently in excellent spirits. He smiled at Mr. Goliadkin-the-first, nodded his head to him, winked his eye, minced slightly with his feet, and looked as if he was all set to efface himself, slip into the next room, and then, perhaps, out the back door, and that would be it...all pursuit would be in vain. In his hand was the last piece of the tenth little pie, which he, right in front of Mr. Goliadkin's eyes, sent into his mouth, smacking with pleasure. "Supplanted me, the scoundrel!" thought Mr. Goliadkin, flaring up like fire with shame. "He's not ashamed in public! Can't they see him? Nobody seems to notice..." Mr. Goliadkin flung down the silver rouble as if it burned his fingers, and, not noticing the significantly impudent smile of the counterman, a smile of triumph and calm strength, tore himself from the crowd, and rushed away without looking back. "Thanks at least that he didn't compromise a man utterly!" thought Mr. Goliadkin Sr. "Thanks to the brigand, to him and to fate, that it still got settled so well. Only the counterman was rude. But then he was within his rights! He was owed a rouble and ten kopecks, so he was within his rights. Meaning, we don't give to anyone without money! Though he could have been more polite, the lout! . . ."

Mr. Goliadkin was saying all this as he went down the stairs to the porch. However, on the last step he stopped as if rooted to the spot and suddenly turned so red from a fit of wounded pride that tears even welled up in his eyes. Having stood for half a minute like a post, he suddenly stamped his foot resolutely, leaped from the porch to the street in a single bound, and, without looking back, breathless, feeling no fatigue, set out for his home on Shestilavochnaya Street. At home, not even taking off his street clothes, contrary to his habit of dressing informally at home, not even taking his pipe first, he immediately sat on the sofa, moved the inkstand towards him, picked up the pen, took out a sheet of writing paper, and began to scribble, in a hand trembling from inner agitation, the following missive:

My dear Yakov Petrovich!

I would never have taken up the pen, if my circumstances and you yourself, my dear sir, had not forced me to do so. Believe me, necessity alone has forced me to enter upon such a discussion with you, and therefore I beg you first of all not to consider this measure of mine, my dear sir, as deliberately intended to insult you, but as a necessary consequence of the circumstances which now bind us.

"Seems good, decent, polite, though not without force and firmness? . . . Nothing offensive to him here, it seems. Besides, I'm within my rights," thought Mr. Goliadkin, rereading what he had written.

Your unexpected and strange appearance, my dear sir, on a stormy night, after my enemies, whose names I omit out of disdain for them, had acted rudely and indecently with me, has been the germ of all the misunderstandings existing between us at the present time. Your stubborn desire, my dear sir, to have your own way and forcibly enter the circle of my existence and all the relations of my practical life even goes beyond the limits demanded by mere politeness and simple sociality. I think there is no point in mentioning here, my dear sir, your theft of my papers and of my own honorable name in order to win favor with our superiors—favor you did not merit. There is no point in mentioning here your deliberate and offensive avoidance of the explanations necessary on such an occasion. Finally, to say all, I do not mention here your last strange, one might say incomprehensible, act in the coffeehouse. Far be it from me to lament the, for me, useless loss of a silver rouble; yet I cannot but express all my indignation at the recollection of your obvious infringement, my dear sir, to the detriment of my honor, and, moreover, in the presence of several persons who, though not of my acquaintance, are yet of quite good tone ...

"Am I not going too far?" thought Mr. Goliadkin. "Won't it be too much; isn't it too offensive—this allusion to good tone, for instance? ... Well, never mind! I must show firmness of character with him. However, to soften it, maybe I'll just flatter him and butter him up a little at the end. We'll see to that."

But I would not weary you, my dear sir, with my letter, if I were not firmly convinced that the nobility of your heart's feelings and your open, straightforward character would point you to the means for setting all omissions to rights and restoring everything as it was before.

In the fullest hopes, I venture to rest assured that you for your part will not take offense at my letter, and with that will not refuse to explain yourself specifically on this occasion in writing, through the mediation of my man.

In expectation, I have the honor of remaining, my dear sir,
Your most humble servant,
Ya. Goliadkin.

"Well, that's all fine. The deed is done; it's even gone as far as writing. But who is to blame? He himself is to blame: he himself has driven a man to the necessity of requesting written documents. And I'm within my rights..."

Having reread the letter for a last time, Mr. Goliadkin folded it, sealed it, and summoned Petrushka. Petrushka appeared, as was his custom, with sleepy eyes and extremely angry at something.

"Here, brother, take this letter... understand?"

Petrushka was silent.

"Take it and bring it to the department; there you'll find the man on duty, Provincial Secretary Vakhrameev. Vakhrameev is on duty today. Do you understand that?"

"I understand."

"'I understand'! You can't say: 'I understand, sir.' You'll ask for the clerk Vakhrameev and tell him, say, thus and so, say, my master sends his respects and humbly asks you to consult our department address book, say, for where Titular Councillor Goliadkin lives."

Petrushka said nothing and, as it seemed to Mr. Goliadkin, smiled.

"Well, so then, Pyotr, you'll ask for the address and find out where the newly hired clerk Goliadkin lives?"

"Yes."

"You'll ask the address, and take the letter to that address. Understand?"

"I understand."

"If there... where you take this letter—the gentleman to whom you give the letter, this Goliadkin... Why are you laughing, blockhead?"

"Why should I laugh? What's it to me? It's nothing, sir. The likes of us oughtn't to go laughing..."

"Well, so then... if that gentleman asks, say, how's your master, how is it with him; what, say, is he sort of... well, if he starts asking questions—you keep mum and answer, say, my master's all right, but he asks, say, for an answer in your own hand. Understand?"

"I understand, sir."

"Well, then, say, my master, say, tell him, he's all right, say, and in good health, and is, say, about to go visiting; but he asks you, say, for an answer in writing. Understand?"

"I understand."

"Well, off you go."

"So I've also got to work on this blockhead! He laughs to himself, and that's the end. What's he laughing at? I've lived my way into trouble, lived my way into trouble like this! However, maybe it will all turn out for the best... That crook will most likely drag about for a couple of hours, or else disappear somewhere. Can't send him anywhere. Ah, such trouble!... ah, such trouble's come over me!..."

Thus, fully aware of his trouble, our hero decided on a passive two-hour role of waiting for Petrushka. For about an hour he paced the room, smoked, then abandoned his pipe and sat down with some book, then lay on the sofa, then picked up his pipe again, then again began to rush about the room. He tried to reason, but was decidedly unable to reason about anything. Finally, the agony of his passive condition reached the ultimate degree, and Mr. Goliadkin decided to take a certain measure. "Petrushka won't come for another hour," he thought. "I can give the key to the caretaker, and meanwhile sort of... investigate the affair, investigate it for my own part." Losing no time and hastening to investigate the affair, Mr. Goliadkin took his hat, left the room, locked the apartment, stopped at the caretaker's, handed him the keys along with ten kopecks—Mr. Goliadkin had somehow become extraordinarily generous—and set off for where he had to go. Mr. Goliadkin set off on foot, first, for the Izmailovsky Bridge. He spent half an hour walking. On reaching the goal of his journey, he went straight into the courtyard of the familiar house and looked at the windows of State Councillor Berendeev's apartment. Except for the three windows hung with red curtains, all the rest were dark. "Olsufy Ivanovich must have no guests today," thought Mr. Goliadkin, "they must all be at home by themselves now." Having stood in the courtyard for some time, our hero was about to decide on something. But the decision was not destined to take place, evidently. Mr. Goliadkin finished thinking, waved his hand, and went back out to the street. "No, this is not where I needed to come. What am I going to do here? ... But now I'd better sort of ... and investigate the affair in person." Having taken such a decision, Mr. Goliadkin set off for his department. The way was not short, moreover it was terribly dirty, and wet snow was pouring down in the thickest flakes. But at the present time, it seems, there were no difficulties for our hero. He did get soaked, true, and also not a little dirty, "but that was just while he was about it, and meanwhile the goal was attained." And indeed Mr. Goliadkin was already nearing his goal. The dark mass of the enormous official building showed black in the distance before him. "Wait!" he thought, "where am I going and what will I do there? Suppose I learn where he lives; and meanwhile Petrushka is probably already back and has brought me the answer. I'm only wasting my precious time for nothing, I've only wasted my time this way. Well, never mind; it can all still be put right. Although, and in fact, shouldn't I go and see Vakhrameev? Well, but no! I can later ... Ehh, there was no need at all to go out! But no, that's my character! Such an urge, whether it's needed or not, to be always trying to run ahead somehow ... Hm ... what time is it? Must be nine already. Petrushka may come and not find me at home. It was sheer stupidity for me to go out ... Ah, really, what a chore!"

Having thus sincerely acknowledged that he had committed a sheer folly, our hero ran back home to Shestilavochnaya. He arrived there weary, worn out. He learned from the caretaker that Petrushka had never dreamed of coming. "Well, so! I anticipated that," our hero thought, "and yet it's already nine o'clock. What a scoundrel! Eternally drinking somewhere! Lord God! what a day has fallen to my miserable lot!" Reflecting and lamenting like this, Mr. Goliadkin unlocked his apartment, fetched a light, got undressed, smoked a pipe, and, exhausted, weary, broken, hungry, lay down on the sofa to wait for Petrushka. The candle burned dimly, light flickered over the walls... Mr. Goliadkin stared and stared, thought and thought, and finally fell asleep like the dead.

He woke up late. The candle had burned down almost entirely, smoked, and was ready at any moment to go out altogether. Mr. Goliadkin jumped up, roused himself, and remembered everything, decidedly everything. From behind the partition came Petrushka's dense snoring. Mr. Goliadkin rushed to the window—not a light anywhere. He opened the vent pane—stillness; the city slept like the dead. Meaning it was around two or three o'clock; and so it was: the clock behind the partition strained and struck two. Mr. Goliadkin rushed behind the partition.

Somehow, though after long efforts, he shook Petrushka awake and managed to sit him up in bed. During that time the candle went out completely. About ten minutes passed before Mr. Goliadkin managed to find another candle and light it. During that time Petrushka managed to fall asleep again. "You rogue, you blackguard!" said Mr. Goliadkin, shaking him awake again. "Get up, wake up, will you?" After half an hour of efforts, Mr. Goliadkin managed, however, to rouse his servant completely and drag him from behind the partition. Only then did our hero see that Petrushka was, as they say, dead drunk and barely able to keep on his feet.

"You lout!" cried Mr. Goliadkin. "You brigand! You've cut off my head! Lord, where did he unload that letter? Ah, God in heaven, what if it... And why did I write it? As if I had to write it! Fool that I am, galloping away with my vanity! There's where I got with my vanity! That's vanity for you, you scoundrel, that's vanity for you!... Hey, you, what did you do with that letter, you brigand! Who did you give it to?"

"I never gave anybody any letter; and I never had any letter... that's what!"

Mr. Goliadkin wrung his hands in despair.

"Listen, Pyotr... you listen, you listen to me..."

"I'm listening..."

"Where did you go? Answer..."

"Where did I go... I went to good people! what else!"

"Ah, Lord God! Where did you go first? Did you go to the department?... Listen, Pyotr, maybe you're drunk?"

"Me drunk? May I die on this spot, not a ti-ti-tittle— so there..."

"No, no, it's nothing that you're drunk...I just asked; it's good that you're drunk; it's nothing to me, Petrusha, it's nothing to me...Maybe you've only just forgotten, but do remember it all. Well, now, try to recall, did you go to see the clerk Vakhrameev—did you or didn't you?"

"I didn't, and there never was any such clerk. Right now you could..."

"No, no, Pyotr! No, Petrusha, it's nothing to me. You see, it's nothing to me...Well, what of it! Well, it's cold outside, damp, well, so a man has a little drink, well, what of it...I'm not angry. I myself had a drink today, brother... Confess, recollect, brother: did you go to the clerk Vakhrameev?"

"Well, if it's come to that now, then really and truly—I did go, right now you could..."

"Well, that's good, Petrusha, it's good you went. You see, I'm not angry...Well, well," our hero went on, cajoling his servant still more, patting him on the shoulder and smiling at him, "well, you had a drop, you blackguard...a ten-kopeck drop, eh? you slyboots! Well, never mind; well, you see, I'm not angry...I'm not angry, brother, I'm not angry..."

"No, as you like, but I'm not a slyboots, sir...I just stopped to see some good people, but I'm no slyboots, and I've never been a slyboots..."

"Right, you're not, you're not, Petrusha! Listen, Pyotr: it's nothing to me, it's not to abuse you that I call you a slyboots. I say it kindly to you, in a noble sense. It's sometimes flattering, Petrusha, to tell a man he's a stitch, a cunning fellow, that there's no flies on him, and he won't let anybody hoodwink him. Some people like it...Well, well, never mind! Well, now tell me, Petrusha, without hiding anything, openly, as to a friend... well, so you went to the clerk Vakhrameev, and he gave you an address?"

"And he gave me an address, he also gave me an address.

A good clerk! And your master, he says, is a good man, very good, he says; tell him, he says—I send greetings, he says, to your master, thank him and tell him, he says, that I love him— see, he says, how I respect your master! because, he says, your master, Petrusha, is a good man, he says, and you, he says, are also a good man, Petrusha—so there . . ."

"Ah, Lord God! And the address, the address, you Judas?" Mr. Goliadkin uttered the last words almost in a whisper.

"And the address . . . and he gave me the address."

"He did? Well, where does he live, this Goliadkin, the clerk Goliadkin, the titular councillor?"

"And your Goliadkin, he says, you'll find on Shestilavochnaya Street. You just go, he says, to Shestilavochnaya, to the right, upstairs, on the fourth floor. There, he says, you'll find your Goliadkin . . ."

"You swindler!" shouted our hero, finally losing patience. "You brigand! But that's me; you're talking about me. But there's another Goliadkin; I'm talking about the other one, you swindler!"

"Well, as you like! What's it to me! Do whatever you like— so there! . . ."

"But the letter, the letter . . . "

"What letter? There was never any letter, I never saw any letter."

"But what did you do with it, you rascal?!"

"I delivered it, I delivered the letter. Greetings, he says, and thanks; a good master, he says, yours is. Greetings, he says, to your master . . ."

"But who said it? Did Goliadkin say it?"

Petrushka paused for a moment and grinned from ear to ear, looking straight into his master's eyes.

"Listen, brigand that you are!" Mr. Goliadkin began, breathless, at a loss from rage. "What have you done to me! Tell me, what have you done to me! You've cut me down, you villain! You've taken my head from my shoulders, you Judas!"

"Well, now, as you like! What's it to me!" Petrushka said in a resolute tone, retiring behind the partition.

"Come here, come here, you brigand!..."

"And I just won't go to you now, I won't go at all. What's it to me! I'll go to good people...Good people live honestly, good people live without falseness, and they never come in twos..."

Mr. Goliadkin's hands and feet turned ice cold, and his breath was taken away ...

"Yes, sir," Petrushka went on, "they never come in twos, they don't offend God and honest people..."

"You lout, you're drunk! Sleep now, you brigand! But you're going to get it tomorrow," Mr. Goliadkin said in a barely audible voice. As for Petrushka, he muttered something more; then he could be heard putting his full weight on the bed, so that the bed creaked, producing a long yawn, stretching out, and finally snoring the sleep of the innocent, as they say. Mr. Goliadkin was neither dead nor alive. Petrushka's behavior, his hints, which were quite strange, though remote, at which, therefore, there was no point in being angry, the less so as it was all spoken by a drunk man, and, finally, the whole malignant turn that affairs were taking—all this shook Mr. Goliadkin to his foundations. "And I just had to go reprimanding him in the middle of the night," our hero said, his whole body trembling with some sort of morbid sensation. "And I just couldn't help dealing with a drunk man! What sense can you expect from a drunk man? His every word is drivel. What was it, however, that he was hinting at, the brigand! Oh, Lord God! And why did I write all those letters, manslayer that I am! suicide that I am! Just couldn't keep quiet! Had to go driveling! What else! You're perishing, you're like an old rag, and yet, no, there's still vanity, say, my honor's suffering, say, you must save your honor! Suicide that I am!"

So spoke Mr. Goliadkin, sitting on his sofa and not daring to stir from fear. Suddenly his eye rested on a certain object that aroused his attention to the highest degree. Fearing that the object which aroused his attention was an illusion, a trick of the imagination, he reached out his hand, with hope, with timidity, with indescribable curiosity...No, it was not a trick!

not an illusion! A letter, precisely a letter, certainly a letter, and addressed to him...Mr. Goliadkin took the letter from the table. His heart was pounding terribly. "That swindler must have brought it," he thought, "and put it here, and then forgotten it; it must have happened that way; that's precisely how it must have happened..." The letter was from the clerk Vakhrameev, a young colleague and erstwhile friend of Mr. Goliadkin's. "However, I anticipated it all beforehand," thought our hero, "and everything that will now be in the letter I've anticipated as well..." The letter went as follows:

Dear sir, Yakov Petrovich,

Your man is drunk, and no sense can be expected from him; for that reason I prefer to reply in writing. I hasten to inform you that I agree to perform with all accuracy and precision the mission you have entrusted to me, which consists in conveying through my hands a letter to an individual known to you. This individual, who is well known to you and who has now replaced a friend for me, and whose name I hereby pass over in silence (because I do not want vainly to blacken the reputation of a totally innocent man), now lodges with us in Karolina Ivanovna's apartment, in that same room which formerly, while you were still with us, was occupied by an infantry officer visiting from Tambov. However, you can find this individual everywhere among honest and open-hearted people—something that cannot be said of others. I intend to terminate my contacts with you as of this date; it is impossible for us to remain in a friendly tone and the former harmonious air of comradeship, and therefore I ask you, my dear sir, immediately upon receipt of this frank letter of mine, to send me the two roubles owing to me for the razors of foreign workmanship that I sold you, if you will kindly remember, seven months ago on credit, still in the time of your living with us at Karolina Ivanovna's, whom I respect with all my soul. I am acting in this manner because you, by the accounts of intelligent people, have lost your pride and reputation and become dangerous to the morality of innocent and uninfected people, for certain individuals do not live by the truth and, above all, their words are falseness and their well-intentioned air suspicious. It is possible always and everywhere to find people capable of interceding for the offense of Karolina Ivanovna—who has always been of good behavior and, secondly, is an honest woman and moreover a virgin, though no longer young, yet of a good foreign family—of which certain individuals have asked me to make mention in this letter of mine, in passing and speaking for my own person. In any case, you will learn everything in due time, if you have not learned it yet, despite the fact that you have disgraced yourself, by the accounts of intelligent people, in all corners of the capital and, consequently, may already have received from many places, my dear sir, appropriate information about yourself. In conclusion of my letter, I inform you, my dear sir, that the individual known to you, whose name I do not mention here for well-known noble reasons, is highly respected by well-minded people; moreover, he is of a cheerful and agreeable character, succeeds as much in service as among all sober-minded people, is true to his word and to friendship, and does not insult in their absence those with whom he is ostensibly on friendly terms.

In all events I remain

Your humble servant,
N. Vakhrameev.

P.S. You should get rid of your man: he is a drunkard and, in all probability, causes you much trouble, and take Evstafy, who used to work for us and is now without a post. Your present servant is not only a drunkard, but moreover a thief, for last week he sold Karolina Ivanovna a pound of lump sugar at a low price, which, in my opinion, he could not have done unless he had stolen it from you on the sly, in small portions, at various times. I write this to you wishing you well, despite the fact that certain individuals know only how to insult and deceive all people, mostly those who are honest and possessed of a good character; moreover, they denounce them in their absence and present them in a reverse sense, solely out of envy and because they cannot be called such themselves.

V.

Having read Vakhrameev's letter, our hero remained for a long time in a motionless position on his sofa. Some sort of new light was breaking through all this vague and mysterious fog that had surrounded him for two days. Our hero was partly beginning to understand ... He tried to get up from the sofa and pace the room once or twice to refresh himself and somehow collect his broken thoughts, to turn them towards a certain subject, and then, having pulled himself together a little, to give mature consideration to his position. But he was just going to get up when at once, in weakness and impotence, he fell back into his former place. "Of course, I anticipated it all beforehand; though what is it he writes and what is the direct meaning of these words? Suppose I know the meaning; but where does it lead? He should say directly: here, say, thus and so, what's required is this and that, and I'd do it. Such an unpleasant turn this affair is taking! Ah, if only we could get quickly to tomorrow and get quickly to this affair! Now I know what to do. Say, thus and so, I'll tell them, I agree with your reasoning, I won't sell my honor, but sort of ... perhaps; how, though, did that one, that well-known individual, that unfavorable person, get mixed up in this? And precisely why did he get mixed up in it? Ah, if only tomorrow would come quickly! They'll disgrace me meanwhile, they're intriguing, they're working against me! Above all—I mustn't lose time, but now, for instance, I should at least write a letter and only let on that, say, this and that, this and that, and I agree to this and that. And tomorrow at first light send it off and go very early ... and work against them from the other side and forestall the dear hearts ... They'll disgrace me, that's just it!"

Mr. Goliadkin drew paper towards him, took the pen, and wrote the following missive in reply to Provincial Secretary Vakhrameev:

Dear sir, Nestor Ignatievich!

With an astonishment that grieves my heart I have read your letter so insulting to me, for I see clearly that, under the name of certain disreputable individuals and other falsely well-intentioned persons, you imply me. With genuine sorrow I see how quickly, successfully, and how far calumny has sent its roots, to the detriment of my well-being, my honor, and my good name. It is the more grievous and insulting that even honest people with a truly noble cast of mind and, above all, endowed with a direct and open character, abandon the interests of noble people and, with the best qualities of their hearts, cling to a pernicious louse—which, unfortunately, in our difficult and immoral time, have multiplied greatly and extremely ill-intentionedly. In conclusion I will say that I consider it my sacred duty to repay the debt you mentioned, two silver roubles, in its entirety.

With regard, my dear sir, to your hints concerning a certain individual of the female sex, concerning the intentions, calculations, and various designs of this individual, I will tell you, my dear sir, that I have understood all these hints vaguely and unclearly. Allow me, my dear sir, to keep my noble cast of mind and my honest name untainted. In any case, I am ready to condescend to personal explanations, preferring the verity of the personal to the written, and, above all, I am ready to enter into various peaceable—and mutual, to be sure—agreements. To that end I ask you, my dear sir, to convey to this individual my readiness for personal agreement and, moreover, to ask her to appoint the time and place of the meeting. It was bitter for me to read, my dear sir, hints that I had supposedly insulted you, betrayed our original friendship, and had spoken of you in bad terms. I ascribe it all to the misunderstanding, vile slander, envy, and ill-will of those whom I may rightly call my bitterest enemies. But they probably do not know that innocence is strong in its very innocence, that the shamelessness, impudence, and exasperating familiarity of certain individuals will sooner or later earn them the universal brand of contempt, and that those individuals will perish from nothing other than their own indecency and depravity of heart. In conclusion I ask you, my dear sir, to convey to those individuals that their strange claim and ignoble, fantastic desire to supplant with their own being the confines occupied by others in this world, and to occupy their place, are deserving of amazement, contempt, regret, and, moreover, the madhouse; that, moreover, such attitudes are strictly forbidden by law, which, in my opinion, is completely just, for everyone should be satisfied with his own place. There are limits to everything, and if this is a joke, it is an indecent joke; I will say more: it is completely immoral, for, I venture to assure you, my dear sir, that my ideas, enlarged upon above, regarding *one's own place*, are purely moral.

In any case, I have the honor to remain

Your humble servant,
Ya. Goliadkin.

CHAPTER X

GENERALLY IT MAY be said that the happenings of the previous day had shaken Mr. Goliadkin to his foundations. Our hero rested very poorly, that is, did not fall completely asleep even for five minutes: as if some joker had put cut-up bristles in his bed. He spent the whole night in some sort of half-sleeping, half-waking state, tossing and turning from side to side, sighing, groaning, falling asleep for a moment, waking up again a moment later, and all this was accompanied by some strange anguish, vague recollections, grotesque visions—in short, every available unpleasantness . . . Now, in some strange, mysterious half-light, the figure of Andrei Filippovich appeared before him—a dry figure, an angry figure, with a dry, hard gaze and a stiffly courteous reproach . . . And Mr. Goliadkin was just about to go up to Andrei Filippovich in order to justify himself before him in some way, by this or by that, and prove to him that he was not at all as his enemies described him, that he was this and he was that, and, on top of his ordinary, innate qualities, even possessed such and such; but just then the person known for his indecent tendency appeared and by some most outrageous means destroyed at one blow all Mr. Goliadkin's preliminaries, thoroughly blackened his reputation, right there, almost in front of Mr. Goliadkin's eyes, trampled his pride in the mud, and then immediately took over his place at work and in society. Now Mr. Goliadkin's head itched from some flick, recently acquired and accepted in all humility, and received either in everyday life or somehow out of duty, against which flick it was difficult to protest . . . And meanwhile, as Mr. Goliadkin began to rack his brain over precisely why it was so difficult to protest at least against such a flick—meanwhile this thought of the flick imperceptibly recast itself into some other form—into the form of some certain small or rather significant meanness, seen, heard of, or even recently performed by himself—and often performed not even on mean grounds, not even from some mean urge, but just so—sometimes, for instance, by chance—out of delicacy; or another time owing to his total defenselessness, well, and, finally, because...because, in short, this Mr. Goliadkin knew very well *why*! Here Mr. Goliadkin blushed in his sleep and, suppressing his blushes, muttered to himself that here, say, for instance, one could show firmness of character, considerable firmness of character could be shown on this occasion...but then concluded that, "say, what of this firmness of character!...say, why mention it now!..." But what enraged and annoyed Mr. Goliadkin most of all was that here, and unfailingly at this moment, summoned or not summoned, the person known for the grotesqueness and lampoonishness of his tendency appeared and also, despite the fact that the matter seemed to be well known—also muttered with an indecent little smile, that, "say, what has firmness of character got to do with it! what firmness of character, say, are you and I going to show, Yakov Petrovich!..." Now Mr. Goliadkin fancied that he was in excellent company, known for the wit and noble tone of all the persons who constituted it; that Mr. Goliadkin in his turn distinguished himself in respect of amiability and wittiness; that everyone loved him—even some of his enemies, who were right there, loved him—which Mr. Goliadkin found very agreeable; that everyone acknowledged his superiority; and that, finally, Mr. Goliadkin himself overheard with pleasure how his host, just then, leading one of the guests aside, praised Mr. Goliadkin...and suddenly, out of the blue, the person known for his ill intentions and beastly impulses appeared again, in the guise of Mr. Goliadkin Jr., and straightaway, at once, in an instant, by his appearance alone, Goliadkin Jr. destroyed all the triumph and glory of Mr. Goliadkin Sr., eclipsed Goliadkin Sr., trampled Goliadkin Sr. in the mud, and, finally, proved clearly that Goliadkin Sr., the real one at that, was not the real one at all but a counterfeit, and that he was the real one, that, finally, Goliadkin Sr. was not at all what he appeared to be, but was this and that, and consequently should not and had no right to belong to the society of well-intentioned and high-toned people. And all this was done so quickly that, before Mr. Goliadkin Sr. managed to open his mouth, everyone had already given themselves body and soul to the grotesque and counterfeit Mr. Goliadkin, and with the profoundest contempt had rejected him, the real and blameless Mr. Goliadkin. Not a person remained whose opinion the grotesque Mr. Goliadkin had not in one instant remade in his own way. Not a person remained, even the most insignificant of the whole company, whom the useless and false Mr. Goliadkin had not sucked up to in his own way, in the sweetest manner, whom he had not sidled up to in his own way, before whom he had not burned, as was his wont, the most sweet and pleasing incense, so that the censed person only sniffed and sneezed to the point of tears as a sign of the highest satisfaction. And, chiefly, all this had been done in an instant: the speed of the suspect and useless Mr. Goliadkin's course was astonishing! He barely manages, for instance, to smooch with one, to earn his good favor—and in the twinkling of an eye he's already with somebody else. He smooches with the second on the quiet, wins a little smile of benevolence, kicks up his short, round, though rather crudely made little leg, and here he is with a third, already paying court to a third, also smooching with him in a friendly way: you haven't managed to open your mouth, haven't managed to feel astonished, and he's already with a fourth, and is on the same terms with the fourth—terrible: witchcraft, that's all! And everybody is glad of him, and everybody loves him, and everybody extols him, and everybody announces in a chorus that his amiability and satirical turn of mind are far better than the amiability and satirical turn of mind of the real Mr. Goliadkin, and they use that to shame the real and blameless Mr. Goliadkin, and they reject the truth-loving Mr. Goliadkin, and they drive out the well-intentioned Mr. Goliadkin, and they shower flicks on the real Mr. Goliadkin, known for loving his neighbor!... In anguish, in terror, in rage, the much-suffering Mr. Goliadkin ran outside and tried to hire a cab to fly straight to his excellency, and if not to him, then at least to Andrei

Filippovich, but—oh, horror!—the cabbies would in no way agree to take Mr. Goliadkin: "Say, master, it's impossible to take two that are completely alike; say, Your Honor, a good man strives to live honorably, and not just anyhow, and he never comes double." In a frenzy of shame, the perfectly honorable Mr. Goliadkin glanced around and indeed convinced himself with his own eyes that the cabbies, and Petrushka in collusion with them, were within their rights; for the depraved Mr. Goliadkin was indeed there beside him, at no great a distance from him, and, in line with his habitual mean morals, here, too, in this critical case, was certainly preparing to do something highly indecent and revealing not the slightest trace of the particular noble character that one usually receives through upbringing—a nobility which the disgusting Mr. Goliadkin-the-second liked to glory in on every convenient occasion. Forgetting himself, in shame and despair, the lost and perfectly righteous Mr. Goliadkin rushed off wherever his legs would carry him, as fate willed, whatever turn it might take; but with every step, with every blow of his feet on the granite pavement, there sprang up as if from under the ground—each an exact and perfect likeness and of a revolting depravity of heart—another Mr. Goliadkin. And all these perfect likenesses, as soon as they appeared, began running after each other, and stretched out in a long line like a string of geese, went hobbling after Mr. Goliadkin Sr., so that there was no escaping these perfect likenesses, so that Mr. Goliadkin, worthy of all compassion, was left breathless with horror—so that, finally, a frightful multitude of perfect likenesses was born—so that the whole capital was flooded, finally, with perfect likenesses, and a policeman, seeing such a violation of decency, was forced to take all these perfect likenesses by the scruff of the neck and put them in the sentry box that happened to be there beside him . . . Stiff and frozen with horror, our hero would wake up and, stiff and frozen with horror, feel that he was hardly going to have a merrier time of it when awake. It was painful, tormenting . . . Such anguish rose in him as though someone was gnawing the heart in his breast . . .

Finally, Mr. Goliadkin could endure no longer. "This will not be!" he shouted, resolutely sitting up in bed, and after this exclamation, he awakened completely.

Day had evidently begun long ago. The room was somehow unusually bright; the sun's rays strained thickly through the frost-covered windowpanes and abundantly flooded the room, which surprised Mr. Goliadkin not a little; for the sun in its due progress peeked in on him only at noontime; previously such exceptions to the course of the heavenly luminary, at least as far as Mr. Goliadkin himself could recall, had almost never occurred. Our hero had just managed to marvel at it, when the wall clock behind the partition began to buzz and thus became completely ready to strike. "Ah, there!" thought Mr. Goliadkin, and in anguished expectation he got ready to listen... But, to Mr. Goliadkin's complete and utter shock, his clock strained and struck only once. "What's this story?" our hero cried, jumping out of bed altogether. Not believing his ears, he rushed behind the partition just as he was. The clock indeed showed one. Mr. Goliadkin glanced at Petrushka's bed; but there was not even a whiff of Petrushka in the room: his bed had evidently long been made and left; there were no boots anywhere—an unquestionable sign that Petrushka was indeed not at home. Mr. Goliadkin rushed to the door: the door was locked. "But where is Petrushka?" he went on in a whisper, in terrible agitation, and feeling a considerable trembling in all his limbs... Suddenly a thought raced through his head... Mr. Goliadkin rushed to his desk, looked it over, searched around—that was it: yesterday's letter to Vakhrameev was not there... Petrushka was also not there at all behind the partition; the wall clock showed one, and in yesterday's letter from Vakhrameev some new points had been introduced which, though vague at first glance, were now quite explainable. Finally, Petrushka, too—obviously, Petrushka had been bribed! Yes, yes, it was so!

"So it was there that the chief knot was tied!" cried Mr. Goliadkin, striking himself on the forehead and opening his eyes wider and wider. "So it's in that niggardly German woman's nest that the chief unclean powers are hidden now! So that means she was only making a strategic diversion when she directed me to the Izmailovsky Bridge—distracting my attention, confusing me (the worthless witch!), and in that way undermining me!!! Yes, it's so! If you look at it from that side, it's all precisely so! And the appearance of the scoundrel is now fully explained: it all goes together. They've been keeping him for a long time, preparing him and saving him for a rainy day. That's how it is now, that's how it all turns out! That's the whole solution! Ah, well, never mind! I still have time!..." Here Mr. Goliadkin recalled with terror that it was already past one in the afternoon. "What if they've now managed to..." A groan burst from his breast... "But no, nonsense, they haven't managed—we'll see..." He dressed haphazardly, seized some paper, a pen, and scribbled the following missive:

My dear Yakov Petrovich!

Either you or me, but two of us is impossible! And therefore I announce to you that your strange, ridiculous, and at the same time impossible wish—to appear my twin and pass yourself off as such—will serve nothing except your total dishonor and defeat. And therefore I beg you, for your own benefit, to step aside and give way to people of true nobility and well-intentioned purposes. In the contrary case, I am prepared to venture even upon the most extreme measures. I lay down my pen and wait... However, I remain ready to be at your service and—to pistols.

Ya. Goliadkin.

Our hero rubbed his hands energetically when he had finished the note. Then, having pulled on his overcoat and put on his hat, he unlocked the door with a spare key and set off for the department. He reached the department, but did not venture to go in; indeed, it was much too late; Mr. Goliadkin's watch showed half-past two. Suddenly a certain, apparently quite unimportant, circumstance resolved some of Mr. Goliadkin's doubts: a breathless and red-faced little figure appeared from around the corner of the office building and stealthily, with a ratlike gait, darted onto the porch and then at once into the front hall. This was the scrivener Ostafyev, a man quite well known to Mr. Goliadkin, a somewhat necessary man and ready to do anything for ten kopecks. Knowing Ostafyev's soft spot and realizing that, after absenting himself on a most urgent necessity, he was now probably still more avid for his ten-kopeck pieces, our hero decided not to be sparing and at once darted onto the porch and then also into the front hall after Ostafyev, called to him, and with a mysterious look invited him to one side, into a nook behind an enormous iron stove. Having led him there, our hero began asking questions.

"Well, so, my friend, how's things there, sort of . . . you understand me?"

"Yes, Your Honor, I wish Your Honor good day."

"Very well, my friend, very well; and I'll reward you, my dear friend. Well, so you see, how are things, my friend?"

"What are you asking, if you please, sir?" Here Ostafyev slightly covered his accidentally opened mouth with his hand.

"You see, my friend, I sort of . . . but don't go thinking anything . . . Well, so, is Andrei Filippovich here? . . ."

"He is, sir."

"And the clerks are here?"

"The clerks also, as they should be, sir."

"And his excellency also?"

"And his excellency also, sir." Here once more the scrivener held his hand over his again opened mouth and looked at Mr. Goliadkin somehow curiously and strangely. At least it seemed so to our hero.

"And there's nothing special, my friend?"

"No, sir, nothing at all, sir."

"So, my dear friend, there isn't anything about me, anything just . . . eh? just so, my friend, you understand?"

"No, sir, I've heard nothing so far." Here the scrivener again held his hand to his mouth and again glanced at Mr. Goliadkin somehow strangely. The thing was that our hero was now trying to penetrate Ostafyev's physiognomy, to read whether there was not something hidden in it. And indeed there seemed to be something hidden; the thing was that Ostafyev was becoming somehow ruder and dryer, and no longer entered into Mr. Goliadkin's interests with the same concern as at the beginning of the conversation. "He's partly within his rights," thought Mr. Goliadkin. "What am I to him? He may already have gotten something from the other side, and that's why he absented himself with such urgency. But now I'll sort of..." Mr. Goliadkin understood that the time for ten-kopeck pieces had come.

"Here you are, my dear friend..."

"I cordially thank Your Honor."

"I'll give you more."

"As you say, Your Honor."

"I'll give you more now, at once, and when the matter's ended, I'll give you as much again. Understand?"

The scrivener said nothing, stood at attention, and looked fixedly at Mr. Goliadkin.

"Well, tell me now: have you heard anything about me?..."

"It seems that, so far...sort of...nothing so far, sir." Ostafyev also replied measuredly, like Mr. Goliadkin, preserving a slightly mysterious look, twitching his eyebrows slightly, looking at the ground, trying to fall into the right tone and, in short, trying with all his might to earn what had been promised, because what had been given he considered his own and definitively acquired.

"And nothing's known?"

"Not so far, sir."

"But listen...sort of...maybe it will be known?"

"Later on, of course, maybe it will be known, sir."

"That's bad!" thought our hero.

"Listen, here's more for you, my dear."

"I heartily thank Your Honor."

"Was Vakhrameev here yesterday?..."

"He was, sir."

"And wasn't there somebody else?...Try to recall, brother!"

The scrivener rummaged in his memory for a moment and recalled nothing suitable.

"No, sir, there was nobody else, sir."

"Hm!" Silence ensued.

"Listen, brother, here's more for you; tell me everything, all the innermost secrets."

"Yes, sir." Ostafyev was now standing there smooth as silk: that was just what Mr. Goliadkin wanted.

"Tell me, brother, what sort of footing is he on now?"

"All right, sir, quite good, sir," replied the scrivener, staring all eyes at Mr. Goliadkin.

"Good in what sense?"

"In that sense, sir." Here Ostafyev twitched his eyebrows significantly. However, he was decidedly at a loss and did not know what more to say. "That's bad!" thought Mr. Goliadkin.

"Haven't they got something further going with this Vakhrameev?"

"It's all as before, sir."

"Think a little."

"They have, so it's said, sir."

"Well, what is it?"

Ostafyev held his hand over his mouth.

"Is there a letter for me from there?"

"Today the caretaker Mikheev went to Vakhrameev's lodgings, to that German woman of theirs, sir, so I'll go and ask if you like."

"Be so kind, brother, for heaven's sake! ... I'm just ... Don't go thinking anything, brother, I'm just ... And ask questions, brother, find out if anything's being prepared there on my account. How does he act? That's what I need to know; you find that out, and then I'll thank you well, my dear friend ..."

"Yes, sir, Your Honor, and today Ivan Semyonovich sat in your place, sir."

"Ivan Semyonovich? Ah! yes! Really?"

"Andrei Filippovich told him to sit there, sir ..."

"Really? By what chance? Find that out, brother, for heaven's sake, find that out; find everything out—and I'll thank you well, my dear; that's what I need to know ... And don't go thinking anything, brother ..."

"Yes, sir, yes, sir, I'll come down here at once, sir. But, Your Honor, won't you be going in today?"

"No, my friend; it's just so, just so, I've just come to have a look, my dear friend, and then I'll thank you well, my dear."

"Yes, sir." The scrivener quickly and zealously ran up the stairs, and Mr. Goliadkin was left alone.

"That's bad," he thought. "Eh, it's bad, bad! Eh, our little affair…it's in such a bad way now! What can it all mean? What precisely can certain of this drunkard's hints mean, for instance, and whose trick is it? Ah! now I know whose trick it is! Here's the trick. They must have found out, and so they sat him there…However, what is it—they sat him there? It was Andrei Filippovich who sat him there, this Ivan Semyonovich; why, however, did he sit him there and with precisely what aim did he sit him? Probably they found out…It's Vakhrameev's work, that is, not Vakhrameev, he's stupid as a pine log, this Vakhrameev; it's all of them working for him, and they set the rogue on for the same purpose; and she complained, the one-eyed German! I've always suspected that this whole intrigue had something behind it, and that all this old-womanish gossip surely had something to it; I said as much to Krestyan Ivano-vich, that, say, they'd sworn to cut a man down, speaking in a moral sense, so they seized on Karolina Ivanovna. No, masters are at work here, you can see! Here, my good sir, there's a master's hand at work, not Vakhrameev. It has already been said that Vakhrameev is stupid, but this…now I know who is working for them all here: it's the rogue, the impostor! That's the one thing he clings to, which partly explains his success in high society. And indeed, I wish I knew what footing he's on now…what is he to them? Only why did they bring in Ivan Semyonovich? Why the devil did they need Ivan Semyonovich? As if they couldn't have come up with somebody else? However, no matter who they sat there, it would all be the same; I only know that I've long suspected this Ivan Semyonovich, I've long noticed that he's such a nasty old codger, such a vile one—they say he lends money on interest and takes interest like a Jew. It's all that bear's doing. The bear got mixed up in this whole circumstance. It started that way. It started by the Izmailovsky Bridge; that's how it started…" Here Mr. Goliadkin winced as if he had bitten into a lemon, probably recalling something highly unpleasant. "Well, never mind, though!" he thought. "And I only go on about my own thing. Why doesn't Ostafyev come? He must have gotten stuck or been stopped somehow. It's partly good that I intrigue this way and undermine them from my side. Ostafyev only has to be given ten kopecks, and he sort of... and he's on my side. Only here's the thing: is he really on my side? Maybe they also, on their side... and in complicity with him, on their side, are conducting an intrigue. He has the look of a brigand, the crook, a sheer brigand! In secret, the rogue! 'No, there's nothing,' he says, 'and, say, I heartily thank Your Honor.' You brigand!"

Noise was heard... Mr. Goliadkin shrank and jumped behind the stove. Someone came down the stairs and went outside. "Who could be leaving like that now?" our hero thought to himself. A moment later someone's footsteps were heard again... Here Mr. Goliadkin could not help himself and stuck the smallest tip of his nose out from behind his breast-work—stuck it out and pulled it back at once, as though someone had pricked his nose with a needle. This time you know who was going by—that is, the rogue, the intriguer and debaucher—walking as usual with his mean, rapid little step, mincing and prancing on his feet as if he was about to kick somebody. "The scoundrel!" our hero said to himself. However, Mr. Goliadkin could not fail to notice that under the scoundrel's arm was an enormous green portfolio belonging to his excellency. "He's on a special mission again," thought Mr. Goliadkin, turning red and shrinking still more from vexation. No sooner did Mr. Goliadkin Jr. flash past Mr. Goliadkin Sr., without noticing him at all, than for a third time someone's footsteps were heard, and this time Mr. Goliadkin guessed that the steps were the scrivener's. Indeed, the slicked-down little figure of a scrivener peeked behind the stove; the little figure, however, was not Ostafyev but another scrivener named Scriverenko. This amazed Mr. Goliadkin. "Why is he mixing others into the secret?" thought our hero. "What barbarians! Nothing's sacred to them!"

"Well, so, my friend?" he said, addressing Scriverenko. "Who are you coming from, my friend?..."

"It's this, sir, on your little affair, sir. So far there's no news from anyone, sir. But if there is, we'll let you know, sir."

"And Ostafyev?..."

"He really couldn't come, Your Honor. His excellency has already made the rounds of the department twice, and I've got no time now."

"Thank you, my dear, thank you... Only tell me..."

"By God, I've got no time, sir... We're asked for every moment, sir... But you please go on standing here, sir, so that if there's anything concerning your little affair, sir, we'll let you know, sir..."

"No, my friend, you tell me..."

"Excuse me, sir; I've got no time, sir," Scriverenko said, trying to tear free of Mr. Goliadkin, who had seized his coat skirt, "really, it's impossible, sir. You kindly go on standing here, and we'll let you know."

"One moment, one moment, my friend! one moment, my dear friend! Here's what now: here's a letter, my friend; and I'll thank you well, my dear."

"Yes, sir."

"Try to hand it to Mr. Goliadkin, my dear."

"To Goliadkin?"

"Yes, my friend, to Mr. Goliadkin."

"Very well, sir; once I've finished up, I'll take it, sir. And you stand here meanwhile. Nobody'll see you here..."

"No, my friend, don't go thinking I...I'm not standing here so that people won't see me. I'll no longer be here, my friend...I'll be in the lane. There's a coffeehouse; I'll be waiting there, and if anything happens, you inform me about it all, understand?"

"Very well, sir. Only let me go; I understand..."

"And I'll thank you well, my dear!" Mr. Goliadkin called after the finally freed Scriverenko... "The rogue seems to have grown ruder towards the end," thought our hero, stealthily coming out from behind the stove. "There's another hitch here.

That's clear... First it was both this and that... However, he really was in a hurry; maybe there was a lot to do there. And his excellency made the rounds of the office twice... What might be the reason for that?... Oof! well, it's nothing! maybe it's nothing, however, but now we're going to see..."

Here Mr. Goliadkin opened the door and was about to step out, when suddenly, at that same instant, his excellency's carriage rumbled up to the porch. Before Mr. Goliadkin managed to recover, the door of the carriage opened from inside and the gentleman sitting in it jumped out onto the porch. The newcomer was none other than the same Mr. Goliadkin Jr., who had absented himself ten minutes earlier. Mr. Goliadkin Sr. remembered that the director's apartment was two steps away. "He's on a special mission," our hero thought to himself. Meanwhile Mr. Goliadkin Jr., taking a fat green portfolio and some other papers from the carriage, and, finally, giving some order to the coachman, opened the door, almost shoving Mr. Goliadkin Sr. with it, and, deliberately ignoring him, and therefore acting this way in order to spite him, started at a trot up the department stairs. "Bad!" thought Mr. Goliadkin. "Eh, our little affair is doing poorly! Look at him, Lord God!" Our hero stood motionless for half a minute; finally, he made up his mind. Not thinking long, though feeling a strong fluttering in his heart and a trembling in all his limbs, he ran after his friend up the stairs. "Ah! let come what may; what is it to me? I have nothing to do with it," he thought, taking off his hat, overcoat, and galoshes in the hall.

When Mr. Goliadkin entered his department, it was already fully dark.[26] Neither Andrei Filippovich nor Anton Antonovich was in the room. They were both in the director's office with their reports; the director, as rumor had it, was hastening in his turn to go to his superior. Owing to this circumstance, and also because there was darkness mixed into it and the business day was almost over, some of the clerks, mostly young men, were occupied at the moment our hero entered with some sort of idleness, clustering together, talking, discussing, laughing, and some of the youngest, that is, of the most rankless rank, on the sly and under cover of the general noise, had even begun a game of pitch-and-toss in the corner by the window. Being a polite man and sensing at the present time some particular need to acquire and to find, Mr. Goliadkin approached some of those with whom he was on better terms, to wish them a good afternoon, and so on. But his colleagues responded to Mr. Goliadkin's greetings somehow strangely. He was unpleasantly struck by a sort of general coldness, dryness, even, one might say, a sort of sternness in the reception. No one shook hands with him. Some simply said "Hello" and walked off; others just nodded, some simply turned away, showing that they had not noticed anything, and, finally, certain—and this was the most offensive thing for Mr. Goliadkin—certain of the lowest ranking young men, boys who, as Mr. Goliadkin correctly observed about them, knew only how to play pitch-and-toss on occasion and to mooch about somewhere—gradually surrounded Mr. Goliadkin, forming a cluster around him and almost blocking his way out. They all gazed at him with some insulting curiosity.

It was a bad sign. Mr. Goliadkin felt that and for his part sensibly prepared not to notice anything. Suddenly one completely unexpected circumstance quite, as they say, finished off and annihilated Mr. Goliadkin.

In the bunch of young colleagues surrounding him, suddenly and, as if on purpose, at the most anguished moment for him, Mr. Goliadkin Jr. appeared, cheerful as always, with a little smile as always, also fidgety as always—in short, a prankster, a leaper, a smoocher, a tittler, light of tongue and foot, as always, as before, just as yesterday, for instance, at a very unpleasant moment for Mr. Goliadkin Sr. Grinning, fidgeting, mincing, with a little smile that as much as said "Good evening" to them all, he wormed his way into the bunch of clerks, shook hands with one, patted another on the shoulder, embraced a third slightly, explained to a fourth precisely on what occasion his excellency had employed him, where he had gone, what he had done, and what he had brought with him; gave the fifth, probably his best friend, a smacking kiss right on the lips—in short, it all happened exactly as in Mr. Goliadkin Sr.'s dream. Having

had his fill of leaping about, having finished with each of them
in his own way, having wound them all into his favor, whether
he needed it or not, having smooched with them all to his
heart's content, Mr. Goliadkin Jr. suddenly, and probably by
mistake, having so far failed to notice his old friend, offered his
hand to Mr. Goliadkin Sr. Probably also by mistake, though,
incidentally, he had managed to notice the ignoble Mr.
Goliadkin Jr. perfectly well, our hero at once eagerly seized the
so unexpectedly proffered hand and shook it in a most firm,
friendly way, with some strange, quite unexpected inner
impulse, with a sort of tearful feeling. Whether our hero had
been deceived by his indecent enemy's first move, or had merely
found nothing better to do, or had sensed and realized deep in
his soul the whole extent of his defenselessness, it is hard to
say. The fact was that Mr. Goliadkin Sr., of sound mind, by his
own will, and before witnesses, solemnly shook hands with the
one he called his mortal enemy. But what was the amazement,
the fury, and the rage, what was the horror and shame of Mr.
Goliadkin Sr., when his adversary, his mortal enemy, the ignoble
Mr. Goliadkin Jr., noticing the mistake of the innocent and
persecuted man whom he had perfidiously deceived, without
any shame, without feeling, without compassion and conscience, suddenly, with insufferable impudence and rudeness,
tore his hand from Mr. Goliadkin Sr.'s hand; what's more, he
shook his hand as if he had dirtied it in something quite unsa-
vory; what's more, he spat to the side, accompanying it all
with a most insulting gesture; what's more, he took out his
handkerchief and right there, in the most outrageous fashion,
wiped all the fingers that had rested for a moment in Mr.
Goliadkin Sr.'s hand. Acting in this way, Mr. Goliadkin Jr.
deliberately looked around, as was his mean custom, making
sure that everyone had seen his conduct, looked everyone in the
eye, and obviously tried to instill in everyone all that was most
unfavorable regarding Mr. Goliadkin. It seemed that the conduct of the disgusting Mr. Goliadkin Jr. aroused general indignation in the surrounding clerks; even the flighty young men
showed their displeasure. Grumbling and talk arose around.

The general stir could not have missed the ears of Mr. Goliadkin Sr.; but suddenly the timely arrival of a joke that boiled up, among other things, on the lips of Mr. Goliadkin Jr., dashed and destroyed our hero's last hopes and again tilted the balance in favor of his mortal and useless enemy.

"This is our Russian Faublas,[27] gentlemen; allow me to introduce to you the young Faublas," squeaked Mr. Goliadkin Jr., mincing and twining with an impudence all his own among the clerks and pointing to the petrified, and at the same time furious, real Mr. Goliadkin. "Give us a kiss, sweetie!" he went on with insufferable familiarity, moving closer to the man he had treacherously insulted. The little joke of the useless Mr. Goliadkin Jr. seemed to have found an echo in the right place, the more so as it contained a perfidious allusion to a circumstance that was already public and known to all. Our hero felt the hand of his enemies heavily on his shoulders. However, he was already resolved. With a burning gaze, a pale face, a fixed smile, he extricated himself somehow from the crowd and, with irregular, hurrying steps, made his way straight to his excellency's office. In the next to last room, he met with Andrei Filippovich, who had just come from his excellency's, and though there were quite a number of persons in the room at that moment who were total strangers to Mr. Goliadkin, our hero did not want to pay any attention to that circumstance. Directly, resolutely, and boldly, almost astonished at himself and inwardly praising himself for his boldness, without wasting any time he accosted Andrei Filippovich, who was quite amazed at such an unexpected assault.

"Ah!...what...what do you want?" asked the head of the office, not listening to Mr. Goliadkin, who had faltered over something.

"Andrei Filippovich, I...may I, Andrei Filippovich, have a talk with his excellency now, at once, and eye-to-eye?" our hero uttered eloquently and distinctly, directing a most resolute glance at Andrei Filippovich.

"What, sir? Of course not, sir." Andrei Filippovich looked Mr. Goliadkin up and down.

"I say all this, Andrei Filippovich, because I'm surprised that no one here will expose an impostor and scoundrel."

"Wha-a-at, sir?"

"A scoundrel, Andrei Filippovich."

"To whom are you pleased to refer in this manner?"

"To a certain person, Andrei Filippovich. I am alluding, Andrei Filippovich, to a certain person; I am within my rights...I think, Andrei Filippovich, that the authorities should encourage such initiative," added Mr. Goliadkin, obviously forgetting himself. "Andrei Filippovich...you probably can see for yourself...Andrei Filippovich, that this noble initiative betokens all possible good intentions in me—to take a superior as a father, Andrei Filippovich, say, I take a beneficent superior as a father and blindly entrust my fate to him. Thus and so, say...that's what..." Here Mr. Goliadkin's voice trembled, his face reddened, and two tears welled up on both of his eyelashes.

Andrei Filippovich was so surprised, listening to Mr. Goliadkin, that he somehow inadvertently drew back a couple of steps. Then he looked around uneasily...It is hard to say how the matter would have ended...But suddenly the door of his excellency's office opened, and he himself emerged, in the company of several clerks. Everyone in the room was drawn after him. His excellency called to Andrei Filippovich and walked beside him, broaching a conversation about some business. When they all started moving and headed out of the room, Mr. Goliadkin came to his senses. Subdued, he took shelter under the wing of Anton Antonovich Setochkin, who in turn hobbled after them all and, as it seemed to Mr. Goliadkin, with a most stern and preoccupied air. "I've said too much again, I've mucked it up again," he thought to himself. "Ah, well, never mind."

"I hope that at least you, Anton Antonovich, will agree to listen to me and enter into my circumstances," he said softly and in a voice still trembling with agitation. "Rejected by all, I turn to you. I'm still puzzled by the meaning of Andrei Filippovich's words, Anton Antonovich. Explain them to me, if you can..."

"Everything will be explained in good time, sir," Anton Antonovich replied sternly and measuredly and, as it seemed to Mr. Goliadkin, with an air which showed clearly that Anton Antonovich had no wish to continue the conversation. "You will learn everything shortly, sir. Today you will be formally notified of everything."

"What do you mean by 'formally,' Anton Antonovich? Why precisely 'formally,' sir?" our hero asked timidly.

"It is not for us to reason, Yakov Petrovich, about what our superiors decide."

"Why our superiors, Anton Antonovich," Mr. Goliadkin asked still more timidly, "why our superiors? I see no reason why there's any need to trouble our superiors here, Anton Antonovich...Maybe you mean to say something about yesterday, Anton Antonovich?"

"No, sir, not about yesterday, sir; there's something else here that's not up to snuff with you."

"What's not up to snuff, Anton Antonovich? It seems to me, Anton Antonovich, that there's nothing that's not up to snuff with me."

"And this being clever with somebody?" Anton Antonovich sharply cut off the totally dumbfounded Mr. Goliadkin. Mr. Goliadkin gave a start and turned white as a sheet.

"Of course, Anton Antonovich," he said in a barely audible voice, "if we heed the voice of calumny and listen to our enemies, without accepting justification from the other side, then, of course...of course, Anton Antonovich, then we can suffer, Anton Antonovich, suffer innocently and for nothing."

"Come, come, sir; and your indecent act to the detriment of the reputation of a noble young lady of a virtuous, respectable, and well-known family that had been your benefactor?"

"What action is that, Anton Antonovich?"

"Come, come, sir. And with regard to another young lady who, though poor, is of honorable foreign extraction, are you also ignorant of your laudable act, sir?"

"Excuse me, Anton Antonovich...be so good, Anton Antonovich, as to hear me out..."

"And your perfidious act and calumny of another person—accusing the other person of that in which your own little sin lay? eh? what is the name for that?"

"I didn't drive him out, Anton Antonovich," our hero said with trepidation, "and I didn't teach Petrushka—that is, my man—any such thing, sir ... He ate my bread, Anton Antonovich; he availed himself of my hospitality," our hero added expressively and with deep feeling, so that his chin trembled slightly and tears were about to well up again.

"You, Yakov Petrovich, are only saying that he ate your bread," Anton Antonovich replied, grinning, and slyness could be heard in his voice, so that something clawed at Mr. Goliadkin's heart.

"Allow me to humbly ask you, Anton Antonovich: has his excellency been informed of this whole affair?"

"What else, sir! However, let me go now, sir. I have no time for you now ... Today you'll learn of everything you ought to know, sir."

"For God's sake, allow me one more little minute, Anton Antonovich ..."

"You can tell me later, sir ..."

"No, Anton Antonovich; I, you see, sir, just listen, Anton Antonovich ... I am not a freethinker, Anton Antonovich, I shun freethinking; I am perfectly ready for my part, and I even slipped in this idea ..."

"All right, sir, all right. I've already heard, sir ..."

"No, sir, this you haven't heard, Anton Antonovich. It's something else, Anton Antonovich, it's good, it's truly good, and pleasant to hear ... I slipped in this idea, as I explained above, Anton Antonovich, that what we have here is God's design creating two perfect likenesses, and our beneficent superiors, seeing God's design, gave shelter to both twins, sir. It's good, Anton Antonovich. You can see that it's very good, Anton Antonovich, and that I'm far from any freethinking. I accept our beneficent superiors as a father. Thus and so, beneficent superiors, say, and you sort of ... the young man needs a job ... Support me, Anton Antonovich, intercede for me, Anton

Antonovich...I don't...Anton Antonovich, for God's sake, one more little word...Anton Antonovich..."

But Anton Antonovich was already far away from Mr. Goliadkin...Our hero did not know where he was standing, what he was hearing, what he was doing, what was being done to him, and what else would be done to him, so confused and shaken he was by all he had heard and all that had happened to him.

With an imploring gaze, he sought Anton Antonovich in the crowd of clerks, in order to justify himself further in his eyes and tell him something extremely well intentioned and highly noble and agreeable concerning himself...However, a new light gradually began to break through Mr. Goliadkin's confusion, a new, terrible light, which illuminated for him suddenly, all at once, a whole perspective of as yet completely unknown and even not in the least suspected circumstances...At that moment someone nudged our completely bewildered hero in the side. He turned. Before him stood Scriverenko.

"A letter, Your Honor."

"Ah!...you already went, my dear?"

"No, this one was brought here in the morning, at ten o'clock, sir. Sergei Mikheev, the caretaker, brought it from the lodgings of Provincial Secretary Vakhrameev."

"All right, my friend, all right, I'll thank you well, my dear."

Having said that, Mr. Goliadkin hid the letter away in the side pocket of his uniform and buttoned all the buttons, then looked around and noticed, to his surprise, that he was already in the front hall of the department, in a little bunch of clerks crowding towards the exit, because the workday was over. Mr. Goliadkin not only did not notice this last circumstance, but did not even notice or remember how it was that he suddenly had his overcoat and galoshes on and his hat in his hand. All the clerks stood motionless and in deferential expectation. The thing was that his excellency had stopped at the bottom of the stairs to wait for his carriage, which was delayed for some reason, and was engaged in a highly interesting conversation with two councillors and Andrei Filippovich. A little distance

away from the two councillors and Andrei Filippovich stood
Anton Antonovich Setochkin and some of the other clerks, full
of smiles, seeing that his excellency was pleased to joke and
laugh. The clerks crowding at the top of the stairs also smiled
and waited for his excellency to laugh again. The only one who
did not smile was Fedoseich, the fat-bellied porter, who kept
himself at attention by the door handle, waiting impatiently for
a portion of his daily satisfaction, which consisted in opening
one half of the door widely all at once, with a sweep of the arm,
and then, bending his back into a curve, deferentially allowing
his excellency to pass by. But apparently the one who was glad-
dest and felt the most satisfaction of all was Mr. Goliadkin's
unworthy and ignoble enemy. At that moment he even forgot
all the clerks, he even stopped mincing and twining among
them, as was his mean custom, he even forgot to make use of
the opportunity to fawn on someone at that moment. He turned
all ears and eyes, shrank somehow strangely, probably so as to
listen more conveniently, not taking his eyes off his excellency,
and his arms, his legs, his head only twitched occasionally with
some barely noticeable spasms, which exposed all the hidden,
inner stirrings of his soul.

"See how worked up he is!" our hero thought. "He has the
look of a favorite, the swindler! I wish I knew precisely how he
gets ahead in high-toned society! No intelligence, no character,
no education, no feeling; he's a lucky rogue! Lord God! how
quickly a man can go ahead, if you think of it, and get in with
everybody! And, I swear, the man will go on, he'll go far, the
rogue, he'll make it—he's a lucky rogue! I wish I knew precisely
what it is he whispers to them all! What secrets has he got with
all these people, and what mysteries do they talk about? Lord
God! Why couldn't I sort of . . . and also with them a little . . . say,
thus and so, to ask him . . . say, thus and so, but I won't do it
anymore; say, I'm to blame, and a young man in our time needs
to work, Your Excellency; and the obscure circumstance doesn't
trouble me in the least—so there! Nor will I protest in any way,
and I'll endure it all with patience and humility—so there!
Is that how I'm to act? . . . No, however, you can't get at this

rogue with any words; you can't hammer any reason into his wayward head... However, let's give it a try. I might happen to fall on a good moment, so why not give it a try..."

In his uneasiness, in anguish and confusion, feeling that it was impossible to remain like this, that the decisive moment was coming, that it was necessary to discuss it with at least someone, our hero gradually began edging towards the place where his unworthy and mysterious friend stood; but just then his excellency's long-awaited carriage rumbled up to the entrance. Fedoseich tore at the door and, bending double, allowed his excellency to pass by him. All the waiting clerks surged at once to the exit and momentarily pushed Mr. Goliadkin Sr. away from Mr. Goliadkin Jr. "You won't escape!" our hero was saying as he broke through the crowd, not taking his eyes off the one he wanted. Finally the crowd parted. Our hero felt himself free and rushed in pursuit of his adversary.

CHAPTER XI

THE BREATH LABORED in Mr. Goliadkin's chest; he flew as on wings after his quickly retreating adversary. He felt in himself the presence of a terrible energy. However, despite the presence of a terrible energy, Mr. Goliadkin could boldly trust that at the present moment even a simple mosquito, had it been able to live at such a season in Petersburg, could quite easily have knocked him down with its wing. He also felt that he was completely limp and feeble, that he was borne up by some completely peculiar and extraneous power, that he was not walking by himself, that, on the contrary, his legs were giving way under him and refused to serve. However, all that might work out for the better. "For better or worse," thought Mr. Goliadkin, almost suffocating from running so fast, "but there's not the slightest doubt that the affair is lost; that I'm totally lost is known, determined, decided, and signed." Despite all that, it was as if our hero had risen from the dead, as if he had endured battle, as if he had snatched away the victory, when he managed to seize the overcoat of his adversary, who had already hoisted one leg into the droshky he had just hired. "My dear sir! my dear sir!" he shouted finally at the ignoble Mr. Goliadkin Jr., caught at last. "My dear sir, I hope that you..."

"No, please don't hope for anything," Mr. Goliadkin's unfeeling adversary replied evasively, one foot standing on one step of the droshky and with the other straining with all his might to get to the other side of the vehicle, waving it vainly in the air, trying to keep his balance and at the same time trying with all his might to detach his overcoat from Mr. Goliadkin Sr., who for his part attached himself to it with all the means granted him by nature.

"Yakov Petrovich! just ten minutes..."

"Excuse me, I have no time, sir."

"You yourself must agree, Yakov Petrovich...please, Yakov Petrovich...for God's sake, Yakov Petrovich...thus and so—to have a talk...on a bold footing...One little second, Yakov Petrovich!..."

"My dear heart, I have no time," Mr. Goliadkin's falsely noble adversary replied with discourteous familiarity, but in the guise of heartfelt kindness, "some other time, believe me, from fullness of soul and purity of heart; but now—really, it's impossible."

"Scoundrel!" thought our hero.

"Yakov Petrovich!" he cried in anguish. "I have never been your enemy. Wicked people have described me unfairly...For my part, I'm ready...Yakov Petrovich, if you wish, you and I, Yakov Petrovich, shall we go in now?...And there, from purity of heart, as you just said correctly, and in a direct, noble tongue...into this coffeehouse: then everything will explain itself—that's what, Yakov Petrovich! Then certainly everything will explain itself..."

"Into the coffeehouse? Very well, sir. I have nothing against it, let's go to the coffeehouse, only on one condition, my joy, on the single condition—that there everything will explain itself. Say, thus and so, my sweet," said Mr. Goliadkin Jr., stepping down from the droshky and shamelessly patting our hero on the shoulder, "my good chum; for you, Yakov Petrovich, I'm ready to go down a little lane (as you, Yakov Petrovich, were pleased to observe correctly once upon a time). What a slyboots, really, he does whatever he wants with a man!" Mr. Goliadkin's false friend went on, fidgeting and twining around him with a slight smile.

Off the main streets, the coffeehouse which the two Mr. Goliadkins entered was at that moment totally empty. A rather fat German woman appeared at the counter as soon as she heard the ringing of the little bell. Mr. Goliadkin and his unworthy adversary passed into the second room, where a puffy-faced boy with cropped hair was fussing with a heap of chips by the stove, trying to revive the dying fire. At the demand of Mr. Goliadkin Jr., hot chocolate was served.

"She's a tasty morsel, that one," said Mr. Goliadkin Jr., winking slyly at Mr. Goliadkin Sr.

Our hero blushed and said nothing.

"Ah, yes, I forgot, forgive me. I know your taste. We, sir, relish thin German women; you and I, you truthful soul, say, we relish thin German women, though, incidentally, not lacking in certain pleasant qualities; we rent their apartments, we seduce their virtue; for bier-zuppe, for milch-zuppe, we dedicate our hearts to them and sign various papers—that's what we do, you Faublas, you traitor, you!"

Mr. Goliadkin Jr. said all this, making thereby a completely useless though villainously cunning allusion to a certain person of the female sex, twining around Mr. Goliadkin, smiling at him in simulated courtesy, making a false display, thereby, of his affability and joy at their meeting. But noticing that Mr. Goliadkin Sr. was by no means so stupid and deprived of education and good-toned manners as to believe him at once, the ignoble man decided to change his tactics and conduct the affair on an open footing. Straightaway, having uttered his abomination, the false Mr. Goliadkin concluded by patting the reliable Mr. Goliadkin on the shoulder with outrageous shamelessness and familiarity, and, not content with that, began flirting with him in a manner completely improper to good-toned society— namely, he was about to repeat the former abomination, that is, despite the resistance and the slight outcries of the indignant Mr. Goliadkin Sr., to pinch his cheek. Seeing such depravity, our hero seethed but said nothing . . . only for a time, however.

"That's how my enemies talk," he finally answered in a trembling voice, sensibly restraining himself. At the same time our hero turned to look anxiously at the door. The thing was that Mr. Goliadkin Jr. was apparently in an excellent state of mind and ready to start all kinds of tricks not admissible in a public place and, generally speaking, not permitted by the laws of society, and chiefly of high-toned society.

"Ah, well, in that case, as you wish," Mr. Goliadkin Jr. retorted gravely to the thought of Mr. Goliadkin Sr., placing his empty cup, which he had drunk with indecent greediness,

on the table. "Well, sir, anyhow there's no point in prolong-
ing…Well, sir, how are you getting along now, Yakov
Petrovich?"

"I can say only one thing to you, Yakov Petrovich," our hero
replied coolly and with dignity, "I have never been your enemy."

"Hm…well, and Petrushka? How now! It's Petrushka, I
believe?—why, yes! So, how is he? Well? Same as before?"

"He's also the same as before, Yakov Petrovich," replied the
slightly astonished Mr. Goliadkin Sr. "I don't know, Yakov
Petrovich…for my part…for the noble, for the sincere part,
Yakov Petrovich, you must agree, Yakov Petrovich…"

"Yes, sir. But you yourself know, Yakov Petrovich," Mr.
Goliadkin Jr. replied in a soft and insinuating voice, thus falsely
making himself out to be a sad, dignified man, filled with
repentance and regret, "you yourself know, our times are
hard…I defer to you, Yakov Petrovich; you're an intelligent
man and will judge fairly," Mr. Goliadkin Jr. put in, basely
flattering Mr. Goliadkin Sr. "Life's not a game—you know
that yourself, Yakov Petrovich," Mr. Goliadkin Jr. concluded
meaningfully, thus pretending to be an intelligent and learned
man who could reason about lofty subjects.

"For my part, Yakov Petrovich," our hero replied with animation, "for my part, scornful of roundabout paths and speaking
boldly and sincerely, speaking a direct, noble language, and
putting the whole affair on a noble level, I will tell you, I can
openly and nobly assert, Yakov Petrovich, that I am completely
clear and that, as you yourself know, a mutual error—anything
can happen—the world's judgment, the opinion of the servile
crowd…I'm speaking sincerely, Yakov Petrovich, anything can
happen. I will also say, Yakov Petrovich, if one judges in this
way, if one looks at the affair from a noble and lofty point of
view, I will say boldly, without false shame, Yakov Petrovich, it
would even be pleasant for me to reveal that I was mistaken,
it would even be pleasant for me to admit it. You yourself know,
you're an intelligent man, and moreover a noble one. Without
shame, without false shame, I am ready to admit it…" our hero
concluded with dignity and nobility.

"Fate, destiny, Yakov Petrovich!...But let's leave all that," Mr. Goliadkin Jr. said with a sigh. "Better let's use the brief moments of our encounter in more useful and pleasant conversation, as befits two colleagues...Really, I somehow haven't managed to exchange two words with you all this time...I'm not to blame for it, Yakov Petrovich..."

"Neither am I," our hero warmly interrupted, "neither am I! My heart tells me, Yakov Petrovich, that I am not to blame for all this. Let's blame destiny for it, Yakov Petrovich," Mr. Goliadkin Sr. added in a completely conciliatory tone. His voice gradually began to weaken and tremble.

"Well, so? How's your health generally?" the wayward one asked in a sweet voice.

"I have a slight cough," our hero replied still more sweetly.

"Take care of yourself. There are these infections going around, it's easy to catch a quinsy, and, I confess to you, I'm beginning to wrap myself in flannel."

"Indeed, Yakov Petrovich, it is easy to catch a quinsy, sir...Yakov Petrovich!" our hero said after a meek pause. "Yakov Petrovich! I see that I was mistaken...I have a fond memory of those happy minutes we managed to pass under my poor but, I dare say, hospitable roof..."

"However, that is not what you wrote in your letter," the perfectly fair (perfectly fair, however, solely in this respect) Mr. Goliadkin Jr. said partly in reproach.

"Yakov Petrovich! I was mistaken...I now see clearly that I was also mistaken in that unfortunate letter of mine. Yakov Petrovich, I am ashamed to look at you, Yakov Petrovich, you won't believe me...Give me that letter so that I can tear it up before your eyes, Yakov Petrovich, or if that is absolutely impossible, I implore you to read it the other way round— quite the other way round, that is, with a deliberately friendly intention, giving the contrary sense to all the words of my letter. I was mistaken. Forgive me, Yakov Petrovich, I was totally... I was grievously mistaken, Yakov Petrovich."

"You were saying?" Mr. Goliadkin Sr.'s perfidious friend asked rather absentmindedly and indifferently.

"I was saying that I was totally mistaken, Yakov Petrovich, and that, for my part, without any false shame, I . . ."

"Ah, well, good! It's very good that you were mistaken," Mr. Goliadkin Jr. replied rudely.

"I even had the idea, Yakov Petrovich," our candid hero added in a noble fashion, totally oblivious of the terrible perfidy of his false friend, "I even had the idea that, say, here two perfect likenesses have been created . . ."

"Ah, so that's your idea! . . ."

Here Mr. Goliadkin Jr., known for his uselessness, got up and seized his hat. Still failing to notice the deceit, Mr. Goliadkin Sr. also got up, smiling simple-heartedly and nobly to his pseudo-friend, trying, in his innocence, to be gentle, to encourage him, and thus to strike up a new friendship with him . . .

"Good-bye, Your Excellency!" Mr. Goliadkin Jr. suddenly cried out. Our hero shuddered, noticing something even bacchic in his enemy's face and, solely to be rid of him, thrust two fingers of his hand into the hand the immoral man held out to him; but here . . . here the shamelessness of Mr. Goliadkin Jr. went beyond all degree. Having seized the two fingers of Mr. Goliadkin Sr.'s hand and pressed them first, the unworthy man straightaway, before Mr. Goliadkin's eyes, ventured to repeat his shameless morning joke. The measure of human patience was exhausted . . .

He was already putting the handkerchief with which he had wiped his fingers into his pocket when Mr. Goliadkin Sr. came to his senses and rushed after him into the next room, where, as was his nasty habit, his implacable enemy had at once hastened to slip away. Cool as a cucumber, he was standing at the counter eating little pies and, like a virtuous man, quite calmly paying court to the German pastry cook. "Impossible in front of ladies," thought our hero, and he also went up to the counter, beside himself with agitation.

"Not a bad-looking wench, in fact! What do you think?" Mr. Goliadkin Jr. began his indecent escapades anew, probably counting on Mr. Goliadkin's endless patience. The fat German woman, for her part, looked at both her customers with senseless, tinny eyes, obviously not understanding Russian and smiling affably. Our hero flared up like fire at the words of the shameless Mr. Goliadkin Jr. and, losing all control, finally hurled himself at him with the obvious intention of tearing him to pieces and thus having done with him definitively, but Mr. Goliadkin Jr., as was his mean custom, was already far away: he had taken to his heels, he was already on the porch. It goes without saying, of course, that after the first momentary stupefaction, which naturally came over Mr. Goliadkin Sr., he recovered and rushed headlong after his offender, who was already getting into a waiting cab, whose driver was obviously in full complicity with him. But at that same moment the fat German woman, seeing the flight of the two customers, shrieked and rang the bell with all her might. Our hero turned back almost on the wing, threw her money for himself and the shameless, unpaying man, not asking for change, and, despite this delay, still managed—though, again, only on the wing—to catch up with his adversary. Clinging to the droshky's mudguard with all the means granted him by nature, our hero went racing down the street for a time, trying to scramble into the carriage, which Mr. Goliadkin Jr. defended with all his might. Meanwhile the cabby, with whip and reins and foot and words, urged on his broken-down nag, who quite unexpectedly went into a gallop, taking the bit in her teeth and kicking up her hind legs, as was her nasty habit, at every third stride. Finally our hero somehow managed to hoist himself into the droshky, face to his adversary, back leaning against the cabby, his knees to the shameless fellow's knees, and with his right hand clutching as best he could the rather shabby fur collar of his depraved and most bitter enemy's overcoat ...

The enemies raced on and for a time were silent. Our hero could barely catch his breath; the road was very bad, and he was jolted at every step, in danger of breaking his neck. On top of that, his bitter adversary still would not admit defeat and tried to push his enemy off into the mud. To complete all the unpleasantnesses, the weather was most terrible. Snow poured down in big flakes and tried all it could, for its part, to get under the flung-open overcoat of the real Mr. Goliadkin. It was murky all around and impossible to see. It was hard to tell where and down what streets they were racing...It seemed to Mr. Goliadkin that something familiar was happening to him. At one point he tried to recall whether he had had any presentiment the day before...in a dream, for instance...Finally, his anguish grew to the ultimate degree of its agony. Leaning his full weight against his merciless adversary, he was about to cry out. But the cry died on his lips...There was a moment when Mr. Goliadkin forgot everything and decided that all this was quite negligible and that it had been done just like that, somehow, in an inexplicable fashion, and to protest on this occasion would be a superfluous and completely wasted business...But suddenly, and almost at the moment when our hero was coming to this conclusion, some careless jolt changed the whole sense of the affair. Mr. Goliadkin tumbled off the droshky like a sack of flour and rolled away somewhere, admitting quite correctly in the moment of his fall that he had really and highly inappropriately lost his temper. Jumping to his feet, finally, he saw that they had arrived somewhere; the droshky was standing in the middle of someone's yard, and our hero noticed at first glance that it was the yard of the house where Olsufy Ivanovich lived. At that same moment he noticed that his companion was already making his way to the porch and probably to Olsufy Ivanovich's. In his indescribable anguish, he was about to rush in pursuit of his adversary, but, fortunately for him, he had sense enough to think better of it in time. Not forgetting to pay the cabby, Mr. Goliadkin rushed out to the street and ran as fast as he could wherever his legs would carry him. Snow poured down in big flakes as before; as before it was murky, damp, and dark. Our hero did not walk but flew, knocking down everyone in his way—peasants, their women, children, and bouncing off of women, peasants, and children in his turn. Around him and behind him he heard frightened talk, shrieks, cries...But it seemed that Mr. Goliadkin was oblivious and did not want to pay any attention to anything...He came to his senses, however, by the Semyonovsky Bridge, and then only because he happened somehow clumsily to brush against and knock down two peasant women with the wares they were carrying, and to fall down himself along with them. "Never mind that," thought Mr. Goliadkin, "all this may very well still work out for the best"—and he straightaway went to his pocket, wishing to get off by paying a silver rouble for the spilled gingerbreads, apples, peas, and various other things. Suddenly a new light dawned on Mr. Goliadkin; in his pocket he felt the letter that the scrivener had handed to him in the morning. Remembering among other things that there was a tavern he knew not far away, he ran to the tavern, sat down without wasting a moment at a little table lit by a tallow candle, and, not paying attention to anything, not listening to the waiter who came to take his order, he broke the seal and began to read what follows below, struck by it to the uttermost.

Noble man, who suffers for me and is forever dear to my heart!
I am suffering, I am perishing—save me! The slanderer, the intriguer, the man known for his useless tendency, entangled me in his net, and I was lost! I fell! But he is repulsive to me, while you . . . ! They separated us, they intercepted my letters to you—and it was all done by the immoral one, making use of his one good quality—his resemblance to you. In any case, a man may be bad-looking, but attractive by his intelligence, strong feeling, and pleasant manners . . . I am perishing! They are giving me away by force, and the one who is intriguing most of all is my parent, my benefactor, the state councillor Olsufy Ivanovich, probably wishing to occupy my place and my relations in high-toned society . . . But I am resolved and I protest with all the means granted me by nature. Wait for me with your carriage tonight, at exactly nine o'clock, by the windows of Olsufy Ivanovich's apartment. There will be a ball again, and the handsome lieutenant will be there. I will come out, and we will fly away. Besides, there are other places of service, where one can still be of use to the fatherland. In any case, remember, my friend, that innocence is already strong in its innocence. Farewell.

Wait with the carriage at the entrance. I will throw myself under the protection of your embrace at exactly two a.m.

Yours till death,

Klara Olsufyevna.

Having read the letter, our hero remained as if dumbfounded for several minutes. In terrible anguish, in terrible agitation, pale as a sheet, the letter in his hands, he paced several times about the room; to complete his disastrous position, our hero failed to notice that he was at the present moment the object of the exclusive attention of all those in the room. Probably the disorder of his clothes, his unrestrained agitation, his pacing, or, rather, running about, gesticulating with both hands, maybe a few mysterious words uttered to the wind and in oblivion— probably all that recommended Mr. Goliadkin quite poorly to the opinion of all the customers; even the waiter himself began to glance at him suspiciously. Coming to his senses, our hero noticed that he was standing in the middle of the room and staring in an almost indecent, impolite fashion at a little old man of quite venerable appearance, who, after having dinner and praying to God before an icon, sat down again and, for his part, fixed his gaze on Mr. Goliadkin. Our hero looked around vaguely and noticed that everyone, decidedly everyone, was looking at him with a most sinister and suspicious air. Suddenly a retired officer with a red collar loudly asked for *The Police Gazette*. Mr. Goliadkin gave a start and blushed: somehow by chance he looked down and saw that his clothes were so indecent that they would have been impossible even in his own home, to say nothing of a public place. His boots, his trousers, and his entire left side were covered with mud; the trouser strap on his right foot had been torn off, and his tailcoat was even ripped in many places. In inexhaustible anguish, our hero went over to the table at which he had been reading and saw a waiter approaching him with an odd and brazenly insistent expression on his face. Totally bewildered and deflated, our hero began to examine the table at which he was standing. There were dishes on the table left after someone's dinner, a dirty napkin lay there, and a just-used knife, fork, and spoon. "Who was having dinner?" thought our hero. "Could it have been me? Anything's possible! I had dinner and didn't notice it: what am I to do?" Raising his eyes, Mr. Goliadkin again saw the waiter standing beside him, about to say something to him.

"How much do I owe, brother?" our hero asked in a trembling voice.

Loud laughter arose around Mr. Goliadkin; the waiter himself grinned. Mr. Goliadkin realized that in this, too, he had flunked and done something awfully stupid. Having realized it all, he became so embarrassed that he had to go to his pocket for a handkerchief, probably so as to do something and not stand there like that; but to his own and everyone else's indescribable amazement, instead of a handkerchief, he took out a vial with some medication prescribed by Krestyan Ivanovich four days earlier. "Medications from the same apothecary," raced through Mr. Goliadkin's head... Suddenly he gave a start and almost cried out in terror. New light was shed... A dark, disgustingly reddish liquid shone with a sinister gleam before Mr. Goliadkin's eyes. The vial fell from his hand and broke at once. Our hero cried out and sprang two steps back from the spilled liquid... he trembled all over, and sweat broke out on his temples and forehead. "That means my life's in danger!" Meanwhile there was movement, commotion in the room; everyone surrounded Mr. Goliadkin, everyone talked to Mr. Goliadkin, some even seized Mr. Goliadkin. But our hero was mute and motionless, saw nothing, heard nothing, felt nothing... Finally, as if tearing himself away, he rushed out of the tavern, shoved aside each and all of those who tried to hold him back, fell almost unconscious into the first droshky that happened along, and flew home.

In the front hall of his apartment he met Mikheev, the department caretaker, with an official envelope in his hand. "I know, my friend, I know everything," our exhausted hero answered in a weak, melancholy voice, "it's official..." The envelope indeed contained an order for Mr. Goliadkin, signed by Andrei Filippovich, to hand over the cases in his charge to

Ivan Semyonovich. Having taken the envelope and given the caretaker a ten-kopeck piece, Mr. Goliadkin went into his apartment and saw Petrushka preparing and gathering into a heap all his trash and rubbish, all his things, obviously intending to leave Mr. Goliadkin and go over from him to Karolina Ivanovna, who had lured him away to replace her Evstafy.

CHAPTER XII

P ETRUSHKA CAME SAUNTERING IN, bearing himself with some strange casualness and with a sort of knavishly solemn expression on his face. It was evident that he had thought up something, felt himself fully within his rights, and looked like a total stranger, that is, anyone else's servant, only in no way the former servant of Mr. Goliadkin.

"Well, so you see, my dear," our hero began breathlessly, "what time is it now, my dear?"

Petrushka silently went behind the partition, then returned and announced in a rather independent tone that it would soon be half-past seven.

"Well, all right, my dear, all right. Well, you see, my dear . . . allow me to tell you, my dear, that it seems everything is now over between us."

Petrushka was silent.

"Well, now, since everything is over between us, tell me candidly now, tell me like a friend, where have you been, brother?"

"Where have I been? Among good people, sir."

"I know, my friend, I know. I have always been satisfied with you, my dear, and I'll give you a reference . . . Well, how are you doing with them now?"

"How am I doing, sir? You know yourself, if you please, sir. Everybody knows a good man won't teach you anything bad."

"I know, my dear, I know. Good people are rare nowadays, my friend; value them, my friend. Well, how are they doing?"

"Everybody knows how, sir . . . Only I can't serve you anymore now, sir; you know that yourself, if you please, sir."

"I know, my dear, I know; I know your zeal and assiduousness; I've seen all that, my friend, I've noticed. I respect you, my friend. I respect a good and honest man, even if he's a servant."

"Why, sir, everybody knows! The likes of us, you know yourself, if you please, sir, go where it's better. So there, sir. What's it to me! Everybody knows, sir, there's no doing without a good man, sir."

"Well, all right, brother, all right; I feel that . . . Well, here's your money and here's your reference. Now let's kiss, brother, let's say good-bye . . . Well, now, my dear, I'll ask one service of you, a last service," Mr. Goliadkin said in a solemn tone. "You see, my dear, anything can happen. Woe also hides in gilded mansions, my friend, and there's no getting away from it. You know, my friend, I believe I've always been nice to you . . ."

Petrushka was silent.

"I believe I've always been nice to you, my dear . . . Well, how much linen have we got now, my dear?"

"It's all there, sir. Six cotton shirts, sir; three pairs of socks; four shirt fronts; a flannel vest; two undershirts, sir. You know it all, sir. There's nothing of yours, sir, that I . . . I look after my master's goods, sir. You and I, sir, sort of . . . it's a known thing, sir . . . but anything wrong on my part—never, sir; you know that yourself, sir."

"Right, my friend, right. I don't mean that, my friend, not that; you see, there's this, my friend . . ."

"Everybody knows, sir; that we know already, sir. Take me, when I was still in General Stolbniakov's service, he dismissed me, sir, having gone to Saratov himself . . . to his family estate there . . ."

"No, my friend, I don't mean that; I never . . . don't go thinking anything, my dear friend . . ."

"Everybody knows, sir. With the likes of us, you know yourself, if you please, sir, you can slander a man in no time, sir. But they've always been satisfied with me, sir. There've been ministers, generals, senators, counts, sir. I've been with them all, sir, with Prince Svinchatkin, with Colonel Pereborkin, also had a go with General Nedobarov, in my native parts, sir. Everybody knows, sir . . ."

"Yes, my friend, yes; very well, my friend, very well. So now I, too, my friend, am leaving . . . There's a different path laid down for each of us, my dear, and no one knows what road a man may wind up on. Well, my friend, give me my clothes now; and also put in my uniform...a second pair of trousers, sheets, blankets, pillows..."

"Will you have me tie it all up in a bundle, sir?"

"Yes, my friend, yes; perhaps in a bundle...Who knows what may happen with us? Well, now, my dear, go out and find a carriage..."

"A carriage, sir?..."

"Yes, my friend, a carriage, a roomy one and for some length of time. And don't go thinking anything, my friend..."

"And do you mean to go a long way, sir?"

"I don't know, my friend, I don't know that either. I suppose you should also put in the feather bed. What do you think, my friend? I'm relying on you, my dear..."

"Might you be pleased to leave at once, sir?"

"Yes, my friend, yes! There's this circumstance...so it is, my dear, so it is..."

"Everybody knows, sir; it was the same with a lieutenant in our regiment—ran off, sir...with a landowner's..."

"Ran off?...What, my dear? You..."

"Yes, ran off, sir, and they got married on another estate. It was all prepared beforehand, sir. They were pursued; only here the late prince stepped in, sir—well, and the matter was settled, sir..."

"Married, hm...but how is it, my dear, how did you come to know it?"

"Why, what do you mean, sir, everybody knows! The earth's full of rumors, sir. Yes, sir, we know everything...of course, nobody's without sin. Only I'll tell you now, sir, allow me in a simple, boorish way to tell you, since we're talking about it, sir, I'll tell you—you've got a rival there, sir, a strong rival..."

"I know, my friend, I know; you know it yourself, my dear...Well, so I'm relying on you. What are we to do, my friend? How would you advise me?"

"So then, sir, if you're now proceeding, shall we say, in such a manner, sir, you'll need to buy a thing or two, sir—well, say, sheets, pillows, another feather bed, a double one, sir, a good blanket, sir—from the neighbor here, sir, downstairs: she's a tradeswoman; she has a good fox-fur woman's coat; you could have a look at it and buy it, you could go now and have a look, sir. You'll need it now, sir; a good satin coat, sir, lined with fox fur..."

"Well, all right, my friend, all right; I agree, my friend, I'm relying on you, relying on you fully; perhaps the coat as well, my dear...Only quickly, quickly! for God's sake, quickly! I'll buy the coat as well, only quickly, please! It will soon be eight o'clock, hurry, for God's sake, my friend! as fast as you can, my friend!..."

Petrushka abandoned the as yet untied bundle of linen, pillows, blanket, sheets, and various trash he was gathering together and tying up, and rushed headlong from the room. Mr. Goliadkin meanwhile snatched out the letter once again—but was unable to read it. Clutching his victorious head in both hands, he leaned against the wall in amazement. He was unable to think of anything, he was also unable to do anything; he did not know what was happening to him. Finally, seeing that time was passing and no Petrushka or fur coat appeared, Mr. Goliadkin decided to go himself. Opening the door to the front hall, he heard noise, talk, argument, and discussion downstairs...Several neighbor women were babbling, shouting, argling and bargling about something—and Mr. Goliadkin knew precisely what about. Petrushka's voice was heard, then someone's footsteps. "My God! They'll invite the whole world here!" moaned Mr. Goliadkin, wringing his hands in despair and rushing back to his room. Running into his room, he fell almost oblivious onto the sofa, his face buried in a cushion. After lying like that for a moment, he jumped up and, not waiting for Petrushka, put on his galoshes, his hat, his overcoat, seized his wallet, and ran headlong down the stairs. "Nothing's needed, nothing, my dear! I'll do it myself, all myself. There's no need for you right now, and meanwhile maybe the affair will get settled for the best," Mr. Goliadkin murmured to Petrushka, meeting him on the stairs; then he ran out to the yard and away

from the house; his heart was sinking; he was still undecided...
What should he do, how should he behave, how should he act
in this present and critical case ...

"This is it! How to act, oh, Lord God? And all this just had
to happen!" he finally cried in despair, hobbling down the street
wherever his legs carried him, "it all just had to happen! If it
weren't for this, precisely for this, everything would have been
settled; all at once, at one stroke, one deft, energetic, firm
stroke, it would have been settled. I'd let them cut my finger
off that it would have been settled. And I even know in
precisely what way it would have been settled. Here's how it
would be: I'd say such and such—thus and so, but for me, my
good sir, with your permission, it's neither here nor there;
say, things aren't done this way; say, my good sir, my very dear
sir, things aren't done this way, and imposture doesn't get
anywhere with us; an impostor, my good sir, is a man who is—
useless and of no use to the fatherland. Do you understand
that? I say, do you understand that, my very dear sir?! That's
how it would be, sort of... But no, however, what am I... that's
not it, not it at all... What am I babbling, like an utter fool!
me, suicide that I am! I say, suicide that you are, it's not that
at all... Though that is how, you depraved man, that is how
things are done nowadays!... Well, where shall I take myself
now? Well, what, for instance, am I to do with myself now?
What am I good for now? What, for instance, are you good
for now, you Goliadkin, you worthless fellow! Well, what now?
I have to hire a carriage; go, she says, and fetch a carriage here;
our little feet, she says, will get wet if there's no carriage ...
There, who'd have thought it? Oh, you young lady! oh, lady
mine! oh, you well-behaved miss! oh, our much-praised one!
You've distinguished yourself, ma'am, I declare, you've distinguished yourself!... And it all comes from immoral upbringing;
and I, as I look closely now and get to the bottom of it all, I
see that it comes from nothing else than immorality. Instead
of a bit of birching from a young age ... every once in a
while ... they give her candy, they stuff her with all sorts of
sweets, and the old fellow slobbers over her: says you're my

this, and you're my that, you good girl, says I'll give you away to a count!...And now she's up and shown us her cards; says here's what our game is! Instead of keeping her at home at a young age, they put her in a boarding school, with a French madame, an émigrée Falbala[28] of some sort; and she learns all kinds of good things from the émigrée Falbala—and so it all turns out this way. She says, go on, rejoice! Says, be there with a carriage at such and such hour in front of the windows and sing a sentimental romance in Spanish style; I'm waiting for you, and I know you love me, and we'll run off together and live in a cabin. But it's impossible, finally; if it's come to that, lady mine, it's impossible, it's against the law to carry off an honest and innocent girl from her parents' home without her parents' permission! And, finally, what for, and why, and where's the need? Well, let her marry the one she ought to, the one she's destined for, and the matter can end there. But I'm in government service; I could lose my job because of it; I, lady mine, could wind up in court because of it! that's what, in case you didn't know! This is the German woman's work. It's from her, the witch, that all this comes, she set the whole forest on fire. Because they're slandering a man, because they've invented some old wives' tale about him, some cock-and-bull story, on Andrei Filippovich's advice, that's where it comes from. Otherwise why is Petrushka mixed up in it? what is it to him? what's the need for that rogue here? No, I can't do it, my lady, I simply can't do it, can't do it for anything...You, my lady, must excuse me somehow this time. It all comes from you, my lady, it doesn't come from the German woman, not from the witch at all, but purely from you, because the witch is a good woman, because the witch is not to blame for anything, it's you, lady mine, who are to blame—that's how it is! You, my lady, are leading me into futility...A man's perishing here, a man's vanishing from his own sight here, and can't control himself—what sort of wedding can there be! And how will it all end? and how will it be settled now? I'd pay dearly to know all that!..."

Thus our hero reasoned in his despair. Suddenly coming to

his senses, he noticed that he was standing somewhere on Liteinaya. The weather was terrible: there was a thaw, heavy snow fell, rain came—exactly as in that unforgettable time, at the dreadful midnight hour, when all of Mr. Goliadkin's misfortunes had begun. "What sort of journey can there be!" thought Mr. Goliadkin, looking at the weather, "this is universal death... Oh, Lord God! where, for instance, am I to find a carriage? There seems to be something black there at the corner. Let's look, examine... Oh, Lord God!" our hero went on, directing his feeble and shaky steps towards where he saw something resembling a carriage. "No, here's what I'll do: I'll go, fall at his feet, if I can, I'll humbly beg. I'll say, thus and so; into your hands I put my fate, into the hands of my superiors; say, Your Excellency, be a benefactor, defend a man; thus and so, say, there's this and that, an illegal act; do not destroy me, I take you as a father, do not abandon me... save my pride, my honor, my name... save me from a villain, a depraved man... He's a different man, Your Excellency, and I'm also a different man; he's separate, and I'm also my own man; I'm really my own man, Your Excellency, really my own man; so there. I'll say, I can't resemble him; change it, if you please, order it changed—and do away with the godless, unwarranted substitute... no example to others, Your Excellency. I take you as my father; our superiors are, of course, beneficent and solicitous and ought to encourage such actions... There's even something chivalrous in it. I'll say, I take you, my beneficent superior, as a father, and entrust my fate to you, and will not object, I entrust myself to you and withdraw from the affair... so there!"

"Well, so, my dear, are you a cabby?"

"I am..."

"A carriage, brother, for the evening..."

"And would you be going far, if you please, sir?"

"For the evening, for the evening; wherever it may be, my dear, wherever it may be."

"Might you be going out of town, if you please, sir?"

"Yes, my friend, maybe out of town, too. I still don't know

for certain myself, my friend, I can't tell you for certain, my dear. You see, my dear, it may all get settled for the best. Everybody knows, my friend..."

"Yes, of course, sir, everybody knows; God grant everybody that."

"Yes, my friend, yes; thank you, my dear; well, how much will you charge, my dear?..."

"Might you be pleased to go now, sir?"

"Yes, now, that is, no, you must wait in a certain place...wait a little, it won't be long, my dear..."

"If you hire me for the whole time, sir, it can't be less than six roubles, considering the weather, sir..."

"All right, my friend, all right; and I'll thank you well, my dear. Well, so you'll take me now, my dear."

"Get in; excuse me, I'll straighten it out a little here; get in now, if you please. Where would you like to go?"

"To the Izmailovsky Bridge, my friend."

The driver clambered up on the box and urged his pair of skinny nags, whom he had trouble tearing away from the hay trough, in the direction of the Izmailovsky Bridge. But Mr. Goliadkin suddenly tugged the bell-pull, stopped the carriage, and asked in a pleading voice to turn back and not go to the Izmailovsky Bridge, but to another street. The driver turned into the other street, and in ten minutes Mr. Goliadkin's newly obtained vehicle stopped in front of the house in which his excellency was quartered. Mr. Goliadkin got out of the carriage, insistently asked his driver to wait, and with a sinking heart ran up to the first floor, tugged the bell-pull, the door opened, and our hero found himself in his excellency's front hall.

"Is his excellency at home, if you please?" asked Mr. Goliadkin, addressing in this way the man who had opened the door for him.

"What is your business, sir?" asked the footman, looking Mr. Goliadkin up and down.

"I, my friend, am sort of...Goliadkin, a clerk, Titular Councillor Goliadkin. Say, thus and so, to explain..."

"Wait; it's impossible, sir..."

"I can't wait, my friend: my business is important, it will brook no delay..."

"But where are you coming from? Have you brought any papers?..."

"No, my friend, I'm on my own... Announce me, my friend, say, thus and so, to explain. And I'll thank you well, my dear..."

"Impossible, sir. I have no orders to receive anyone; they're having guests, sir. Please come in the morning at ten o'clock, sir..."

"Announce me, my dear; I can't, it's impossible for me to wait... You'll answer for it, my dear..."

"Go and announce him; what, are you sorry for your boots or something?" said the other footman, who was sprawled on a bench and so far had not said a word.

"Wear out my boots! He gave no orders to receive anyone, you know? Their turn's in the morning."

"Announce him. Your tongue won't fall off."

"So I'll announce him: my tongue won't fall off. But he gave no orders, I told you, he gave no orders. Come in, then."

Mr. Goliadkin went into the first room; there was a clock on the table. He looked: it was half-past eight. His heart ached in his breast. He was about to retreat; but at that moment the lanky footman, standing on the threshold of the next room, loudly pronounced Mr. Goliadkin's name. "What a gullet!" our hero thought in indescribable anguish... "Well, he might have said: sort of... say, thus and so, came most obediently and humbly to explain—sort of... be so good as to receive... But now the whole affair is ruined, and it's all gone to the winds; however... ah, well—never mind..." There was no point in reasoning, however. The footman came back, said, "This way please," and led Mr. Goliadkin into the study.

When our hero went in, he felt as if he had been blinded, for he could see decidedly nothing. Two or three figures, however, flashed before his eyes. "These must be the guests," flashed through Mr. Goliadkin's head. Finally, our hero began to make out clearly the star on his excellency's black tailcoat, then, still as gradually, he passed on to the black tailcoat, and finally acquired the ability of full contemplation ...

"What is it, sir?" the familiar voice spoke over Mr. Goliadkin.

"Titular Councillor Goliadkin, Your Excellency."

"Well?"

"I've come to explain..."

"How?...What?..."

"Just that. Say, thus and so, I've come to explain, Your Excellency, sir..."

"But you...but who on earth are you?"

"M-m-mr. Goliadkin, Your Excellency, a titular councillor."

"Well, what is it you want?"

"Say, thus and so, I take his excellency as a father; I withdraw from the affair, and protect me from my enemy—so there!"

"What is this?..."

"Everybody knows..."

"Knows what?"

Mr. Goliadkin was silent; his chin began to twitch slightly ...

"Well?"

"I thought it was chivalrous, Your Excellency...That here, say, it was chivalrous, and I take my superior as a father...say, thus and so, protect me, I en...entreat you in te...tears, and that such sti...stirrings sho...should be en...en... encouraged..."

His excellency turned away. For a few moments our hero was unable to look at anything with his eyes. His chest was tight. His breath failed him. He did not know where he was standing...He felt somehow sad and ashamed. God knows what happened then...Having recovered, our hero noticed that his excellency was talking with his guests and seemed to be discussing something sharply and forcefully. One of the guests Mr. Goliadkin recognized at once. It was Andrei Filippovich. The other he did not; however, the face also seemed familiar— a tall, thickset figure, of a certain age, endowed with extremely bushy eyebrows and side-whiskers and a sharp, expressive gaze. There was a decoration hung on the stranger's neck and a cigar in his mouth. The stranger was smoking and, without taking the cigar out of his mouth, nodded his head significantly, glancing now and then at Mr. Goliadkin. Mr. Goliadkin felt somehow awkward. He looked away and at once saw yet another extremely strange guest. In a doorway which till then our hero had been taking for a mirror, as had happened to him once before—*he* appeared—we all know who, an extremely close acquaintance and friend of Mr. Goliadkin's. Mr. Goliadkin Jr. had in fact been in another little room up to then, hurriedly writing something; now he must have been needed—and he appeared, with papers under his arm, went over to his excellency, and quite deftly, expecting exclusive attention to his person, managed to worm his way into the conversation and concilium, taking his position slightly behind Andrei Filippovich and partly masked by the stranger smoking the cigar. Evidently Mr. Goliadkin Jr. took great interest in the conversation, to which he now listened in a noble manner, nodding his head, mincing his feet, smiling, glancing every moment at his excellency, his eyes as if pleading that he be allowed to put in his own half-word. "The scoundrel!" thought Mr. Goliadkin, and he involuntarily took a step forward. Just then his excellency turned and rather hesitantly approached Mr. Goliadkin himself.

"Well, all right, all right; go with God. I'll look into your affair, and order that you be accompanied..." Here the general glanced at the stranger with the bushy side-whiskers. He nodded in agreement.

Mr. Goliadkin felt and understood clearly that he was being taken for something else, and not at all as he ought to have been. "One way or another, an explanation is called for," he thought, "thus and so, say, Your Excellency." Here, in his perplexity, he lowered his eyes to the ground and, to his extreme amazement, saw considerable white spots on his excellency's boots. "Can they have split open?" thought Mr. Goliadkin. Soon, however, Mr. Goliadkin discovered that his excellency's boots were not split open at all, but only had bright reflections—a phenomenon explained completely by the fact that the boots were of patent leather and shone brightly. "That's called a *high-light*," thought our hero. "The term is used especially in artists' studios; elsewhere this reflection is called a *bright gleam*." Here Mr. Goliadkin raised his eyes and saw that it was time to speak, otherwise the affair might take a bad turn... Our hero stepped forward.

"I say, thus and so, Your Excellency," he said, "but imposture doesn't get anywhere in our age."

The general did not reply, but tugged strongly on the bell-pull. Our hero took another step forward.

"He's a mean and depraved man, Your Excellency," said our hero, forgetting himself, sinking with fear, and, for all that, pointing boldly and resolutely at his unworthy twin, who at that moment was mincing around his excellency, "thus and so, say, but I'm alluding to a certain person."

Mr. Goliadkin's words were followed by a general stir. Andrei Filippovich and the unknown figure nodded their heads; his excellency was impatiently tugging at the bell-pull with all his might, summoning people. Here Mr. Goliadkin Jr. stepped forward in his turn.

"Your Excellency," he said, "I humbly ask your permission to speak." There was something extremely resolute in Mr. Goliadkin Jr.'s voice; everything about him showed that he felt himself completely within his rights.

"Permit me to ask you," he began, in his zeal forestalling his excellency's reply and this time addressing Mr. Goliadkin, "permit me to ask you, in whose presence are you making such comments? before whom are you standing? whose study are you in?..." Mr. Goliadkin Jr. was all in extraordinary agitation, all red and flushed with indignation and wrath; tears even showed in his eyes.

"Mr. and Mrs. Bassavriukov!"[29] a footman bellowed at the top of his lungs, appearing in the doorway of the study. "A good noble family, of Little Russian extraction," thought Mr. Goliadkin, and just then he felt someone lay a hand on his back in a highly friendly manner; then another hand was laid on his back; Mr. Goliadkin's mean twin was bustling ahead of them, showing the way, and our hero saw clearly that he was being steered towards the big doors of the study. "Just as at Olsufy

Ivanovich's," he thought, and found himself in the front hall. Looking around, he saw his excellency's two footmen and one twin.

"Overcoat, overcoat, overcoat, my friend's overcoat! my best friend's overcoat!" the depraved man chirped, tearing the overcoat from one of the men's hands and flinging it, in mean and unpleasant mockery, right over Mr. Goliadkin's head. Struggling out from under his overcoat, Mr. Goliadkin Sr. clearly heard the laughter of the two footmen. But, not listening or paying attention to anything extraneous, he was already leaving the front hall and found himself on the lighted stairway. Mr. Goliadkin Jr. followed him out.

"Good-bye, Your Excellency!" he called after Mr. Goliadkin Sr.

"Scoundrel!" said our hero, beside himself.

"Well, yes, a scoundrel..."

"Depraved man!"

"Well, yes, a depraved man..." Thus the unworthy adversary responded to the worthy Mr. Goliadkin and, with a meanness all his own, looked from the top of the stairs, directly and without batting an eye, into the eyes of Mr. Goliadkin, as if asking him to go on. Our hero spat in indignation and ran out to the porch; he was so crushed that he simply did not remember by whom and how he was put into the carriage. Coming to his senses, he saw that he was being driven along the Fontanka. "So we're going to the Izmailovsky Bridge?" thought Mr. Goliadkin... Here Mr. Goliadkin wanted to think of something else as well, but it was impossible; it was something so terrible that there was no way to explain it... "Well, never mind!" our hero concluded and drove to the Izmailovsky Bridge.

CHAPTER XIII

...It seemed that the weather wanted to change for the better. Indeed, the wet snow that had been pouring down till then in great heaps gradually began to thin out, thin out, and finally ceased almost entirely. The sky became visible, and little stars sparkled on it here and there. Only it was wet, dirty, damp, and suffocating, especially for Mr. Goliadkin, who even without that could barely catch his breath. From his wet and heavy overcoat some unpleasantly warm dampness penetrated all his limbs, and its weight bent his legs, which were badly weakened without that. Some feverish trembling went through his whole body with sharp and biting prickles; weariness made him break into a cold, sickly sweat, so that Mr. Goliadkin forgot to make use of this good opportunity to repeat, with his characteristic firmness and resolution, his favorite phrase, that perhaps all of this might somehow, certainly and unfailingly, work out and be settled for the best. "However, so far it's all not so bad," our sturdy and undaunted hero added, wiping from his face the drops of cold water that ran in all directions from the brim of his round hat, which was so sodden that it no longer repelled any water. Adding that it was all nothing, our hero tried to seat himself on a rather thick block of wood that lay near the pile of firewood in Olsufy Ivanovich's courtyard. Of course, there was no point in thinking about Spanish serenades and silk ladders; but he did have to think about a cosy nook, maybe not very warm, but at least comfortable and concealed. He was strongly tempted, be it said in passing, by that same nook on the landing of Olsufy Ivanovich's apartment where previously, almost at the beginning of this truthful story, our hero had stood through his two hours between the wardrobe and the old screens, among all sorts of useless household trash, litter, and junk. The thing was that now, too, Mr. Goliadkin had already

been standing and waiting for a whole two hours in Olsufy
Ivanovich's courtyard. But with regard to that former cosy and
comfortable nook there now existed certain inconveniences
which had not existed previously. The first inconvenience was
that this place had probably been spotted and certain preventive
measures taken about it since the time of the incident at Olsufy
Ivanovich's last ball; and second, he had to wait for the prearranged signal from Klara Olsufyevna, because there certainly
must have existed some such prearranged signal. It was always
done that way, and "we're not the first and we won't be the last."
Just then Mr. Goliadkin incidentally had a fleeting recollection
of some novel he had read long ago, in which the heroine gave
a prearranged signal to Alfred in exactly the same circumstances
by tying a pink ribbon to the window. But a pink ribbon now,
at night, and in the St. Petersburg climate, known for its dampness and unreliability, could not enter the picture and, in short,
was quite impossible. "No, it won't come to silk ladders,"
thought our hero. "I'd better stand here, just so, cosily and
quietly...I'd better stand here, for instance," and he chose a
place in the courtyard, across from the windows, by the pile of
stacked firewood. Of course, there were many other people
walking about the courtyard, postilions, coachmen; besides,
there was the rattling of wheels and the snorting of horses, and
so on; but even so, the place was convenient; whether they
noticed him or not, for the time being there was this advantage,
that the thing was going on in the shadows, and nobody could
see Mr. Goliadkin, while he himself could see decidedly everything. The windows were brightly lit; there was some solemn
gathering at Olsufy Ivanovich's. However, there was no music
to be heard yet. "So it's not a ball, and they've just gathered on
some other occasion," our hero thought with a partly sinking
heart. "Was it today, though?" raced through his head. "Did I
get the date wrong? It's possible, anything's possible...That's
just it, that anything's possible... It's possible that the letter was
written yesterday and didn't reach me, and it didn't reach me
because that rogue Petrushka got mixed up in it! Or it was
written tomorrow, meaning that I... that it was all to be done

tomorrow, that is, the waiting with the carriage..." Here our hero turned definitively cold and went to his pocket for the letter, so as to check. But, to his surprise, the letter was not in his pocket. "How's that?" whispered the half-dead Mr. Goliadkin. "Where did I leave it? So I've lost it? Just what I needed!" he finally moaned in conclusion. "And what if it now falls into unfriendly hands? (And maybe it already has!) Lord! what will come of it! It will be something that... Ah, my detestable fate!" Here Mr. Goliadkin trembled like a leaf at the thought that maybe his indecent twin, as he threw the overcoat over his head, had precisely the aim of stealing the letter, which he had somehow gotten wind of from Mr. Goliadkin's enemies. "What's more, he intercepted it," thought our hero, "and the evidence... but who cares about the evidence!..." After the first fit and stupefaction of terror, the blood rushed to Mr. Goliadkin's head. With a moan and a gnashing of teeth, he clutched his hot head, sank onto his chunk of wood, and began thinking about something... But the thoughts somehow did not connect in his head. Some faces flashed in his memory, now vaguely, now sharply, some long-forgotten events, the melodies of some stupid songs kept coming into his head... Anguish, there was an unnatural anguish! "My God! My God!" our hero thought, somewhat recovered, stifling a muffled sobbing in his breast, "grant me firmness of spirit in the inexhaustible depths of my calamities! That I've perished, vanished completely—of that there's no doubt, and it's all in the order of things, for it couldn't be any other way... First, I've lost my job, I've certainly lost it, there's no way I could not have lost it... Well, let's suppose that will get settled somehow. The bit of money I have, let's suppose, will be enough to start with; I'll rent some other apartment, a bit of furniture's also needed... Petrushka won't be with me. I can do without the rogue... rent a room; well, that's good! I can come and go when I please, and Petrushka won't grumble about my coming late—so there; that's what's good about renting a room... Well, suppose it's all good; only why am I talking about something that's not it, not it at all?" Here the thought of his present situation again lit up in

Mr. Goliadkin's memory. He looked around. "Oh, Lord God! Lord God! what am I talking about now?" he thought, totally at a loss and clutching his hot head ...

"Might you be leaving soon, if you please, sir?" a voice spoke over Mr. Goliadkin. Mr. Goliadkin gave a start; but before him stood his cabby, also soaked and chilled to the bone, who, in his impatience and having nothing to do, had decided to visit Mr. Goliadkin behind the woodpile.

"I, my friend, am all right ... soon, my friend, very soon, just wait a little ..."

The cabby left, muttering under his nose. "What's he muttering about?" Mr. Goliadkin thought through his tears. "I hired him for the evening, I'm sort of ... within my rights now ... so there! I hired him for the evening, and that's the end of the matter. Even if he just stands there, it's all the same. It's as I will. I'm free to go, and free not to go. And that I'm now standing behind the woodpile—that, too, is quite all right ... and don't you dare say anything; I say, the gentleman wants to stand behind the woodpile, so he stands behind the woodpile ... and it's no taint to anybody's honor—so there! So there, lady mine, if you'd like to know. Thus and so, I say, but in our age, lady mine, nobody lives in a hut. So there! In our industrial age, lady mine, you can't get anywhere without good behavior, of which you yourself serve as a pernicious example ... You say one must serve as a chief clerk and live in a hut on the seashore. First of all, lady mine, there are no chief clerks on the seashore, and second, you and I can't possibly get to be a chief clerk. For, to take an example, suppose I apply, I show up—thus and so, as a chief clerk, say, sort of ... and protect me from my enemy ... and they'll tell you, my lady, say, sort of ... there are lots of chief clerks, and here you're not at some émigrée Falbala's, where you learned good behavior, of which you yourself serve as a pernicious example. Good behavior, my lady, means sitting at home, respecting your father, and not thinking of any little suitors before it's time. Little suitors, my lady, will be found in due time! So there! Of course, one must indisputably have certain talents, to wit: playing the piano on occasion, speaking French, some history, geography, catechism, and arithmetic—so there!—but not more. Also cooking; cooking should unfailingly be part of every well-behaved young girl's knowledge! But what do we have here? First of all, my beauty, my dearest madam, you won't get away with it, you'll be pursued, and then trumped into a convent. And then what, lady mine? Then what would you have me do? Would you have me follow some stupid novels, lady mine, and go to a neighboring hill, and dissolve in tears gazing at the cold walls of your confinement, and finally die, following the custom of certain bad German poets and novelists, is that it, my lady? Then, first of all, allow me to tell you in a friendly way that that is not how things are done, and, second, I'd have you and your parents soundly thrashed for giving you French books to read; for French books don't teach anything good. There's poison in them...noxious poison, lady mine! Or do you think, if I may be permitted to ask, do you think that, say, thus and so, we'll run away with impunity, and sort of... there'll be a cabin on the seashore for you and we'll start cooing and discussing various feelings; and spend our whole life like that, in prosperity and happiness; and then there'll be a youngling, so that we'll sort of...say, thus and so, our parent and state councillor, Olsufy Ivanovich, here, say, a youngling has come along, so on this good occasion why don't you lift your curse and bless the couple? No, my lady, again that's not how things are done, and the first thing is that there'll be no cooing, kindly don't expect it. Nowadays, lady mine, a husband is the master, and a good and well-behaved wife must oblige him in everything. And gentilities, my lady, are not in favor nowadays, in our industrial age; say, the time of Jean-Jacques Rousseau[30] is past. Nowadays a husband comes home from work hungry—isn't there a bite to eat, darling, he says, a glass of vodka, some pickled herring? So you, my lady, have to have vodka and herring ready at once. The husband relishes his snack and doesn't even glance at you, but says: off to the kitchen, my little kitten, and see to dinner—and he kisses you maybe once a week and even that indifferently...There's how we do it, lady mine! and even that, say, indifferently!...That's how it will be, if we start reasoning like this, if it's already gone so far that you begin looking at things this way . . . And what has it to do with me? Why, my lady, have you mixed me up in your caprices? 'A beneficent man, say, suffering for my sake, and in all ways dear to my heart, and so on.' First of all, lady mine, I'm not right for you, you know that yourself, I'm no expert at paying compliments, I don't like uttering all those perfumed trifles for ladies, I'm not in favor of philanderers, and, I confess, my looks are not very winning. You won't find any false boasting or shame in us, and we are confessing to you now in all sincerity. Say, so there, what we have is a direct and open character and common sense; we don't get involved in intrigues. I am not an intriguer, and I'm proud of it—so there! . . . I go among good people without a mask, and to tell you all . . ."

Suddenly Mr. Goliadkin gave a start. The red and thoroughly sodden beard of his driver again peeked behind the woodpile . . .

"Right away, my friend; at once, you know, my friend; I'll come at once, my friend," Mr. Goliadkin answered in a trembling and weary voice.

The driver scratched the top of his head, then stroked his beard, then stepped another step forward . . . stopped, and looked mistrustfully at Mr. Goliadkin.

"Right away, my friend; you see, I . . my friend . . . I'll sit here a little longer, my friend, you see, only a second longer . . . you see, my friend . . ."

"Might you not be going anywhere at all?" the driver said finally, accosting Mr. Goliadkin resolutely and definitively . . .

"No, my friend, I'll come right away. You see, my friend, I'm waiting . . ."

"Yes, sir . . ."

"You see, my friend . . . what village are you from, my dear?"

"We're house serfs . . ."

"And are they good masters? . . ."

"Sure enough . . ."

"So, my friend; stay here, my friend. You see, my friend, have you been in Petersburg long?"

"I've been driving for a year now . . ."

"And it suits you well, my friend?"

"Sure enough..."

"Yes, my friend, yes. Thank providence, my friend. You, my friend, should be looking for a good man. Good men have become rare, my dear; a good man will wash you, feed you, and give you a drink, that's what he'll do, my dear... And sometimes you see that tears even pour through gold, my friend... you behold a lamentable example of that; so there, my dear..."

The cabby looked as if he felt sorry for Mr. Goliadkin.

"If you please, I'll wait, sir. Might you be waiting long, sir?"

"No, my friend, no; you know, I sort of... I'm not going to keep waiting, my dear. What do you think, my friend? I'll rely on you. I'm not going to keep waiting here..."

"Might you not be going anywhere at all?"

"No, my friend; no, but I'll thank you well, my dear... so there. What do I owe you, my dear?"

"The same as what we agreed on, sir, if you please. I waited a long time, sir; you wouldn't offend a man, sir."

"Well, here you are, my dear, here you are." Mr. Goliadkin gave the cabby a whole six silver roubles and, resolving seriously not to lose any more time, that is, to get away safe and sound, the more so as the affair was definitively resolved and the cabby had been dismissed, and therefore there was nothing more to wait for, he left the yard, went through the gates, turned left, and without looking back, breathless and rejoicing, broke into a run. "Maybe it will still work out for the best," he thought, "and this way I've avoided trouble." Indeed, Mr. Goliadkin somehow suddenly felt an extraordinary lightness of heart. "Ah, if only it would work out for the best!" thought our hero, though hardly believing in his own words. "So I'll sort of..." he thought. "No, I'd better do it like this, and the other way... Or maybe I'd better do it this way?..." Thus doubting and seeking for the key and the solution to his doubts, our hero ran as far as the Semyonovsky Bridge, and having reached the Semyonovsky Bridge, he decided sensibly and definitively to go back. "That will be better," he thought. "I'd better look at it the other way, that is, like this. Here's what I'll do—I'll be an onlooker from outside, and that's the end of it; say, I'm an onlooker, an outsider, and only that; and whatever happens there—it's not my fault. So there! That's how it's going to be now!"

Having decided to go back, our hero actually went back, the more readily in that, according to his happy thought, he had now established himself as a complete outsider. "And it's better this way: you're not answerable for anything, and you'll see what follows . . . so there!" That is, the calculation was most sure, and that was the end of it. Calming himself, he again got into the peaceful shadow of his comforting and protective woodpile and began looking attentively at the windows. This time he did not have to watch and wait for long. Suddenly, in all the windows at once, a strange commotion manifested itself, figures flashed, curtains opened, whole groups of people crowded to Olsufy Ivanovich's windows, all of them searching and looking for something in the courtyard. From the safety of his woodpile, our hero in his turn also began watching the general commotion with curiosity and craning his neck to right and left concernedly, at least as far as the short shadow of the woodpile that covered him would permit. Suddenly he was dumbstruck, gave a start, and almost sat down where he was from terror. He fancied— in short, he fully figured out—that they were not searching for something or somebody, they were quite simply searching for him, Mr. Goliadkin. Everybody is looking his way, everybody is pointing his way. It was impossible to flee: they would see him . . . The dumbstruck Mr. Goliadkin pressed himself as close as he could to the woodpile, and only then did he notice that the treacherous shadow had betrayed him, that it did not cover all of him. Our hero would now have agreed with the greatest pleasure to crawl into some mouse hole between the logs and sit there peaceably, if only it were possible. But it was decidedly impossible. In his agony he finally began to stare resolutely and directly at all the windows at once; that was better . . . And suddenly he burned with the uttermost shame. He was completely noticed, they all noticed him at once, they all waved their hands at him, they all nodded their heads at him, they all called to him; now several vent panes clicked and opened; several voices at once shouted something to him... "I'm surprised these girls aren't thrashed starting from childhood," our hero murmured to himself, quite at a loss. Suddenly *he* (we know who) ran down the porch in nothing but his uniform, hatless, out of breath, bustling, mincing and hopping, perfidiously proclaiming his terrible joy at finally seeing Mr. Goliadkin.

"Yakov Petrovich," the man known for his uselessness chirped. "Yakov Petrovich, you here? You'll catch cold. It's cold here, Yakov Petrovich. Please come inside!"

"Yakov Petrovich! No, sir, I'm all right, Yakov Petrovich," our hero murmured in a humble voice.

"No, sir, impossible, Yakov Petrovich: they beg, they humbly beg, they're waiting for us. 'Make us happy,' they say, 'bring Yakov Petrovich here.' That's what, sir."

"No, Yakov Petrovich; you see, I'd do better... It would be better if I went home, Yakov Petrovich..." our hero said, roasting on a slow fire and freezing from shame and terror, all at the same time.

"No, no, no, no!" the repulsive man chirped. "No, no, no, not for anything! Come on!" he said resolutely and dragged Mr. Goliadkin Sr. towards the porch. Mr. Goliadkin Sr. did not want to go at all; but since everyone was watching, and it would have been stupid to resist and protest, our hero went—however, it is impossible to say he went, because he himself decidedly did not know what was happening to him. But never mind, he did it anyway!

Before our hero had time to straighten himself and come to his senses, he was in the reception room. He was pale, disheveled, in shreds; with dull eyes he looked around at the whole crowd—terrible! That room, all the rooms—all, all of them were filled to overflowing. There were multitudes of people, a whole orangery of ladies; all this clustered around Mr. Goliadkin, all this strained towards Mr. Goliadkin, all this bore Mr. Goliadkin on its shoulders, he noticed quite clearly that he was being urged in a certain direction. "It's not towards the

door," raced through Mr. Goliadkin's head. Indeed, he was not
being urged towards the door, but straight to Olsufy Ivanovich's
easy chair. On one side of the chair stood Klara Olsufyevna,
pale, languid, sad, though magnificently attired. Especially
striking to Mr. Goliadkin's eyes were the little white flowers
in her black hair, which made an excellent effect. Vladimir
Semyonovich kept himself on the other side of the chair, in a
black tailcoat, with his new decoration in the buttonhole. Mr.
Goliadkin was being taken under the arms and, as was said
above, straight to Olsufy Ivanovich—on one side Mr. Goliadkin
Jr., who assumed an extremely well-behaved and well-
intentioned air, which caused our hero no end of joy, while on
the other side he was escorted by Andrei Filippovich with a
most solemn look on his face. "What can this be?" thought Mr.
Goliadkin. But when he saw that he was being led to Olsufy
Ivanovich, it was as if lightning suddenly flashed. The thought
of the intercepted letter flew into his head... In inexhaustible
agony, our hero stood before Olsufy Ivanovich's chair. "What
am I to do now?" he thought to himself. "Of course, it must all
be on a bold footing, that is, with frankness, but not without
nobility; say, thus and so, and so on." But what our hero
evidently feared did not happen. Olsufy Ivanovich seemed
to receive Mr. Goliadkin very well and, though he did not
offer him his hand, at least shook his gray-haired and respect-
inspiring head as he looked at him—shook it with some sort of
solemnly mournful but at the same time benevolent air. So at
least it seemed to Mr. Goliadkin. It even seemed to him that a
tear glistened in Olsufy Ivanovich's dim eyes; he looked up and
saw that a little tear also seemed to be glistening on the eyelashes
of Klara Olsufyevna, who was standing right there, and that
there also seemed to be something similar in Vladimir
Semyonovich's eyes—that, finally, the calm and imperturbable
dignity of Andrei Filippovich was tantamount to the general
tearful sympathy—that, finally, the young man who once greatly
resembled an important councillor was now weeping bitterly,
taking advantage of the present moment... Or maybe all this
only seemed so to Mr. Goliadkin because he himself had turned

quite tearful and clearly felt the hot tears running down his cold cheeks . . . In a voice filled with sobbing, reconciled with people and fate, and feeling great love at the present moment not only for Olsufy Ivanovich, not only for all the guests taken together, but even for his pernicious twin, who now, evidently, was not pernicious at all and not even Mr. Goliadkin's twin, but a total outsider and an extremely amiable man in himself, our hero made as if to address Olsufy Ivanovich with a touching outpouring of his soul; but from the fullness of all that had accumulated in him, he was unable to explain anything at all, but only pointed silently with a highly eloquent gesture to his heart . . . Finally, Andrei Filippovich, probably wishing to spare the gray-haired old man's feelings, led Mr. Goliadkin a little aside and left him, seemingly, however, in a completely independent position. Smiling, murmuring something under his nose, slightly perplexed, but in any case almost completely reconciled with people and fate, our hero began to make his way somewhere through the dense mass of guests. They all gave way to him, they all looked at him with a sort of strange curiosity and a sort of inexplicable, mysterious sympathy. Our hero went into the next room—the same attention everywhere; he dimly heard how the whole crowd pressed after him, noticing his every step, discussing something highly engaging among themselves, wagging their heads, talking, argling, bargling, and whispering. Mr. Goliadkin would have liked very much to know what they were all argling and bargling and whispering about. Turning around, our hero noticed Mr. Goliadkin Jr. nearby. Feeling a need to take his arm and draw him aside, Mr. Goliadkin insistently begged the other Yakov Petrovich to assist him in all his future undertakings and not to abandon him on critical occasions. Mr. Goliadkin Jr. nodded gravely and firmly pressed Mr. Goliadkin Sr.'s hand. The heart in our hero's breast throbbed from an excess of feelings. However, he was suffocating, he felt hemmed in, hemmed in; all those eyes turned on him were somehow oppressing and crushing him . . . Mr. Goliadkin caught a fleeting glimpse of the councillor who wore a wig. The councillor looked at him with a stern, searching gaze not at all softened by the general sympathy... Our hero decided to go straight to him, smile at him, and immediately have a talk with him; but the thing somehow did not work out. For a moment, Mr. Goliadkin almost became oblivious, lost both memory and feeling... Recovering, he noticed that he was turning about in a wide circle of surrounding guests. Suddenly someone called Mr. Goliadkin from the next room; the call passed at once through the whole crowd. Everything became agitated, noisy, everybody rushed to the doors of the first room; our hero was almost carried out, and the hard-hearted councillor in the wig turned up right beside Mr. Goliadkin. Finally, he took him by the arm and sat him down next to himself and across from Olsufy Ivanovich's seat, though at a rather significant distance from him. Everyone who had been in the rooms sat down in several rows around Mr. Goliadkin and Olsufy Ivanovich. Everything became hushed and subdued, everyone preserved a solemn silence, everyone kept glancing at Olsufy Ivanovich, obviously expecting something not entirely ordinary. Mr. Goliadkin noticed that the other Mr. Goliadkin and Andrei Filippovich had placed themselves next to Olsufy Ivanovich's chair and also directly across from the councillor. The silence continued; they really were expecting something. "Just as in some family, when somebody's about to go on a long journey; all that remains now is to stand up and pray," thought our hero. Suddenly an extraordinary commotion arose and interrupted all of Mr. Goliadkin's reflections. Something long expected occurred. "He's coming, he's coming!" passed through the crowd. "Who's coming?" passed through Mr. Goliadkin's head, and he shuddered from some strange sensation. "It's time," said the councillor, looking attentively at Andrei Filippovich. Andrei Filippovich, for his part, looked at Olsufy Ivanovich. Olsufy Ivanovich nodded his head gravely and solemnly. "Let us stand," said the councillor, getting Mr. Goliadkin to his feet. Everybody stood up. Then the councillor took Mr. Goliadkin Sr. by the arm, and Andrei Filippovich took Mr. Goliadkin Jr., and they both solemnly brought together the two completely identical men, in the midst of the crowd that surrounded them and was turned towards them in expectation.

Our hero looked around in perplexity, but was immediately stopped and directed towards Mr. Goliadkin Jr., who held out his hand to him. "They want us to make peace," thought our hero, and, deeply moved, he held out his hand to Mr. Goliadkin Jr.; then, then he held out his face to him. The other Mr. Goliadkin did the same... Here it seemed to Mr. Goliadkin Sr. that his perfidious friend was smiling, that he winked fleetingly and slyly to the crowd around them, that there was something sinister in the face of the indecent Mr. Goliadkin Jr., that he even made a grimace at the moment of his Judas's kiss... Mr. Goliadkin's head rang, his eyes went dark; it seemed to him that a multitude, an endless string of completely identical Goliadkins was bursting noisily through all the doors of the room; but it was too late... A ringing, treacherous kiss resounded, and...

Here a quite unexpected circumstance occurred... The door of the reception room opened noisily, and on the threshold appeared a man the very sight of whom turned Mr. Goliadkin to ice. His feet became rooted to the ground. A cry died in his constricted breast. However, Mr. Goliadkin had known it all beforehand and had long anticipated something like it. The stranger gravely and solemnly approached Mr. Goliadkin... Mr. Goliadkin knew this figure very well. He had seen it, had seen it very often, had seen it that same day... The stranger was a tall, solidly built man, in a black tailcoat, with an important cross on his neck, and endowed with bushy, very black side-whiskers; all he lacked to complete the resemblance was a cigar in his mouth... Yet the stranger's gaze, as has already been said, froze Mr. Goliadkin with terror. With a grave and solemn mien, the fearsome man came up to the lamentable hero of our story... Our hero offered him his hand; the stranger took his hand and pulled him with him... Our hero looked around with a lost, mortified face...

"This, this is Krestyan Ivanovich Rutenspitz, doctor of medicine and surgery, your old acquaintance, Yakov Petrovich!" someone's disgusting voice chirped right in Mr. Goliadkin's ear. He turned: it was Mr. Goliadkin's twin, repulsive in the mean qualities of his soul. An indecent, sinister joy shone in his face; with delight he rubbed his hands, with delight he turned his head around, with delight he minced among all and sundry; he seemed ready to begin dancing straightaway from delight; finally, he leaped forward, snatched a candle from one of the servants, and went ahead, lighting the way for Mr. Goliadkin and Krestyan Ivanovich. Mr. Goliadkin clearly heard how all that was in the reception room rushed after him, how they all pressed and jostled each other, and all together loudly began repeating behind Mr. Goliadkin: "Never mind; don't be afraid, Yakov Petrovich, it's just your old friend and acquaintance, Krestyan Ivanovich Rutenspitz..." Finally they went out to the brightly lit main stairway; on the stairway there was also a mass of people; the doors to the porch were noisily flung open, and Mr. Goliadkin found himself on the porch along with Krestyan Ivanovich. At the entrance stood a carriage harnessed with four horses, which were snorting with impatience. The gleeful Mr. Goliadkin Jr. ran down the steps in three bounds and opened the carriage door himself. With an admonitory gesture, Krestyan Ivanovich invited Mr. Goliadkin to get in. However, there was no need for an admonitory gesture; there were enough people to help him in... Sinking with terror, Mr. Goliadkin turned to look back: the entire brightly lit stairway was strung with people; curious eyes looked at him from everywhere; Olsufy Ivanovich himself presided from his easy chair on the upper landing, and watched what was happening with attention and strong concern. Everyone was waiting. A murmur of impatience passed through the crowd when Mr. Goliadkin looked back.

"I hope there's nothing here... nothing reprehensible... or that might be cause for severity... and the attention of everyone regarding my official relations?" our hero said, at a loss. Talk and noise arose around him; everyone wagged their heads in the negative. Tears gushed from Mr. Goliadkin's eyes.

"In that case, I'm ready... I fully entrust... and hand over my fate to Krestyan Ivanovich..."

Mr. Goliadkin had only just said that he fully handed over his fate to Krestyan Ivanovich, when a terrible, deafening, joyful

shout burst from everyone around him, and its sinister echo
passed through the whole expectant crowd. Here Krestyan
Ivanovich on the one side and Andrei Filippovich on the other
took Mr. Goliadkin under the arms and began putting him into
the carriage; his double, as was his mean custom, helped from
behind. The unfortunate Mr. Goliadkin Sr. cast a last glance at
everyone and everything and, trembling like a kitten that has
been doused with cold water—if the comparison be permitted—
got into the carriage. Krestyan Ivanovich at once got in behind
him. The carriage door slammed, the whip cracked over the
horses, the horses tore the vehicle from its place... everything
rushed after Mr. Goliadkin. The piercing, furious shouts of all
his enemies came rolling after him in the guise of a farewell.
For a certain time faces still flashed around the carriage that was
bearing Mr. Goliadkin away; but they gradually dropped behind,
dropped behind, and finally disappeared completely. Mr.
Goliadkin's indecent twin held out longer than anyone else. His
hands in the pockets of his green uniform trousers, he ran along
with a pleased look, skipping now on one side of the carriage,
now on the other; sometimes, taking hold of the window frame
and hanging on, he would thrust his head through the window
and blow Mr. Goliadkin little farewell kisses; but he, too, began
to tire, appeared more and more rarely, and finally disappeared
completely. The heart in Mr. Goliadkin's breast ached dully; a
hot stream of blood rushed to his head; he gasped for air, he
wanted to unbutton himself, to bare his chest, to pour snow and
cold water on it. He fell, finally, into oblivion... When he
came to, he saw that the horses were bearing him along some
unfamiliar road. To right and left a forest blackened; it felt
desolate and deserted. Suddenly he went dead: two fiery eyes
gazed at him from the darkness, and those two eyes shone with
sinister, infernal glee. This was not Krestyan Ivanovich! Who
was it? Or was it him? Him! It was Krestyan Ivanovich, only
not the former, but another Krestyan Ivanovich! This was a
terrible Krestyan Ivanovich! ...

"Krestyan Ivanovich, I...I seem to be all right, Krestyan
Ivanovich," our hero began timidly and with trepidation,

wishing to appease the terrible Krestyan Ivanovich at least
somewhat with submissiveness and humility.

"You vill haf a gofernment apartment, mit firewood, mit licht,
und mit serfices, vich you don't deserf," Krestyan Ivanovich's
reply came sternly and terribly, like a verdict.

Our hero cried out and clutched his head. Alas! he had long
foreseen it!

THE GAMBLER

A Novel

(From a Young Man's Notes)

CHAPTER I

I'VE FINALLY COME BACK from my two-week absence. Our people have already been in Roulettenburg for three days. I thought they would be waiting for me God knows how eagerly, but I was mistaken. The general had an extremely independent look, spoke to me condescendingly, and sent me to his sister. It was clear they had got hold of money somewhere. It even seemed to me that the general was a little ashamed to look at me. Marya Filippovna was extremely busy and scarcely spoke with me; she took the money, however, counted it, and listened to my whole report. Mezentsov, the little Frenchman, and some Englishman or other were expected for dinner; as usual, when there's money, then at once it's a formal dinner; Moscow-style. Polina Alexandrovna, seeing me, asked what had taken me so long, and went off somewhere without waiting for an answer. Of course, she did it on purpose. We must have a talk, however. A lot has accumulated.

I've been assigned a small room on the fourth floor of the hotel. It's known here that I belong to *the general's suite.* By all appearances, they've managed to make themselves known. The general is regarded by everyone here as a very rich Russian grandee. Before dinner he managed, among other errands, to give me two thousand-franc notes to have changed. I changed them in the hotel office. Now they'll look at us as millionaires for at least a whole week. I was about to take Misha and Nadya for a walk, but on the stairs I was summoned to the general; he had seen fit to inquire where I was going to take them. The man is decidedly unable to look me straight in the eye; he would very much like to, but I respond each time with such an intent— that is, irreverent—gaze, that he seems disconcerted. In a highly pompous speech, piling one phrase on another and finally becoming totally confused, he gave me to understand that I should stroll with the children somewhere in the park, a good distance from the vauxhall.[1] He finally became quite angry and added abruptly: "Or else you might just take them to the vauxhall, to the roulette tables. Excuse me," he added, "but I know you're still rather light-minded and perhaps capable of gambling. In any case, though I am not your mentor, and have no wish to take that role upon myself, I do at any rate have the right to wish that you not, so to speak, compromise me..."

"But I don't even have any money," I said calmly. "To lose it, you have to have it."

"You shall have it at once," the general replied, blushing slightly. He rummaged in his desk, consulted a ledger, and it turned out that he owed me about a hundred and twenty roubles.

"How are we going to reckon it up?" he began. "It has to be converted into thalers. Here, take a hundred thalers, a round figure—the rest, of course, won't get lost."

I silently took the money.

"Please don't be offended by my words, you're so touchy... If I made that observation, it was, so to speak, to warn you, and, of course, I have a certain right to do so..."

Coming back home with the children before dinner, I met a whole cavalcade. Our people had gone to have a look at some ruins. Two excellent carriages, magnificent horses! Mlle Blanche in the same carriage with Marya Filippovna and Polina; the little Frenchman, the Englishman, and the general on horseback. Passersby stopped and looked; an effect was produced; only it won't come to any good for the general. I calculated that with the four thousand francs I had brought, plus whatever they had evidently managed to get hold of here, they now had seven or eight thousand francs. That is too little for Mlle Blanche.

Mlle Blanche is also staying in our hotel, along with her mother; our little Frenchman is here somewhere as well. The servants call him "M. le comte," Mlle Blanche's mother is called "Mme la comtesse"; well, maybe they really are comte and comtesse.*

---

*Count and countess.

I just knew that M. le comte would not recognize me when we gathered for dinner. The general, of course, did not even think of introducing us or of presenting me to him; and M. le comte himself has visited Russia and knows what small fry an *outchitel**—as they call it—is there. He knows me very well, however. But, I must confess, I appeared at dinner uninvited; it seems the general forgot to give orders, otherwise he would surely have sent me to eat at the *table d'hôte.*† I appeared on my own, so that the general looked at me with displeasure. Kindly Marya Filippovna showed me to a place at once; but my having met Mr. Astley helped me, and willy-nilly I wound up making part of their company.

I first met this strange Englishman in Prussia, on a train where we sat opposite each other, when I was catching up with our people; then I ran into him on entering France, and finally in Switzerland; twice in the course of these two weeks—and now I suddenly met him in Roulettenburg. Never in my life have I met a shyer man; he's shy to the point of stupidity, and, of course, he knows it himself, because he's not at all stupid. However, he's very nice and quiet. I got him to talk at our first meeting in Prussia. He announced to me that he had been at Nordkap that summer, and that he would like very much to go to the Nizhny Novgorod fair. I don't know how he became acquainted with the general; I believe he's boundlessly in love with Polina. When she came in, he flushed a flaming crimson. He was very glad that I sat down beside him at the table, and it seems he considers me a bosom friend.

At table the Frenchman set the tone extraordinarily; he was careless and pompous with everyone. And in Moscow, I remember, he just blew soap bubbles. He talked terribly much about finance and Russian politics. The general sometimes ventured to contradict—but modestly, only enough so as not to definitively damage his own importance.

I was in a strange state of mind. Of course, before dinner

*Teacher or tutor [Russian in French transliteration].
†Common table.

was half-through, I managed to ask myself my customary and habitual question: "How come I hang around with this general and didn't leave them long, long ago?" Now and then I glanced at Polina Alexandrovna; she ignored me completely. It ended with me getting angry and deciding to be rude.

It began with me suddenly, for no rhyme or reason, interfering in their conversation, loudly and without being asked. Above all, I wanted to quarrel with the little Frenchman. I turned to the general and suddenly, quite loudly and distinctly, and, it seems, interrupting him, observed that in hotels this summer it was almost impossible for Russians to dine at the *table d'hôte*. The general shot me an astonished glance.

"If you're a self-respecting man," I let myself go on, "you will unavoidably invite abuse and will have to put up with being exceedingly slighted. In Paris, on the Rhine, even in Switzerland, there are so many little Poles and sympathizing little Frenchmen at the *table d'hôte* that it's impossible to utter a word, if you happen to be a Russian."

I said it in French. The general looked at me in perplexity, not knowing whether he should get angry or merely be astonished that I had forgotten myself so.

"That means that somebody somewhere has taught you a lesson," the little Frenchman said carelessly and contemptuously.

"In Paris I began by quarreling with a Pole," I replied, "then with a French officer who supported the Pole. And then some of the Frenchmen took my side, when I told them how I wanted to spit in the monseigneur's coffee."

"Spit?" the general asked with pompous perplexity, and even looked around. The little Frenchman studied me mistrustfully.

"Just so, sir," I replied. "Since I was convinced for a whole two days that I might have to go to Rome briefly to take care of our business, I went to the office of the Holy Father's embassy in Paris to get a visa in my passport.[2] There I was met by a little abbé, about fifty years old, dry and with frost in his physiognomy, who, having heard me out politely, but extremely dryly, asked me to wait. Though I was in a hurry, I did sit down, of course, took out *L'Opinion nationale*,[3] and began reading some terrible abuse of Russia. Meanwhile, I heard someone go through the next room to see monseigneur; I saw my abbé bow to him. I addressed him with my former request; again, still more dryly, he asked me to wait. A little later another stranger came, but on business—some Austrian. He was listened to and at once taken upstairs. Then I became extremely vexed. I stood up, went over to the abbé, and told him resolutely that since monseigneur was receiving, he could finish with me as well. The abbé suddenly drew back from me in extraordinary surprise. It was simply incomprehensible to him how a Russian nonentity dared to put himself on a par with monseigneur's visitors. In the most insolent tone, as if glad that he could insult me, he looked me up and down and cried: 'Can you possibly think that Monseigneur would interrupt his coffee for you?' Then I, too, cried, but still louder than he: 'Let it be known to you that I spit on your monseigneur's coffee! If you do not finish with my passport this very minute, I'll go to him myself.'

"'What! Just when the cardinal is sitting with him!' the abbé cried, recoiling from me in horror, rushed to the door, and spread his arms crosswise, showing that he would sooner die than let me pass.

"Then I answered him that I was a heretic and a barbarian, '*que je suis hérétique et barbare*,' and that to me all these arch-bishops, cardinals, monseigneurs, etc., etc.—were all the same. In short, I showed him that I would not leave off. The abbé gave me a look of boundless spite, then snatched my passport and took it upstairs. A minute later it had a visa in it. Here, sirs, would you care to have a look?" I took out the passport and showed the Roman visa.

"Really, though," the general began ...

"What saved you was calling yourself a barbarian and a heretic," the little Frenchman observed, grinning. "*Cela n'était pas si bête.*"*

"What, should I look to our Russians? They sit here, don't dare peep, and are ready, perhaps, to renounce the fact that

*That was not so stupid.

they're Russians. At any rate in my hotel in Paris they began to treat me with much greater attention when I told everybody about my fight with the abbé. The fat Polish *pan*,* the man most hostile to me at the *table d'hôte*, faded into the background. The Frenchmen even put up with it when I told them that about two years ago I saw a man whom a French chasseur had shot in the year twelve[4]—simply so as to fire off his gun. The man was a ten-year-old child then, and his family hadn't managed to leave Moscow."

"That cannot be," the little Frenchman seethed, "a French soldier would not shoot a child!"

"Yet so it was," I replied. "It was told to me by a respectable retired captain, and I myself saw the scar from the bullet on his cheek."

The Frenchman began talking much and quickly. The general tried to support him, but I recommended that he read, for instance, bits from the *Notes* of General Perovsky,[5] who was taken prisoner by the French in the year twelve. Finally, Marya Filippovna started talking about something, so as to disrupt the discussion. The general was very displeased with me, because the Frenchman and I had almost begun to shout. But it seemed that Mr. Astley liked my argument with the Frenchman very much; getting up from the table, he suggested that he and I drink a glass of wine. In the evening, I duly managed to have a fifteen-minute talk with Polina Alexandrovna. Our talk took place during a stroll. Everybody went to the park near the vauxhall. Polina sat down on a bench opposite the fountain and sent Nadenka to play not far away with some children. I also let Misha play by the fountain, and we were finally alone.

At first we began, naturally, with business. Polina simply became angry when I gave her only seven hundred guldens in all. She was sure I'd bring her from Paris, in pawn for her diamonds, at least two thousand guldens or even more.

"I need money at all costs," she said, "and I must get it; otherwise I'm simply lost."

*Gentleman.

I started asking about what had happened in my absence.

"Nothing, except that we received two pieces of news from Petersburg, first, that grandmother was very unwell, and, two days later, that it seemed she had died. This was news from Timofei Petrovich," Polina added, "and he's a precise man. We're waiting for the final, definitive news."

"So everyone here is in expectation?" I asked.

"Of course: everyone and everything; for the whole six months that's the only thing they've hoped for."

"And you're hoping, too?" I asked.

"Why, I'm not related to her at all, I'm only the general's stepdaughter. But I know for certain that she'll remember me in her will."

"It seems to me you'll get a lot," I said affirmatively.

"Yes, she loved me; but why does it seem so to *you*?"

"Tell me," I answered with a question, "our marquis, it seems, is also initiated into all the family secrets?"

"And why are you interested in that?" asked Polina, giving me a stern and dry look.

"Why not? If I'm not mistaken, the general has already managed to borrow money from him."

"You've guessed quite correctly."

"Well, would he lend him money if he didn't know about grandma? Did you notice, at dinner: three times or so, speaking about grandmother, he called her 'grandma'—'*la baboulinka*.' Such close and friendly relations!"

"Yes, you're right. As soon as he learns that I'm also getting something in the will, he'll immediately propose to me. Is that what you wanted to find out?"

"Only then? I thought he proposed a long time ago."

"You know perfectly well he hasn't!" Polina said testily. "Where did you meet this Englishman?" she asked after a moment's silence.

"I just knew you'd ask about him right away."

I told her about my previous meetings with Mr. Astley during my trip. "He's shy and amorous and, of course, already in love with you?"

"Yes, he's in love with me," Polina replied.

"And he's certainly ten times richer than the Frenchman. What, does the Frenchman really have anything? Isn't that open to doubt?"

"No, it's not. He has some sort of château. The general told me that yesterday. Well, so, is that enough for you?"

"In your place, I'd certainly marry the Englishman."

"Why?" asked Polina.

"The Frenchman's handsomer, but he's meaner; and the Englishman, on top of being honest, is also ten times richer," I snapped.

"Yes, but then the Frenchman is a marquis and more intelligent," she replied with the greatest possible equanimity.

"Is that true?" I went on in the same way.

"Perfectly."

Polina terribly disliked my questions, and I saw that she wanted to make me angry with her tone and the wildness of her answer. I told her so at once.

"Why, it does indeed amuse me to see you in a fury. You ought to pay for the fact alone that I allow you to put such questions and make such surmises."

"I do indeed consider it my right to put all sorts of questions to you," I replied calmly, "precisely because I'm prepared to pay for them however you like, and my own life I now count for nothing."

Polina burst out laughing:

"Last time, on the Schlangenberg, you told me you were ready at my first word to throw yourself down headfirst, and I believe it's a thousand-foot drop. One day I'll speak that word, solely to see how you're going to pay, and you may be sure I'll stand firm. You are hateful to me—precisely because I've allowed you so much, and more hateful still, because I need you so much. But for the time being I do need you—I must take good care of you."

She went to get up. She had spoken with irritation. Lately she has always finished a conversation with me with spite and irritation, with real spite.

"Allow me to ask you, what is this Mlle Blanche?" I asked, not wanting to let her go without an explanation.

"You know yourself what Mlle Blanche is. Nothing more has been added. Mlle Blanche will probably become Madame la Générale—naturally, if the rumor of grandmother's death is confirmed, because Mlle Blanche, and her mother, and her second cousin, the marquis, all know very well that we are ruined."

"And the general is definitively in love?"

"That's not the point now. Listen and remember: take these seven hundred florins and go gambling, win me as much as you can at roulette; I need money now at all costs."

Having said this, she called Nadenka and went to the vauxhall, where she joined our whole company. I, however, turned into the first path to the left, pondering and astonished. It was as if I'd been hit on the head, after the order to go and play roulette. Strange thing: I had enough to ponder, and yet I immersed myself wholly in an analysis of my feelings for Polina. Really, it had been easier for me during those two weeks of absence than now, on the day of my return, though on the way I had longed for her like a madman, had thrashed about like a man in a frenzy, and even in sleep had seen her before me every moment. Once (this was in Switzerland), I had fallen asleep on the train, and it seems I began talking aloud with Polina, which made all my fellow travelers laugh. And now once more I asked myself the question: do I love her? And once more I was unable to answer it, that is, better to say, I answered myself again, for the hundredth time, that I hated her. Yes, she was hateful to me. There were moments (and precisely each time at the end of our conversations) when I would have given half my life to strangle her! I swear, if it had been possible to sink a sharp knife slowly into her breast, it seems to me I'd have snatched at it with delight. And yet, I swear by all that's holy, if on the Schlangenberg, on the fashionable *point*,* she had actually said to me: "Throw yourself down," I would have thrown myself

*Overlook.

down at once, and even with delight. I knew that. One way or another this has to be resolved. She understands all this astonishingly well, and the thought that I have a fully correct and distinct awareness of all her inaccessibility to me, all the impossibility of the fulfillment of my fantasies—this thought, I'm sure, affords her extraordinary pleasure; otherwise how could someone so prudent and intelligent be on such intimate and frank terms with me? It seems to me that she has looked at me so far like that ancient empress who began to undress in front of her slave, not regarding him as a human being. Yes, many times she has not regarded me as a human being ...

However, I had her commission—to win at roulette at all costs. There was no time to reflect on why and how soon I had to win, and what new considerations had been born in that eternally calculating head. Besides, during these two weeks, evidently, no end of new facts had accrued, of which I still had no idea. All this had to be figured out, it all had to be grasped, and as soon as possible. But meanwhile now there was no time: I had to go to the roulette table.

CHAPTER II

I CONFESS, THIS WAS unpleasant for me. Though I had decided that I would play, it was not at all my intention to begin by playing for others. It even threw me off somewhat, and I went into the gaming rooms with a most vexatious feeling. At first sight, I disliked everything there. I can't stand this lackeyishness in the gossip columns of the whole world, and mainly in our Russian newspapers, where almost every spring our columnists tell about two things: first, the extraordinary magnificence and splendor of the gaming rooms in the roulette towns on the Rhine, and second, the heaps of gold that supposedly lie on the tables. They're not paid for that; they simply do it out of disinterested obsequiousness. There is no magnificence in these trashy rooms, and as for the gold, not only are there no heaps on the tables, but there's scarcely even the slightest trace. Of course, now and then during the season some odd duck suddenly turns up, an Englishman, or some sort of Asiatic, a Turk, as happened this summer, and suddenly loses or wins a great deal; the rest all play for small change, and, on the average, there's usually very little money lying on the table. As I had only just entered the gaming room (for the first time in my life), I did not venture to play for a while. Besides, it was crowded. But if I had been alone, even then I think I would sooner have left than started playing. I confess, my heart was pounding, and I was not coolheaded; I knew for certain and had long resolved that I would not leave Roulettenburg just so; something radical and definitive was bound to happen in my fate. So it must be, and so it would be. Ridiculous as it is that I should expect to get so much from roulette, it seems to me that the routine opinion, accepted by all, that it is stupid and absurd to expect anything at all from gambling, is even more ridiculous. Why is gambling worse than any other way of making money—trade, for instance? It's true that only one in a hundred wins. But what do I care about that?

In any case, I decided to look on at first and not start anything serious that evening. That evening, if something did happen, it would be accidental and slight—and that's what I settled on. Besides, I had to study the game itself; because, despite the thousands of descriptions of roulette I had always read with such avidity, I understood decidedly nothing of how it worked until I saw it myself.

First, it all seemed so filthy to me—somehow morally nasty and filthy. I am by no means speaking of those greedy and restless faces that stand in dozens, even in hundreds, around the gaming tables. I see decidedly nothing filthy in the desire to win sooner and more; I have always found very stupid the thought of one well-nourished and prosperous moralist, who, in response to someone's excuse that "they play for low stakes," replied: so much the worse, because there's little interest. As if little interest and big interest were not the same. It's a matter of proportion. What's small for Rothschild, is great wealth for me, and as for gains and winnings—people everywhere, not only at the roulette table, do nothing but gain or win something from each other. Whether gain and profit are vile in themselves—is another question. But I won't decide it here. Since I myself was possessed in the highest degree by a desire to win, all this interest and all this interested filth, if you wish, was for me, as I entered the room, somehow the more helpful, the more congenial. It's really nice when people don't stand on ceremony, but act in an open and unbuttoned way with each other. And why should one deceive oneself? It's the most futile and ill-calculated occupation! Especially unattractive, at first sight, in all this roulette riffraff was the respect for what they were doing, the grave and even deferential way they all stood around the tables. That's why there is a sharp distinction here between the kind of gambling known as *mauvais genre** and the kind permissible to a respectable man. There are two sorts of gambling—one gentlemanly, the other

*The bad sort.

plebeian, mercenary, a gambling for all kinds of riffraff. Here they are strictly distinguished, and in essence how mean that distinction is! A gentleman, for instance, may stake five or ten louis d'or, rarely more; however, he may also stake a thousand francs, if he's very rich, but only for the game itself, only for amusement, only to watch the process of winning or losing; but by no means should he be interested in the actual winnings. Having won, he may, for instance, laugh aloud, make a remark to someone around him, he may even stake again and double it again, but solely out of curiosity, to observe the chances, to calculate, and not out of a plebeian desire to win. In short, he should look at all these gaming tables, roulette wheels, and *trente et quarante** not otherwise than as an amusement set up solely for his pleasure. He should not even suspect the interests and traps on which the bank is founded and set up. It would even be far from a bad thing if, for instance, he fancied that all these other gamblers, all this trash that trembles over every gulden, were just as rich and gentlemanly as he is, and gambled solely for diversion and amusement. This total ignorance of reality and innocent view of people would, of course, be extremely aristocratic. I saw how many mamas pushed forward innocent and graceful young ladies of fifteen and sixteen, their daughters, and, giving them a few gold coins, taught them how to play. The young lady would win or lose, unfailingly smile, and go away very pleased. Our general approached the table solidly and pompously; an attendant rushed to offer him a chair, but he ignored the attendant; he spent a very long time taking out his purse, spent a very long time taking three hundred francs in gold from the purse, staked them on black, and won. He didn't pick up his winnings but left them on the table. It came up black again; he didn't take them this time either, and when the third time it came up red, he lost twelve hundred francs at one go. He walked away with a smile and controlling his temper. I'm convinced there was a gnawing in his heart, and had the stake been two or three times bigger, he would have lost control and shown his

*Thirty and forty.

emotion. However, in my presence a Frenchman won and then lost as much as thirty thousand francs gaily and without any emotion. A true gentleman, even if he loses his entire fortune, must not show emotion. Money should be so far beneath the gentlemanly condition that it is almost not worth worrying about. Of course, it would be highly aristocratic to pay absolutely no attention to all the filth of all this riffraff and all the surroundings. However, sometimes the reverse method is no less aristocratic: to notice, that is, to observe, even to scrutinize, for instance, through a lorgnette, all this riffraff; but not otherwise than taking all this crowd and all this filth as its own sort of diversion, as a performance set up for gentlemanly amusement. You can knock about in this crowd yourself, but look around with the perfect conviction that you are in fact an observer and by no means make up one of its components. However, you oughtn't to observe too closely: again that would not be gentlemanly, because in any case the spectacle isn't worth too great or close an inspection. And in general, few spectacles are worth too close an inspection by a gentleman. And yet to me personally it seemed that all this was very much worth quite a close inspection, especially for someone who did not come only to observe, but sincerely and conscientiously counted himself among all this riffraff. As for my innermost moral convictions, in my present reflections there is, of course, no place for them. Let it be so; I say it to clear my conscience. But I will note this: that all this time recently, it has been terribly disgusting for me to match my acts and thoughts to any moral standard. Something else has guided me...

The riffraff do indeed play very filthily. I'm even not averse to the thought that a lot of the most common thievery goes on here at the table. The croupiers who sit at the ends of the table, look after the stakes, and make the payments, have a terrible amount of work. There's more riffraff for you! For the most part they're Frenchmen. However, I'm observing and making remarks here not at all in order to describe roulette; I'm attuning myself, in order to know how to behave in the future. I noticed, for instance, that there was nothing more ordinary than for someone's hand suddenly to reach out from behind the table and take what you've won. An argument begins, there's often shouting, and—I humbly ask you to prove, to find witnesses, that the stake is yours!

At first this was all Chinese to me; I only guessed and figured out somehow that one can stake on numbers, odds and evens, and colors. That evening I decided to try a hundred guldens of Polina Alexandrovna's money. The thought that I was setting out to play for someone else somehow threw me off. The sensation was extremely unpleasant, and I wanted to be done with it quickly. I kept fancying that by starting out for Polina I was undermining my own luck. Is it really impossible to touch a gaming table without being infected at once with superstition? I began by taking out five friedrichs d'or, that is, fifty guldens, and staking them on evens. The wheel spun and it came up thirteen—I lost. With some morbid feeling, solely to be done with it somehow and leave, I staked another five friedrichs d'or on red. It came up red. I staked all ten friedrichs d'or—again it came up red. I again staked it all at once, and again it came up red. I took the forty friedrichs d'or and staked twenty on the twelve middle numbers, not knowing what would come of it. I was paid triple. Thus, from ten friedrichs d'or, I had suddenly acquired eighty. Some extraordinary and strange sensation made it so unbearable for me that I decided to leave. It seemed to me that I would play quite differently if I were playing for myself. Nevertheless, I staked all eighty friedrichs d'or once more on evens. This time it came up four; they poured out another eighty friedrichs d'or for me, and, taking the whole heap of a hundred and sixty friedrichs d'or, I went to look for Polina Alexandrovna.

They had all gone for a stroll somewhere in the park, and I managed to see her only at supper. This time the Frenchman wasn't there, and the general made a display of himself; among other things, he found it necessary to observe to me again that he did not wish to see me at the gaming table. In his opinion, it would be very compromising for him if I somehow lost too much; "but even if you were to win a lot, then, too, I would be compromised," he added significantly. "Of course, I have no right to control your actions, but you must agree..." Here, as usual, he didn't finish. I answered dryly that I had very little money and that, consequently, I could not lose too conspicuously, even if I should gamble. On the way to my room upstairs, I managed to hand Polina her winnings and declared to her that I would not play for her another time.

"Why not?" she asked anxiously.

"Because I want to play for myself," I replied, studying her with astonishment, "and this hampers me."

"So you resolutely go on being convinced that roulette is your salvation and your only way out?" she asked mockingly. I answered again very seriously that, yes; that as for my absolute assurance of winning, let it be ridiculous, I agree, "so long as I'm left alone."

Polina Alexandrovna insisted that I absolutely must share today's winnings half and half with her, and wanted to give me eighty friedrichs d'or, suggesting that we go on playing in the future on that condition. I refused the half resolutely and definitively, and declared that I could not play for others, not because I didn't want to, but because I was sure to lose.

"However, I myself, stupid as it may be, also hope almost only in roulette," she said pensively. "And therefore you absolutely must go on playing half and half with me, and—of course—you will." Here she left me, not listening to my further objections.

CHAPTER III

Howenver, for the whole day yesterday she didn't say a word to me about gambling. And she generally avoided talking with me yesterday. Her earlier manner with me did not change. The same complete carelessness of attitude when we met, and even something scornful and hateful. Generally she doesn't wish to conceal her loathing for me; I can see that. In spite of that, she also doesn't conceal from me that she needs me for something and is saving me for something. Some sort of strange relations have been established between us, in many ways incomprehensible to me—considering her pride and arrogance with everyone. She knows, for instance, that I love her madly, she even allows me to speak of my passion—and, of course, she could in no way express her scorn of me more fully than by this permission to speak to her of my love unhindered and uncensored. "Meaning," so to say, "I hold your feelings of so little account that it is decidedly all the same to me what you speak to me about and what you feel for me." Of her own affairs she talked a lot with me before as well, but she was never fully candid. What's more, there were the following subtleties in her disregard for me: she knows, let's say, that I'm aware of some circumstance of her life or of something that troubles her greatly; she will even tell me something of her circumstances herself, if she needs to use me somehow for her own purposes, like a slave, or for running errands; but she will always tell me exactly as much as someone needs to know who is used for running errands, and—if the whole sequence of events is still unknown to me, if she sees herself how I suffer and worry over her sufferings and worries, she will never deign to set me fully at ease by friendly candor, though, as she often employed me on not only troublesome but even dangerous errands, she was obliged, in my opinion, to be candid with me. And was it worth caring about my feelings, about the fact that I also worried, and maybe cared and suffered three times more over her cares and misfortunes than she did herself?

Three weeks ago I already knew of her intention to play roulette. She even warned me that I was to play in her place, because it was indecent for her to play. By the tone of her words I noticed then that she had some serious concern, and not merely a wish to win money. What was money in itself to her! There's a goal here, some circumstance that I may guess at, but that I don't yet know. Of course, the humiliation and slavery in which she holds me could give me (quite often do give me) the possibility of questioning her crudely and directly. Since I'm a slave to her and all too insignificant in her eyes, there is no point in her being offended at my crude curiosity. But the thing is that, while she allows me to ask questions, she doesn't answer them. Sometimes she doesn't notice them at all. That's how it is with us!

Yesterday there was a lot of talk among us about a telegram sent to Petersburg four days ago and to which there has been no reply. The general is visibly worried and pensive. It has to do, of course, with grandmother. The Frenchman is worried as well. Yesterday, for instance, they had a long and serious talk after dinner. The Frenchman's tone with us all was extraordinarily arrogant and careless. Precisely as in the proverb: invite a pig to the table and he'll put his feet on it. Even with Polina he was careless to the point of rudeness; however, he enjoys taking part in general strolls in the vauxhall or in cavalcades and drives out of town. I have long been informed of some of the circumstances binding the Frenchman and the general: in Russia they were going to start a factory together; I don't know whether their project has fallen through or they're still talking about it. Besides that, I chanced to learn part of a family secret: the Frenchman actually helped the general out last year and gave him thirty thousand to make up a deficit in government funds as he handed over his post. And so, of course, the general is in his clutches; but now, right now, the main role in all this is being played all the same by Mlle Blanche, and in that I'm sure I'm not mistaken.

Who is Mlle Blanche? Among us here they say she's a French noblewoman, who goes around with her mother and has a colossal fortune. It is also known that she is some sort of relation of our marquis, only a very distant one, some sort of cousin or second cousin. They say that before my trip to Paris, contacts between the Frenchman and Mlle Blanche were somehow much more ceremonious, they seemed to be on a much more refined and delicate footing; while now their acquaintance, friendship, and family connection have emerged as somehow more coarse, more intimate. Maybe our situation seems so bad to them that they no longer find it necessary to be too ceremonious with us and to hide things. I noticed two days ago how Mr. Astley was studying Mlle Blanche and her mother. It seemed to me that he knew them. It even seemed to me that our Frenchman had met Mr. Astley previously as well. However, Mr. Astley is so shy, prudish, and reserved that one can virtually count on him— he won't wash any dirty linen in public. The Frenchman, at any rate, barely greets him and almost doesn't look at him; which means he's not afraid of him. That's understandable; but why is it that Mlle Blanche almost doesn't look at him either? The more so as yesterday the marquis let something slip: in general conversation he suddenly said, I don't remember on what occasion, that Mr. Astley was colossally rich and he knew it for a fact; and so Mlle Blanche might well look at Mr. Astley! The general is now thoroughly worried. It's clear what a telegram about his aunt's death could mean for him now!

Though it seemed certain to me that Polina was avoiding conversation with me, as if on purpose, I myself assumed a cold and indifferent air as well: I kept thinking she was just about to approach me. Instead, yesterday and today I turned all my attention predominantly to Mlle Blanche. The poor general, he's utterly lost! To fall in love with such strong passion at the age of fifty-five is of course a misfortune. Add to that his widowerhood, his children, his completely ruined estate, his debts, and, finally, the woman he had to fall in love with. Mlle Blanche is quite beautiful. But I don't know whether I'll be understood if I say that hers is one of those faces that can be frightening. At any rate I have always been afraid of such women. She must be about twenty-five. She is tall and well built, with shapely shoulders; her neck and bosom are luxuriant; her complexion is a swarthy yellow; her hair is black as ink, and there is a terrible amount of it, enough for two coiffures. Her eyes are black, the whites are yellowish, her gaze is insolent, her teeth are very white, her lips always rouged; she smells of musk. She dresses showily, richly, with *chic*, but with great taste. Her feet and hands are astonishing. Her voice is a husky contralto. She sometimes bursts out laughing, and with that shows all her teeth, but usually she looks on silently and insolently—at any rate in the presence of Polina and Marya Filippovna. (A strange rumor: Marya Filippovna is leaving for Russia.) It seems to me that Mlle Blanche is without any education, is maybe not even intelligent, but instead is suspicious and cunning. It seems to me that her life has not been without adventures. If we're to say all, it may be that the marquis is no relation of hers, and her mother is not her mother. But there is information that in Berlin, where we met them, she and her mother had some respectable acquaintances. As for the marquis himself, though to this day I have my doubts that he is a marquis, his belonging to decent society, as with us, for example, in Moscow, and in some places in Germany, does not seem open to doubt. I don't know what he is in France. They say he has a château. I thought that in these two weeks a lot of water would have flowed, and yet I still don't know for certain whether anything decisive has been said between Mlle Blanche and the general. Everything now depends generally on our fortune, that is, on whether the general can show them a lot of money. If, for instance, news came that grandmother hasn't died, I'm sure Mlle Blanche would disappear at once. I find it astonishing and ridiculous, however, that I've become such a gossip. Oh, how disgusting this all is to me! With what pleasure I'd drop everyone and everything! But how can I leave Polina, how can I stop spying around her? Spying is mean, of course, but—what do I care!

I also found Mr. Astley curious yesterday and today. Yes, I'm convinced that he is in love with Polina! It's curious and ridiculous how much the gaze of a prudish and painfully chaste man, touched by love, can sometimes express, and that precisely at a moment when the man would, of course, sooner be glad to fall through the earth than say or express anything with a word or a look. We run into Mr. Astley very often during our walks. He doffs his hat and passes by, dying, naturally, from the desire to join us. If he's invited, he immediately declines. At resting places, in the vauxhall, at a concert, or near the fountain, he unfailingly stops somewhere not far from our bench, and wherever we may be, in the park, in the woods, or on the Schlangenberg—you need only raise your eyes, look around, and unfailingly somewhere, on the nearest path, or behind a bush, a little corner of Mr. Astley will appear. He seems to be seeking an occasion to speak with me privately. This morning we met and exchanged a couple of words. He sometimes speaks somehow extremely abruptly. Without even a "good morning," he began by declaring:

"Ah, Mlle Blanche!... I've seen many women like Mlle Blanche!"

He fell silent, looking at me significantly. What he wanted to say by that, I don't know, because when I asked him what it meant, he nodded with a sly smile and added: "Quite so. Is Mlle Pauline very fond of flowers?"

"I don't know, I simply don't know," I replied.

"What? You don't know that either?" he cried in great amazement.

"I don't know, I simply never noticed," I repeated, laughing.

"Hm, that gives me a particular thought." Here he nodded and walked on. He looked pleased, however. We speak to each other in the most vile French.

CHAPTER IV

Today was a ridiculous, outrageous, absurd day. Now it's eleven o'clock at night. I'm sitting in my little room and remembering. It started with my having to go in the morning and play roulette for Polina Alexandrovna. I took all her hundred and sixty friedrichs d'or, but on two conditions: first, that I did not want to go halves, that is, if I won, I'd take nothing for myself; and second, that in the evening Polina would explain to me precisely why she has such a need to win and precisely how much money. I still can in no way suppose that it is simply for the sake of money. Money is obviously necessary here, and as soon as possible, for some particular purpose. She promised to explain, and I went. There was a terrible crowd in the gaming rooms. How insolent they all are, and how greedy! I pushed my way to the middle and stood right next to the croupier; then I began timidly to play, staking two or three coins. Meanwhile I observed and took note; it seemed to me that calculation meant rather little in itself and had none of the importance many gamblers attach to it. They sit with ruled sheets of paper, note down the stakes, calculate, deduce the chances, reckon up, finally place their bet, and—lose in exactly the same way as we simple mortals, who play without calculation. But, on the other hand, I drew one conclusion that seems to be correct: in the sequence of accidental chances, there is indeed, if not a system, at any rate the semblance of some order—which, of course, is very strange. For instance, it happens that after the twelve middle numbers come the twelve last ones; twice, let's say, the ball lands on these twelve last ones, and then goes on to the twelve first. Having landed on the twelve first, it goes on again to the twelve middle numbers, lands three or four times on the twelve middle ones, then again goes on to the twelve last, from where again, after landing twice, it goes on to the first, lands there once, goes on to land three times on the middle ones, and so it continues for an hour and a half, for two hours. One, three, and two; one, three, and two. It's very amusing. One day or one morning it goes, for instance, so that red alternates with black and vice versa, every moment almost without any order, so that the ball doesn't land on the same color more than two or three times in a row. But the next day, or the next evening, it happens, for instance, that it lands on red alone up to twenty-two times in a row, and it's sure to go on that way for some time—a whole day, for instance. A lot of this was explained to me by Mr. Astley, who spent the whole morning at the gaming tables, but did not stake once himself. As for me, I lost everything, and very quickly. I straight away staked twenty friedrichs d'or on evens and won, staked five and won again, and so it went two or three more times. I think about four hundred friedrichs d'or came into my hands in some five minutes. I should have walked away right then, but some strange sensation was born in me, some defiance of fate, some desire to give it a flick, to stick my tongue out at it. I placed the biggest stake permitted, four thousand guldens, and lost. Then, getting excited, I took out all I had left, staked it in the same way, and lost again, after which I left the table as if stunned. I didn't even understand what had happened to me, and announced my loss to Polina Alexandrovna only just before dinner. The time till then I spent loitering in the park.

At dinner I was again in an agitated state, just as three days ago. The Frenchman and Mlle Blanche were again dining with us. It turned out that Mlle Blanche had been in the gaming rooms that morning and had seen my exploits. This time she talked with me somehow more attentively. The Frenchman was more straightforward and simply asked me if I had really gambled away my own money. It seems to me he suspects Polina. In short, there's something there. I lied at once and said it was my money.

The general was extremely surprised: where had I gotten so much money? I explained that I had begun with ten friedrichs d'or, that six or seven wins in a row, doubled, gained me five or six thousand guldens, and that I had then lost it all in two turns.

All that, of course, was probable. While explaining it, I looked at Polina, but could make out nothing in her face. However, she let me lie and did not correct me; from that I concluded that I did have to lie and conceal that I was playing for her. In any case, I thought to myself, she owed me an explanation and this morning had promised to reveal something or other to me.

I thought the general would make some remark, but he kept silent; instead I noticed worry and uneasiness in his face. Maybe, in his tough circumstances, it was simply hard for him to hear that such a respectable pile of gold had come and gone in a quarter of an hour for such a wasteful fool as me.

I suspect that a heated controversy had taken place between him and the Frenchman yesterday evening. They had locked themselves in and talked hotly about something for a long time. The Frenchman had come out looking vexed at something, and early this morning had gone to the general again—probably in order to continue yesterday's conversation.

Hearing of my loss, the Frenchman observed to me caustically and even spitefully that I ought to be more sensible. He added, I don't know why, that while many Russians gamble, in his opinion, Russians are incapable even of gambling.

"And in my opinion, roulette is just made for Russians," I said, and when the Frenchman smirked scornfully at my response, I observed to him that, of course, the truth was on my side, because, in speaking of Russians as gamblers, I was abusing them much more than praising them, and that meant I could be believed.

"On what do you base your opinion?" asked the Frenchman.

"On the fact that the ability to acquire capital entered the catechism of virtues and merits of the civilized Western man historically and almost as the main point. While a Russian is not only incapable of acquiring capital, but even wastes it somehow futilely and outrageously. Nevertheless, we Russians also need money," I added, "and therefore we are very glad of and very prone to such methods as, for instance, roulette, where one can get rich suddenly, in two hours, without any work. We find that very attractive; but since we also gamble futilely, without working at it, we lose!"

"That is partly true," the Frenchman observed smugly.

"No, it's not true, and it's shameful to speak that way of your fatherland," the general observed sternly and imposingly.

"For pity's sake," I answered him, "is it really not clear yet which is more vile—Russian outrageousness, or the German way of accumulation through honest work?"

"What an outrageous thought!" exclaimed the general.

"What a Russian thought!" exclaimed the Frenchman.

I laughed, I wanted terribly to egg them on.

"And I'd rather spend all my life roaming about in a Kirghiz tent," I cried, "than worship a German idol."

"What idol?" cried the general, beginning to get seriously angry.

"The German way of accumulating wealth. I haven't been here long, but, nevertheless, all the same, what I've managed to observe and verify here arouses the indignation of my Tartar blood. By God, I don't want such virtues! I managed to make a seven-mile tour here yesterday. Well, it's exactly the same as in those moralizing little German picture books: everywhere here each house has its *Vater*, terribly virtuous and extraordinarily honest. So honest it's even frightening to go near him. I can't stand honest people whom it's frightening to go near. Each such *Vater* has a family, and in the evening they all read edifying books aloud. Over their little house, elms and chestnuts rustle. A sunset, a stork on the roof, and all of it extraordinarily poetic and touching . . .

"Now, don't be angry, General, let me tell it as touchingly as possible. I myself remember my late father reading such books aloud to me and my mother in the evenings, under the lindens, in the front garden . . . I can judge it properly myself. Well, so every such family here is in total slavery and obedience to a *Vater*. They all work like oxen, and they all save money like Jews. Suppose the *Vater* has already saved up so many guldens and is counting on passing on his trade or bit of land to the elder son. For that the daughter is deprived of a dowry, and she remains an old maid. For that the younger son is sold into bondage or the army, and the money is joined to the family capital. Really, they do that here; I've asked around. All this is done not otherwise than out of honesty, out of exaggerated honesty, to the point that the sold younger son piously believes he was sold not otherwise than out of honesty—and that is the ideal thing, when the victim himself rejoices that he is being led to the slaughter. What next? Next is that for the elder son it's also not easy: he's got this Amalchen there, with whom his heart is united—but they can't get married, because they haven't saved so many guldens yet. They wait befittingly and sincerely, and with a smile go to the slaughter. Amalchen's cheeks are sunken by now; she's wasting away. Finally, after some twenty years, their fortune has multiplied; the guldens have been honestly and virtuously saved up. The *Vater* blesses the forty-year-old elder son and the thirty-five-year-old Amalchen, with her dried-up breasts and red nose... With that he weeps, pronounces a moral, and dies. The elder son himself turns into a virtuous *Vater*, and the same story begins all over again. In some fifty or seventy years the grandson of the first *Vater* is indeed possessed of a considerable capital and passes it on to his son, he to his, he to his, and in some five or six generations out comes Baron Rothschild himself, or Hoppe and Co.,[6] or the devil knows what. Well, sir, isn't that a majestic sight: a hundred- or two-hundred-year succession of work, patience, intelligence, honesty, character, firmness, calculation, a stork on the roof! What more do you want, there's nothing higher than that, and they themselves begin to judge the whole world from that standpoint, and the guilty, that is, those just slightly unlike themselves, they punish at once. Well, sir, the thing is this: I'd rather debauch Russian-style or win at roulette. I don't want to be a Hoppe and Co. in five generations. I need money for myself, and I don't consider myself as something necessary to and accessory to capital. I know I've said a whole heap of terrible things, but so be it. Such are my convictions."

"I don't know if there's much truth in what you've said," the general observed pensively, "but I know for certain that you begin showing off insufferably as soon as you're allowed to forget yourself the least bit . . ."

As was usual with him, he did not finish what he was saying. If our general began speaking about something just a bit more significant than ordinary conversation, he never finished. The Frenchman listened carelessly, goggling his eyes slightly. He understood almost nothing of what I said. Polina looked on with some sort of haughty indifference. It seemed she heard nothing that was said, not only by me, but by anyone else at the table this time.

CHAPTER V

S HE WAS UNUSUALLY PENSIVE, but as soon as we left the table, she told me to accompany her on a walk. We took the children and went to the fountain in the park.

As I was particularly agitated, I blurted out a question stupidly and crudely: why is it that our marquis des Grieux, the little Frenchman, not only doesn't accompany her now, when she goes out somewhere, but doesn't even speak to her for whole days at a time?

"Because he's a scoundrel," she answered strangely. I had never before heard such an opinion about des Grieux from her, and I kept silent, afraid to understand this irritability.

"And did you notice that he's not on good terms with the general today?"

"You want to know what's the matter?" she answered dryly and irritably. "You do know that the general is entirely mortgaged to him, everything he owns is his, and if grandmother doesn't die, the Frenchman immediately comes into possession of all that's mortgaged to him."

"Ah, so it's really true that everything's mortgaged? I'd heard, but didn't know it was decidedly everything."

"But of course!"

"And with that it's good-bye Mlle Blanche," I observed. "She won't be a generaless then! You know what: it seems to me the general is so in love that he might shoot himself if Mlle Blanche abandons him. At his age it's dangerous to be so in love."

"I think myself that something will happen to him," Polina Alexandrovna observed pensively.

"And how splendid that is," I cried. "She couldn't show more crudely that she had consented to marry only for money. Here even decencies weren't observed, it all happened quite without ceremony. A wonder! And as for grandmother, what could be more comical and filthy than to send telegram after telegram, asking: 'Is she dead, is she dead?' Eh? How do you like it, Polina Alexandrovna?"

"That's all nonsense," she said with disgust, interrupting me. "On the contrary, I'm astonished that you're in such a merry mood. What are you glad about? Can it be because you lost my money?"

"Why did you give it to me to lose? I told you I couldn't play for others, the less so for you. I'll obey whatever orders you give me; but the result doesn't depend on me. I warned you that nothing would come of it. Tell me, are you very crushed to have lost so much money? What do you need so much for?"

"Why these questions?"

"But you yourself promised me to explain... Listen: I'm perfectly convinced that when I start playing for myself (I have twelve friedrichs d'or), I'll win. Then take as much as you need from me."

She made a scornful face.

"Don't be angry with me," I went on, "for such an offer. I'm so pervaded by the awareness that I'm a zero before you, that is, in your eyes, that you can even accept money from me. A present from me cannot offend you. Besides, I lost yours."

She gave me a quick glance and, noticing that I was speaking irritably and sarcastically, changed the subject again:

"There's nothing interesting for you in my circumstances. If you want to know, I simply owe the money. I borrowed money and would like to pay it back. I had the crazy and strange notion that I was sure to win here at the gaming table. Why I had that notion I don't understand, but I believed in it. Who knows, maybe I believed because I had no other choice."

"Or because there was all too much *need* to win. It's exactly like a drowning man grasping at a straw. You must agree that if he weren't drowning, he wouldn't take a straw for the branch of a tree."

Polina was surprised.

"Why," she asked, "aren't you hoping for the same thing yourself? Two weeks ago you yourself once spoke to me, a lot and at length, about your being fully convinced of winning here at roulette, and tried to persuade me not to look at you as a madman—or were you joking then? But I remember you spoke so seriously that it couldn't possibly have been taken for a joke."

"That's true," I answered pensively. "To this day I'm fully convinced of winning. I'll even confess to you that you've just now led me to a question: precisely why has my senseless and outrageous loss today not left me with any doubts? I'm still fully convinced that as soon as I start playing for myself, I'm sure to win."

"Why are you so completely certain?"

"If you like—I don't know. I know only that I *need* to win, that it's also my one way out. Well, so maybe that's why it seems to me that I'm sure to win."

"Which means you also have all too much *need* to win, if you're so fanatically convinced."

"I'll bet you doubt I'm capable of feeling a serious need."

"It's all the same to me," Polina replied quietly and indifferently. "If you like—*yes*, I doubt that you could seriously suffer from anything. You may suffer, but not seriously. You're a disorderly and unsettled man. What do you need money for? I found nothing serious in any of the reasons you gave me then."

"By the way," I interrupted, "you said you had to repay a debt. A nice debt, then! Not to the Frenchman?"

"What are these questions? You're particularly sharp today. You're not drunk, are you?"

"You know I allow myself to say anything and sometimes ask very frank questions. I repeat, I am your slave, one is not ashamed with slaves, and a slave cannot give offense."

"That's all rubbish! And I can't stand this 'slave' theory of yours!"

"Note that I speak of my slavery not because I wish to be your slave, but just so—as of a fact that does not depend on me at all."

"Tell me straight out, why do you need money?"

"And why do you want to know that?"

"As you like," she replied and proudly tossed her head.

"You can't stand the slave theory, but you demand slavery: 'Answer and don't argue!' Very well, so be it. Why money, you ask? What do you mean, why? Money's everything!"

"I understand, but not falling into such madness from desiring it! You also reach the point of frenzy, of fatalism! There's something in it, some special goal. Speak without meandering, I want it that way."

It was as if she was beginning to get angry, and I liked terribly that she put so much heart into her questioning.

"Of course there's a goal," I said, "but I'm unable to explain what it is. No more than that with money I'll become a different person for you, and not a slave."

"What? How are you going to achieve that?"

"How achieve it? What, you don't even understand how I can achieve that you look at me otherwise than as a slave? Well, that's just what I don't want, such surprises and perplexities."

"You said this slavery was a pleasure for you. I thought so myself."

"You thought so," I cried with some strange pleasure. "Ah, how good such naïveté is coming from you! Well, yes, yes, to be enslaved to you is a pleasure. There is, there is pleasure in the ultimate degree of humiliation and insignificance!" I went on raving. "Devil knows, maybe there is in the knout, too, when the knout comes down on your back and tears your flesh to pieces ... But maybe I want to try other pleasures as well. Earlier at the table, in your presence, the general read me a lesson, because of the seven hundred roubles a year which I still may not even get from him. The marquis des Grieux raises his eyebrows, scrutinizes me, and at the same time doesn't notice me. And maybe I, for my part, passionately desire to take the marquis des Grieux by the nose in your presence?"

"A milksop's talk. One can behave with dignity in any situation. If there's a struggle involved, it's elevating, not humiliating."

"Straight out of a copybook! Just try to suppose that I may not know how to behave with dignity. That is, perhaps I'm a dignified man, but I don't know how to behave with dignity.

Do you understand that it may be so? All Russians are that way, and you know why? Because Russians are too richly and multifariously endowed to be able to find a decent form for themselves very quickly. It's a matter of form. For the most part, we Russians are so richly endowed that it takes genius for us to find a decent form. Well, but most often there is no genius, because generally it rarely occurs. It's only the French, and perhaps some few other Europeans, who have so well-defined a form that one can look extremely dignified and yet be a most undignified man. That's why form means so much to them. A Frenchman can suffer an insult, a real, heartfelt insult, and not wince, but a flick on the nose he won't suffer for anything, because it's a violation of the accepted and time-honored form of decency. That's why our young ladies fall so much for French-men, because they have good form. In my opinion, however, there's no form there, but only a rooster, *le coq gaulois.*[*][7] However, that I cannot understand, I'm not a woman. Maybe roosters are fine. And generally I'm driveling, and you don't stop me. Stop me more often; when I talk with you, I want to say everything, everything, everything. I lose all form. I even agree that I have not only no form, but also no merits. I announce that to you. I don't even care about any merits. Everything in me has come to a stop now. You yourself know why. I don't have a single human thought in my head. For a long time I haven't known what's going on in the world, either in Russia or here. I went through Dresden and don't remember what Dresden is like. You know yourself what has swallowed me up. Since I have no hope and am a zero in your eyes, I say outright: I see only you everywhere, and the rest makes no difference to me. Why and how I love you—I don't know. Do you know, maybe you're not good at all? Imagine, I don't even know whether you're good or not, or even good-looking? Your heart probably isn't good; your mind isn't noble; that may very well be."

"Maybe that's why you count on buying me with money," she said, "since you don't believe in my nobility?"

[*]The Gallic cock.

"When did I ever count on buying you with money?" I cried.

"Your tongue ran away with you and you lost your thread. If it's not me, it's my respect you think you can buy with money."

"Well, no, that's not so at all. I told you, it's hard for me to explain. You intimidate me. Don't be angry at my babbling. You see why it's impossible to be angry with me: I'm simply mad. But, anyhow, it's all the same to me if you are angry. When I'm upstairs in my little room, I only have to remember and imagine the rustle of your dress, and I'm ready to bite my hands. And why are you angry with me? Because I call myself a slave? Avail yourself, avail yourself of my slavery, avail yourself! Someday I'll kill you, do you know that? Not because I've fallen out of love or become jealous, but—just so, simply kill you, because I sometimes long to eat you up. You're laughing..."

"I'm not laughing at all," she said with wrath. "I order you to be silent."

She stopped, barely able to breathe from wrath. By God, I don't know whether she was good-looking or not, but I always liked looking at her when she stood before me like that, and so I often liked to provoke her wrath. I told her that.

"What filth!" she exclaimed with disgust.

"It makes no difference to me," I went on. "Do you know, too, that it's dangerous for us to go about together: many times I've had an irrepressible longing to beat you, to mutilate you, to strangle you. And what do you think, won't it come to that? You'll drive me to delirium. Am I afraid of a scandal? Of your wrath? What is your wrath to me? I love without hope, and I know that after that I'll love you a thousand times more. If I ever kill you, I'll have to kill myself, too; well, so—I'll put off killing myself for as long as I can, in order to feel this unbearable pain of being without you. Do you know an incredible thing: I love you *more* every day, and yet that's almost impossible. Can I not be a fatalist after that? Remember, two days ago on the Schlangenberg you challenged me, and I whispered: say the word and I'll jump into this abyss. If you had said the word then, I would have jumped. You don't believe I'd have jumped?"

"What stupid babble!" she cried.

"It's none of my affair whether it's stupid or intelligent," I cried. "I know that in your presence I have to talk, talk, talk— and so I talk. I lose all self-respect in your presence, and it makes no difference to me."

"Why should I make you jump off the Schlangenberg?" she said dryly and somehow especially offensively. "It would be completely useless to me."

"Splendid!" I cried. "You said that splendid 'useless' on purpose, in order to intimidate me. I see right through you. Useless, you say? But pleasure is always useful, and wild, boundless power—if only over a fly—is also a pleasure of a certain sort. Man is a despot by nature and likes to play the torturer. You like it terribly."

I remember she studied me with some especially close attention. It must be that my face then expressed all my senseless and absurd feelings. I recall now that our conversation actually went on like that almost word for word, as I've described it here. My eyes were bloodshot. Froth clotted on the edges of my lips. And as for the Schlangenberg, I swear on my honor even now: if she had ordered me to throw myself down then, I would have done it! If she had said it only as a joke, said it with contempt, spitting on me—even then I would have jumped!

"No, why, I believe you," she said, but as only she knows how to speak sometimes, with such contempt and sarcasm, with such arrogance, that, by God, I could have killed her at that moment. She was taking a risk. I also wasn't lying about that, talking to her.

"Are you a coward?" she asked me suddenly.

"I don't know, maybe I am. I don't know . . . I haven't thought about it for a long time."

"If I told you: kill this man, would you kill him?"

"Who?"

"Whoever I wanted."

"The Frenchman?"

"Don't ask, answer—whoever I point to. I want to know whether you were speaking seriously just now." She waited so seriously and impatiently for my reply that I felt somehow strange.

"But will you tell me, finally, what's going on here?" I cried. "Are you afraid of me, or what? I myself can see all the disorders here. You're the stepdaughter of a ruined and crazy man, infected with a passion for that she-devil—Blanche; then there's this Frenchman with his mysterious influence over you, and— now you ask me so seriously... such a question. At any rate let me know: otherwise I'll go mad right here and do something. Or are you ashamed to honor me with your candor? Can you really be ashamed with me?"

"I'm not talking about that at all. I asked you and I'm waiting for a reply."

"Of course I'll kill," I cried, "whoever you order me to, but can you really... would you really order that?"

"What do you think, that I'll feel sorry for you? I'll order you to do it, and stay out of it myself. Can you bear that? No, how could you! You might kill on orders and then come and kill me for having dared to send you."

It was as if something hit me on the head at these words. Of course, even then I considered her question half as a joke, as a challenge; but all the same she said it much too seriously. All the same, I was struck by her speaking it out like that, by her having such a right over me, accepting such power over me, and saying so directly: "Go to your ruin, and I'll stay out of it." There was something so cynical and frank in these words that, in my opinion, it was far too much. So that's how she looks at me then? This was going beyond the bounds of slavery and nonentity. To have such a view is to raise a man to one's own level. And however absurd, however unbelievable our whole conversation was, my heart shook.

Suddenly she burst out laughing. We were sitting on a bench then in front of the playing children, across from the place where carriages stopped and unloaded the public on the avenue before the vauxhall.

"Do you see that fat baroness?" she cried. "It's Baroness Wurmerhelm. She came only three days ago. See her husband:

a long, dry Prussian with a stick in his hand? Remember him looking us over two days ago? Go now, walk over to the baroness, take off your hat, and say something to her in French."

"Why?"

"You swore you'd jump off the Schlangenberg; you swear you're ready to kill if I order it. Instead of all these killings and tragedies, I want only to laugh. Go without any excuses. I want to see the baron beat you with his stick."

"You're challenging me; you think I won't do it?"

"Yes, I'm challenging you, go, that's how I want it!"

"I'll go, if you please, though it's a wild fantasy. Only here's the thing: won't there be trouble for the general, and for you through him? By God, I don't worry about myself, but about you, well—and the general. And what is this fantasy of going and insulting a woman?"

"No, you're a mere babbler, I can see," she said contemptuously. "Your eyes became bloodshot earlier—however, maybe that's because you drank a lot of wine at dinner. As if I don't understand myself that it's stupid, and trite, and that the general will get angry? I simply want to laugh. Well, I want to, that's all! And why should you insult a woman? You'll sooner get beaten with a stick."

I turned and silently went to do her bidding. Of course it was stupid, and of course I failed to get out of it, but as I went up to the baroness, I remember something seemed to egg me on, namely, schoolboy prankishness. And I was terribly worked up, as if drunk.

CHAPTER VI

Two days have now gone by since that stupid day. And so much shouting, noising, knocking, talking! And it's all such disorder, confusion, stupidity, and banality, and I'm the cause of it all. However, sometimes it seems funny—to me at any rate. I'm unable to give myself an accounting for what has happened to me, whether I'm indeed in a state of frenzy, or have simply jumped off the rails and gone on a rampage till they tie me up. At times it seems I'm going mad. And at times it seems I'm still not far from childhood, from the schoolbench, and it's simply crude prankishness.

It's Polina, it's all Polina! Maybe there would be no schoolboy pranks if it weren't for her. Who knows, maybe I'm doing it all out of despair (however stupid it is to reason this way). And I don't understand, I don't understand what's so good about her! Good-looking she is, though; yes, it seems she's good-looking. Others lose their minds over her, too. She's tall and trim. Only very thin. It seems to me you could tie her in a knot or bend her double. The print of her foot is narrow and long—tormenting. Precisely tormenting. Her hair has a reddish tint. Her eyes—a real cat's, but how proud and arrogant she can look with them. Four months ago, when I had just entered their service, she had a long and heated conversation with des Grieux one evening in the drawing room. And she looked at him in such a way . . . that later, when I went to my room to go to bed, I imagined that she had given him a slap—given it a moment before, then stood in front of him and looked at him . . . That evening I fell in love with her.

However, to business.

I went down the path to the avenue, stood in the middle of the avenue, and waited for the baroness and baron. From five paces away I took off my hat and bowed.

I remember the baroness was wearing a silk dress of boundless circumference, light gray in color, with flounces, a crinoline, and a train. She was short and extraordinarily fat, with a terribly fat, pendulous chin, so that her neck couldn't be seen at all. A purple face. Small eyes, wicked and insolent. She walks along as if she's doing everyone an honor. The baron is dry, tall. His face, as German faces usually are, is crooked and covered with a thousand tiny wrinkles; eyeglasses; forty-five years old. His legs begin almost at the level of his chest; that takes breeding. Proud as a peacock. A bit clumsy. Something sheeplike in the expression of his face, which in its way replaces profundity.

All this flashed in my eyes within three seconds.

My bow and the hat in my hand at first barely caught their attention. Only the baron knitted his brows slightly. The baroness just came sailing towards me.

"*Madame la baronne,*" I said loudly and clearly, rapping out each word, "*j'ai l'honneur d'être votre esclave.*"*

Then I bowed, put my hat on, and walked past the baron, politely turning my face to him and smiling.

She had told me to take off my hat, but the bowing and prankishness were all my own. Devil knows what pushed me. It was as if I was flying off a hilltop.

"*Hein!*" cried, or, better, grunted the baron, turning to me with angry surprise.

I turned and stopped in respectful expectation, continuing to look at him and smile. He was obviously perplexed and raised his eyebrows to the *ne plus ultra.*[†] His face was darkening more and more. The baroness also turned towards me and stared in wrathful perplexity. Passersby began to look. Some even stopped.

"*Hein!*" the baron grunted again with a redoubled grunt and with redoubled wrath.

"*Jawohl!*"[‡] I drawled, continuing to look him straight in the face.

---

*Madame baroness . . . I have the honor of being your slave.
†Utmost.
‡Yes indeed.

"*Sind Sie rasend?*"* he cried, waving his stick and, it seemed, beginning to turn a bit cowardly. He might have been thrown off by my outfit. I was very decently, even foppishly, dressed, like a man fully belonging to the most respectable public.

"*Jawo-o-ohl!*" I suddenly shouted with all my might, drawing out the *O* as Berliners do, who constantly use the expression *jawohl* in conversation, with that more or less drawn out letter *O* expressing various nuances of thought and feeling.

The baron and baroness quickly turned and all but fled from me in fright. Some of the public started talking, others looked at me in perplexity. However, I don't remember it very well.

I turned and walked at an ordinary pace towards Polina Alexandrovna. But I was still about a hundred yards from her bench when I saw her get up and go towards the hotel with the children.

I caught up with her by the porch.

"I performed . . . the foolery," I said, drawing even with her.

"Well, what of it? Now you can deal with it," she replied, without even looking at me, and went up the stairs.

That whole evening I spent walking in the park. Through the park and then through the woods, I even walked to another principality.[8] In one cottage I ate scrambled eggs and drank wine. For this idyll I was fleeced as much as one and a half thalers.

I came home only at eleven o'clock. The general sent for me at once.

Our people occupy two suites in the hotel; they have four rooms. The first—a big one—is the salon, with a grand piano. Next to it another big room—the general's study. He was waiting for me there, standing in the middle of the study in an extemely majestic attitude. Des Grieux was sprawled on the sofa.

"My dear sir, allow me to ask, what you have done?" the general began, addressing me.

"I would like you to get straight to the point, General," I

*Are you crazy?

said. "You probably want to speak of my encounter with a certain German today?"

"A certain German?! This German is Baron Wurmerhelm and an important person, sir! You were rude to him and to the baroness."

"Not in the least."

"You frightened them, my dear sir," cried the general.

"Not at all. Back in Berlin this *jawohl* got stuck in my ear, which they constantly repeat after every word and draw out so disgustingly. When I met him in the avenue, for some reason this *jawohl* suddenly popped up in my memory and had an irritating effect on me ... Besides, three times now the baroness, on meeting me, has had the habit of walking straight at me as if I was a worm that could be crushed underfoot. You must agree that I, too, may have my self-respect. I took off my hat and politely (I assure you it was politely) said: '*Madame, j'ai l'honneur d'être votre esclave.*' When the baron turned and shouted '*Hein!*'—I also suddenly felt pushed to shout: '*Jawohl!*' So I shouted it twice, the first time in an ordinary way, and the second time drawing it out with all my might. That's all."

I confess, I was terribly glad of this highly schoolboyish explanation. I had an astonishing wish to smear the whole story around as absurdly as possible.

And the further it went, the more I got a taste for it.

"Are you laughing at me, or what?" shouted the general. He turned to the Frenchman and told him in French that I was decidedly inviting a scandal. Des Grieux smiled contemptuously and shrugged his shoulders.

"Oh, don't think that, it's nothing of the sort!" I cried to the general. "My act was not nice, of course, and I admit it to you frankly in the highest degree. My act may even be called stupid and indecent prankishness, but—nothing more. And you know, General, I'm repentant in the highest degree. But there's one circumstance here which, in my eyes, almost even spares me any repentance. Lately, for some two or even three weeks, I've been feeling unwell: sick, nervous, irritable, fantastic, and on some occasions I even lose all control of myself. Really, I've sometimes wanted terribly to address the marquis des Grieux all at once and... However, there's no point in saying it; he may get offended. In short, these are signs of illness. I don't know whether Baroness Wurmerhelm will take that circumstance into consideration when I offer my apologies (because I intend to apologize). I suppose she won't, the less so in that, from what I know, this circumstance has lately been misused in the legal world: in criminal trials, lawyers have begun quite frequently to justify their clients, the criminals, by saying that at the moment of the crime they remembered nothing and that it was supposedly some such illness. 'He beat someone,' they say, 'and remembers nothing.' And imagine, General, medical science agrees with them—it really confirms that there is such an illness, such a temporary madness, when a man remembers almost nothing, or half-remembers, or a quarter-remembers. But the baron and baroness are people of the older generation, and Prussian Junkers and landowners to boot. They must still be unfamiliar with this progress in the legal and medical world, and therefore will not accept my explanations. What do you think, General?"

"Enough, sir!" the general uttered sharply and with restrained indignation, "enough! I will try to rid myself once and for all of your prankishness. Apologize to the baron and baroness you will not. Any relations with you, even if they consist solely of your asking forgiveness, would be too humiliating for them. The baron, having learned that you belong to my household, already had a talk with me in the vauxhall, and, I confess to you, a little more and he would have demanded satisfaction from me. Do you realize what you have subjected me to—me, my dear sir? I, I was forced to offer my apologies to the baron and give him my word that, immediately, this very day, you would cease to belong to my household..."

"Pardon me, pardon me, General, so it was he himself who absolutely demanded that I not belong to your household, as you're pleased to put it?"

"No; but I myself considered it my duty to give him that satisfaction, and, naturally, the baron remained pleased. We are parting, my dear sir. I still owe you those four friedrichs d'or

and three florins in local currency. Here's the money, and here's
the paper with the accounting; you may verify it. Good-bye.
We are strangers from here on out. I have seen nothing from
you but trouble and unpleasantness. I will summon the desk
clerk at once and announce to him that starting tomorrow I do
not answer for your hotel expenses. I have the honor to remain
your obedient servant."

I took the money, the paper on which the accounting was
penciled, bowed to the general, and said to him quite gravely:

"General, the matter cannot end this way. I am very sorry
that you were subjected to unpleasantness by the baron, but—
excuse me—you yourself are to blame for it. How is it that you
took it upon yourself to answer to the baron for me? What is
the meaning of the expression that I belong to your household?
I am simply a tutor in your house, and only that. I am not your
son, I am not under your guardianship, and you cannot answer
for my acts. I am a legally competent person. I am twenty-five
years old, I have a university degree, I am a nobleman, I am a
perfect stranger to you. Only my boundless respect for your
merits keeps me from demanding satisfaction from you right
now and a further accounting for the fact that you took upon
yourself the right to answer for me."

The general was so dumbfounded that he spread his arms,
then turned to the Frenchman and told him hurriedly that I
had just all but challenged him to a duel. The Frenchman
guffawed loudly.

"But I do not intend to let the baron off," I continued with
perfect equanimity, not embarrassed in the least by M. des
Grieux's laughter, "and since you, General, by consenting today
to listen to the baron's complaint, and thereby entering into his
interests, have put yourself in the position of a participant, as it
were, in this whole business, I have the honor to inform you
that, no later than tomorrow morning, I will, in my own name,
demand a formal explanation from the baron of the reasons
why, having business with me, he bypassed me and addressed
himself to another person, as if I could not or was not worthy
to answer him for myself."

What I anticipated happened. The general, hearing this new silliness, became terribly scared.

"What, can you really intend to go on with this cursed business?" he cried. "But what are you doing to me, oh, Lord! Don't you dare, don't you dare, my dear sir, or I swear to you!... There are authorities here, too, and I...I...in short, by my rank... and the baron also...in short, you'll be arrested and sent away from here by the police, so that you won't make a row! Understand that, sir!" And though he was choking with wrath, all the same he was terribly scared.

"General," I replied, with an equanimity intolerable to him, "one cannot be arrested for rowdiness before there's any rowdiness. I have not yet begun my talk with the baron, and it is as yet completely unknown to you in what manner and on what basis I intend to go about the business. My only wish is to clarify the offensive suggestion that I am under the guardianship of a person who supposedly has power over my free will. You needn't trouble and worry yourself so much."

"For God's sake, for God's sake, Alexei Ivanovich, drop this senseless intention!" the general muttered, suddenly changing his wrathful tone to a pleading one and even seizing me by the hands. "Well, imagine what will come of it? Another unpleasantness! You must agree, I have to behave myself in a special manner here, especially now!... especially now!... Oh, you don't know, you don't know all my circumstances!... When we leave here, I'm prepared to take you back. It's only just so, well, in short—you do understand the reasons!" he cried desperately. "Alexei Ivanovich, Alexei Ivanovich!..."

Retreating to the door, I again earnestly begged him not to worry, promised that everything would turn out well and decently, and hastened to leave.

Russians abroad are sometimes much too cowardly and are terribly afraid of what will be said of them, and how they'll be looked at, and whether this or that will be proper; in short, they behave as if they're in corsets, especially those who make claims to significance. What they like most is some preconceived, pre-established form, which they follow slavishly—in hotels, on promenades, at assemblies, while traveling... But on top of that the general had let slip that he had some special circumstances, that he somehow had to "behave specially." That was why he was suddenly so pusillanimous and cowardly and changed his tone with me. I took that into consideration and made note of it. And, of course, tomorrow he might foolishly turn to some authorities, so that I indeed had to be careful.

However, I had no interest at all in angering the general himself; but I did want to anger Polina a little now. Polina had dealt so cruelly with me, and had pushed me onto such a stupid path, that I wanted very much to drive her to the point of asking me to stop. My prankishness might finally compromise her as well. Besides that, some other sensations and desires were taking shape in me. If, for instance, I voluntarily vanish into nothing before her, that does not at all mean that I'm a wet chicken before people, and it is certainly not for the baron to "beat me with a stick." I wanted to make fun of them all and come out as a fine fellow. Let them see. Never fear! she'll be afraid of a scandal and call for me again. And if she doesn't, she'll still see that I'm not a wet chicken ...

(Astonishing news: I've just heard from our nanny, whom I met on the stairs, that Marya Filippovna set off today for Karlsbad, all by herself, on the evening train, to visit her cousin. What kind of news is that? The nanny says she had been intending to for a long time; but how is it no one knew? However, maybe only I didn't know. The nanny let slip that Marya Filippovna had had a big talk with the general two days ago. I understand, sir. It's probably—Mlle Blanche. Yes, something decisive is coming for us.)

CHAPTER VII

THE NEXT MORNING I sent for the desk clerk and told him that my account should be kept separately. My room was not so expensive that I should get very frightened and leave the hotel. I had sixteen friedrichs d'or, and there . . . there, maybe, lay riches! Strange thing, I haven't won yet, but I act, feel, and think like a rich man, and I can't imagine myself otherwise.

I planned, despite the early hour, to go at once and see Mr. Astley at the Hôtel d'Angleterre, very near us, when suddenly des Grieux came into my room. This had never happened before, and, on top of that, the gentleman and I had lately been in the most alienated and strained relations. He plainly did not conceal his contempt for me, even made an effort not to conceal it; while I—I had my own reasons not to favor him. In short, I hated him. His visit surprised me very much. I realized at once that something very special was brewing.

He came in very amiably and paid my room a compliment. Seeing that I had my hat in my hand, he inquired if I was really going for a walk so early. When he heard that I was going to see Mr. Astley on business, he reflected, understood, and his face acquired an extremely preoccupied look.

Des Grieux was like all Frenchmen, that is, cheerful and amiable when it was necessary and profitable, and insufferably dull when the necessity to be cheerful and amiable ceased. A Frenchman is rarely amiable by nature; he is always amiable as if on command, out of calculation. If, for instance, he sees the necessity of being fantastic, original, out of the ordinary, then his fantasy, being most stupid and unnatural, assembles itself out of *a priori* accepted and long-trivialized forms. The natural Frenchman consists of a most philistine, petty, ordinary positiveness—in short, the dullest being in the world. In my opinion, only novices, and Russian young ladies in particular,

are attracted to Frenchmen. Any decent being will at once
notice and refuse to put up with this conventionalism of the
pre-established forms of salon amiability, casualness, and gaiety.

"I've come to see you on business," he began extremely inde-
pendently, though, by the way, politely, "and I will not conceal
that I've come as an ambassador or, better to say, a mediator
from the general. Knowing Russian very poorly, I understood
almost nothing yesterday; but the general explained it to me in
detail, and I confess..."

"Listen, M. des Grieux," I interrupted him, "here you've
undertaken to be a mediator in this business as well. I am, of
course, '*un outchitel,*' and have never claimed the honor of being
a close friend of this house or on any especially intimate relations, and therefore I do not know all the circumstances; but
explain to me: can it be that you now fully belong to the mem-
bers of this family? Because, finally, you take such interest in
absolutely everything, you unfailingly become a mediator in it
all straight away..."

He didn't like my question. It was only too transparent for
him, and he didn't want to let anything slip.

"I am connected with the general partly by business, partly
by *certain special* circumstances," he said dryly. "The general has
sent me to ask you to drop your intentions of yesterday. Everything you thought up was, of course, very clever; but he has
precisely asked me to represent to you that it will be a total
failure; moreover, the baron will not receive you, and, finally, in
any case, he has every means of ridding himself of any further
unpleasantness on your part. You'll agree yourself. Why go on
with it, tell me? The general has promised you that he will
certainly take you back into his household at the first conve-
nience, and until that time will credit you for your salary, *vos
appointements.** Rather profitable, is it not?"

I objected to him quite calmly that he was somewhat mistaken; that maybe I would not be chased out of the baron's, but,
on the contrary, be listened to; and I asked him to admit that

---

*Your emoluments.

he had probably come in order to worm out of me precisely how I was going to set about this whole business.

"Oh, God, since the general is so involved, he would certainly like to know what you are going to do and how! It's so natural!"

I started to explain, and he began to listen, sprawling, cocking his head slightly towards me, with an obvious, unconcealed ironic nuance in his face. In general, he behaved with extreme haughtiness. I tried with all my might to pretend that I looked at the business from the most serious point of view. I explained that, since the baron had addressed a complaint against me to the general, as though I was the general's servant, he had, first of all, deprived me thereby of my post, and, second, treated me as a person who is unable to answer for himself and is not worth talking to. Of course, I am justified in feeling myself offended; however, understanding the difference in age, of position in society, and so on, and so forth (I could barely keep from laughing at this point), I do not want to take another frivolity upon myself, that is, directly demand satisfaction from the baron, or even merely suggest it to him. Nevertheless, I consider myself perfectly within my rights in offering him, and especially the baroness, my apologies, the more so in that lately I have indeed been feeling unwell, upset, and, so to speak, fantastic, and so on, and so forth. However, by offensively addressing the general yesterday and insisting that the general deprive me of my post, the baron has put me in such a position that I can no longer offer him and the baroness my apologies, because he, and the baroness, and the whole world would probably think I am coming with my apologies out of fear, in order to get my post back. It follows from all this that I now find myself forced to ask the baron to apologize to me first, in the most moderate terms—for instance, by saying he had by no means wished to offend me. And once the baron speaks it out, then I, my hands now untied, will offer him my openhearted and sincere apologies. In short, I concluded, I ask only that the baron untie my hands.

"Fie, such scrupulousness and such subtleties! And why should you apologize? Well, you will agree, *Monsieur...Monsieur...*

that you are starting it all on purpose to vex the general ... or perhaps you have some sort of special goals ... *mon cher monsieur, pardon, j'ai oublié votre nom, monsieur Alexis? ... n'est-ce pas?*"*

"Excuse me, *mon cher marquis,* but what business is that of yours?"

"*Mais le général ...*"

"And what is it to the general? He said something yesterday about having to keep himself on some sort of footing ... and he was so alarmed ... but I understood nothing."

"Here there is ... here precisely there exists a special circumstance," des Grieux picked up in a pleading tone, in which more and more vexation could be heard. "Do you know Mlle de Cominges?"

"You mean Mlle Blanche?"

"Well, yes, Mlle Blanche de Cominges ... *et madame sa mère*† ... you must agree, the general ... in short, the general is in love and even ... the marriage may even take place here. And, imagine, at the same time various scandals, stories ..."

"I don't see any scandals or stories here that have anything to do with his marriage."

"But *le baron est si irascible, un caractère prussien, vous savez, enfin il fera une querelle d'Allemand.*‡"

"It will be with me, then, not with you, since I no longer belong to the household ..." (I deliberately tried to be as muddle-headed as possible.) "But, excuse me, so it's decided that Mlle Blanche will marry the general? What are they waiting for? I mean to say—why conceal it, at any rate from us, the household?"

"I cannot tell you ... however, it is still not entirely ... though ... you know, they are waiting for news from Russia; the general must arrange his affairs ..."

"Aha! *la baboulinka!*"

---

*My dear monsieur, forgive me, I've forgotten your name, monsieur Alexis? ... isn't it?

†Madame her mother.

‡The baron is so irascible, a Prussian character, you know, he will finally make a German-style quarrel.

Des Grieux looked at me with hatred.

"In short," he interrupted, "I fully trust in your innate courtesy, your intelligence, your tact...you will, of course, do it for the family, in which you were like their own, were loved, respected..."

"Good God, I've been thrown out! You insist now that it was for the sake of appearances; but you must agree that if you say: 'Of course, I don't want to box your ears, but for the sake of appearances allow me to box your ears...' Well, isn't it almost the same?"

"If so, if no entreaties have any influence on you," he began sternly and presumptuously, "then allow me to assure you that measures will be taken. There are authorities here, you will be sent away today—*que diable! un blanc-bec comme vous** wants to challenge a person like the baron to a duel! And you think you will be left alone? And, believe me, nobody here is afraid of you! If I asked, it was more on my own behalf, because you have troubled the general. And can you, can you possibly think that the baron will not simply ask a footman to throw you out?"

"But I won't go myself," I replied with extraordinary calm, "you're mistaken, M. des Grieux, it will all work out with much greater decency than you think. I will now go to Mr. Astley and ask him to be my mediator, in short, to be my second. The man likes me and certainly will not refuse me. He will go to the baron, and the baron will receive him. If I myself am *un outchitel* and seem something of a *subalterne*, well, and, finally, without protection, Mr. Astley is the nephew of a lord, a real lord, that is known to everyone, Lord Pibroch, and that lord is here. Believe me, the baron will be polite to Mr. Astley and hear him out. And if he doesn't, Mr. Astley will count it as a personal insult (you know how tenacious Englishmen are) and send a friend to the baron on his own behalf, and he has good friends. Consider now that things may not come out quite the way you reckon."

The Frenchman was decidedly scared; indeed, it all very

*Devil take it! a greenhorn like you ...

much resembled the truth, and consequently it appeared that I really was capable of starting a whole story.

"But I beg you," he began in a thoroughly pleading voice, "drop it all! It is as if you are pleased that a whole story will come of it! It is not satisfaction you want, but a story! I told you, it will come out amusing and even clever—which is maybe what you are after—but, in short," he concluded, seeing that I had stood up and was taking my hat, "I have come to convey to you these few words from a certain person. Read them. I was told to wait for an answer."

So saying, he took from his pocket a little note, folded and sealed with wax, and handed it to me.

It was written in Polina's hand:

> I have the impression that you intend to go on with this story. You're angry and are beginning to behave like a school-boy. But there are certain special circumstances here, and later maybe I will explain them to you; so please stop it and calm yourself. How stupid this all is! I have need of you, and you have promised to obey. Remember the Schlangenberg. I beg you to be obedient, and, if need be, I order it.
>
> Your P.
>
> P.S. If you are angry with me about yesterday, forgive me.

Everything seemed to turn upside down as I read these lines. My lips went white, and I began to tremble. The cursed French-man looked on with an exaggeratedly modest air and averted his eyes from me, as if in order not to see my confusion. It would have been better if he had burst out laughing at me.

"Very well," I said, "tell *mademoiselle* not to worry. Allow me, however, to ask you," I added sharply, "why you took so long to give me this note? Instead of talking about trifles, it seems to me, you ought to have begun with it ... since you came precisely on that errand."

"Oh, I wanted ... generally this is all so strange that you must pardon my natural impatience. I wanted the sooner to learn your intentions for myself, from you personally. However, I do

not know what is in this note, and thought I would always have
time to give it to you."

"I see, you were simply told to give it to me as a last resort,
and not to give it if you could settle it verbally. Right? Talk
straight, M. des Grieux!"

"*Peut-être*,"* he said, assuming an air of some special restraint
and giving me some sort of special look.

I took my hat; he inclined his head and left. I fancied there
was a mocking smile on his lips. And how could it be otherwise?

"We'll settle accounts, Frenchy, we'll measure forces!" I muttered, going down the stairs. I still couldn't grasp anything, as
if I'd been hit on the head. The fresh air revived me a little.

After a couple of minutes, when I just began to grasp things
clearly, two thoughts distinctly presented themselves to me:
first, that from such trifles, from a few prankish, improbable
threats from a mere boy, uttered the day before in passing,
such a *general* alarm had arisen! and the *second* thought—what
influence, anyhow, does this Frenchman have on Polina? One
word from him, and she does everything he wants, writes a
note, and even *begs* me. Of course, their relations had always
been an enigma to me from the very beginning, ever since I got
to know them; however, in these last few days I'd noticed in her
a decided loathing and even contempt for him, while he didn't
even look at her, was even simply impolite to her. I'd noticed
that. Polina herself spoke to me of her loathing; extremely
significant confessions have burst from her... That means he's
simply got her in his power, he keeps her in some sort of
chains ...

*Perhaps.

CHAPTER VIII

ON THE PROMENADE, as they call it here, that is, the chest-nut avenue, I met my Englishman.

"Oho!" he began when he saw me, "I'm going to you, and you to me. So you've already parted from your people?"

"Tell me, first of all, how you know about all this," I asked in surprise. "Can it be that everybody knows all about it?"

"Oh, no, everybody does not know; and it's better if they don't. Nobody's talking about it."

"Then how do you know?"

"I know because I chanced to learn. Now where are you going to go from here? I like you, that's why I was coming to see you."

"You're a nice man, Mr. Astley," I said (though I was terribly struck: where did he find out?), "and since I haven't had my coffee yet, and you probably did a poor job on yours, let's go to the vauxhall café, sit there, have a smoke, and I'll tell you everything, and . . . you'll also tell me."

The café was a hundred paces away. Coffee was brought, we sat down, I lit a cigarette, Mr. Astley didn't light anything and, fixing his eyes on me, prepared to listen.

"I'm not going to go anywhere, I'm staying here," I began.

"I was just sure you'd stay," Mr. Astley said approvingly.

On my way to see Mr. Astley, I had had no intention and even purposely did not want to tell him anything about my love for Polina. In all those days I had scarcely said a single word to him about it. Besides, he was very shy. I had noticed from the first that Polina had made a great impression on him, but he never mentioned her name. But, strangely, suddenly, now, as soon as he sat down and fixed me with his intent, tinny gaze, an urge came over me, I don't know why, to tell him everything, that is, all my love and with all its nuances. I spent a whole half-hour telling him, and I found it extremely pleasant to be telling about it for the first time! Noticing that in some especially ardent places he became embarrassed, I deliberately increased the ardor of my story. One thing I regret: I may have said some unnecessary things about the Frenchman ...

Mr. Astley listened, sitting opposite me, without moving, without uttering a word or a sound, and looking me in the eye; but when I started speaking of the Frenchman, he suddenly cut me short and asked sternly whether I had the right to mention this extraneous circumstance. Mr. Astley always put his questions in a very strange way.

"You're right: I'm afraid I don't," I replied.

"You can say nothing precise about this marquis and Miss Polina, apart from mere surmises?"

Again I was surprised at such a categorical question from such a shy man as Mr. Astley.

"No, nothing precise," I replied, "of course not."

"If so, you have done a wrong thing not only in talking about it with me, but even in thinking about it to yourself."

"All right, all right! I acknowledge it; but that's not the point now," I interrupted, surprised in myself. Here I told him the whole of yesterday's story in all its details, Polina's escapade, my adventure with the baron, my dismissal, the general's extraordinary cowardice, and finally I gave him a detailed account of today's visit from des Grieux, with all its nuances; in conclusion, I showed him the note.

"What do you make of it?" I asked. "I was precisely coming to learn your thoughts. As for me, I think I could kill that little Frenchman, and maybe I will."

"And I, too," said Mr. Astley. "As for Miss Polina ... you know, we enter into relations even with people we hate, if necessity demands it of us. Here there may be relations unknown to you, which depend on extraneous circumstances. I think you can rest easy—in part, to be sure. As for her action yesterday, it is, of course, strange—not because she wanted to get rid of you and sent you under the baron's stick (which he didn't use, though I don't understand why, since he had it in his hand), but because such an escapade from such a ... from such an excellent miss...is improper. Naturally, she couldn't have foreseen that you would literally carry out her jesting wish..."

"You know what?" I cried suddenly, peering intently at Mr. Astley. "I have the feeling that you've already heard about all this, and do you know from whom?—from Miss Polina herself!"

Mr. Astley looked at me in surprise.

"Your eyes flash, and I read suspicion in them," he said, recovering his former equanimity at once, "but you haven't the least right to reveal your suspicions. I cannot acknowledge that right, and I totally refuse to answer your question."

"Well, enough! And you needn't!" I cried, strangely agitated and not understanding why that had popped into my mind! And when, where, how could Mr. Astley have been chosen by Polina as a confidant? Lately, however, I had partially let Mr. Astley slip from sight, and Polina had always been an enigma to me—so much an enigma that now, for instance, in setting out to tell Mr. Astley the whole history of my love, I was suddenly struck, during the telling, by the fact that I could say almost nothing precise and positive about my relations with her. On the contrary, everything was fantastic, strange, insubstantial, and even bore no resemblance to anything.

"Well, all right, all right; I'm confused, and now there are still many things I can't grasp," I replied as if breathlessly. "However, you're a good man. Now it's a different matter, and I ask your—not advice, but opinion."

I paused and began:

"Why do you think the general got so scared? Why did they make such a story out of my most stupid mischievousness? Such a story that even des Grieux himself found it necessary to interfere (and he interferes only in the most important cases), visited me (how about that!), begged, pleaded with me—he, des Grieux, with me! Finally, note for yourself that he came at nine o'clock, just before nine, and Miss Polina's note was already in his hands. When, may I ask, was it written? Maybe Miss Polina was awakened just for that! Besides, from that I can see that Miss Polina is his slave (because she even asked my forgiveness!)—besides that, what is all this to her, to her personally?

Why is she so interested? Why are they afraid of some baron? And so what if the general is marrying Mlle Blanche de Cominges? They say they have to behave in some *special* way, owing to this circumstance—but this is much too special, you must agree! What do you think? I'm convinced by your eyes that here, too, you know more than I do."

Mr. Astley smiled and nodded his head.

"Indeed, it seems that in this, too, I know a great deal more than you do," he said. "This whole business concerns Mlle Blanche alone, and I'm sure it's perfectly true."

"Well, what about Mlle Blanche?" I cried impatiently (I suddenly had a hope that something would be revealed now about Mlle Polina).

"It seems to me that Mlle Blanche has at the present moment a special interest in avoiding any kind of meeting with the baron and baroness—all the more so an unpleasant meeting, worse still a scandalous one."

"Well? Well?"

"Two years ago, Mlle Blanche was here in Roulettenburg during the season. And I also happened to be here. Mlle Blanche was not known as Mlle de Cominges then, nor was her mother, Madame *la veuve* Cominges, then in existence. At any rate there was no mention of her. Des Grieux—there was no des Grieux either. I nurse the profound conviction that they are not only not related to each other, but even became acquainted quite recently. Des Grieux also became a marquis quite recently—I am sure of that because of one circumstance. It may even be supposed that he became known as des Grieux quite recently as well. I know a man here who met him under a different name."

"But he does have a respectable circle of acquaintances?"

"Oh, that may be. Even Mlle Blanche may. But two years ago Mlle Blanche, on a complaint from this same baroness, received an invitation from the local police to leave town, and leave she did."

"How was that?"

"She appeared here first then with an Italian, some sort of

prince with a historic name something like *Barberini* or something similar. A man all in rings and diamonds, and not even
fake. They drove around in an astonishing equipage. Mlle
Blanche played at *trente et quarante*,* successfully at first, but
then luck began to let her down badly; so I recall. I remember
one evening she lost a considerable sum. But, worst of all, *un
beau matin*† her prince vanished no one knew where; the horses
and equipage vanished, everything vanished. The hotel bill was
terrible. Mlle Zelmà (instead of Barberini she suddenly turned
into Mlle Zelmà) was in the last degree of despair. She howled
and shrieked for the whole hotel to hear and tore her dress in
rage. A certain Polish count (all traveling Poles are counts) was
staying right there in the hotel, and Mlle Zelmà, who was tearing
her dress and scratching her face like a cat with her beautiful
perfume-washed hands, made a certain impression on him. They
talked, and by dinnertime she was comforted. That evening he
appeared arm in arm with her in the vauxhall. Mlle Zelmà
laughed, as was her custom, quite loudly, and her manner showed
a somewhat greater casualness. She entered directly into that
category of roulette-playing ladies, who, as they come to the
table, will shove a player aside as hard as they can with their
shoulder in order to clear a space for themselves. That's especially
chic here among these ladies. You've noticed them, of course?"

"Oh, yes."

"They're not worth noticing. To the vexation of the decent
public, there's no lack of them here, at any rate those of them
who change thousand-franc notes at the tables every day. However, as soon as they stop changing notes, they're immediately
asked to leave. Mlle Zelmà still went on changing notes; but
her game went still more unluckily. Note that these ladies are
quite often lucky at gambling; they have astonishing self-
control. However, my story is over. One day, exactly like the
prince, the count, too, vanished. Mlle Zelmà appeared in the
evening to play alone; this time no one appeared to offer her

*Thirty and forty.
†One fine morning.

his arm. In two days she lost everything. Having staked her last louis d'or and lost it, she looked around and saw Baron Wurmerhelm nearby, studying her with great attention and deep indignation. But Mlle Zelmà did not perceive the indignation and, turning to the baron with a certain kind of smile, asked him to put ten louis d'or on red for her. As a result of that, on the baroness's complaint, she received that evening an invitation not to appear in the vauxhall anymore. If it surprises you that I know all these small and completely indecent details, it is because I finally heard them from Mr. Feeder, a relation of mine, who that same evening took Mlle Zelmà in his carriage from Roulettenburg to Spa. Now understand: Mlle Blanche wants to become the general's wife, probably, so that she will never again receive such invitations as she did two years ago from the vauxhall police. Now she no longer gambles; but that is because, by all tokens, she now has capital, which she lends to local gamblers on interest. That is much more prudent. I even suspect that the unfortunate general owes her money. Maybe des Grieux does, too. Maybe des Grieux is her associate. You must agree that, at least until the wedding, she would not wish to attract the attention of the baron or the baroness for any reason. In short, in her position scandal is the least profitable thing for her. You are connected with their household, and your acts could cause a scandal, the more so as she appears every day in public arm in arm with the general or with Miss Polina. Now do you understand?"

"No, I don't!" I cried, banging the table with all my might, so that the frightened *garçon* came running.

"Tell me, Mr. Astley," I repeated in frenzy, "if you know this whole story, and consequently know by heart what Mlle Blanche de Cominges is—how is it that you haven't warned at least me, the general himself, and above all Miss Polina, who has appeared here in the vauxhall, in public, arm in arm with Mlle Blanche? Can this be possible?"

"There was no point in warning you, because there was nothing you could do," Mr. Astley replied calmly. "And anyhow, what was there to warn you about? The general may know more about Mlle Blanche than I do, and all the same he goes strolling with her and Miss Polina. The general is an unfortunate man. Yesterday I saw Mlle Blanche riding a splendid horse with M. des Grieux and that little Russian prince, and the general riding behind them on a chestnut. In the morning he had said that his legs hurt, but he sat his horse well. And at that moment the thought suddenly occurred to me that this was a completely lost man. Moreover, this is all none of my business, and I had the honor of meeting Miss Polina only recently. However," Mr. Astley suddenly caught himself, "I've already told you that I cannot acknowledge your right to certain questions, though I sincerely like you . . ."

"Enough," I said, getting up. "It's clear as day to me now that Miss Polina also knows all about Mlle Blanche, but she can't part with her Frenchman, and therefore ventures to stroll with Mlle Blanche. Believe me, no other influence would induce her to stroll with Mlle Blanche and beg me in a note not to touch the baron. Here there must be precisely that influence before which everything bows! And yet it was she who loosed me on the baron! Devil take it, nothing can be sorted out here!"

"You forget, first, that this Mlle de Cominges is the general's fiancée, and, second, that Miss Polina, the general's step-daughter, has a little brother and sister, the general's own children, totally abandoned by this crazy man and, it seems, robbed as well."

"Yes, yes, that's so! Leaving the children means abandoning them completely, staying means protecting their interests, and maybe saving shreds of the estate as well. Yes, yes, that's all true! But still, still! Oh, I understand why they're all now so interested in *baboulinka*!"

"In whom?" asked Mr. Astley.

"In that old witch in Moscow who won't die and about whom they're expecting a telegram that she's dead."

"Well, yes, of course, the whole interest converges in her. The whole point lies in the inheritance! When the inheritance is announced, the general will get married; Miss Polina will be unbound, and des Grieux . . ."

"Well, and des Grieux?"

"Des Grieux will be paid his money; that's all he's waiting for here."

"All! You think that's all he's waiting for?"

"I know nothing more." Mr. Astley fell stubbornly silent.

"But I know, I know!" I repeated in a rage. "He's also waiting for the inheritance, because Polina will get a dowry, and once she gets the money, she'll immediately throw herself on his neck. Women are all like that! And the proudest of them come out as the most banal slaves! Polina is capable only of loving passionately and nothing more! That's my opinion of her! Look at her, especially when she's sitting alone, deep in thought: it's something predestined, foredoomed, accursed! She's capable of all the horrors of life and passion . . . she . . . she . . . but who's that calling me?" I suddenly exclaimed. "Who's shouting? I heard somebody shout 'Alexei Ivanovich!' in Russian. A woman's voice, listen, listen!"

At that moment we were approaching our hotel. We had left the café long ago, almost without noticing it.

"I heard a woman shout, but I don't know who she's calling; it was in Russian. Now I can see where it's coming from," Mr. Astley was pointing, "it's that woman shouting, the one sitting in a big armchair and who has just been carried up to the porch by so many footmen. They're carrying her suitcases behind her; that means the train has just arrived."

"But why is she calling me? She's shouting again; look, she's waving to us."

"I see that she's waving," said Mr. Astley.

"Alexei Ivanovich! Alexei Ivanovich! Ah, Lord, what a dolt!" desperate cries came from the porch of the hotel.

We almost ran to the entrance. I reached the landing and . . . my arms dropped in amazement, and my feet became rooted to the stone.

CHAPTER IX

ON THE UPPER LANDING of the wide hotel porch, carried up the steps in a chair and surrounded by manservants and maidservants and the numerous, obsequious hotel staff, in the presence of the manager himself, who had come out to meet the exalted guest arriving with so much flurry and noise, with her own servants and with so many suitcases and valises, sat—*grandmother*! Yes, it was she herself, formidable and rich, seventy-five years old, Antonida Vassilyevna Tarassevichev, a landowner and a Moscow grande dame, *la baboulinka*, about whom telegrams were sent and received, who was dying and did not die, and who suddenly, herself, in person, appeared like fresh snow on our heads. She appeared, though she couldn't walk, carried in an armchair as she had always been for the last five years, but, as was her custom, brisk, perky, self-satisfied, straight-backed, shouting loudly and commandingly, scolding everybody—well, exactly as I had had the honor of seeing her twice since the time I was taken into the general's household as a tutor. Naturally, I stood before her dumbstruck with amazement. But she had made me out with her lynx eyes from a hundred paces away, as they carried her up in her chair, had recognized me and called me by my name and patronymic—which, as was her custom, she had also memorized once and for all. "And she's the one they expected to see in a coffin, buried, and having left an inheritance," flitted through my mind, "yet she'll outlive us all and the whole hotel! But, God, what will become of all our people now, what will become of the general! She'll stand the whole hotel on its ear!"

"Well, what are you doing, dearie, standing in front of me with your eyes popping out!" grandmother went on yelling at me. "You don't know how to bow and greet a body, eh? Or you've grown proud and don't want to? Or maybe you don't recognize me? You hear, Potapych," she turned to a gray-haired old man in a tailcoat and white tie and with a pink bald spot, her butler, who had accompanied her on her journey, "you hear, he doesn't recognize me! They've got me buried! They send one telegram after another: is she dead or not? I know everything! And here, you see, I'm as alive as can be!"

"Good heavens, Antonida Vassilyevna, why would I wish you ill?" I answered cheerfully, coming to my senses. "I was only surprised... And how not marvel at such an unexpected..."

"But what's so surprising for you? I got on the train and came. It's a quiet ride, no jolts. You've been for a walk, have you?"

"Yes, I strolled to the vauxhall."

"It's nice here," said grandmother, looking around, "warm, and there's a wealth of trees. I like that. Are our people at home? The general?"

"Oh, yes! at this hour they're probably all at home."

"So they've established a schedule here and all the cere-monies? Setting the tone. I've heard they keep a carriage, *les seigneurs russes*!* Blew all their money and went abroad! Is Praskovya[9] with him?"

"Yes, Polina Alexandrovna, too."

"And the little Frenchman? Well, I'll see them all for myself, Alexei Ivanovich, show me the way straight to him. Do you find it nice here?"

"So so, Antonida Vassilyevna."

"And you, Potapych, tell that dolt of a manager to give me comfortable quarters, nice ones, not too high up, and carry my things there at once. Why is everybody in a rush to carry me? Why are they getting at me? Eh, what slaves! Who's that with you?" she turned to me again.

"This is Mr. Astley," I replied.

"Who is this Mr. Astley?"

"A traveler, my good acquaintance; he also knows the general."

"An Englishman. That's why he's staring at me and doesn't

*The Russian gentlefolk.

unclench his teeth. I like Englishmen, though. Well, drag me upstairs, straight to their place; where are they?"

Grandmother was carried; I walked ahead up the wide hotel stairway. Our procession was very impressive. Everyone who came our way stopped and looked at us all eyes. Our hotel was considered the best, the most expensive, and the most aristocratic at the spa. On the stairs and in the corridors one always met magnificent ladies and important Englishmen. Many made inquiries downstairs of the manager, who, for his own part, was deeply impressed. He, of course, replied to all who asked that this was an important foreign lady, *une russe, une comtesse, grande dame*, and that she would occupy the same suite which a week before had been occupied by *la grande duchesse de N.* Grandmother's commanding and imperious figure, borne up in her chair, was the cause of the main effect. Each time she met a new person, she at once measured him with a curious gaze, and she loudly questioned me about them all. Grandmother belonged to a large breed, and though she never got up from her chair, one could tell, looking at her, that she was quite tall. She held her back straight as a board, and did not recline in the chair. Her big gray head, with its large and sharp features, was held erect; her glance was somehow even haughty and defiant; and one could see that her gaze and gestures were perfectly natural. Despite her seventy-five years, her face was quite fresh, and even her teeth had not suffered much. She was dressed in a black silk gown and a white bonnet.

"She interests me greatly," Mr. Astley whispered to me, going up the stairs beside me.

"She knows about the telegrams," I thought, "she's also been informed about des Grieux, but it seems she still knows little about Mlle Blanche." I immediately communicated this to Mr. Astley.

Sinful man! My first surprise had no sooner passed, than I rejoiced terribly at the thunderbolt we were about to produce at the general's. It was as if something was egging me on, and I led the way extremely cheerfully.

Our people were quartered on the second floor. I made no

announcement, did not even knock at the door, but simply thrust it open, and grandmother was carried in in triumph. As if on purpose, they were all gathered in the general's study. It was twelve o'clock, and they seemed to be planning an excursion—some were going in carriages, others on horseback, the entire company; besides that, other acquaintances had been invited. Besides the general, Polina with the children, their nanny, there were in the study: des Grieux, Mlle Blanche, again in a riding habit, her mother Mme *la veuve* Cominges, the little prince, and also some learned traveler, a German, whom I saw with them for the first time. The chair with grandmother was set down right in the middle of the study, three paces from the general. God, I'll never forget this impression! Before we came in, the general had been telling some story, and des Grieux had been correcting him. It should be noted that for two or three days Mlle Blanche and des Grieux had for some reason been paying much court to the little prince—*à la barbe du pauvre général*,* and the company was tuned, though perhaps artificially, to the most merry and cordially familial pitch. At the sight of grandmother, the general was suddenly dumbfounded, opened his mouth, and stopped in the middle of a phrase. He stared at her, his eyes popping, as though spellbound by a basilisk's gaze. Grandmother also looked at him silently, fixedly—but what a triumphant, defiant, and mocking gaze it was! They stared at each other like that for a whole ten seconds, amid the profound silence of everyone around them. Des Grieux was petrified at first, but soon an extraordinary uneasiness flashed in his face. Mlle Blanche raised her eyebrows, opened her mouth, and gazed wildly at grandmother. The prince and the scholar contemplated the whole picture in deep perplexity. Polina's gaze expressed great astonishment and perplexity, but suddenly she turned white as a sheet; a moment later the blood quickly rushed to her face and suffused her cheeks. Yes, this was a catastrophe for them all! The only thing I did was shift my eyes from grandmother to everyone around and back. Mr.

---

*Under the poor general's nose.

Astley stood to one side, as was his custom, calmly and decorously.

"Well, here I am! Instead of a telegram!" grandmother burst out at last, breaking the silence. "What, you didn't expect me?"

"Antonida Vassilyevna...auntie:...but how on earth..." the unfortunate general murmured. If grandmother hadn't begun speaking for a few seconds more, he might have had a stroke.

"What do you mean, how? I got on the train and came. What's the railroad for? And you all thought I'd stretched out my bones and left you an inheritance? I know how you sent telegrams from here. Paid a lot of money for them, I suppose. It's not cheap from here. But I shouldered my old bones and came here. Is this that Frenchman? M. des Grieux, I believe?"

"*Oui, madame*," des Grieux picked up, "*et croyez, je suis si enchanté...vôtre santé...c'est un miracle...vous voir ici, une surprise charmante...*"*

"Hm, *charmante*. I know you, you mountebank, only I don't believe you even that much!" and she showed her little finger. "Who's this?" she turned, pointing to Mlle Blanche. The showy Frenchwoman in the riding habit, with a crop in her hand, apparently impressed her. "Are you a local, or what?"

"This is Mlle Blanche de Cominges, and this is her mother, Mme de Cominges; they're staying at this hotel," I reported.

"Is the daughter married?" grandmother inquired without ceremony.

"Mlle de Cominges is unmarried," I replied as respectfully as I could, purposely lowering my voice.

"A merry girl?"

I didn't understand the question at first.

"She's not boring to be with? Does she understand Russian? This des Grieux picked up a smattering of it with us in Moscow."

I explained to her that Mlle de Cominges had never been to Russia.

---

*Yes, Madame...and believe me, I am so delighted...your health...it's a miracle...to see you here, a charming surprise...

"*Bonjour!*" said grandmother, suddenly and abruptly addressing Mlle Blanche.

"*Bonjour, madame,*" Mlle Blanche curtsied decorously and gracefully, hastening, under the cover of extraordinary modesty and politeness, to display with the whole expression of her face and figure her extreme astonishment at such a strange question and manner of address.

"Ah, she's lowered her eyes, she's mincing and prancing; you can tell the bird at once; some sort of actress. I'm staying downstairs in this hotel," she suddenly turned to the general, "I shall be your neighbor; are you glad or not?"

"Oh, auntie! Believe in the sincere feeling . . . of my pleasure," the general picked up. He had already recovered somewhat, and since he was capable on occasion of speaking aptly, imposingly, and with a claim to a certain effect, he began expatiating now as well. "We were so alarmed and struck by the news of your ill health . . . We received such hopeless telegrams, and suddenly . . ."

"Lies, lies!" grandmother interrupted at once.

"But how is it," the general also hastened to interrupt and raised his voice, trying to ignore this "lies," "how is it, though, that you ventured upon such a journey? You must agree that at your age and with your health . . . at any rate it's all so unexpected that our astonishment is comprehensible. But I'm so glad . . . and we all" (he started smiling sweetly and rapturously) "will try as hard as we can to make your season here pass most pleasantly . . ."

"Well, enough empty chatter; laying it on thick as usual; I can get along by myself. However, I have nothing against you; I don't bear any grudges. How, you ask? What's so surprising? In the simplest way. Why are they all so surprised? Hello, Praskovya. What are you doing here?"

"Hello, grandmother," said Polina, going up to her. "Was it a long trip?"

"Well, this one has asked the smartest question, none of this oh and ah! You see, I lay and lay, got treated and treated, then I chased the doctors away and summoned the sacristan from

St. Nicholas's. He had cured one woman of the same illness with hay dust. Well, and he helped me; on the third day I sweated all over and got up. Then all my Germans gathered again, put on their spectacles, and began to opinionate: 'If you were to go abroad now to a spa and take a cure,' they said, 'your gripes would go away completely.' And why not? I thought. The Fool-Blazers start their oh-ing: 'You can't go so far!' they say. Well, so there! In one day I got ready and on Friday last week I took my maid, and Potapych, and the footman Fyodor, only in Berlin I chased this Fyodor home, because I saw there was simply no need for him, I could get here all by myself . . . I'm riding in a separate compartment, and there are porters at all the stations, they'll carry me wherever I like for twenty kopecks. Look, what quarters you occupy!" she concluded, glancing around. "With what money are you paying for it, dearie? Everything you've got is mortgaged. You owe quite a lump to this little Frenchman alone! I know everything, everything!"

"Auntie . . ." the general began, all embarrassed, "I'm astonished, auntie . . . it seems that, even without anyone's control, I can . . . what's more, my expenses do not exceed my means, and here we . . ."

"Don't exceed your means? Come now! You must have robbed the children of their last penny—a fine guardian!"

"After this, after such words . . ." the general began indignantly, "I really don't know . . ."

"He doesn't know! I'll bet you never leave the roulette tables here! Have you blown it all?"

The general was so astounded that he almost spluttered from the rush of his agitated feelings.

"Roulette! I? With my importance . . . I? You forget yourself, auntie, you must still be unwell . . ."

"Lies, lies; I'll bet they can't drag you away; it's all lies! I'm going to have a look at what this roulette is right today. You, Praskovya, tell me what there is to be seen here, and Alexei Ivanovich will show me, and you, Potapych, write down all the places to go. What's there to see here?" she suddenly turned to Polina again.

"There are the ruins of a castle nearby, then there's the Schlangenberg."

"What is this Schlangenberg? A woods, or what?"

"No, not a woods, it's a mountain; there's a *point* ..."

"What sort of *point*?"

"The highest part of the mountain, an enclosed place. The view from there is magnificent."

"That means dragging the armchair up the mountain. Can it be done, or not?"

"Oh, it should be possible to find porters," I replied.

At that moment, Fedosya, the nanny, came up to greet grandmother, bringing the general's children.

"Well, there's no need for smooching! I don't like to kiss children, they're all snotty! How are you getting on here, Fedosya?"

"It's vur-ry, vur-ry nice here, Antonida Vassilyevna, ma'am," Fedosya replied. "And how have you been, ma'am? We've been grieving over you so."

"I know, you're a simple soul. What have you got here, all guests, or something?" she turned to Polina again. "This runty one in the spectacles?"

"That's Prince Nilsky, grandmother," Polina whispered to her.

"A Russian? And I thought he wouldn't understand! Maybe he didn't hear! I've already seen Mr. Astley. Here he is again," grandmother caught sight of him again. "Hello!" she suddenly addressed him.

Mr. Astley silently bowed to her.

"Well, do you have something nice to say to me? Say something! Translate for him, Polina."

Polina translated.

"That I am looking at you with great pleasure and rejoicing that you are in good health," Mr. Astley replied gravely, but with great readiness. It was translated for grandmother, and she obviously liked it.

"Englishmen always answer well," she observed. "For some reason I've always liked Englishmen, no comparison with these little Frenchmen! Call on me," she turned to Mr. Astley again.

"I'll try not to bother you too much. Translate it for him and tell him that I'm downstairs here, downstairs here—you hear, downstairs, downstairs," she repeated to Mr. Astley, pointing down with her finger.

Mr. Astley was extremely pleased with the invitation.

Grandmother looked Polina over from head to foot with an attentive and satisfied gaze.

"I could love you, Praskovya," she said suddenly, "you're a nice girl, better than all of them, but what a little character you've got—oof! Well, yes, I have my character, too; turn around; that's not a hairpiece, is it?"

"No, grandmother, it's my own."

"Hm, I don't like this stupid modern fashion. You're a very pretty girl. I'd fall in love with you if I were a young man. How is it you don't get married? However, it's time I was off. I want to go outside, it's been nothing but the train, the train ... Well, what's with you, still angry?" she turned to the general.

"Come now, auntie, for pity's sake!" the happy general roused himself. "I understand, at your age ..."

"*Cette vieille est tombée en enfance,*"* des Grieux whispered to me.

"I want to have a look at everything here. Will you lend me Alexei Ivanovich?" grandmother continued to the general.

"Oh, for as long as you like, but I myself ... and Polina, and M. des Grieux ... we'll all consider it a pleasure to accompany you ..."

"*Mais, madame, cela sera un plaisir,*"† des Grieux popped up with a charming smile.

"Hm, *plaisir.* I find you ridiculous, dearie. By the way, I won't give you any money," she suddenly added to the general. "Well, now to my suite: I must look the rooms over, and then we'll set out for all those places. Well, lift me up."

Grandmother was lifted up again, and the whole crowd of us set out, following the armchair down the stairs. The general

---

*This old woman has fallen into dotage.
†But, madame, it will be a pleasure.

walked as if stunned by the blow of a bludgeon on the head. Des Grieux was mulling something over. Mlle Blanche made as if to stay, but then for some reason decided to go with everybody else. The prince at once set out after her, and only the German and Mme *la veuve* Cominges stayed upstairs in the general's suite.

CHAPTER X

AT SPAS—AND, IT SEEMS, all over Europe—hotel adminis-
trators and managers, when assigning rooms to their
guests, are guided not so much by their demands and wishes as
by their own personal view of them; and, it must be noted, they
are rarely mistaken. But grandmother, God knows why, was
given such rich quarters that they even overdid it: four magnificently decorated rooms, with a bathroom, servants' quarters, a
special room for the maid, and so on, and so forth. Indeed, a
week earlier some *grande duchesse* had stayed in these rooms,
which fact, of course, was at once announced to the new guests,
to raise the price of the suite. Grandmother was carried, or
rather rolled, through all the rooms, and she examined them
attentively and sternly. The manager, an older man with a bald
head, respectfully accompanied her on this first inspection.

I don't know who they took grandmother for, but it seems
they thought her an extremely important and, above all, a very
rich personage. They at once entered in the register: "*Madame
la générale princesse de Tarassévitchev*," though grandmother had
never been a princess. Her prestige probably began with her
having her own servants, a separate compartment on the train,
the endless number of unnecessary valises, suitcases, and even
trunks that arrived with her; and the chair, grandmother's
brusque tone and voice, her eccentric questions, asked with
a most unabashed air and brooking no objections, in short,
grandmother's whole figure—erect, brusque, imperious—
rounded out the universal awe in which she was held. During
the inspection, grandmother sometimes ordered them to stop
the chair, pointed at some piece of furniture, and addressed
unexpected questions to the respectfully smiling manager, who
was already beginning to turn coward. Grandmother put her
questions in French, which she spoke, however, quite poorly, so

that I usually translated. The manager's answers were for the most part not to her liking and seemed unsatisfactory. Besides, she somehow kept asking not about essentials, but about God knows what. For instance, she suddenly stopped before a painting—a rather weak copy of some famous original on a mythological subject.

"Whose portrait is that?"

The manager declared that it was probably some countess.

"How is it you don't know? You live here and you don't know? What's it doing here? Why is she cross-eyed?"

The manager was unable to give satisfactory answers to all these questions and was even at a loss.

"What a blockhead!" grandmother retorted in Russian.

They carried her further on. The same story was repeated with a Saxony statuette, which grandmother inspected for a long time and then ordered to be removed, no one knew why. She finally badgered the manager about the cost of the bedroom carpets and where they had been made. The manager promised to find out.

"What asses!" grandmother grumbled and turned all her attention to the bed.

"Such a magnificent canopy! Unmake it."

The bed was unmade.

"Go on, go on, unmake it all. Take away the pillows, the pillowcases, lift up the feather bed."

Everything was turned upside down. Grandmother inspected it all attentively.

"A good thing they don't have bedbugs. Take off all the linen! Remake it with my linen and my pillows. Anyhow, it's all much too magnificent, an old woman like me doesn't need such a suite: I'll be bored by myself. Alexei Ivanovich, come and see me often, when you're done teaching the children."

"Since yesterday I no longer work for the general," I replied, "and I'm living in the hotel completely on my own."

"Why's that?"

"The other day a distinguished German baron and the baroness, his wife, came here from Berlin. Yesterday on the promenade I addressed him in German without keeping to the Berlin accent."

"Well, what of it?"

"He considered it insolent and complained to the general, and the general dismissed me the same day."

"What, did you abuse him, this baron, or something? (Even if you did, it wouldn't matter!)"

"Oh, no. On the contrary, the baron raised his stick at me."

"And you, you dribbler, allowed your tutor to be treated that way," she suddenly turned on the general, "and dismissed him from his post to boot! You're dunderheads—you're all dunderheads, I can see."

"Don't worry, auntie," the general replied with a slight tinge of haughty familiarity, "I know how to handle my own affairs. Besides, Alexei Ivanovich did not report it to you quite accurately."

"And you just let it pass?" she turned to me.

"I wanted to challenge the baron to a duel," I replied as modestly and calmly as I could, "but the general was against it."

"Why were you against it?" grandmother turned to the general again. "(And you may go, dearie, come back when you're called," she also turned to the manager, "no point in standing there gaping. I can't stand his Nuremberg mug!)" The man bowed and left, without, of course, understanding grandmother's compliment.

"Good heavens, auntie, duels really aren't possible," the general answered with a smile.

"Why aren't they? Men are all cocks, so they ought to fight. You're all dunderheads. I can see, you don't know how to stand up for your country. Well, lift me up! Potapych, arrange it so that two porters are always ready, hire them and settle it. No need for more than two. They'll only have to carry me on the stairs, but on the level, on the street, they can roll me—tell them that; and pay them in advance, they'll be more respectful. You yourself must always be with me, and you, Alexei Ivanovich, show me this baron on the promenade: I'd at least like to see what sort of von baron he is. Well, so where's this roulette?"

I explained that the roulette tables were in rooms of the vauxhall. Then followed questions: how many are there? do many people play? Does it go on all day? How is it set up? I answered, finally, that it would be best of all to see it with her own eyes, and that it was quite difficult to describe it just like that.

"Well, then carry me straight there! Lead the way, Alexei Ivanovich!"

"Why, auntie, are you not even going to rest after the trip?" the general asked solicitously. He seemed to be in a bit of a flutter, and they were all somehow perplexed and began exchanging glances. They probably found it slightly ticklish, even shameful, to accompany grandmother straight to the vauxhall, where she, of course, was capable of committing all sorts of eccentricities, but now in public. However, they themselves had all volunteered to accompany her.

"Why should I rest? I'm not tired; I've been sitting for five days as it is. And then we'll go to look at what sort of springs and medicinal waters they've got and where they are. And then... what was it you said, Praskovya—a *point*, was it?"

"A *point*, grandmother."

"Well, if it's *point*, it's *point*. And what else is there here?"

"There are lots of things, grandmother," Polina hesitated.

"Eh, you don't know yourself! Marfa, you'll also come with me," she said to her maid.

"Why should she go, auntie?" the general suddenly began bustling. "And, finally, it's forbidden; it's unlikely Potapych will be allowed in the vauxhall either."

"Well, nonsense! Just because she's a servant, I should abandon her! She's also a human being; we've been riding the rails for a week now, she also wants to see things. Who will she go with, if not me? Alone she won't dare peek outside."

"But, grandmother..."

"What, are you ashamed to come with me? Stay home then, nobody's inviting you. Look, what a general; I'm a general's widow myself. And why indeed should I go dragging such a train behind me? I'll look at everything with Alexei Ivanovich..."

But des Grieux resolutely insisted that we all escort her, and produced the most amiable phrases about the pleasure of accompanying her and so on. We all set off.

"*Elle est tombée en enfance,*" des Grieux kept saying to the general, "*seule elle fera des bêtises...*"* I didn't hear any more, but he obviously had some sort of intentions, and maybe his hopes had even returned.

It was about a quarter of a mile to the vauxhall. The way led us down the chestnut avenue to the green, beyond which one went straight into the vauxhall. The general calmed down a bit, because our procession, though eccentric enough, was nevertheless decorous and decent. And there was nothing surprising in the fact of an ailing person with paralyzed legs appearing at the spa. But the general was obviously afraid of the vauxhall: why should an ailing person with paralyzed legs, and an old woman at that, go to the roulette tables? Polina and Mlle Blanche walked on either side of her, beside the rolling chair. Mlle Blanche laughed, was modestly merry, and from time to time even played up quite amiably to grandmother, so that she finally praised her. Polina, on the other hand, was obliged to answer grandmother's constant and innumerable questions, such as: "Who's that man walking by? who's that woman driving by? how big is the town? how big is the garden? What trees are those? What mountains are these? Are there eagles here? What's that funny roof?" Mr. Astley was walking beside me and whispered to me that he expected much from this morning. Potapych and Marfa walked behind, just after the chair— Potapych in his tailcoat and white tie, but in a peaked cap, and Marfa, a forty-year-old maiden, red-cheeked but already beginning to go gray, in a bonnet, a cotton dress, and creaking kidskin shoes. Grandmother turned and spoke to them very often. Des Grieux and the general lagged behind a little and talked about something with great vehemence. The general was very downcast; des Grieux talked with a resolute air. Maybe he was trying to encourage the general; obviously he was giving

---

*Alone she'll do stupid things.

him advice. But earlier grandmother had already uttered the fatal phrase: "I won't give you any money." This news may have seemed incredible to des Grieux, but the general knew his aunt. I noticed that des Grieux and Mlle Blanche continued to exchange winks. I caught sight of the prince and the German traveler at the very end of the avenue: they lagged behind and made off from us somewhere.

We arrived at the vauxhall in triumph. The doorman and the attendants showed the same deference as the servants in the hotel. They looked at us, however, with curiosity. Grandmother first of all ordered them to carry her around all the rooms; some things she praised, to others she remained completely indifferent; about everything she asked questions. They finally reached the gaming rooms. The footman who was standing guard by the closed doors suddenly, as if in astonishment, flung them open.

Grandmother's appearance in the gambling hall made a deep impression on the public. There were maybe a hundred and fifty or two hundred players crowding in several rows around the roulette tables and at the other end of the room where the table for *trente et quarante* stood. Those who managed to push their way close to the table itself usually stood firm and did not relinquish their places until they lost everything; for to stand there just as simple spectators and occupy a gambling place for nothing was not allowed. Though chairs are placed around the gaming table, few of the players sit down, especially if the public gathers in large numbers—because standing people can squeeze closer together and thus gain space, and it's more convenient for placing stakes. The second and third rows crowded behind the first, waiting and keeping an eye out for their turn; but sometimes in impatience someone would thrust his arm through the first row to place his bet. Even from the third row people contrived to thrust their stakes through in this way; owing to which not ten or even five minutes would go by without some "story" over a disputed stake beginning at one end of the table or another. The vauxhall police, however, were rather good. Crowding, of course, cannot be avoided; on the contrary, the influx of the public is welcomed, because it's profitable; but the eight croupiers who sit around the table keep a sharp eye on the betting, they do the reckoning as well, and they settle disputes whenever they arise. In extreme cases, the police are summoned, and the matter is ended in a few minutes. The police are stationed right there in the hall, in plain clothes, among the spectators, so they can't be recognized. They watch out especially for pilferers and professional thieves, who are especially numerous at the roulette table, it being unusually suited to their profession. Indeed, elsewhere thefts are made from pockets or locked places—and that, in case of failure, can end very bothersomely. While here it's quite simple, you need only go up to the table, start playing, then suddenly, openly and publicly, pick up somebody else's winnings and put them in your pocket; if a dispute starts, the crook loudly and vociferously insists that the stake was his. If the thing is done deftly and the witnesses hesitate, the thief very often succeeds in awarding himself the money— if, of course, the sum is not very considerable. In the latter case, it would certainly have been noticed earlier by the croupiers or some of the other players. But if the sum is not so considerable, the real owner, wary of a scandal, sometimes even simply declines to prolong the dispute and walks away. But if a thief is exposed, he is at once removed with a scandal.

Grandmother observed all this from a distance, with wild curiosity. She liked it very much that the thieves were removed. *Trente et quarante* aroused little curiosity in her; she much preferred roulette and the way the little ball rolled about. She wanted, finally, to have a closer look at the game. I don't understand how it happened, but the attendants and some other busybodies (mostly little Poles who had lost their money and now foisted their services on lucky players and all foreigners) at once found and cleared a place for grandmother, despite all that crowd, right at the middle of the table, next to the head croupier, and rolled her chair there. Numerous visitors who were not playing themselves, but watched the play from outside (mostly Englishmen and their families), at once pushed their way to the table to get a look at grandmother from behind the players.

Numerous lorgnettes turned towards her. Hopes were born in the croupiers: such an eccentric gambler really seemed to promise something extraordinary. A seventy-year-old woman, crippled and wishing to gamble, was, of course, not an ordinary case. I also pushed my way to the table and established myself by grandmother. Potapych and Marfa stayed somewhere far to the side, among the people. The general, Polina, des Grieux, and Mlle Blanche also stationed themselves to the side, among the spectators.

Grandmother began by examining the players. She asked me sharp, abrupt questions in a half-whisper: who's that man? who's that woman? She especially liked one very young man at the end of the table, who played a very big game, staked thousands, and had already won, as the whisper went around, up to forty thousand francs, which lay in a heap before him, in gold and banknotes. He was pale; his eyes flashed and his hands trembled; he staked now without any calculation, as much as his hands snatched up, and yet he kept winning and winning, raking and raking it all in. Attendants bustled about him, put a chair behind him, cleared a space around him so that he would have more room and not be crowded—all this in expectation of a rich reward. Certain players, when they're winning, will sometimes give them money without counting, just like that, out of joy, also as much as their hand snatches from their pocket. A little Pole had already settled himself next to the young man, bustling with all his might, and whispered something to him, respectfully but constantly, probably telling him how to stake, advising and directing the play—naturally, also hoping for a handout afterwards. But the gambler scarcely looked at him, staking at random and raking it all in. He was obviously becoming flustered.

Grandmother observed him for several minutes.

"Tell him," grandmother suddenly fluttered up, giving me a nudge, "tell him to quit, to take the money and leave quickly. He'll lose, he'll lose everything now!" she fussed, nearly breathless with agitation. "Where's Potapych? Send Potapych to him! Tell him, tell him," she nudged me, "no, where indeed is

Potapych? *Sortez, sortez,"* she herself began shouting to the
young man. I bent down to her and whispered resolutely that
it was not permitted to shout like that here, nor even to raise
one's voice a little, because it interfered with the counting, and
that we'd be turned out at once.

"How vexing! The man's lost, which means he wants it that
way himself...I can't watch him, I'm all upset. What a dolt!"
And grandmother quickly turned in another direction.

There, to the left, on the other side of the table, among the
players, a young lady could be noticed and beside her some sort
of dwarf. Who this dwarf was, I don't know: a relation of hers
perhaps, or else just brought along for effect. I had noticed the
lady before; she came to the gaming table every day at one in
the afternoon and left at exactly two; she played for one hour
every day. They knew her by now and offered her a chair at
once. She would take some gold from her pocket, some thousand-franc notes, and begin to stake quietly, coolly, with calculation, marking the numbers on a paper with her pencil and trying
to find the system by which the chances were grouped at the
moment. She staked significant amounts. Every day she won
one, two, at the most three thousand francs, not more, and,
having won, she immediately left. Grandmother studied her for
a long time.

"Well, that one's not going to lose! that one there's not going
to lose! What is she? You don't know? Who is she?"

"A Frenchwoman, must be, or the like," I whispered.

"Ah, you can tell a bird by its flight. You can see her little
nails are sharpened. Now explain to me what every turn means
and how to stake."

I explained to grandmother, as far as possible, the meaning
of the numerous combinations of stakes, *rouge et noir, pair et
impair, manque et passe,*† and, finally, various nuances in the
system of numbers. Grandmother listened attentively, memorized, asked again, and learned by heart. Each system of stakes

---

*Leave, leave.
†Red and black, even and odd, below and above eighteen.

could be illustrated at once by an example, so that many things could be learned and memorized very easily and quickly. Grandmother remained quite pleased.

"And what is *zéro*? Why did this croupier, the head one, the curly one, cry *zéro* just now? And why did he rake in everything that was on the table? Such a pile, and he took it all for himself? What's that?"

"It's *zéro*, grandmother, the bank's profit. If the ball lands on *zéro*, everything that was put on the table goes to the bank without counting it up. True, another spin is permitted so as to restart the game, but the bank pays nothing."

"Fancy that! And I don't get anything?"

"No, grandmother, if you staked on *zéro* beforehand, and it comes up *zéro*, they pay you thirty-five times the amount."

"What, thirty-five times? And does it come up often? The fools, why don't they stake on it?"

"The odds are thirty-six to one, grandmother."

"That's rubbish! Potapych! Potapych! Wait, I have money on me—here!" She took a tightly stuffed purse from her pocket and took out a friedrich d'or. "Here, stake it right now on *zéro*."

"Grandmother, *zéro* just came up," I said, "that means it won't come up for a long time now. You'll lose heavily; wait awhile at least."

"Eh, lies, go on, stake!"

"As you wish, but it may not come up till evening, you'll lose as much as a thousand, such things happen."

"Eh, nonsense, nonsense! Nothing ventured, nothing gained. What? you lost? Stake again!"

We lost the second friedrich d'or; staked a third. Grandmother could barely sit still, she simply fastened her burning eyes on the ball bouncing over the grooves of the turning wheel. We lost the third as well. Grandmother was beside herself, she simply couldn't sit still, she even banged her fist on the table when the croupier announced *trente-six** instead of the hoped-for *zéro*.

*Thirty-six.

"Drat it!" grandmother said angrily, "won't that cursed little *zéro* come up sometime soon? I'll wait for it even if it's the death of me! It's all this cursed curly croupier's doing, he never gets it to come up! Alexei Ivanovich, stake two gold pieces at once! If we stake so little, then, even if *zéro* does come up, there won't be any gain."

"Grandmother!"

"Stake them, stake them! They're not yours."

I staked two friedrichs d'or. The ball rolled around the wheel for a while, then began bouncing over the grooves. Grandmother froze and squeezed my hand, and suddenly—plop!

"*Zéro*," announced the croupier.

"You see, you see!" grandmother quickly turned to me, beaming all over and very pleased. "I told you, I told you! The Lord himself put it into my head to stake two gold pieces. Well, how much will I get now? Why don't they give it to me? Potapych, Marfa, where are they? Where have all our people gone? Potapych, Potapych!"

"Later, grandmother," I whispered. "Potapych is by the door, they won't let him in here. Look, grandmother, they're giving you your money, take it!" They tossed her a heavy roll of fifty friedrichs d'or sealed in dark blue paper and counted out another twenty unsealed friedrichs d'or. I raked it all towards grandmother.

"*Faites le jeu, messieurs! Faites le jeu, messieurs! Rien ne va plus?*"* proclaimed the croupier, inviting the stakes and preparing to spin the wheel.

"Lord! we're too late! They're about to spin it! Stake, stake!" grandmother fussed. "Don't dawdle, be quick," she was getting beside herself, nudging me with all her might.

"Stake on what, grandmother?"

"On *zéro*, on *zéro*! on *zéro* again! Stake as much as possible! How much do we have? Seventy friedrichs d'or? No point in saving them, stake twenty friedrichs d'or at one go."

"Collect yourself, grandmother! Sometimes it doesn't come

---

*Place your bets, gentlemen! Place your bets, gentlemen! No more bets?

up once in two hundred turns! I assure you, you'll lose all your capital."

"Eh, lies, lies! stake it! Don't wag your tongue! I know what I'm doing." Grandmother was even shaking with frenzy.

"According to the rules, you're not allowed to stake more than twelve friedrichs d'or at a time on *zéro*, grandmother—so that's what I'm staking."

"How not allowed? You wouldn't be lying, would you? Moosieu, moosieu!" she began nudging the croupier, who was sitting just to her left and preparing to spin, "*combien zéro? douze? douze?*"*

I hastened to explain her question in French.

"*Oui, madame*," the croupier confirmed politely, "just as no single stake may exceed four thousand florins at a time, according to the rules," he added in explanation.

"Well, no help for it, stake twelve."

"*Le jeu est fait!*"† cried the croupier.

The wheel spun, and thirteen came up. We lost!

"Again! again! again! stake again!" cried grandmother. I no longer objected and, shrugging my shoulders, staked another twelve friedrichs d'or. The wheel spun for a long time. Grandmother simply trembled as she watched it. "Does she really think she'll win again on *zéro*?" I thought, looking at her in astonishment. A decided conviction of winning shone in her face, an unfailing expectation that there was just about to be a cry of "*Zéro!*" The ball jumped into the groove.

"*Zéro!*" cried the croupier.

"So there!!!" grandmother turned to me in furious triumph.

I myself was a gambler; I felt it that same moment. My hands and feet were trembling, my head throbbed. Of course, it was a rare case that *zéro* should pop up three times in some ten turns; but there was nothing especially surprising about it. I myself had witnessed, two days ago, how *zéro* came up three times *in a row*, and one of the players, who zealously noted down all the

*How much zero? twelve? twelve?
†The betting is closed!

turns on papers, observed aloud that no longer ago than the previous day that same *zéro* had come up just once in a whole twenty-four hours.

As grandmother had won the most significant sum, they paid her with particular attention and deference. She was to receive exactly four hundred and twenty friedrichs d'or, that is, four thousand florins and twenty friedrichs d'or. She was given the twenty friedrichs d'or in gold and the four thousand in banknotes.

This time grandmother did not call Potapych; she was otherwise occupied. She didn't even nudge me or tremble outwardly. She trembled—if it's possible to put it so—inwardly. She was all concentrated on something, aiming at it:

"Alexei Ivanovich! he said one can stake only four thousand florins a time? Here, take and put this whole four thousand on red," grandmother decided.

It was useless to try talking her out of it. The wheel spun.

"*Rouge!*" announced the croupier.

Again a win of four thousand florins, meaning eight in all. "Give me four here, and put four on red again," grandmother commanded.

I staked four thousand again.

"*Rouge!*" the croupier announced once more.

"A total of twelve! Give it all here. Pour the gold here, into this purse, and put away the banknotes.

"Enough! Home! Roll on!"

CHAPTER XI

THE CHAIR WAS ROLLED to the door at the other end of the room. Grandmother was beaming. All our people crowded around her at once with congratulations. However eccentric grandmother's behavior was, her triumph covered up a lot, and the general no longer feared compromising himself in public by being related to such an odd woman. With a condescending and familiarly cheerful smile, as if placating a child, he congratulated grandmother. However, he was evidently struck, as were all the spectators. The people around were talking and pointing at grandmother. Many walked past her in order to get a closer look. Mr. Astley, standing to one side, was talking about her with two Englishmen of his acquaintance. Several majestic spectators, ladies, gazed at her as at some wonder, with majestic perplexity. Des Grieux simply dissolved in smiles and congratulations.

"*Quelle victoire!*"* he kept saying.

"*Mais, madame, c'était du feu!*"† Mlle Blanche added with a flirtatious smile.

"Yes, ma'am, I just up and won twelve thousand florins! Twelve, nothing, what about the gold? With the gold it comes out to nearly thirteen. How much is that in our money? Some six thousand, eh?"

I reported that it was over seven and, with the exchange what it was, maybe even eight.

"No joking, eight thousand! And you dunderheads sit here and do nothing! Potapych, Marfa, did you see?"

"Dearie, but how can it be? Eight thousand roubles!" Marfa exclaimed, twining about.

"Take, here's five gold pieces from me for each of you, here!"

*What a victory!
†But, madame, it was fire [exciting, brilliant].

Potapych and Marfa rushed to kiss her hands.

"The porters get one friedrich d'or each. Give them a gold piece each, Alexei Ivanovich. What's that attendant bowing for, and the other one also? Congratulating me? Give them each a friedrich d'or as well."

"*Madame la princesse...un pauvre expatrié...malheur continuel...les princes russes sont si généreux,*"* a person twined about the armchair, in a shabby frock coat, a motley waistcoat, a mustache, holding a peaked cap in his outstretched hand, and with an obsequious smile ...

"Give him a friedrich d'or as well. No, give him two; well, enough, there'll be no end to it. Up and carry! Praskovya," she turned to Polina Alexandrovna, "tomorrow I'll buy you stuff for a dress, and also for this Mlle ... how's she called, Mlle Blanche, or something, I'll also buy her stuff for a dress. Translate, Praskovya!"

"*Merci, madame,*" Mlle Blanche curtsied sweetly, twisting her mouth into a mocking smile, which she sent to des Grieux and the general. The general was a bit embarrassed and was terribly glad when we reached the avenue.

"Fedosya, I'm thinking how surprised Fedosya will be now," said grandmother, remembering her acquaintance, the general's nanny. "She should also be given money for a dress. Hey, Alexei Ivanovich, Alexei Ivanovich, give something to this beggar!"

Some ragamuffin with a bent back was going down the road and looking at us.

"Maybe he's not a beggar, grandmother, but some sort of rascal."

"Give! give! give him a gulden!"

I went over and gave it to him. He gazed at me in wild perplexity, though he silently took the gulden. He reeked of wine.

"And you, Alexei Ivanovich, have you tried your luck yet?"

"No, grandmother."

*Madame princess...a poor expatriate...continual misfortune...Russian princes are so generous.

"Your eyes were burning, I saw it."

"I'll try it yet, grandmother, for certain, later on."

"And stake directly on *zéro*! You'll see! How much capital do you have?"

"Only twenty friedrichs d'or, grandmother."

"Not much. I'll lend you fifty friedrichs d'or, if you like. Here's that same roll, take it, and you, dearie, don't get your hopes up, I won't give you anything!" she suddenly turned to the general.

The man was as if bowled over, but he said nothing. Des Grieux frowned.

"*Que diable, c'est une terrible vieille!*"* he whispered to the general through his teeth.

"A beggar, a beggar, again a beggar!" cried grandmother. "Alexei Ivanovich, give this one a gulden, too."

This time we met a gray-haired old man on a wooden leg, in some sort of long-skirted blue frock coat and with a long cane in his hand. He looked like an old soldier. But when I offered him a gulden, he stepped back and examined me menacingly.

"*Was ist's der Teufel!*"† he cried, adding another dozen oaths.

"Eh, the fool!" cried grandmother, waving her hand. "Drive on! I'm hungry! I'll have dinner right now, then loll about for a bit and go back again."

"You want to gamble again, grandmother?" I cried.

"What do you think? You all sit here and mope, so I've got to look at you?"

"*Mais, madame,*" des Grieux came closer, "*les chances peuvent tourner, une seule mauvaise chance et vous perdrez tout . . . surtout avec votre jeu . . . c'était terrible!*"‡

"*Vous perdrez absolument,*"§ chirped Mlle Blanche.

---

*Devil take it, she's a terrible old woman!

†What the devil is this!

‡But, madame . . . luck can turn, one stroke of bad luck and you will lose everything . . . above all the way you play . . . it was terrible!

§You'll surely lose.

"What is it to all of you? It's my money I'll be losing, not yours! And where is that Mr. Astley?" she asked me.

"He stayed at the vauxhall, grandmother."

"A pity; he's such a nice man."

On reaching home, grandmother, meeting the manager while still on the stairs, called to him and boasted of her win; then she called Fedosya, gave her three friedrichs d'or and ordered dinner served. Fedosya and Marfa simply dissolved before her during dinner.

"I'm watching you, dearie," Marfa rattled out, "and I say to Potapych, what is it our dearie means to do? And all that money on the table, all that money, saints alive! in my whole life I never saw so much money, and gentlefolk all around, nothing but gentlefolk. How is it, Potapych, I say, it's all such gentlefolk here? Mother of God, I think, help her. I'm praying for you, dearie, and my heart sinks, it just sinks, I'm trembling, I'm trembling all over. Grant her, Lord, I think, and so here the Lord sent it to you. And till now I'm still trembling, dearie, just trembling all over."

"Alexei Ivanovich, after dinner, at around four, get ready and we'll go. Meanwhile, good-bye—oh, yes, and don't forget to send me some little doctor, I also have to drink the waters. Or else you may forget."

I left grandmother's as if in a daze. I tried to imagine what would happen now with all our people and what turn affairs would take. I saw clearly that they (the general mainly) had not yet managed to collect their senses, even from the first impression. The fact of grandmother's appearance, instead of the telegram about her death (and therefore about the inheritance as well) that had been expected at any moment, had so shattered the whole system of their intentions and already-made decisions, that they treated grandmother's further exploits at roulette with decided perplexity and a sort of stupor, which had come over them all. And yet this second fact was almost more important than the first, because, though grandmother had twice repeated that she would give no money to the general, who could tell—all the same they should not lose hope yet. Des

Grieux, who was involved in all the general's affairs, had not. I was sure that Mlle Blanche, who was also quite involved (what else: a general's wife and a considerable inheritance!) would not lose hope and would use all the seductions of coquetry on grandmother—in contrast to the proud and unyielding Polina, who was not given to tenderness. But now, now, when grandmother had performed such exploits at roulette, now, when grandmother's personality was stamped so clearly and typically before them (an obstinate, domineering old woman, *et tombée en enfance*)—now perhaps all was lost: why, she was pleased, like a child, to have gotten down to it, and, as usually happens, would lose her shirt. God! I thought (and, Lord forgive me, with the most malicious laughter), God, every friedrich d'or grandmother had staked today had left a sore spot in the general's heart, had infuriated des Grieux, and had driven Mlle de Cominges, who felt the spoon going past her mouth, to a frenzy. Here is another fact: even after winning, in her joy, when grandmother had given money to everybody and had taken every passerby for a beggar, even then she had let slip to the general: "But all the same I won't give you anything!" Which meant she was stubbornly fixed on this thought, had promised it to herself—dangerous! dangerous!

All these considerations wandered through my head while I was going up the central stairway from grandmother's to the topmost floor, to my little room. All this concerned me greatly; though, of course, I could guess in advance the main, the thickest threads connecting the actors before me, I still did not ultimately know all the means and secrets of this game. Polina was never fully trusting with me. Though, true, it did happen that she would open her heart to me occasionally, as if inadvertently, I noticed that often, even almost always, after being open, she either turned everything she had said to ridicule, or deliberately made it look confused and false. Oh, she concealed a lot! In any case, I sensed that the finale was approaching for this whole mysterious and tense situation. One more stroke and everything would be finished and revealed. About my own fate, which was also caught up in it all, I almost didn't worry. I was in a strange mood: in my pocket a total of twenty friedrichs d'or; I'm far away in a foreign land, with no post and no means of existence, no hopes, no plans and—it doesn't worry me! If it hadn't been for the thought of Polina, I would simply have surrendered myself entirely to the comic interest of the coming denouement and laughed my head off. But Polina confounds me. Her fate is being decided, I can feel that, but, I confess, it's not at all her fate that troubles me. I'd like to penetrate her secrets; I'd like her to come to me and say: "I love you," and if not, if that madness is unthinkable, then . . . well, what should I wish for? Do I know what to wish for? I'm as if lost myself; all I need is to be near her, in her aura, in her radiance, forever, always, all my life. Beyond that I know nothing! And can I possibly leave her?

On the third floor, in their corridor, it was as if something nudged me. I turned and, twenty or more paces away, saw Polina coming out the door. She seemed to have been waiting and watching for me, and immediately beckoned to me.

"Polina Alexandrovna . . ."

"Quiet!" she warned.

"Imagine," I whispered, "it's as if something just nudged me in the side; I turn around—it's you! As if you give off some kind of electricity!"

"Take this letter," Polina said with a preoccupied and frowning air, probably without hearing what I had just said, "and deliver it personally to Mr. Astley right away. Be quick, I beg you. No reply is needed. He himself . . ."

She didn't finish. "To Mr. Astley?" I repeated in astonishment.

But Polina had already disappeared through the door.

"Aha, so they correspond!" Naturally, I ran at once to look for Mr. Astley, first in his hotel, where I didn't find him, then in the vauxhall, where I ran around all the rooms, and finally, in vexation, almost in despair, on my way home, I met him by chance in a cavalcade of some English men and ladies, on horseback. I beckoned to him, stopped him, and gave him the letter. We had no time even to exchange glances. But I suspect that Mr. Astley deliberately hastened to urge his horse on.

Was I tormented by jealousy? I was indeed in the most broken state of mind. I didn't even want to know what they corresponded about. So he was her confidant! "A friend he may be," I thought, and that was clear (and when had he found time to become one?), "but is there love in it?" "Of course not," reason whispered to me. But reason alone is not enough in such cases. In any case, this, too, was to be clarified. The business was becoming unpleasantly complicated.

I no sooner entered the hotel than the doorman and the manager, coming out of his room, informed me that I was being asked for, looked for, that three times there had been an inquiry about where I was, and a request that I go as quickly as possible to the general's suite. I was in the nastiest state of mind. In the general's study, besides the general himself, I found des Grieux and Mlle Blanche, alone, without her mother. The mother was decidedly a dummy personage, used only for display; when it came to real *business*, Mlle Blanche managed by herself. And the woman scarcely knew anything about her presumed daughter's affairs.

The three of them were hotly conferring about something, and the door of the study was even shut, something that had never happened before. Approaching the door, I heard loud voices—the brazen and caustic talk of des Grieux, the impudently abusive and furious shouting of Blanche, and the pitiful voice of the general, who was apparently trying to justify himself for something. On my appearance, they all seemed to restrain themselves and put themselves to rights. Des Grieux put his hair to rights and made his angry face into a smiling one—with that nasty, officially courteous French smile I hate so much. The general, crushed and at a loss, assumed a dignified air, but somehow mechanically. Mlle Blanche alone made scarcely a change in her anger-flashing physiognomy and only fell silent, directing her gaze at me with impatient expectation. I will note that till then she had treated me with incredible negligence, had not even responded to my greetings—simply hadn't noticed me.

"Alexei Ivanovich," the general began in a gently upbraiding tone, "allow me to declare to you that it is strange, strange in the highest degree ... in short, your behavior regarding me and my family ... in short, strange in the highest degree ..."

"*Eh! ce n'est pas ça,*"* des Grieux interrupted with vexation and contempt. (He decidedly had the upper hand in everything!) "*Mon cher monsieur, notre cher général se trompe†* when he lapses into this tone" (I continue his speech in Russian), "but he wanted to tell you ... that is, to warn you, or, better to say, to earnestly beg you not to ruin him—oh, yes, not to ruin! I am using precisely this expression ..."

"But how, how?" I interrupted.

"Good heavens, you've undertaken to be the guide (or how do they say?) of this old woman, *cette pauvre terrible vieille,*" des Grieux himself became confused, "but she will lose; she will lose her shirt and everything! You've seen yourself, you've witnessed the way she plays! If she begins to lose, she won't leave the table, out of stubbornness, out of anger, and she'll keep on playing, keep on playing, and in such cases one can win nothing back, and then ... then ..."

"And then," the general picked up, "then you will ruin the entire family! Me and my family, we're her heirs, she has no closer relations. I'll tell you frankly: my affairs are in disarray, extreme disarray. You partly know yourself ... If she loses a considerable sum, or even perhaps the whole fortune (oh, God!), what will become of them then, of my children!" (the general turned to des Grieux) "of me!" (He looked at Mlle Blanche, who turned away from him with contempt.) "Alexei Ivanovich, save us, save us! ..."

"But how, General, tell me, how can I ... What do I amount to here?"

"Refuse, refuse, drop her! ..."

"Then she'll find somebody else!" I cried.

"*Ce n'est pas ça, ce n'est pas ça,*" des Grieux interrupted again, "*que diable!* No, don't drop her, but at any rate exhort her, talk

---

*Eh! it's not that.
†My dear sir, our dear general is mistaken ...

to her, distract her ... Well, finally, don't let her lose too much, distract her somehow."

"But how can I do that? If you were to take it upon yourself, M. des Grieux," I added as naïvely as I could.

Here I noticed the quick, fiery, questioning glance Mlle Blanche gave des Grieux. In des Grieux's own face something peculiar flashed, something frank, which he was unable to hold back.

"That's just it, that she won't take me now!" des Grieux cried, waving his hand. "If only! ... later ..."

Des Grieux glanced quickly and significantly at Mlle Blanche.

"*Oh, mon cher Monsieur Alexis, soyez si bon,*"* Mlle Blanche *herself* stepped towards me with an enchanting smile, seized me by both hands, and pressed them firmly. Damn it all, that devilish face knew how to change in a single second! She instantly acquired such a pleading face, so sweet, childishly smiling, and even mischievous; at the end of the phrase she gave me a sly wink, in secret from everyone; did she mean to undercut me all at once, or what? And it didn't come off badly—only it was crude, terribly crude.

The general jumped up after her—precisely jumped:

"Alexei Ivanovich, forgive me for speaking to you like that earlier, I meant to say something else ... I beg you, I implore you, I bow down before you Russian-style—you, you alone can save us! Mlle de Cominges and I implore you—you understand? you do understand?" he implored, indicating Mlle Blanche to me with his eyes. He was very pitiful.

At that moment there came three quiet and respectful knocks at the door; they opened—the floorboy had knocked, and a few steps behind him stood Potapych. The ambassadors were from grandmother. There was a request to find me and deliver me immediately—"she being angry," Potapych informed me.

"But it's still only half-past three!"

"She couldn't sleep, kept tossing, then suddenly got up,

*Oh, my dear Monsieur Alexis, be so good.

demanded her chair, and sent for you. She's already on the porch, sir..."

"*Quelle mégère!*"* cried des Grieux.

Indeed, I found grandmother already on the porch, losing patience over my absence. She couldn't wait till four o'clock.

"Well, lift me up!" she cried, and we set off again for the roulette tables.

*What a shrew!

CHAPTER XII

GRANDMOTHER WAS IN AN impatient and irritable state of mind; it was clear that roulette had lodged itself firmly in her head. She paid no attention to anything else, and was generally extremely distracted. For instance, she didn't ask questions about anything on the way, as she had earlier. Seeing a very rich carriage that raced past us like the wind, she raised her hand and asked: "What's that? Whose is it?"—but didn't seem to hear my reply; her pensiveness was constantly broken by abrupt and impatient movements and actions. When I pointed out Baron and Baroness Wurmerhelm in the distance, as we were approaching the vauxhall, she looked distractedly and said quite indifferently: "Ah!"—and, turning quickly to Potapych and Marfa, who were walking behind her, said sharply:

"Well, why are you tagging along? You needn't be taken every time! Go home! You're enough for me," she added to me, when the other two hastily bowed and returned home.

Grandmother was already expected in the vauxhall. She was at once allotted the same place next to the croupier. It seems to me that these croupiers, who are always so decorous and pretend to be ordinary officials for whom it is decidedly almost all the same whether the bank wins or loses, are not at all indifferent to the bank's losses and, of course, are furnished with certain instructions for attracting gamblers and keeping better watch over the establishment's interests—for which they certainly receive prizes and awards. At any rate they already looked upon grandmother as a nice little victim. Thereupon, what had been assumed of us—happened.

Here's how it went.

Grandmother fell directly on *zéro* and straight away ordered me to stake twelve friedrichs d'or. We staked once, twice, three times—*zéro* wouldn't come up. "Go on, stake!" grandmother nudged me impatiently. I obeyed.

"How many times have we lost?" she asked finally, grinding her teeth in impatience.

"That was the twelfth stake, grandmother. We've lost a hundred and forty-four friedrichs d'or. I tell you, grandmother, it may not be till evening..."

"Silence!" grandmother interrupted. "Stake on *zéro*, and right now stake a thousand guldens on red. Here, take the banknote."

Red came up, but the *zéro* lost again; we won back a thousand guldens.

"See, see!" whispered grandmother, "we won back almost everything we lost. Stake again on *zéro*; we'll stake ten more times and drop it."

But by the fifth time grandmother had become quite bored.

"To hell with it, drop that nasty little *zéro*. Here, stake all four thousand guldens on red," she ordered.

"Grandmother! it's too much, what if red doesn't come up?" I implored; but grandmother nearly hit me. (However, she nudged me so hard that one could almost call it beating.) There was nothing to be done, I staked all the four thousand guldens we had won earlier on red. The wheel spun. Grandmother sat calmly and proudly erect, not doubting the certainty of winning.

"*Zéro*," announced the croupier.

At first grandmother didn't understand, but when she saw the croupier rake in her four thousand guldens along with everything that was on the table, and learned that the *zéro* which had taken so long to come up, and on which we had lost almost two hundred friedrichs d'or, had popped up, as if on purpose, just when grandmother denounced it and dropped it, she cried "Ah!" and clasped her hands for the whole hall to see. People around her even laughed.

"Saints alive! The cursed thing had to pop up just now!" grandmother yelled. "What a fiendish, fiendish thing! It's you! It's all you!" she fell upon me ferociously, shoving me. "You talked me out of it."

"Grandmother, I talked sense to you, how can I be responsible for all the chances?"

"I'll give you your chances!" she whispered threateningly. "Get out of here!"

"Good-bye, grandmother," I turned to leave.

"Alexei Ivanovich, Alexei Ivanovich, stay! Where are you going? Well, what is it? what is it? Look, he's angry! Fool! Stay, stay awhile, don't be angry, I'm a fool myself! Well, tell me, what am I to do now?"

"I won't venture to tell you, grandmother, because you're going to accuse me. Play on your own; order me, and I'll stake."

"Well, well! so stake another four thousand guldens on red! Here's my wallet, take it." She took the wallet from her pocket and gave it to me. "Well, take it quickly, there's twenty thousand roubles in cash here."

"Grandmother," I whispered, "such amounts..."

"I'll win it back if it kills me. Stake!" We staked and lost.

"Stake, stake, stake the whole eight thousand!"

"I can't, grandmother, the biggest stake is four!..."

"Stake four then!"

This time we won. Grandmother took heart. "See, see!" she nudged me. "Stake four again."

We staked and lost; staked again and lost again.

"Grandmother, the whole twelve thousand is gone," I reported.

"I see it's gone," she said in some sort of calm fury, if I may put it so, "I see, dearie, I see," she muttered, staring fixedly in front of her and as if pondering. "Eh, even if it kills me, stake another four thousand guldens!"

"But we have no money, grandmother; there are some Russian five percent notes and some postal money orders in the wallet, but no money."

"And in the purse?"

"Only small change left, grandmother."

"Do they have exchange bureaus here? I was told I could cash any Russian papers here," grandmother asked resolutely.

"Oh, as much as you like! But you'll lose so much on the exchange that...the Jew himself will be horrified."

"Rubbish! I'll win it back. Take me. Call those blockheads!"

I rolled the chair away, the porters appeared, and we rolled out of the vauxhall. "Hurry, hurry!" grandmother commanded. "Show the way, Alexei Ivanovich, the shortest...is it far?"

"Two steps away, grandmother."

But at the turn from the green into the avenue, we met our whole company: the general, des Grieux, and Mlle Blanche with her mama. Polina Alexandrovna was not with them, nor was Mr. Astley.

"Well, well, well! no stopping!" shouted grandmother. "Well, what do you care? I have no time for you!"

I walked behind; des Grieux sprang over to me.

"She lost all she won in the morning and blew twelve thousand guldens of her own. We're on our way to exchange the five percent notes," I whispered to him hurriedly.

Des Grieux stamped his foot and dashed to tell the general. We went on rolling grandmother.

"Stop her, stop her!" the general whispered in a frenzy.

"You go and try stopping her," I whispered to him.

"Auntie!" the general approached, "auntie...we're just... we're just..." his voice trembled and faltered, "going to hire horses and drive out of town...A most delightful view...a *point*...we were on our way to invite you."

"Eh, you and your *point!*" grandmother waved him away irritably.

"There's a village...we'll have tea..." the general went on, now in total despair.

"*Nous boirons du lait, sur l'herbe fraîche,*"* des Grieux added with ferocious spite.

Du lait, de l'herbe fraîche—that's all a Parisian bourgeois has of the ideally idyllic; therein, as everybody knows, lies his view of "*la nature et la vérité!*"†[10]

---

*We'll drink milk, in the fresh grass.
†Nature and truth.

"Eh, you and your milk! Go and guzzle it yourself, it gives me a bellyache. Why are you bothering me?!" cried grandmother. "I tell you, I have no time!"

"Here we are, grandmother!" I cried. "This it it!"

We rolled up to the house where the banker's office was. I went to exchange the notes; grandmother stayed waiting by the entrance; des Grieux, the general, and Blanche stood to one side, not knowing what to do. Grandmother looked at them wrathfully, and they went off down the road to the vauxhall.

I was offered such terrible terms that I didn't dare accept and went back to grandmother to ask for instructions.

"Ah, the robbers!" she cried, clasping her hands. "Well! Never mind! Exchange them!" she cried resolutely. "Wait, call the banker to me!"

"Maybe one of the clerks, grandmother?"

"All right, a clerk, it's all the same. Ah, the robbers!"

The clerk agreed to come out, having learned that he had been asked by a paralyzed old countess who couldn't walk. Grandmother reproached him for thievery, at length, wrathfully, and loudly, and bargained with him in a mixture of Russian, French, and German, with me helping to translate. The grave clerk kept looking at the two of us and silently wagging his head. He gazed at grandmother even with a much too intent curiosity—which was impolite. Finally, he began to smile.

"Well, away with you!" cried grandmother. "Choke on my money! Exchange with him, Alexei Ivanovich, there's no time, otherwise we could go elsewhere..."

"The clerk says others will give still less."

I don't remember the figures exactly, but it was terrible. I exchanged about twelve thousand florins in gold and notes, took the receipt, and brought it to grandmother.

"Well! well! well! No point in counting it," she waved her hands, "quick, quick, quick!"

"I'll never stake on that cursed *zéro*, nor on red either," she said as we approached the vauxhall.

This time I tried as hard as I could to persuade her to make smaller stakes, insisting that, with a turn of the chances, there would always be a moment for staking a big amount. But she was so impatient that, though she agreed at first, it was impossible to hold her back during the play. As soon as she began to win stakes of ten or twenty friedrichs d'or, "Well, there! Well, there!" she began nudging me, "well, there, we've won— if we'd staked four thousand instead of ten, we'd have won four thousand, and what now? It's all you, all you!"

And vexed as I was, watching her play, I finally decided to keep quiet and give no more advice.

Suddenly des Grieux sprang over. The three of them were nearby; I noticed that Mlle Blanche and her mama were standing to one side, exchanging courtesies with the little prince. The general was obviously out of favor, almost in the doghouse. Blanche didn't even want to look at him, though he fidgeted about her with all his might. Poor general! He turned pale, red, trembled, and even no longer followed grandmother's play. Blanche and the little prince finally left; the general ran after them.

"*Madame, madame,*" des Grieux whispered to grandmother in a honeyed voice, having pushed his way close to her ear. "*Madame,* stake no go that way...no, no, no possible..." he spoke in distorted Russian, "no!"

"And how, then? Go on, teach me!" grandmother turned to him. Des Grieux suddenly began babbling rapidly in French, giving advice, fussing, saying one had to wait for the chance, started calculating some numbers...Grandmother understood nothing. He turned to me constantly, asking me to translate; jabbed his finger at the table, pointing, finally snatched a pencil and was beginning to work something out on paper. Grandmother finally lost patience.

"Well, away, away with you! it's all rubbish! *Madame, madame*—and he doesn't understand a thing himself. Away!"

"*Mais, madame,*" chirped des Grieux, and again he began nudging and pointing. He was all worked up.

"Well, stake once as he says," grandmother told me, "let's see; maybe it will really work."

Des Grieux wanted only to distract her from big stakes: he

suggested staking on numbers singly and in groups. I staked, at his direction, one friedrich d'or on each of the series of odd numbers from one to twelve, and five friedrichs d'or on groups of numbers between twelve and eighteen, and between eighteen and twenty-four: in all we staked sixteen friedrichs d'or.

The wheel spun. "*Zéro*," cried the croupier. We lost everything.

"What a blockhead!" cried grandmother, turning to des Grieux. "Vile little Frenchman that you are! You and your fiendish advice! Away, away! He doesn't understand a thing, and he pokes his nose into it anyway!"

Terribly offended, des Grieux shrugged his shoulders, gave grandmother a contemptuous look, and walked off. He felt ashamed now that he had gotten involved; he just couldn't help it.

An hour later, despite all our efforts, we had lost everything.

"Home!" cried grandmother.

She didn't say a word till we got to the avenue. In the avenue and already approaching the hotel, exclamations began to escape her.

"What a fool! what a great big fool! You old fool, you!"

We had only just entered the suite: "Bring me tea!" grandmother cried, "and get ready at once! We're going!"

"Where would you be pleased to be going, dearie?" Marfa tried to ask.

"What business is that of yours? To your last, shoemaker! Potapych, pack up everything, all the luggage! We're going back to Moscow! I've *verspieled** away fifteen thousand roubles!"

"Fifteen thousand, dearie! My God!" cried Potapych, clasping his hands touchingly, probably hoping to oblige.

"Well, well, you fool! None of this sniveling! Silence! Get ready! The bill, quickly, quickly!"

"The next train leaves at half-past nine, grandmother," I reported, to stop her furor.

"And what is it now?"

---

*Gambled away (distortion of the German *verspielt*).

"Half-past seven."

"How vexing! Well, never mind! Alexei Ivanovich, I haven't a kopeck. Here are two more notes, run off to that place, exhange them for me. Otherwise I'll have nothing for the road."

I went. Half an hour later, on returning to the hotel, I found all our people at grandmother's. Having learned that grandmother was leaving altogether for Moscow, they seemed to be even more struck than by her losses. Suppose that going away would save her fortune, but what would become of the general now? Who would pay des Grieux? Mlle Blanche certainly wouldn't wait until grandmother died, and would probably slip away now with the little prince or somebody else. They were all standing in front of her, comforting her, trying to talk sense into her. Polina again was not there. Grandmother was shouting furiously at them.

"Leave me alone, you devils! What business is it of yours? Why is this goat-beard getting at me?" she shouted at des Grieux. "And you, you shank of a girl, what do you want?" she turned to Mlle Blanche. "What are you fussing about?"

"*Diantre!*"* whispered Mlle Blanche, her eyes flashing with rage, but she suddenly burst out laughing and left.

"*Elle vivra cent ans!*"† she cried to the general from the doorway.

"Ah, so you're counting on my death?" grandmother screamed at the general. "Get out! Throw them all out, Alexei Ivanovich! Is it any of your business? I've blown my money, not yours!"

The general shrugged his shoulders, stooped, and left. Des Grieux followed.

"Call Praskovya," grandmother told Marfa.

Five minutes later Marfa returned with Polina. All this time Polina had been sitting in her room with the children and, it seems, had purposely decided not to go out all day. Her face was serious, sad, and preoccupied.

"Praskovya," grandmother began, "is it true, what I learned

*The deuce!
†She'll live a hundred years!

from someone today, that your fool of a stepfather supposedly wants to marry that silly French fidget—an actress, isn't she, or something still worse? Tell me, is it true?"

"I don't know for certain, grandmother," Polina answered, "but from the words of Mlle Blanche herself, who finds concealment unnecessary, I conclude..."

"Enough!" grandmother interrupted energetically, "I understand everything! I always reckoned he was up to just that, and always considered him the emptiest and flightiest of men. He goes around swaggering that he's a general (he got the rank after he retired as a colonel), and putting on airs. I know it all, my dear, how you sent telegram after telegram to Moscow— 'Will the old crone turn her toes up soon?' They were waiting for the inheritance; without money, that mean wench—what's her name?—de Cominges or something, wouldn't even take him as a lackey, with false teeth at that. They say she has heaps of money herself, lends it on interest, having earned it in a nice way. I don't blame you, Praskovya; it wasn't you who sent the telegrams; nor do I want to remember old wrongs. I know what a nasty character you've got—a wasp! it swells when you sting, but I feel sorry for you, because I loved your late mother Katerina. Well, do you want to drop all this here and come with me? You've got nowhere to go; and it's improper for you to be with them now. Wait!" grandmother interrupted Polina, who was about to begin a reply, "I haven't finished yet. I won't demand anything of you. My house in Moscow you know— it's a palace, you can have a whole floor and not come down to see me for weeks, if you don't fancy my character. Well, do you want to or not?"

"Allow me to ask you first: do you really mean to leave right now?"

"Do you think I'm joking, dearie? I said I'd leave, and I'll leave. I've dumped fifteen thousand roubles today at your thrice-cursed roulette. Five years ago I promised to replace the wooden church on my estate near Moscow with a stone one, and instead I whistled it away here. Now, dearie, I'm going to go and build that church."

"And the waters, grandmother? Haven't you come to take the waters?"

"Eh, you and your waters! Don't vex me, Praskovya; are you doing it on purpose, or what? Tell me, will you come along?"

"I thank you very, very much, grandmother," Polina began with feeling, "for the refuge you're offering me. You've partly guessed my situation. I'm so grateful that, believe me, I may even come to you soon; but now there are reasons...important ones...and I can't decide at once, this minute. If you were staying two weeks..."

"You mean you don't want to?"

"I mean I can't. Besides, in any case I can't leave my brother and sister, and since...since...since they may indeed be all but abandoned, then...if you'll take me with the little ones, grandmother, I'll certainly come to you, and, believe me, I'll come to deserve it of you," she added warmly, "but without the children I can't, grandmother."

"Well, don't snivel!" (Polina had never thought of sniveling, and she never cried.) "There'll be room for the chicks as well; it's a big chicken coop. Besides, it's time they went to school. Well, so you're not coming now? Well, Praskovya, watch out! I'd like to wish you well, but I know why you're not coming. I know everything, Praskovya! That little Frenchman won't bring you any good."

Polina flushed. I gave a start. (Everybody knows! I alone, therefore, know nothing!)

"Well, well, don't frown. I won't embroider on it. Only watch out that nothing bad happens, understand? You're a smart girl; I'd be sorry for you. Well, enough, I don't even want to look at you all! Go! Good-bye!"

"I'll still come to see you off, grandmother," said Polina.

"No need to; don't bother me, I'm sick of you all."

Polina kissed grandmother's hand, but she pulled her hand away and kissed Polina on the cheek.

As she passed me, Polina glanced at me quickly and at once turned away.

"Well, good-bye to you, too, Alexei Ivanovich! It's only an

hour till the train. And you're tired of me, I think. Here, take these fifty gold pieces."

"I humbly thank you, grandmother, I'm ashamed to ..."

"Well, well!" cried grandmother, but so energetically and menacingly that I didn't dare refuse and accepted.

"In Moscow, when you're running around without a job, come to me; I'll recommend you to someone. Well, out with you!"

I went to my room and lay down on the bed. I think I lay for half an hour on my back, my hands thrust behind my head. The catastrophe had broken out, there was something to think about. I decided imperatively to talk with Polina tomorrow. Ah! the little Frenchman? So then it's true! What could there be to it, though? Polina and des Grieux! Lord, what a juxtaposition!

All this was simply unbelievable. I suddenly jumped up, beside myself, to go looking for Mr. Astley at once and make him speak at all costs. Here, too, of course, he knows more than I do. Mr. Astley? There's another riddle for me!

But suddenly there came a knock at my door. I looked— Potapych.

"Alexei Ivanovich, my dear: the mistress, she's calling."

"What is it? Is she leaving or something? It's still twenty minutes till the train."

"She's restless, my dear, can barely sit still. 'Quick, quick!'— meaning you, my dear; for Christ's sake, don't delay."

I raced downstairs at once. Grandmother had already been rolled out to the corridor. She had the wallet in her hands.

"Alexei Ivanovich, lead the way, come on! ..."

"Where to, grandmother?"

"It may kill me, but I'll win back what I lost! Well, march, no questions! They play till midnight there, don't they?"

I was dumbfounded, reflected, but made up my mind at once.

"As you will, Antonida Vassilyevna, but I won't go."

"Why not? What's this now? Are you all moonstruck or something?"

"As you will, but afterwards I'd reproach myself; I don't want to! I don't want either to witness it or to participate in it; spare me, Antonida Vassilyevna. Here are your fifty friedrichs d'or back; good-bye!" And, placing the roll of friedrichs d'or right there on a little table next to grandmother's chair, I bowed and left.

"What rubbish!" grandmother cried after me. "Don't come then, if you please, I'll find the way myself! Potapych, come with me! Well, pick me up, get going."

I didn't find Mr. Astley and went back home. Late, past midnight, I learned from Potapych how grandmother's day had ended. She had lost everything I had exchanged for her earlier, that is, another ten thousand roubles, by our reckoning. That same little Pole to whom she had given two friedrichs d'or had attached himself to her and guided her play the whole time. First, before the little Pole, she had made Potapych stake for her, but soon chased him away; it was then that the little Pole popped up. As luck would have it, he understood Russian and could even chatter in a mixture of three languages, so that they somehow managed to understand each other. Grandmother scolded him mercilessly all the time, and though he constantly "laid himself out at my lady's feet," he was "no comparison with you, Alexei Ivanovich," Potapych recounted. "She treated you *as a gentleman*, but that one—I saw it with my own eyes, God strike me dead—he stole from her right there at the table. She caught him twice and railed at him, my dear, railed at him with all sorts of words, and even pulled his hair once, really, I'm not lying, so that there was laughter all around. She lost everything, my dear; everything she had, everything you exchanged for her. We brought her here, the dear lady—she just asked for a drink of water, crossed herself, and went to bed. Wore herself out, must be, fell asleep at once. May God send her angelic dreams! Ah, these foreign parts!" Potapych concluded. "I said no good would come of it. We ought to hurry back to our Moscow! We've got everything at home in Moscow. A garden, flowers such as don't exist here, fragrance, apples ripening, vastness—no, she had to go abroad! Oh, oh, oh!..."

CHAPTER XIII

I T'S ALMOST A WHOLE month now since I've touched these notes of mine, begun under the effect of strong though disorderly impressions. The catastrophe, the approach of which I anticipated then, did come, but a hundred times more drastically and unexpectedly than I had thought. It was all something strange, ugly, and even tragic, at any rate for me. Certain things happened to me that were almost miraculous; so at least I look at them to this day—though from another point of view, and especially judging by the whirl I was then spinning in, they were at most only somewhat out of the ordinary. But most miraculous of all for me was the way I regarded these events. To this day I don't understand myself! And it all flew away like a dream—even my passion, and yet it really was strong and true, but ... where has it gone now? Indeed, the thought occasionally flits through my head: "Didn't I go out of my mind then and spend the whole time sitting in a madhouse somewhere, and maybe I'm sitting there now—so that for me it was all a *seeming* and only *seems* to this day ..."

I collected and reread my pages. (Who knows, maybe so as to convince myself that I hadn't written them in the madhouse?) Now I'm all alone. Autumn is coming, the leaves are turning yellow. I'm sitting in this dreary little town (oh, how dreary little German towns are!), and instead of thinking over the next step, I live under the influence of feelings just past, under the influence of fresh memories, under the influence of all this recent whirl, which drew me into that turbulence then, and threw me out of it again somewhere. It still seems to me at times that I'm spinning in the same whirl, and that the storm is about to rush upon me, snatch me up with its wing in passing, and I will again break out of all order and sense of measure, and spin, spin, spin ...

However, maybe I'll settle somehow and stop spinning, if I give myself as precise an account as possible of all that happened this month. I'm drawn to my pen again; and sometimes there's nothing at all to do in the evenings. Strangely, in order to occupy myself with at least something, I go to the mangy local library and take out the novels of Paul de Kock[11] (in German translation!), which I can barely stand, but I read them and—marvel at myself: it's as if I'm afraid to spoil the charm of what has only just passed by a serious book or some serious occupation. As if this ugly dream and all the impressions it left behind are so dear to me that I'm even afraid to touch it with something new, lest it vanish in smoke! Is it so dear to me, or what? Yes, of course it is; maybe I'll remember it even forty years later ...

And so, I set about writing. However, all this can now be told partially and more briefly: the impressions are not at all the same ...

First, to finish with grandmother. The next day she definitively lost everything. That's how it had to happen: once that kind of person starts out on this path, then, like sliding down a snowy hill on a sled, it all goes faster and faster. She played all day, until eight o'clock in the evening; I wasn't present when she played and know it only from hearsay.

Potapych attended her at the vauxhall the whole day. The little Poles who guided grandmother changed several times that day. She started by chasing away the previous day's little Pole, whose hair she had pulled, and taking another one, but he turned out to be almost worse. Having chased that one away and taken back the first one, who hadn't left and poked about during the whole time of his banishment right there behind her chair, thrusting his head in every moment—she finally fell into decided despair. The second chased-away little Pole also refused to leave; one stationed himself to her right, the other to her left. They quarreled and abused each other all the time over stakes and strategy, called each other *łajdak** and other Polish

*Scoundrel.

compliments, then made peace again, threw money around without any order, gave directions in vain. When they quarreled, they each staked on his own side, one, for instance, on red, and the other, at the same time, on black. The end was that they got grandmother completely muddled and thrown off, so that she finally turned to the old croupier, all but in tears, asking him to protect her and chase them away. They were, in fact, chased away at once, despite their shouts and protests: they both shouted in unison, trying to prove that grandmother owed them money, that she had deceived them in some way, had acted dishonestly, meanly. Miserable Potapych told it to me in tears, that very evening after they lost, complaining that the Poles had stuffed their pockets with money, that he himself had seen them stealing shamelessly and constantly shoving money into their pockets. One, for instance, would wheedle five friedrichs d'or from grandmother for his labors and straight away stake them on the roulette table next to grandmother's stakes. Grandmother would win, and he would shout that it was his stake that had won, and grandmother's had lost. When they were chased out, Potapych stepped forward and reported that they had pockets full of gold. Grandmother at once asked the croupier to take measures, and though both little Poles began squawking (just like two snatched roosters), the police appeared and their pockets were emptied at once in grandmother's favor. All that day, until she lost everything, grandmother had enjoyed a conspicuous authority with the croupiers and the whole vauxhall administration. Her renown had gradually spread through the town. All the visitors to the spa, from all nations, the ordinary and the most notable, flocked to look at *"une vieille comtesse russe tombée en enfance,"* who had already lost "several million."

But grandmother gained very, very little from having rid herself of the two Poles. In their place a third Pole appeared at once to serve her, speaking perfectly pure Russian, dressed like a gentleman, though he smacked of the footman all the same, with enormous mustaches and with *gonor.** He, too, kissed "the

*Honor (Polish).

pani's feet"* and "laid himself out at the *pani*'s feet," but he treated everyone around him with arrogance, gave despotic orders—in short, he established himself at once not as grand-mother's servant, but as her master. Every moment, with every round, he turned to her and swore terrible oaths that he was a *gonorable pan*† and would not take a kopeck of grandmother's money. He repeated these oaths so often that she finally became frightened. But since this *pan* at first actually seemed to improve her play and began to win a little, grandmother herself could no longer part with him. An hour later the two previous little Poles, who had been taken out of the vauxhall, appeared once more behind grandmother's chair, again offering their services, if only to run errands. Potapych swore by God that the *gonorable pan* exchanged winks with them and even put something in their hands. Since grandmother had had no dinner and had hardly ever left her chair, one of the Poles actually proved useful: he ran next door to the vauxhall dining room and fetched her a cup of bouillon, and later tea as well. They both went, however. But towards the end of the day, when everybody could see that she was about to lose her last banknote, there were as many as six little Poles standing behind her chair, never seen or heard of before. And by the time grandmother was losing her last coins, they all not only didn't listen to her, but didn't even notice her, reached out to the table right over her, grabbed the money them-selves, gave orders and placed stakes themselves, argued and shouted, chatted with the *gonorable pan* in a *pan*-brotherly way, while the *gonorable pan* even all but forgot about grandmother's existence. Even when, having lost everything, grandmother was returning to the hotel at eight o'clock in the evening, three or four little Poles still refused to leave her and ran on both sides of her chair, shouting with all their might and insisting in a quick patter that grandmother had cheated them in some way and had to pay them something. Thus they came right up to the hotel, where, at last, they were driven away.

*The lady's feet.
†Honorable gentleman (distorted Polish).

By Potapych's reckoning, grandmother lost in that day a total of ninety thousand roubles, besides the money she had lost the day before. All her bonds—the five percent bonds, the state bonds, all the shares she had brought with her—she had cashed one after the other. I marveled at her ability to hold out for the whole seven or eight hours, sitting in her chair and hardly ever leaving the table, but Potapych told me that, on some three occasions, she had actually begun to win heavily, and, borne up by renewed hope, had no longer been able to leave. However, gamblers know how a man can sit almost around the clock in the same place over cards, without taking his eyes off the right one or the left.

Meanwhile, all that day quite decisive things were happening with us in the hotel. In the morning, before eleven o'clock, when grandmother was still at home, our people—that is, the general and des Grieux—resolved upon an ultimate step. Learning that grandmother had no thought of leaving, but, on the contrary, was setting out again for the vauxhall, the whole conclave of them (except for Polina) came to talk things over with her definitively and even *openly*. The general, trembling and his heart sinking in view of the terrible consequences for him, even overdid it: after half an hour of begging and pleading, and even having openly acknowledged everything, that is, all his debts, and even his passion for Mlle Blanche (he was totally lost), the general suddenly assumed a threatening tone and even began shouting and stamping his feet at grandmother; he shouted that she had disgraced their name, that she had become a scandal for the whole town, and finally... finally: "You have disgraced the name of Russia, madam!" shouted the general, "and there are police for that!" Grandmother finally drove him out with a stick (a real stick). That morning the general and des Grieux conferred once or twice more, interested precisely in whether it might in fact be possible to use the police. That is, thus and so, the unfortunate but venerable old lady has lost her wits, is gambling away her last money, and so on. In short, mightn't it be possible to petition for some sort of custody or restriction?... But des Grieux only shrugged his shoulders and laughed in the face of the general, who was now pouring out complete drivel and running up and down the study. Finally, des Grieux waved his hand and disappeared somewhere. In the evening it turned out that he had left the hotel altogether, having first talked things over quite decisively and mysteriously with Mlle Blanche. As for Mlle Blanche, she had taken definitive measures that same morning: she had thrust the general away from her altogether and did not even allow him to come into her presence. When the general ran after her to the vauxhall and met her arm in arm with the little prince, neither she nor Mme *la veuve* Cominges recognized him. The little prince also did not bow to him. All that day Mlle Blanche probed and worked on the prince, so that he would finally declare himself decisively. But, alas! She was cruelly deceived in counting on the prince! This minor catastrophe took place in the evening; it was suddenly discovered that the prince was naked as a worm, and was counting on borrowing money from her on a promissory note and playing roulette. Blanche indignantly threw him out and locked herself in her room.

That same morning I went to see Mr. Astley, or, better to say, I spent the whole morning looking for Mr. Astley, but couldn't find him anywhere. He was neither at home, nor in the vauxhall, nor in the park. He did not dine at his hotel that day. Between four and five, I suddenly saw him coming from the railway platform straight to the Hôtel d'Angleterre. He was hurrying and very preoccupied, though it was hard to make out the preoccupation or any sort of perplexity in his face. He offered me his hand affably, with his usual exclamation: "Ah!" but without stopping in the road and continuing on his way at a rather quick pace. I tagged along behind him; but he was somehow able to answer me in such a way that I didn't manage to ask him about anything. Besides, for some reason I was terribly ashamed to ask about Polina; he didn't ask a word about her himself. I told him about grandmother; he listened attentively and gravely, and shrugged his shoulders.

"She'll lose everything," I observed.

"Oh, yes," he replied, "she already went to play earlier, as

I was leaving, and so I knew for certain that she'd lose. If I have time I'll stop by the vauxhall to have a look, because it's curious..."

"Where did you go?" I cried, amazed that I hadn't asked till then.

"I was in Frankfurt."

"On business?"

"Yes, on business."

Well, what more was there for me to ask? However, I was still walking beside him, but he suddenly turned into the Hôtel des Quatre Saisons, which stood on the road, nodded to me, and disappeared. On the way home I gradually realized that, even if I talked with him for two hours, I would learn decidedly nothing, because... I had nothing to ask him! Yes, of course, it was so! There was no way I could now formulate my question.

All that day, Polina either walked in the park with the children and the nanny, or sat at home. She had long been avoiding the general and barely spoke to him, at any rate about anything serious. I had long noticed it. But, knowing the situation the general was in that day, I thought he couldn't pass her by, that is, it was impossible for there not to be any important family discussions. Nevertheless, when, on returning to the hotel after my conversation with Mr. Astley, I met Polina and the children, her face reflected the most untroubled calm, as if all the family storms had passed by her alone. In response to my bow she nodded her head. I came to my room totally angry.

Of course, after the incident with the Wurmerhelms, I avoided talking with her and never once got together with her. In that I was partly showing off and posturing; but as time went on, real indignation seethed in me more and more. Even if she didn't love me in the least, it still seemed wrong to trample on my feelings that way and receive my declarations with such contempt. She does know that I truly love her; she herself has allowed, has permitted me to speak that way with her! True, it began somehow strangely with us. Sometime long ago now, a good two months back, I began to notice that she wanted to make me her friend, a confidant, and she was even partly testing me. But for some reason it didn't get going between us then; and instead it has remained in these present strange relations; that was why I began to speak that way with her. But if she's repulsed by my love, why not forbid me outright to speak of it?

She doesn't forbid me; she herself even occasionally initiated a conversation with me, and...of course, did it to make fun of me. I know for certain, I firmly noted it—it was a pleasure for her to listen to me and exacerbate me painfully, to stun me suddenly with a show of the greatest contempt and negligence. And she knows that I can't live without her. It's three days now since the story with the baron, and I can no longer bear our *separation*. When I met her just now near the vauxhall, my heart beat so hard that I turned pale. But she can't survive without me either! She needs me and—can it be, can it be only as a buffoon Balakirev?[12]

She has a secret—that's clear! Her conversation with grandmother pricked my heart painfully. A thousand times I've invited her to be frank with me, and she knew that I was actually ready to lay down my life for her. But she always got off with near contempt, or, instead of the sacrifice of my life, which I had offered her, demanded escapades from me like that time with the baron! Isn't it outrageous? Can it be that for her the whole world is in this Frenchman? And Mr. Astley? But here the affair was becoming decidedly incomprehensible, and meanwhile—God, how I suffered!

Having come home, in a fit of rage I seized a pen and scribbled the following:

> Polina Alexandrovna, I see clearly that the denouement has come, which will, of course, affect you as well. I repeat for the last time: do you need my life or not? If you need me *for anything at all*—I am at your disposal, and meanwhile I'll be sitting in my room, at least most of the time, and won't go anywhere. If need be—write me or send for me.

I sealed this note and sent it with the floorboy, with orders that he put it directly into her hands. I didn't expect an answer, but three minutes later the floorboy came back, saying that "the lady sends her greetings."

Sometime after six I was summoned to the general.

He was in his study and dressed as if he was about to go out. His hat and stick lay on the sofa. I fancied, as I came in, that he was standing in the middle of the room, his legs straddled, his head bowed, saying something aloud to himself. But as soon as he saw me, he rushed to me all but with a shout, so that I involuntarily drew back and was about to run away; but he seized me by both hands and pulled me to the sofa; he sat down on the sofa himself, seated me directly opposite him in an armchair, and, without letting go of my hands, with trembling lips, with tears suddenly glistening on his eyelashes, said to me in a pleading voice:

"Alexei Ivanovich, save me, save me, spare me!"

For a long time I could understand nothing; he kept talking, talking, talking, and kept repeating: "Spare me, spare me!" I finally realized that he expected something like advice from me; or, better to say, abandoned by everybody, anguished and anxious, he had remembered me and summoned me in order to talk, talk, talk.

He had gone crazy, or at any rate was bewildered in the highest degree. He clasped his hands and was ready to throw himself on his knees before me to persuade me to—what do you think?—to go at once to Mlle Blanche and beg her, exhort her to return to him and marry him.

"For pity's sake, General," I cried, "it may well be that Mlle Blanche hasn't noticed me up to now! What can I do?"

But it was useless to object: he didn't understand what was said to him. He began talking about grandmother as well, only it was terribly incoherent; he still stood by the notion of sending for the police.

"With us, with us," he began, suddenly boiling over with indignation, "in short, with us, in our well-organized state, where authorities do exist, such old women would immediately be taken into custody! Yes, my dear sir, yes," he went on, suddenly lapsing into a scolding tone, jumping up and pacing the room, "you still don't know that, my dear sir," he turned to some imaginary dear sir in the corner, "so now you'll learn...yes, sir...with us such old women get tied in a knot, yes, a knot, a knot, sir...oh, devil take it!"

And he threw himself down on the sofa again, but a minute later, all but spluttering, breathless, he hastened to tell me that Mlle Blanche wouldn't marry him because grandmother had come instead of a telegram, and it was now clear that he would get no inheritance. He thought I still didn't know any of it. I tried to mention des Grieux; he waved his hand: "Gone! Everything I own is mortgaged to him; I'm naked as a worm! That money you brought...that money—I don't know how much is left, I think about seven hundred francs, and—enough, sir, that's it, and beyond that I don't know, I don't know, sir!..."

"How are you going to pay for the hotel?" I cried in alarm, "and...then what?"

He glanced around pensively, but didn't seem to understand, and maybe hadn't even heard me. I tried to start talking about Polina Alexandrovna, about the children; he hurriedly answered, "Yes! yes!" but at once began talking about the prince again, about the fact that Blanche was now going off with him, and then..."and then...what am I to do, Alexei Ivanovich?" he suddenly turned to me. "I swear to God! What am I to do?— tell me, that's really ungrateful! isn't it ungrateful?"

Finally, he dissolved in a flood of tears.

There was nothing to be done with a man like that; to leave him alone was also dangerous; something might happen to him. However, I somehow got rid of him, but gave the nanny to know that she should look in on him often, and besides that I told the floorboy, a very sensible fellow, who for his part also promised me to keep an eye on him.

I no sooner left the general than Potapych came to me with a summons from grandmother. It was eight o'clock, and she had just come back from the vauxhall after losing definitively. I went to her: the old woman was sitting in her chair, totally exhausted, and evidently sick. Marfa served her a cup of tea, which she almost forced her to drink. Grandmother's voice and tone were markedly changed.

"Good evening, dearest Alexei Ivanovich," she said, inclining her head slowly and gravely, "forgive me for troubling you once more, forgive an old woman. I, my dear, left everything there, nearly a hundred thousand roubles. You were right not to go with me yesterday. I have no money now, not a penny. I don't want to delay for a moment, I'll leave at half-past nine. I've sent to that Englishman of yours, Astley or whatever, and want to borrow three thousand francs from him for a week. You persuade him, so he doesn't get some notion and say no. I'm still quite rich, my dear. I have three estates and two houses. And some money can be found, I didn't take it all with me. I say it so that he won't have doubts of some sort ... Ah, here he is! You can tell a good man when you see one."

Mr. Astley came hurrying at grandmother's first summons. Without much reflection or talk, he at once counted out three thousand francs against a promissory note which grandmother proceeded to sign. The business concluded, he bowed and hurriedly left.

"And now you go, too, Alexei Ivanovich. There's a little more than an hour left—I want to lie down, my bones ache. Don't judge me too harshly, fool that I am. Now I'll never accuse young people of light-mindedness, and it would also be a sin now for me to accuse that unfortunate fellow, that general of yours. Even so I won't give him any money, as he wants, because in my opinion he's as foolish as they come, though I'm no smarter than he is, old fool that I am. Truly, God judges old age as well and punishes pride. Well, good-bye. Marfusha, lift me up."

I wished to see grandmother off, however. Besides, I was in some sort of expectation, I kept expecting that something was about to happen. I couldn't sit in my room. I went out to the corridor several times, even went out for a moment to wander in the avenue. My letter to her had been clear and decisive, and the present catastrophe was, of course, definitive. In the hotel I heard of des Grieux's departure. Finally, if she rejects me as a friend, maybe she won't reject me as a servant. She does need me, at any rate to run errands; I'll be useful, it can't be otherwise!

By train time I ran to the station and got grandmother seated. They all settled in a special family car. "Thank you, dearie, for your disinterested concern," she said at parting, "and tell Praskovya what I said to her yesterday—I'll be waiting for her."

I went home. Passing by the general's suite, I met the nanny and inquired about the general. "Him, dearie? He's all right," she answered glumly. I stepped in anyhow, but in the doorway to the study I stopped in decided amazement. Mlle Blanche and the general were laughing their heads off over something. *La veuve* Cominges was sitting right there on the sofa. The general was obviously out of his wits with joy, babbled all sorts of nonsense, and kept dissolving in long, nervous laughter, which made his face crease into a countless number of wrinkles and his eyes disappear somewhere. Later I learned from Blanche herself that, having chased the prince away and learning of the general's weeping, she decided to comfort him and stopped to see him for a moment. But the poor general didn't know then that his fate had been decided and Blanche had already started packing in order to fly off to Paris on the first morning train.

Having paused on the threshold of the general's study, I decided not to go in and went away unnoticed. Going up to my room and opening the door, I suddenly noticed some figure in the semidarkness, sitting on a chair in the corner by the window. It didn't get up when I appeared. I quickly approached, looked, and—my breath was taken away: it was Polina!

CHAPTER XIV

I CRIED OUT.

"What is it? What is it?" she asked strangely. She was pale and looked gloomy.

"What do you mean, what? You? here, in my room?"

"If I come, I come *entirely*. That's my way. You'll see it presently; light a candle."

I lit a candle. She stood up, went to the table, and placed an unsealed letter before me.

"Read it," she ordered.

"This—this is des Grieux's hand!" I cried, snatching the letter. My hands shook, and the lines leaped before my eyes. I've forgotten the exact terms of the letter, but here it is, if not word for word, at least thought for thought.

Mademoiselle [wrote des Grieux], unfortunate circumstances have forced me to leave immediately. You, of course, noticed yourself that I deliberately avoided a final talk with you until all the circumstances had been clarified. The arrival of your old relative [*de la vielle dame*] and her preposterous action put an end to all my perplexities. My own unsettled affairs forbid me definitively to nourish any further the sweet hopes in which I allowed myself to revel for some time. I regret the past, but I hope you will find nothing in my behavior unworthy of a gentleman and an honest man [*gentil-homme et honnête homme*]. Having lost almost all my money in loans to your stepfather, I find myself in extreme necessity of making use of what remains to me: I have already told my friends in Petersburg to make immediate arrangements for the sale of the property mortgaged to me; knowing, however, that your light-minded stepfather has squandered your own money, I have decided to forgive him fifty thousand francs, and I am returning to him part of the mortgage papers in that sum, so that it is now possible for you to regain everything you have lost by suing him for your property through the courts. I hope, *mademoiselle*, that in the present state of affairs my action will prove quite profitable for you. I hope also that by acting thus I am fully fulfilling the obligations of an honest and noble man. Rest assured that the memory of you is forever imprinted on my heart.

"Well, it's all clear," I said, turning to Polina, "not that you could have expected anything else," I added indignantly.

"I wasn't expecting anything," she replied with apparent calm, but something seemed to tremble in her voice. "I resolved everything long ago; I read his mind and knew what he thought. He thought that I was seeking...that I'd insist..." She stopped and, without finishing, bit her lip and fell silent. "I purposely doubled my contempt for him," she began again, "I waited for what he would do. If the telegram about the inheritance had come, I would have flung my idiot stepfather's debt at him and chased him away! He's been hateful to me for a long, long time. Oh, this was not the man of before, a thousand times not, and now, and now!...Oh, what happiness it would be now to fling that fifty thousand in his mean face, and spit...and smear it around!"

"But the paper—that mortgage for fifty thousand he returned—isn't it with the general? Take it and give it to des Grieux."

"Oh, that's not it! That's not it!"

"Yes, true, that's not it! And what use is the general now? But what about grandmother?" I cried suddenly.

Polina looked at me somehow distractedly and impatiently.

"Why grandmother?" Polina said with vexation. "I can't go to her...And I don't want to ask anyone's forgiveness," she added irritably.

"What's to be done, then?" I cried. "And how, how could you love des Grieux! Oh, the scoundrel, the scoundrel! Well, if you like, I'll kill him in a duel! Where is he now?"

"He's in Frankfurt and will be there for three days."

"One word from you, and I'll go tomorrow by the first train," I said in some sort of stupid enthusiasm.

She laughed.

"Why, he might just say: first return the fifty thousand francs. And why would he fight? . . . What nonsense!"

"But where, then, where can we get these fifty thousand francs?" I repeated, grinding my teeth, as if one could just suddenly pick them up off the floor. "Listen: Mr. Astley?" I asked, turning to her with the beginnings of some strange idea.

Her eyes flashed.

"What, do *you yourself* really want me to leave you for that Englishman?" she said, looking into my face with piercing eyes and smiling bitterly. It was the first time in my life she had spoken so intimately.

It seems at that moment her head began spinning from agitation, and she suddenly sat down on the sofa as if in exhaustion.

It was like being struck by lightning: I stood there and couldn't believe my eyes, couldn't believe my ears! So it meant she loved me! She came *to me*, not to Mr. Astley! She, alone, a young girl, came to my room, in a hotel—meaning she had compromised herself publicly—and I stand before her and still don't understand!

A wild thought flashed in my head.

"Polina! Give me just one hour! Wait here for only one hour and . . . I'll come back! It's . . . it's necessary! You'll see! Stay here, stay here!"

And I ran out of the room without responding to her astonished, questioning look; she called out something after me, but I didn't go back.

Yes, sometimes the wildest thought, the seemingly most impossible thought, gets so firmly settled in your head that you finally take it for something feasible . . . Moreover, if the idea is combined with a strong, passionate desire, you might one day take it, finally, for something fatal, inevitable, predestined, for something that can no longer not be and not happen! Maybe there's also something else, some combination of presentiments, some extraordinary effort of will, a self-intoxication by your own fantasy, or whatever else—I don't know; but on that evening (which I will never forget as long as I live) a miraculous event took place. Though it is perfectly justified arithmetically, nonetheless for me it is still miraculous. And why, why did this certainty lodge itself so deeply and firmly in me then, and now so long ago? I surely must have thought of it, I repeat to you, not as an event that might happen among others (and therefore also might not happen), but as something that simply could not fail to happen!

It was a quarter-past ten; I entered the vauxhall in such firm hopes and at the same time in such excitement as I had never experienced before. There were still enough people in the gaming rooms, though twice less than in the morning.

After ten o'clock, those left around the gaming tables are the real, desperate gamblers, for whom nothing exists at the spa except roulette, who come for the sake of it alone, who give poor notice to what happens around them, and are interested in nothing else during the whole season, but only play from morning till night, and would be ready, perhaps, to play all night till dawn, if it were possible. And they always go away grudgingly when the roulette closes at midnight. And when, around midnight, before closing the roulette, the head croupier announces: "*Les trois derniers coups, messieurs!*"* they are some-times ready to gamble away all they have in their pockets on these last three rounds—and it's actually here that they lose the most. I went to the same table where grandmother had sat earlier. It wasn't very crowded, so that I very quickly found a place to stand at the table. Right in front of me on the green baize, the word *Passe* was written. *Passe* is the series of numbers from nineteen to thirty-six inclusive. The first series, from one to eighteen inclusive, is called *Manque*; but what business was that of mine? I didn't calculate, I didn't even hear what number had come up on the last round, and I didn't ask about it as I began to play—as any slightly calculating gambler would have

*The last three rounds, gentlemen!

done. I took out all my twenty friedrichs d'or and threw them on the *passe* that lay in front of me.

"*Vingt-deux!*"* cried the croupier.

I won—and again staked everything: the previous money and the winnings.

"*Trente-et-un!*"† cried the croupier. I won again! That meant I had eighty friedrichs d'or in all! I pushed all eighty onto the twelve middle numbers (triple the winnings, but the chances are two to one against you), the wheel spun, and twenty-four came up. They handed me three rolls of fifty friedrichs d'or and ten gold pieces; in all, with the previous money, I wound up with two hundred friedrichs d'or.

I was as if in a fever and pushed this whole pile of money onto red—and suddenly came to my senses! And for the only time that whole evening, in all that playing, fear sent a chill over me and came back as a trembling in my hands and legs. With terror I sensed and instantly realized what it meant for me now to lose! My whole life was at stake!

"*Rouge!*" cried the croupier—and I drew a deep breath, fiery needles pricked me all over. They paid me in banknotes; I therefore had four thousand florins and eighty friedrichs d'or! (I could still follow the reckoning.)

Then, I remember, I staked two thousand florins on the twelve middle numbers again and lost; I staked my gold and eighty friedrichs d'or and lost. Rage came over me: I seized the last remaining two thousand florins and staked them on the twelve first numbers—just so, in case, like that, without calculation! However, there was one moment of expectation, perhaps similar in impression to that experienced by Mme Blanchard, in Paris, as she fell to the ground from a hot-air balloon.[13]

"*Quatre!*"‡ cried the croupier. In all, including the former stake, I again had six thousand florins. I had the air of a conqueror, I feared nothing, nothing at all now, and I threw four

*Twenty-two!
†Thirty-one!
‡Four!

thousand florins on black. Some nine people, following me, also rushed to stake on black. The croupiers exchanged glances and remarks. There was talk and anticipation around me.

It came up black. Here I no longer remember either my reckoning or the order of my stakes. I only remember, as in a dream, that it seems I won sixteen thousand florins; then, in three unlucky turns, I blew twelve of them; then I pushed the remaining four thousand onto *passe* (but almost feeling nothing as I did it; I only waited somehow mechanically, without thinking)—and won again; then I won four more times in a row. I remember only that I raked in money by the thousands; I also recall that the twelve middle numbers came up most often, and I attached myself to them. They appeared somehow regularly—three, four times in a row without fail—then disappeared a couple of times, then came back again three or four times in a row. This astonishing regularity sometimes occurs in spells—and it's this that throws off the seasoned gamblers, who calculate with a pencil in their hands. And what a terrible mockery of fate sometimes happens here!

I think no more than half an hour had gone by since my arrival. Suddenly the croupier informed me that I had won thirty thousand florins, and since the bank could not answer for more at one time, it meant that the roulette would close till the next morning. I grabbed all my gold, poured it into my pockets, grabbed all the banknotes, and at once moved to another table, in another room, where there was another roulette; a whole crowd flocked after me; a place was cleared for me at once, and I began staking again, anyhow and without calculating. I have no idea what saved me!

Occasionally, however, calculation began to flash in my head. I would latch on to certain numbers and choices, but soon abandoned them and staked again almost unawares. I must have been very distracted; I remember that the croupiers corrected my play several times. I made bad mistakes. My temples were damp with sweat, and my hands shook. Little Poles ran up to me with their services, but I didn't listen to anyone. My luck held out! Suddenly loud talk and laughter arose around me.

"Bravo, bravo!" everyone cried, some even clapped their hands. I won thirty thousand florins here as well, breaking the bank, which was closed till the next day!

"Leave, leave," someone's voice whispered to me on my right. It was some Frankfurt Jew; he had been standing next to me all the while and, it seems, had occasionally helped me to play.

"For God's sake, leave," another voice whispered in my left ear. I glanced up fleetingly. It was a quite modestly and decently dressed lady of about thirty, with a sickly pale, weary face, but even now recalling her wonderful former beauty. At that moment I was stuffing my pockets with banknotes, which I just crumpled up, and gathering the gold that was left on the table. Seizing the last roll of fifty friedrichs d'or, I managed, quite unnoticed, to put it into the pale lady's hand; I wanted terribly to do that then, and I remember her slender, thin fingers pressed my hand hard as a sign of warmest gratitude. All this took only a moment.

Having gathered up everything, I quickly went on to the *trente et quarante*.

Trente et quarante is where the aristocratic public sits. It's not roulette, it's cards. Here the bank is answerable for a hundred thousand thalers a time. The biggest stake is also four thousand florins. I was totally ignorant of the game, and among the stakes knew only red and black, which were here as well. I latched on to them. The whole vauxhall crowded around. I don't remember whether I thought even once about Polina during that time. I felt some sort of insuperable pleasure then in grabbing and raking in banknotes, which were heaping up in front of me.

It actually seemed that fate was urging me on. This time, as if on purpose, a certain circumstance occurred, which, however, is repeated rather often in gambling. Luck attaches itself, for instance, to red, and doesn't leave it for ten, even fifteen times in a row. I had heard two days earlier that, a week before, red had come up twenty-two times in a row; no one even remembered such a thing happening at roulette, and it was retold with amazement. Naturally, everyone abandoned red at once, and after ten times, for instance, almost no one dared to stake on it. But no experienced gambler would have staked on black then as opposed to red. An experienced gambler knows what this "whim of chance" means. For instance, it would seem that, after sixteen reds, the seventeenth is bound to be black. Novices fall upon it in crowds, doubling and tripling their stakes, and lose terribly.

But I, by some strange whim, noticing that red had come up seven times in a row, deliberately latched on to it. I'm convinced that it was half vanity; I wanted to astonish the spectators with an insane risk, and—oh, strange feeling—I distinctly remember that suddenly, indeed without any challenge to my vanity, I was overcome by a terrible thirst for risk. Maybe, having gone through so many sensations, my soul was not sated but only exacerbated by them, and demanded more sensations, ever stronger and stronger, to the point of utter exhaustion. And, I'm truly not lying, if the rules of the game had allowed me to stake fifty thousand florins at once, I would certainly have staked them. Around me they cried that it was insane, that red had already come up fourteen times!

"*Monsieur a gagné déjà cent mille florins,*"* someone's voice said next to me.

I suddenly came to my senses. What? I had won a hundred thousand florins that evening! What did I need more for? I fell upon the banknotes, crumpled them into my pocket without counting, raked up all my gold, all the rolls, and ran out of the vauxhall. Around me everyone laughed as I passed through the rooms, looking at my bulging pockets and my uneven gait owing to the weight of the gold. I think it weighed over seventeen pounds. Several hands reached out to me; I gave money away by the handful, as much as I got hold of. Two Jews stopped me at the exit.

"You're bold! You're very bold!" they said to me. "But leave tomorrow morning without fail, otherwise you'll lose it all . . ."

I didn't listen to them. The avenue was so dark that I couldn't see my own hand. It was about a quarter of a mile to the hotel.

---

*The gentleman has already won a hundred thousand florins.

I had never been afraid of thieves or robbers, even when I was little; I didn't think of them now either. However, I don't remember what I thought about on the way; there were no thoughts. My only sensation was of some terrible pleasure— luck, victory, power—I don't know how to express it. The image of Polina flashed before me as well; I remembered and was conscious that I was going to her, that I would presently be together with her and would be telling her, showing her . . . but I barely remembered what she had said to me earlier, and why I had gone, and all those recent sensations, which had been there an hour and a half ago, now seemed to me something long past, corrected, outdated—of which we would make no further mention, because now everything would start anew. Almost at the end of the avenue fear suddenly came upon me: "What if I'm murdered and robbed right now!" With each step, my fear redoubled. I nearly ran. Suddenly at the end of the avenue our hotel shone all at once, lit up by countless lights— thank God: home!

I ran up to my floor and quickly opened the door. Polina was there, sitting on my sofa in front of a lighted candle, her arms crossed. She looked at me in amazement, and I certainly was a strange sight at that moment. I stopped before her and began flinging my whole pile of money on the table.

CHAPTER XV

I REMEMBER SHE LOOKED terribly intently into my face, but without moving, without even changing her position.

"I won two hundred thousand francs," I cried, flinging down my last roll. The enormous pile of banknotes and rolls of gold covered the whole table, and I couldn't take my eyes off it; at moments I completely forgot about Polina. Now I'd begin putting all those heaps of banknotes in order, stacking them together, now I'd gather the gold into one common heap; then I'd abandon it all and begin pacing the room in quick strides, lapsing into thought; then I'd suddenly go up to the table and begin counting the money again. Suddenly, as if coming to my senses, I rushed to the door and quickly locked it, turning the key twice. Then I stopped, pondering, before my little suitcase.

"Shouldn't I put it in the suitcase till tomorrow?" I asked, suddenly turning to Polina, and I suddenly remembered about her. She went on sitting without stirring, in the same place, but was watching me intently. The expression on her face was somehow strange; I didn't like that expression! I wouldn't be mistaken if I said there was hatred in it.

I quickly went over to her.

"Polina, here's twenty-five thousand florins—that's fifty thousand francs, even more. Take it, fling it in his face tomorrow."

She didn't answer me.

"If you like, I'll take it myself, early in the morning. Shall I?"

She suddenly began to laugh. She laughed for a long time.

I looked at her with astonishment and sorrowful feeling. This laughter was very much like her recent, frequent, mocking laughter at me, which always came at the time of my most passionate declarations. Finally, she stopped and frowned; she looked me over sternly from under her eyebrows.

"I won't take your money," she said contemptuously.

"How's that? What's wrong?" I cried. "Why, Polina?"

"I don't take money for nothing."

"I'm offering it to you as a friend; I'm offering you my life."

She looked at me with a long, searching gaze, as if she wanted to pierce me through.

"You're paying too much," she said, smiling, "des Grieux's mistress isn't worth fifty thousand francs."

"Polina, how can you speak to me like that!" I cried in reproach. "Am I des Grieux?"

"I hate you! Yes...yes!...I dislike you more than des Grieux," she cried, suddenly flashing her eyes.

Here she suddenly covered her face with her hands and went into hysterics. I rushed to her.

I realized that something had happened to her in my absence. It was as if she was not at all in her right mind.

"Buy me! You want to? you want to? for fifty thousand francs, like des Grieux?" she burst out with convulsive sobs. I embraced her, kissed her hands, her feet, fell on my knees before her.

Her hysterics were passing. She put both hands on my shoulders and studied me intently. It seemed as if she wanted to read something in my face. She listened to me, but apparently without hearing what I said to her. Some sort of care and pensiveness appeared in her face. I feared for her; it decidedly seemed to me that her mind was becoming deranged. She would suddenly begin to draw me gently to her; a trustful smile would wander over her face; then she would suddenly push me away, and again start peering at me with a darkened look.

Suddenly she rushed to embrace me.

"You do love me, don't you?" she said. "Why, you wanted... you wanted to fight with the baron over me!" And she suddenly burst out laughing—as if something funny and dear had suddenly flashed in her memory. She wept and laughed at the same time. Well, what was I to do? I was as if in a fever myself. I remember she began saying something to me, but I could understand almost nothing. It was some kind of raving, some kind of prattle—as if she wanted to tell me something quickly— raving interrupted now and then by the merriest laughter, which

began to frighten me. "No, no, you're a dear, a dear!" she
repeated. "You're my faithful one!" and she again put her hands
on my shoulders, again peered at me and went on repeating:
"You love me . . . love me . . . will you love me?" I couldn't take
my eyes off her; I had never yet seen her in these fits of tenderness and love; true, it was, of course, raving, but . . . noticing my
passionate look, she would suddenly begin to smile slyly; for no
reason at all she would start talking about Mr. Astley.

However, she mentioned Mr. Astley constantly (especially
earlier, when she had tried to tell me something), but precisely
what it was, I couldn't grasp; it seemed she even laughed at
him; she constantly repeated that he was waiting . . . and did I
know that he was certainly standing under the window now?
"Yes, yes, under the window—well, open it, look, look, he's
here, here!" She pushed me towards the window, but as soon as
I made as if to go to it, she dissolved in laughter, and I stayed
by her, and she rushed to embrace me.

"So we're leaving? Aren't we leaving tomorrow?" suddenly
came anxiously to her head. "Well . . ." (and she fell to thinking),
"well, will we catch up with grandmother, do you think? In
Berlin, I think, we'll catch up with her. What do you think
she'll say when we catch up with her and she sees us? And Mr.
Astley? . . . Well, that one won't jump off the Schlangenberg, do
you think?" (She laughed loudly.) "Well, listen: do you know
where he's going next summer? He wants to go to the North
Pole for scientific research, and he invited me to go with him,
ha, ha, ha! He says that without the Europeans we Russians
don't know anything and can't do anything . . . But he's also kind!
You know, he excuses the 'general'; he says that Blanche . . . that
passion—well, I don't know, I don't know," she suddenly
repeated as if wandering and at a loss. "Poor things, I'm so sorry
for them and for grandmother . . . No, listen, listen, who are you
to go killing des Grieux? And did you really and truly think
you'd kill him? Oh, silly boy! Could you possibly think I'd let
you fight with des Grieux? And you wouldn't kill the baron
either," she added, suddenly bursting into laughter. "Oh, how
ridiculous you were then with the baron; I watched the two of

you from my bench; and how reluctant you were to go then, when I sent you. How I laughed then, how I laughed," she added, laughing loudly.

And again she suddenly kissed me and embraced me, again she pressed her face to mine passionately and tenderly. I no longer thought or heard anything. My head was spinning...

I think it was about seven o'clock in the morning when I came to my senses; the sun was shining into the room. Polina was sitting next to me and looking around strangely, as if coming out of some darkness and collecting her memories. She also had only just woken up and gazed intently at the table and the money. My head was heavy and ached. I was about to take Polina's hand; she suddenly pushed me away and jumped up from the sofa. The beginning day was overcast; it had rained before dawn. She went to the window, opened it, thrust out her head and chest, and, propping herself on her hands, her elbows resting on the windowsill, stayed that way for about three minutes, without turning to me or listening to what I was saying to her. With fear it came to my head: what will come now and how will it end? Suddenly she got up from the window, went over to the table, and, looking at me with an expression of boundless hatred, her lips trembling with anger, said to me:

"Well, now give me my fifty thousand francs!"

"Again, again, Polina!" I tried to begin.

"Or have you changed your mind? Ha, ha, ha! Maybe you're sorry now?"

The twenty-five thousand florins, already counted out last night, were lying on the table. I took them and gave them to her.

"So it's mine now? Is it? Is it?" she asked me spitefully, holding the money in her hands.

"But it has always been yours," I said.

"Well, then, here's your fifty thousand francs!" She swung and sent them flying at me. The wad struck me painfully in the face and scattered over the floor. Having done that, Polina ran out of the room.

I know, of course, she was not in her right mind at that

moment, though I don't understand this temporary madness. True, even now, a month later, she's still unwell. What, however, was the cause of this condition and, above all, of this escapade? Injured pride? Despair over the fact that she had even ventured to come to me? Did I look to her as if I was glorying in my success and indeed, just like des Grieux, wanted to get rid of her by giving her fifty thousand francs? But that wasn't so, I know it by my own conscience. I think that part of the blame here lay in her vanity: vanity prompted her not to believe me and to insult me, though all this may have presented itself to her quite vaguely. In that case, of course, I answered for des Grieux, and was to blame, maybe, without much blame. True, all this was only delirium; it's also true that I knew she was delirious, and ... paid no attention to that circumstance. Maybe now she can't forgive me for it? Yes, but that's now; but then, then? Her delirium and illness were not so strong that she totally forgot what she was doing when she came to me with des Grieux's letter? So she knew what she was doing.

Carelessly, hastily, I stuffed all my paper money and my whole heap of gold into the bed, covered it, and left some ten minutes after Polina. I was sure she had run home, and wanted to get to their suite quietly and ask the nanny in the front room about the young lady's health. What was my amazement when, meeting the nanny on the stairs, I learned that Polina had not returned home yet and that the nanny herself was coming to my room to fetch her.

"Just now," I said to her, "she left me only just now, some ten minutes ago, where could she have gone?"

The nanny looked at me reproachfully.

And meanwhile a whole story had come out, which had already spread through the hotel. In the porter's lodge and at the manager's it was whispered that, at six o'clock in the morning, the *Fräulein* came running out of the hotel, in the rain, and ran off in the direction of the Hôtel d'Angleterre. From their words and hints, I noticed that they already knew she had spent the whole night in my room. However, there was already talk about the general's whole family: it became known that the general had lost his mind the day before and wept for the whole hotel to hear. The talk also was that the grandmother who had come was his mother, who had appeared on purpose from Russia itself to forbid her son to marry Mlle de Cominges, and in case he disobeyed, to deprive him of his inheritance, and since he hadn't obeyed, the countess, before his eyes, had deliberately lost all her money at roulette, so that there was nothing to leave him. "*Diese Russen!*"* the manager repeated in indignation, shaking his head. Others laughed. The manager was making out the bill. Everybody already knew about my winning; Karl, my floorboy, was the first to congratulate me. But I couldn't be bothered with them. I raced to the Hôtel d'Angleterre.

It was still early; Mr. Astley was not receiving anyone; learning that it was I, he came out to me in the corridor and stood before me, silently aiming his tinny gaze at me, waiting for what I was going to say. I inquired at once about Polina.

"She's ill," Mr. Astley replied, looking at me point-blank as before and not taking his eyes off me.

"So she's really here with you?"

"Oh, yes, with me."

"So, then, you . . . you intend to keep her with you?"

"Oh, yes, I do."

"Mr. Astley, this will cause a scandal; this is impossible. Besides, she's quite ill; maybe you haven't noticed?"

"Oh, yes, I have, and I've already told you she's ill. If she weren't ill, she wouldn't have spent the night with you."

"So you know that, too?"

"I know that. She was on her way here yesterday, and I would have taken her to my female relation, but since she was ill, she went to you by mistake."

"Imagine that! Well, I congratulate you, Mr. Astley. By the way, you've given me an idea: didn't you spend the whole night standing under the window? Miss Polina kept telling me all night to open the window and see whether you were standing there, and she laughed terribly."

*These Russians!

"Really? No, I wasn't standing under the window; but I waited in the corridor and walked about."

"But she needs to be treated, Mr. Astley."

"Oh, yes, I've already sent for a doctor, and if she dies, you will give me an accounting for her death."

I was amazed.

"For pity's sake, Mr. Astley, what is it you want?"

"Is it true that you won two hundred thousand thalers yesterday?"

"Only one hundred thousand florins in all."

"Well, you see! So, then, go to Paris this morning."

"What for?"

"All Russians go to Paris when they have money," Mr. Astley explained in a voice and tone as if he was reading it from a book.

"What will I do in Paris now, in the summer? I love her, Mr. Astley! You know it yourself."

"Really? I'm convinced that you don't. Besides, if you stay here, you're certain to lose everything, and you won't have the money to go to Paris. But good-bye, I'm perfectly convinced that you'll go to Paris today."

"Very well, good-bye, only I won't go to Paris. Think, Mr. Astley, about how it will be for us now. In short, the general . . . and now what's happend with Miss Polina—why, it will get all over town."

"Yes, all over town. The general, I think, doesn't think about it and couldn't care less. Besides, Miss Polina is fully entitled to live wherever she likes. As for this family, it would be correct to say that this family no longer exists."

I walked along and chuckled at this Englishman's strange certainty that I would go to Paris. "Anyhow he wants to shoot me in a duel," I thought, "if Mlle Polina dies—there's another business!" I swear I felt sorry for Polina, but, strangely, since the moment I touched the gaming table the night before and began to rake in wads of money, it was as if my love moved into the background. I say that now; but at the time I still hadn't noted it all clearly. Can it be that I'm really a gambler, can it be that I indeed . . . loved Polina so strangely? No, I love her even now, by God! And at that moment, when I left Mr. Astley and walked home, I sincerely suffered and blamed myself. But...but here I got involved in an extremely strange and stupid story.

I was hurrying to the general's when a door suddenly opened near their suite and someone called out to me. It was Mme *la veuve* Cominges, and she called me on Mlle Blanche's orders. I went into Mlle Blanche's suite.

They had a small two-room suite. I could hear the laughter and cries of Mlle Blanche from the bedroom. She was getting up.

"*Ah, c'est lui! Viens donc, béta!* Is it true that *tu as gagné d'or et d'argent? J'aimerais mieux l'or.*"*

"I did win," I answered, laughing.

"How much?"

"A hundred thousand florins."

"*Bibi, comme tu es bête.* But do come in, I can't hear a thing. *Nous ferons bombance, n'est-ce pas?*"†

I went into her room. She was lying under a pink satin spread, from which her swarthy, healthy, astonishing shoulders protruded—shoulders such as can only be seen in a dream—negligently covered by a batiste nightgown trimmed with the whitest lace, which went wonderfully with her swarthy skin.

"*Mon fils, as-tu du coeur?*"‡ she cried, seeing me, and laughed loudly. She always laughed very gaily and sometimes even sincerely.

"*Tout autre...*"§ I began, paraphrasing Corneille.[14]

"You see, *vois tu*," she suddenly began chattering, "first, find my stockings, help me into my shoes, and second, *si tu n'est pas trop bête, je te prends à Paris.*¶ You know, I'm going right now."

"Now?"

"In half an hour."

---

*Ah, it's him! Come then, you ninny!...you won gold and silver? I'd prefer the gold.

†Bibi, how stupid you are...We'll have a beanfeast, won't we?

‡My son, have you a heart?

§Anyone else...

¶If you're not too stupid, I'll take you to Paris.

Indeed, everything was packed. All her suitcases and things were standing ready. Coffee had been served long ago.

"*Eh bien!* If you want, *tu verra Paris. Dis donc qu'est-ce que c'est qu'un outchitel? Tu étais bien bête quand tu étais outchitel.** But where are my stockings? So, help me on with them!"

She stuck out a really delightful little foot, swarthy, small, not misshapen, like almost all those little feet that look so cute in shoes. I laughed and began to pull a silk stocking onto it. Mlle Blanche meanwhile sat on the bed and chattered.

"*Eh bien, que feras-tu, si je te prends avec?* First, *je veux cinquante mille francs.* You'll give them to me in Frankfurt. *Nous allons à Paris;* there we'll live together *et je te ferais voir des étoiles en plein jour.*† You'll see women such as you've never seen before. Listen . . ."

"Wait, so I give you fifty thousand francs, and what am I left with?"

"*Et cent cinquante mille francs*, you've forgotten, and, on top of that, I agree to live in your apartment for a month, two months, *que sais-je!* Of course, in two months we'll go through that hundred and fifty thousand francs. You see, *je suis bonne enfant* and am telling you beforehand, *mais tu verras des étoiles.*"‡

"What, all in two months?"

"What? So it frightens you? *Ah, vil esclave!* You don't know that one month of that life is better than your whole existence? One month—*et après le déluge!*[15] *Mais tu ne peux comprendre, va!* Off with you, you're not worthy of it! *Aie, que fais-tu?*" §

At that moment I was putting a stocking on her other foot, but I couldn't help myself and kissed it. She pulled it back and began flicking me in the face with her toe. Finally, she drove me out altogether.

*Well, then! . . . you'll see Paris. But tell me, what's an outchitel? You were quite stupid when you were an outchitel.
†Well, then, what will you do if I take you along? . . . I want fifty thousand francs . . . We'll go to Paris . . . and I'll make you see stars in broad daylight.
‡Another hundred and fifty thousand francs . . . who knows? . . . I'm a good girl . . . but you'll see stars.
§Ah, vile slave! . . . and afterwards the deluge! But you can't understand, go! . . . Aie, what are you doing?

"*Eh bien, mon outchitel, je t'attends, si tu veux*,*" I'm leaving in a quarter of an hour!" she called after me.

Returning home, I was already as if in a whirl. What, then, was it my fault that Mlle Polina had thrown the whole wad in my face and already yesterday had preferred Mr. Astley to me? Some stray banknotes still lay on the floor; I picked them up. At that moment the door opened and the manager himself (who wouldn't even look at me before) came with an invitation: wouldn't I like to move downstairs to an excellent suite in which Count V. had just been staying?

I stood and thought a moment.

"The bill!" I cried. "I'm leaving right now, in ten minutes." "If it's Paris, let it be Paris," I thought to myself, "it must have been written down at my birth!"

A quarter of an hour later the three of us were indeed sitting in a family compartment: myself, Mlle Blanche, and Mme *la veuve* Cominges. Mlle Blanche laughed loudly, looking at me, to the point of hysterics. *La veuve* Cominges seconded her. I wouldn't say that I felt very gay. My life was breaking in two, but since the previous day I had become accustomed to staking all I had. Maybe it was really true that the money was too much for me and got me into a whirl. *Peut-être, je ne demandais pas mieux.*[†] It seemed to me that for a time—but only for a time—the stage set was being changed. "But in a month I'll be back here, and then . . . then I'll still have it out with you, Mr. Astley!" No, as I remember it now, I felt terribly sad then, though I did laugh my head off with that little fool Blanche.

"But what is it to you? How stupid you are! oh, how stupid!" cried Blanche, interrupting her laughter and beginning to scold me seriously. "Well, yes, yes, we'll go through your two hundred thousand francs, but to make up for it, *mais tu seras heureux, comme un petit roi*;[‡] I'll tie your necktie myself and introduce you to Hortense. And when we've gone through all our money,

*Well, then, my outchitel, I'm waiting for you, if you want.
†Maybe I was asking for no better.
‡But you'll be happy, like a little king.

you'll come back here and break the bank again. What did those Jews tell you? It's boldness above all, and you have it, and you'll be coming to Paris bringing me money more than once. *Quant à moi, je veux cinquante mille francs de rente et alors...* *

"And the general?" I asked her.

"And the general, as you know yourself, goes to fetch me a bouquet every day at this hour. Today I purposely told him to find the rarest flowers. The poor thing will come back, and the bird will have flown. He'll fly after us, you'll see. Ha, ha, ha! I'll be very glad. He'll be useful to me in Paris; here Mr. Astley will pay for him..."

And so it was that I left for Paris then.

*As for me, I want an allowance of fifty thousand francs and then ...

CHAPTER XVI

WHAT SHALL I SAY about Paris? It was all, of course, both delirium and foolery. I lived in Paris for only a little more than three weeks, and in that time my hundred thousand francs were completely finished. I'm speaking of only a hundred thousand; the remaining hundred thousand I gave to Mlle Blanche in straight cash—fifty thousand in Frankfurt, and three days later in Paris I handed her the other fifty thousand francs in a promissory note, for which, however, she took the money from me a week later, "*et les cent mille francs qui nous restent, tu les mangeras avec moi, mon outchitel.*"* She always called me *outchitel*. It's hard to imagine anything in the world more calculating, mean, and stingy than the category of beings like Mlle Blanche. But that's with regard to her own money. As for my hundred thousand francs, she later declared to me straight out that she needed it in order to establish herself initially in Paris. "So that now I'm standing on a decent footing once and for all, and it will be a long time before anybody throws me off, so at least I've arranged things," she added. However, I scarcely saw that hundred thousand; she kept the money herself all the while, and my purse, which she visited every day, never held more than a hundred francs, and almost always less.

"What do you need money for?" she said occasionally with a most artless look, and I didn't argue with her. Instead, she decorated her apartment very, very nicely on this money, and later when she moved me to the new place, she said, as she was showing me the rooms: "See what can be done, with calculation and taste, on the scantiest means." This scantiness added up, however, to exactly fifty thousand francs. The other fifty

*And the hundred thousand francs we have left, you'll eat up with me, my outchitel.

thousand she spent on a carriage and horses, and besides that we threw two balls, that is, two evening parties, to which Hortense, and Lisette, and Cléopatre came—women remarkable in many, many respects, and even far from bad. At these two parties I was forced to play the utterly stupid role of host, to meet and entertain some rich and extremely dull merchants, impossibly ignorant and shameless army lieutenants of various sorts, and pathetic little authors and magazine midges, who arrived in fashionable tailcoats, straw-colored gloves, and with a vanity and conceit of dimensions inconceivable even in Petersburg—which is saying a lot. They even ventured to make fun of me, but I got drunk on champagne and lay about in the back room. All this was loathsome to me in the highest degree. "*C'est un outchitel,*" Blanche said of me, "*il a gagné deux cent mille francs,*[*] and without me he wouldn't know how to spend it. And afterwards he'll become an *outchitel* again—does anyone know of a post? We must do something for him." I began resorting to champagne quite often, because I was very sad and extremely bored all the time. I lived in the most bourgeois, in the most mercantile milieu, where every sou was counted and measured out. For the first two weeks, Blanche disliked me very much, I noticed that; true, she got me smartly dressed and tied my necktie every day, but in her heart she sincerely despised me. I didn't pay the slightest attention to that. Bored and despondent, I got into the habit of going to the Château des Fleurs,[16] where regularly, every evening, I got drunk and practiced the cancan (which they dance most vilely there) and later on even achieved some celebrity in that line. Finally, Blanche got to the bottom of me: she had somehow formed an idea for herself beforehand that during our cohabitation, I would walk behind her with a pencil and paper in my hand and keep an account of how much she spent, how much she stole, how much she was going to spend, and how much more she was going to steal, and, of course, she was sure that we would have battles over every ten francs. To each of my assaults, which she

[*]He won two hundred thousand francs.

imagined beforehand, she had prepared timely objections; but seeing no assaults from me, at first she herself started to object. Sometimes she would begin very hotly, but seeing that I kept silent—most often lying on the sofa and staring fixedly at the ceiling—she would finally even become astonished. At first she thought I was simply stupid, an *outchitel*, and simply broke off her objections, probably thinking to herself: "He's stupid; there's no point in suggesting anything, if he doesn't understand for himself." She would leave, but about ten minutes later would come back again (this happened during the time of her most furious spending, spending completely beyond our means: for instance, she changed horses and bought a pair for sixteen thousand francs).

"Well, so, Bibi, you're not angry?" she came up to me.

"No-o-o! How bo-o-oring!" I said, moving her away with my hand, but this made her so curious that she at once sat down beside me:

"You see, if I decided to pay so much, it's because they were a good deal. They can be sold again for twenty thousand francs."

"I believe you, I believe you; they're splendid horses; and now you've got a nice turnout; it will be useful; well, and enough."

"So you're not angry?"

"At what? It's smart of you to stock up on a few things you need. It will all be of use later. I see you really have to put yourself on such a footing, otherwise you'll never make a million. Here our hundred thousand francs is only a beginning, a drop in the ocean."

Blanche, who least of all expected such talk from me (instead of shouts and reproaches!), looked as if she'd fallen from the sky.

"So you . . . so that's how you are! *Mais tu as l'esprit pour comprendre! Sais-tu, mon garçon,** you're an *outchitel*, but you should have been born a prince! So you're not sorry our money's going so quickly?"

"Who cares, the quicker the better!"

"*Mais . . . sais-tu . . . mais dis donc*, are you rich? *Mais sais-tu,*

---

*Why, you have the wits to understand. You know, my boy . . .

you really despise money too much. *Qu'est-ce que tu feras après, dis donc?"**

"*Après*, I'll go to Homburg and win another hundred thousand francs."

"*Oui, oui, c'est ça, c'est magnifique!*[†] And I know you'll certainly win and bring it all here. *Dis donc*, you'll make it so that I really fall in love with you! *Eh bien*, since that's the way you are, I'll love you all the while and won't be unfaithful even once. You see, all this while, though I didn't love you, *parce que je croyais que tu n'est qu'un outchitel (quelque chose comme un laquais, n'est-ce pas?)*, but even so I was faithful to you, *parce que je suis bonne fille.*"[‡]

"No, lies! And with Albert, that swarthy little officer—as if I didn't see it last time?"

"*Oh, oh, mais tu es . . .*"

"No, lies, lies; and what do you think, that I'm angry? I spit on it; *il faut que jeunesse se passe.*[§] You can't chase him away, if he was there before me and you love him. Only don't give him any money, you hear?"

"So you're not angry about that either? *Mais tu es un vrai philosophe, sais tu? Un vrai philosophe!*" she cried in delight. "*Eh, bien, je t'aimerai, je t'aimerai—tu verras, tu sera content!*"[¶]

And, indeed, since then it was even as if she really did become attached to me, even in a friendly way, and so we spent our last ten days. The promised "stars" I didn't see; but in some respects she really kept her word. Moreover, she got me acquainted with Hortense, who was even all too remarkable a woman in her own way and in our circle was known as *Thérèse-philosophe . . .*[17]

However, there's no point expanding on it; all this could

---

*But . . . you know . . . but tell me . . . But you know . . . What will you do afterwards, tell me?

†Yes, yes, that's it, that's magnificent!

‡Because I thought you were just an outchitel (something like a lackey, isn't it?) . . . because I'm a good girl.

§Youth must pass.

¶Why, you're a real philosopher, you know? A real philosopher . . . Well, then, I'm going to love you, I'm going to love you—you'll see, you'll be pleased.

make up a special story, with a special coloring, which I don't want to put into this story. The thing is that I wished with all my might that it would all be over soon. But our hundred thousand francs lasted, as I've already said, for almost a month— at which I was genuinely surprised: at least eighty thousand of this money Blanche spent buying things for herself, and we lived on no more than twenty thousand francs, and even so it was enough. Blanche, who towards the end was even almost candid with me (at least in certain things she didn't lie to me), confessed that at least the debts she had had to incur wouldn't fall on me. "I didn't give you any bills or promissory notes to sign," she said to me, "because I felt sorry for you; another woman would certainly have done that and packed you off to prison. You see, you see how I've loved you and how kind I am! This damned wedding alone is going to cost me quite a bit!"

We did indeed have a wedding. It took place at the very end of our month, and I suppose the last dregs of my hundred thousand francs went on it; with that the affair ended, that is, with that our month ended, after which I was formally dismissed.

It happened like this: a week after we installed ourselves in Paris, the general came. He came straight to Blanche and from the very first visit all but stayed with us. True, he had his own little apartment somewhere. Blanche greeted him joyfully, with shrieks and loud laughter, and even rushed to embrace him; as things turned out, she herself wouldn't let him go, and he had to follow her everywhere: to the boulevards, and for carriage rides, and to the theater, and to see acquaintances. The general was still fit for this employment; he was rather stately and respectable—almost tall, with dyed side-whiskers and enormous mustaches (he served formerly in the cuirassiers), with a distinguished though somewhat flabby face. His manners were excellent, he wore a tailcoat very smartly. In Paris he started wearing his decorations. With such a man, to stroll down the boulevard was not only possible, but, if one may put it so, even *recommandable*. The kind and muddle-headed general was terribly pleased with it all; he had by no means counted on that when he appeared before us on his arrival in Paris. He appeared then all but trembling with fear; he thought Blanche would start shouting and order him thrown out; and therefore, seeing such a turn of affairs, he went into raptures and spent the whole month in some sort of senselessly rapturous state; and in such a state I left him. I was already here when I learned in detail how, after our sudden departure then from Roulettenburg, that same morning something like a fit came over him. He fell unconscious, and then for a whole week was almost like a crazy man and talked nonsense. He was treated, but he suddenly dropped everything, got on the train, and showed up in Paris. Naturally, Blanche's reception of him proved the best medicine; but some signs of illness remained long afterwards, despite his joyful and rapturous state. He was completely unable to reason or even merely conduct any sort of slightly serious conversation; on such occasions he merely added a "Hm!" to every word spoken and nodded his head—and he got off with that. He often laughed, but it was some sort of nervous, morbid laughter, as if he was going into a fit; other times he would sit for whole hours as gloomy as night, knitting his bushy eyebrows. Many things he even didn't remember at all; he became outrageously absentminded and adopted the habit of talking to himself. Only Blanche could revive him; and the fits of a gloomy, sullen state, when he hid in the corner, meant only that he hadn't seen Blanche for a long time, or that Blanche had gone somewhere and hadn't taken him with her, or hadn't been nice to him as she was leaving. Yet he himself couldn't say what he wanted and didn't know he was gloomy and sad. Having sat for an hour or two (I noticed it twice when Blanche left for the whole day, probably to see Albert), he would suddenly start looking around, fussing, glancing over his shoulder, recalling, and seemed as if he wanted to find someone; but seeing no one and just not recalling what he wanted to ask, he would again lapse into oblivion, until Blanche suddenly appeared, gay, frolicsome, dressed up, with her loud, ringing laughter. She would run to him, start pulling at him, and even kiss him—a favor, however, that she rarely bestowed on him. Once the general was so glad to see her that he even burst into tears—I even marveled at him.

As soon as he appeared at our place, Blanche at once began acting as his advocate before me. She even waxed eloquent. She reminded me that she had been unfaithful to the general because of me, that she had almost been his fiancée, had given him her word; that because of her he had abandoned his family, and that, finally, I worked for him and should be sensible of that, and—shame on me . . . I kept silent, and she rattled on terribly. Finally, I burst out laughing, and the matter ended there, that is, at first she thought I was a fool, but towards the end she arrived at the notion that I was a very good and agreeable man. In short, I had the luck, towards the end, decidedly to earn the full good favor of this worthy girl. (However, Blanche was in fact a most kind girl—only in her own way, of course; I didn't appreciate her at first.) "You're an intelligent and kind man," she used to say to me towards the end, "and . . . and . . . it's too bad you're such a fool! You'll never, never be rich!"

"*Un vrai russe, un calmouk*"*[18]—several times she sent me out to walk the general, just like a lackey with her greyhound. However, I also took him to the theater, and to the Bal Mabille,[19] and to restaurants. For this Blanche even supplied money, though the general had his own, and he liked very much to take out his wallet in front of people. Once I was almost obliged to use force to keep him from paying seven hundred francs for a brooch he had become enamored of in the Palais Royal[20] and wanted at all costs to give to Blanche. Well, what did she need a seven-hundred-franc brooch for? The general had no more than a thousand francs in all. I could never find out where he got it from. I suppose it was from Mr. Astley, the more so as he had paid their hotel bill. As for the way the general looked at me all the while, it seems to me that he never even suspected my relations with Blanche. Though he had heard somehow vaguely that I had won a fortune, he probably supposed I was some sort of private secretary to Blanche, or maybe even a servant. At any rate he always spoke to me condescendingly, as before, like a superior, and occasionally even began to

*A true Russian, a Kalmuck.

upbraid me. Once he made Blanche and me laugh terribly, at our place, over morning coffee. He was not at all quick to take offense; but here he suddenly took offense at me—for what, I still don't understand. But, of course, he didn't understand himself. In short, he started talking without beginning or end, *à batons rompus*,* shouted that I was a mere boy, that he would teach me...that he would make me understand...and so on, and so forth. But no one could understand anything. Blanche rocked with laughter; finally we somehow managed to calm him down and took him for a walk. I noticed many times, however, that he felt sad, was sorry for someone or something, missed someone, even despite Blanche's presence. In those moments, he started talking with me himself a couple of times, but never could explain anything sensibly, recalled his service, his late wife, his management, his estate. He would latch on to some word—and rejoice, and repeat it a hundred times a day, though it didn't express his feelings or his thoughts at all. I tried to speak with him about his children; but he would get off with his former patter and quickly pass on to another subject: "Yes, yes! the children, the children, you're right, the children!" Only once did he wax emotional—he and I were going to the theater: "They're unfortunate children," he suddenly began, "yes, sir, yes, they're un-for-tunate children!" And several times later that evening he repeated the words: "Unfortunate children!" When I began talking once about Polina, he even flew into a rage. "She's an ungrateful woman," he exclaimed, "she's wicked and ungrateful! She has disgraced our family! If we had laws here, I'd have tied her in knots! Yes, sir, yes, sir!" As far as des Grieux was concerned, he couldn't even hear his name. "He has ruined me," he said, "he has robbed me, he has killed me! He was my nightmare for two whole years! For whole months in a row I saw him in my dreams! He...he...Oh, never speak to me of him!"

I saw that things were coming along between them, but kept silent as usual. Blanche was the first to announce it to me: this

*At sixes and sevens.

was exactly a week before we parted. "*Il a de la chance,*"* she rattled out to me, "*babouchka* is really sick now and will certainly die. Mr. Astley sent a telegram. You must admit that he is her heir after all. And even if he's not, he won't hinder anything. First, he has his pension, and second, he'll live in the side room and be perfectly happy. I'll be '*madame la générale.*' I'll get into a good circle" (Blanche constantly dreamed of that), "later on I'll become a Russian landowner, *j'aurai un château, des moujiks, et puis j'aurai toujours mon million.*"†

"Well, but if he begins to get jealous, demands . . . God knows what—you understand?"

"Oh, no, *non, non, non!* he won't dare! I've taken measures, don't worry. I've already made him sign several promissory notes in Albert's name. One slip—and he'll be punished at once; but he won't dare!"

"Well, so marry him . . ."

The wedding was quiet and familial, with no great pomp. Among those invited were Albert and a few close acquaintances. Hortense, Cléopatre, and the rest were decidedly excluded. The groom was exceedingly concerned with his position. Blanche herself tied his necktie, pomaded him, and in his tailcoat and white waistcoat he looked *très comme il faut.*

"*Il est pourtant très comme il faut,*"‡ Blanche herself announced to me, coming out of the general's room, as if the idea that the general was *très comme il faut* struck even her. I entered so little into the details, taking part in it all in the capacity of such a lazy spectator, that I've forgotten much that went on. I only remember that Blanche turned out not to be de Cominges at all, just as her mother was not *la veuve* Cominges at all, but du Placet. Why they were both de Cominges up to then, I don't know. But the general remained pleased with that as well, and liked du Placet even more than de Cominges. The morning of the wedding, already fully dressed, he kept pacing the reception

*He's in luck.
†I'll have a mansion, muzhiks [peasants], and besides I'll still have my million.
‡All the same, he's very proper.

room, repeating to himself with an extremely grave and important air: "Mlle Blanche du Placet! Blanche du Placet! Du Placet! Miss Blanca du Placet! . . ." And a certain self-satisfaction shone in his face. In church, at the mayor's, and at home over the hors d'oeuvres, he was not only joyful and content, but even proud. Something happened with the two of them. Blanche also acquired an air of some special dignity.

"I must behave quite differently now," she said to me with extreme seriousness, "*mais vois-tu,* I haven't thought about this one nasty thing: imagine, I still can't learn my new last name: Zagoryansky, Zagoziansky, *madame la générale de Sago-Sago, ces diables des noms russe, enfin madame la générale à quatorze consonnes! Comme c'est agréable, n'est-ce pas?*"*

Finally we parted, and Blanche, that silly Blanche, even became tearful, saying good-bye to me. "*Tu étais bon enfant,*" she said, snuffling. "*Je te croyais bête et tu en avais l'air,*† but it suits you." And, already pressing my hand for the last time, she suddenly exclaimed: "*Attends!*", rushed to her boudoir and a moment later brought me out two thousand-franc banknotes. I would never have believed it! "This may come in handy. You may be a very learned *outchitel,* but you're a very stupid man. I won't give you more than two thousand, because you'll gamble it away in any case. Well, good-bye! *Nous serons toujours bons amis,* and if you win again, be sure to come to me, *et tu seras heureux!*"‡

I still have about five hundred francs left; besides, I have a magnificent watch worth a thousand francs, diamond cuff links and the like, so I may still last a rather long time without worrying about anything. I've purposely lodged myself in this little town in order to pull myself together, but I'm mainly waiting for Mr. Astley. I've learned for certain that he'll be passing through and will stop here for a day on business. I'll

---

*These devilish Russian names, well, then . . . with fourteen consonants! Pleasant, isn't it?

†You've been a good boy . . . I thought you were stupid, and you look it . . .

‡We'll always be good friends . . . and you'll be happy!

find out about everything...and then—then go straight to Homburg. I won't go to Roulettenburg, or not until next year. Indeed, they say it bodes ill to try your luck twice in a row at one and the same table, and Homburg is also where the real gambling is.

CHAPTER XVII

I T's A YEAR AND eight months since I've looked at these notes, and only now, out of anguish and grief, has it occurred to me to divert myself and by chance read through them. So I left off then on the point of going to Homburg. God! with what a—comparatively speaking—light heart I wrote those last lines then! That is, not really with a light heart—but with what self-assurance, with what unshakable hopes! Did I at least have some doubts of myself? And here over a year and a half has gone by, and in my opinion I'm much worse than a beggar! What's a beggar! Spit on beggary! I've simply ruined myself! However, there's hardly anything that compares to it, and there's no point in reading moral lessons to myself! Nothing could be more absurd than moral lessons at such a moment! Oh, self-satisfied people: with what proud self-satisfaction such babblers are ready to utter their pronouncements! If they only knew to what degree I myself understand all the loathsomeness of my present condition, they wouldn't have the heart to teach me. Well, what, what new thing can they say to me that I don't know myself? And is that the point? The point here is that—one turn of the wheel, and everything changes, and these same moralizers will be the first (I'm sure of it) to come with friendly jokes to congratulate me. And they won't all turn away from me as they do now. Spit on them all! What am I now? *Zéro.* What may I be tomorrow? Tomorrow I may rise from the dead and begin to live anew! I may find the man in me before he's lost!

I actually went to Homburg then, but . . . later I was in Roulettenburg again, I was in Spa as well, I was even in Baden, where I went as the valet of the councillor Hintze, a scoundrel and my former master here. Yes, I was also a lackey, for five whole months! That happened right after prison. (I got to prison in Roulettenburg for a debt I incurred here. An unknown person bought me out—who was it? Mr. Astley? Polina? I don't know, but the debt was paid, two hundred thalers in all, and I was released.) Where was I to go? I went to work for this Hintze. He's a young and flighty man, likes to be lazy, and I can speak and write in three languages. I began working for him as some sort of secretary, for thirty guldens a month; but I ended in real lackeydom with him: he didn't have the means to keep a secretary, and he lowered my salary; since I had nowhere to go, I stayed—and thus turned myself into a lackey. I ate little and drank little while with him, and that way I saved seventy guldens in five months. One evening in Baden, I announced to him that I wished to part with him; that same evening I went to play roulette. Oh, how my heart throbbed! No, it wasn't money that was dear to me! My only wish then was that the next day all those Hintzes, all those hotel managers, all those magnificent Baden ladies—that they would all be talking about me, telling my story, astonished at me, praising me, and bowing before my new winnings. That was all childish dreams and concerns, but...who knows, maybe I'd meet Polina, too, and tell her, and she'd see that I was above all these absurd jolts of fate...Oh, it's not money that's dear to me! I'm sure I would have frittered it all away on some Blanche again and driven around Paris for three weeks with my own pair of horses worth sixteen thousand francs. I know for certain that I'm not stingy: I even think I'm a spendthrift—and yet, even so, with what trepidation, with what a sinking heart I listen to the cry of the croupier: *trente-et-un, rouge, impaire et passe,* or *quatre, noir, pair et manque!* With what greed I look at the gaming table, scattered with louis d'or, friedrichs d'or, and thalers, at the stacks of gold, when the croupier's rake breaks it up into piles, burning like fire, or the two-foot stacks of silver lying around the wheel. Already as I approach the gaming room, from two rooms away, the moment I hear the clink of spilling money—I almost go into convulsions.

Oh, that evening when I carried my seventy guldens to the gaming table was also remarkable. I began with ten guldens, and again with *passe.* I have a prejudice for *passe.* I lost. I was left with sixty guldens in silver coins; I pondered—and chose *zéro*. I began staking five guldens a time on *zéro*; at the third stake *zéro* suddenly came up, I nearly died of joy, receiving a hundred and seventy-five guldens; when I won a hundred thousand guldens, I wasn't that glad. I at once put a hundred guldens on *rouge*—it won; all two hundred on *rouge*—it won; all four hundred on *noir*—it won; all eight hundred on *manque*—it won; counting what I'd had before, it came to one thousand seven hundred guldens, and that in less than five minutes! But in such moments you forget all your previous failures! For I had obtained it at the risk of more than life, I had dared to risk and—here I was numbered among the human beings again!

I took a room, locked myself in, and sat till three o'clock counting my money. The next morning I woke up a lackey no more. I decided that same day to leave for Homburg: there I had never served as a lackey or sat in prison. Half an hour before the train, I went to make two stakes, no more, and lost fifteen hundred florins. However, I still moved to Homburg, and it's a month now that I've been here . . .

I live, of course, in constant anxiety, play for the smallest stakes, and am waiting for something, I calculate, I stand for whole days at the gaming table and *watch* the play, I even dream about it, but for all that it seems to me that I've turned to wood, gotten stuck in some mire. I conclude that from the impression of my meeting with Mr. Astley. We hadn't seen each other since that very time, and we met by chance; here's how it was. I was walking in the garden and reckoning that now I was almost out of money, but that I did have fifty guldens—besides, two days before I had paid up fully at the hotel, where I occupied a small room. And so I was left with the possibility of going only once now to play roulette—if I won at least something, I could go on playing; if I lost—I would have to become a lackey again, if I didn't at once find Russians who needed a tutor. Occupied with this thought, I went for my daily walk through the park and through the woods to the neighboring principality. Sometimes I'd spend four hours walking like that and return to Homburg tired and hungry. I had just walked out of the garden into the park, when I suddenly saw Mr. Astley sitting on a bench. He noticed me first and called to me. I sat down beside him. Noticing a certain gravity in him, I at once restrained my gladness; for I had been terribly glad to see him.

"So you're here! I just thought I'd meet you," he said to me. "Don't bother telling me: I know, I know everything; your whole life for the past year and eight months is known to me."

"Hah! see how you keep track of old friends!" I replied. "It's to your credit that you don't forget . . . Wait, though, that gives me an idea—was it you who bought me out of the Roulettenburg prison, where I was sent for a debt of two hundred guldens? Some unknown person bought me out."

"No, oh, no! I didn't buy you out of the Roulettenburg prison, where you were sent for a debt of two hundred guldens, but I knew you had been sent to prison for a debt of two hundred guldens."

"So all the same you know who bought me out."

"Oh, no, I can't say as I know who bought you out."

"Strange; our Russians don't know me, and the Russians here probably wouldn't buy anyone out; it's there in Russia that Orthodox people buy out their own. So I thought it might have been some odd Englishman, out of eccentricity."

Mr. Astley listened to me with some astonishment. It seems he expected to find me crestfallen and crushed.

"However, I'm very glad to see you have completely preserved all your independence of mind and even your gaiety," he said with a rather unpleasant look.

"That is, you're inwardly gnashing your teeth in vexation because I'm not crushed and humiliated," I said, laughing.

He didn't understand at once, but when he did, he smiled.

"I like your observations. I recognize in those words my former intelligent, rapturous, and at the same time cynical friend. Russians alone are able to combine so many opposites in themselves at one and the same time. Actually, man likes seeing his best friend humiliated before him; friendship is mostly based on humiliation; and that is an old truth known to all intelligent people. But in the present case, I assure you, I am sincerely glad that you are not crestfallen. Tell me, do you intend to give up gambling?"

"Oh, devil take it! I'll give it up at once, as soon as . . ."

"As soon as you win? So I thought. Don't finish—I know you said it inadvertently, and therefore spoke the truth . . . Tell me, besides gambling, is there nothing that occupies you?"

"No, nothing . . ."

He began testing me. I knew nothing, I hardly ever looked at the newspapers, and in all that time I had positively not opened a single book.

"You've turned to wood," he observed, "you've not only renounced life, your own interests and society's, your duty as a citizen and a human being, your friends (all the same you did have them), you've not only renounced any goal whatsoever apart from winning, but you've even renounced your memories. I remember you in an ardent and strong moment of your life; but I'm sure you've forgotten all your best impressions then; your dreams, your most essential desires at present don't go beyond *pair* and *impair, rouge, noir,* the twelve middle numbers, and so on, and so forth—I'm sure of it!"

"Enough, Mr. Astley, please, please don't remind me," I cried in vexation, all but in anger. "Know that I've forgotten precisely nothing; but I've driven it all out of my head for a time, even the memories—until I've radically improved my circumstances. Then . . . then you'll see, I'll rise from the dead!"

"You'll still be here ten years from now," he said. "I'll make you a bet that I'll remind you of it, if I live, right here on this bench."

"Well, enough," I interrupted him impatiently, "and to prove to you that I'm not so forgetful of the past, allow me to ask: where is Miss Polina now? If it wasn't you who bought me out, then it must have been her. Since that time I've had no news of her."

"No, oh, no! I don't think she bought you out. She's in Switzerland now, and you will give me great pleasure if you stop asking me about Miss Polina," he said resolutely and even crossly.

"That means she's wounded you badly as well!" I laughed involuntarily.

"Miss Polina is the best being of all beings most worthy of respect, but, I repeat, you will give me great pleasure if you stop asking me about Miss Polina. You never knew her, and I consider her name on your lips an insult to my moral sense."

"So that's how it is! You're wrong, however; and, just think, what else am I to talk to you about except that? That's all our memories consist of. Don't worry, by the way, I don't need any of your innermost secret matters . . . I'm interested only in Miss Polina's external situation, only in her present external circumstances. That can be said in a couple of words."

"If you please, provided that these couple of words will end it all. Miss Polina was ill for a long time; she's ill now, too. For some time she lived with my mother and sister in the north of England. Six months ago her granny—that same crazy woman, you remember—died and left to her personally a fortune of seven thousand pounds. Now Miss Polina is traveling with the family of my sister, who has since married. Her little brother and sister were also provided for by the granny's inheritance and are studying in London. A month ago the general, her stepfather, died of a stroke in Paris. Mlle Blanche treated him well, but managed to transfer everything he got from the granny to her own name . . . that, it seems, is all."

"And des Grieux? Isn't he also traveling in Switzerland?"

"No, des Grieux is not traveling in Switzerland, and I don't know where des Grieux is; besides, I warn you once and for all to avoid such hints and ignoble juxtapositions, otherwise you will certainly have to deal with me."

"What! despite our former friendly relations?"

"Yes, despite our former friendly relations."

"A thousand pardons, Mr. Astley. Excuse me, however: there's nothing offensive or ignoble; I don't blame Miss Polina for anything. Besides that, a Frenchman and a Russian young lady, generally speaking—that is such a juxtaposition, Mr. Astley, as neither you nor I can resolve or understand definitively."

"If you will not mention the name of des Grieux together

with the other name, I would ask you to explain to me what you mean by the expression 'a Frenchman and a Russian young lady.' What sort of 'juxtaposition' is it? Why precisely a Frenchman and a Russian young lady?"

"You see, you've become interested. But this is lengthy stuff, Mr. Astley. Here you have to know a lot beforehand. However, it's an important question—ridiculous as it all is at first sight. A Frenchman, Mr. Astley, is a finished, beautiful form. You, as a Briton, might disagree with that; I, as a Russian, also disagree— well, let's say, out of envy; but our young ladies may be of a different opinion. You may find Racine[21] affected, distorted, and perfumed; you probably wouldn't even bother to read him. I, too, find him affected, distorted, and perfumed, even ridiculous from a certain point of view; but he's charming, Mr. Astley, and, above all—he's a great poet, whether we like it or not. The national form of the Frenchman, that is, the Parisian, began composing itself into a graceful form while we were still bears. The revolution was heir to the nobility. Nowadays even the most banal little Frenchman may have manners, ways, expressions, and even thoughts of a fully graceful form, without partaking in that form either with his own initiative, or with his soul, or with his heart; he has come into it all by inheritance. In himself he may be emptier than the emptiest and lower than the lowest. Well, Mr. Astley, sir, I shall now inform you that there is no being in the world more trustful and candid than a good, clever, and not too affected Russian young lady. A des Grieux, appearing in some sort of role, appearing masked, can win her heart with extraordinary ease; he is of graceful form, Mr. Astley, and the young lady takes this form for his very soul, for the natural form of his soul and heart, and not for clothing that has come to him through inheritance. To your greatest displeasure, I must confess that Englishmen are for the most part angular and graceless, while Russians have a rather keen ability to discern beauty and to fall for it. But to discern the beauty of a soul and the originality of a person—for that one needs incomparably more independence and freedom than our women, especially young ladies, possess—and in any case more experience. And

Miss Polina—forgive me, what's said can't be unsaid—needs a very, very long time to decide that she prefers you to the scoundrel des Grieux. She will appreciate you, will become your friend, will open all her heart to you, but even so in that heart will reign the hateful blackguard, the nasty and petty money-grubber des Grieux. This will even persist, so to speak, out of obstinacy and vanity alone, because the same des Grieux once appeared to her in the aureole of a graceful marquis, a disenchanted liberal, who (supposedly!) ruined himself helping her family and the light-minded general. All these tricks were uncovered afterwards. But never mind that they were uncovered: even so, give her the former des Grieux now—that's what she wants! And the more she hates the present des Grieux, the more she pines for the former one, though the former one existed only in her imagination. Are you in sugar, Mr. Astley?"

"Yes, I'm a partner in the well-known sugar refinery Lowell and Co."

"Well, so you see, Mr. Astley. On one side there's a sugar refiner, on the other—the Apollo Belvedere.[22] All this somehow doesn't hang together. And I'm not even a sugar refiner; I'm simply a petty gambler at roulette, and was even a lackey, which is certainly already known to Miss Polina, because she seems to have good police."

"You're bitter, that's why you talk all this nonsense," Mr. Astley said coolly, having pondered. "Besides, there's no originality in your words."

"I agree! But that's the horror of it, my noble friend, that all these accusations of mine, however outdated, however banal, however farcical—are still true! You and I still never got anywhere!"

"That's vile nonsense... because, because... be it known to you!" Mr. Astley pronounced in a trembling voice and flashing his eyes, "be it known to you, ungrateful and unworthy, petty and unhappy man, that I have come to Homburg especially on her orders, so as to see you, have a long and heartfelt talk with you, and report everything to her—your feelings, thoughts, hopes and... memories!"

"It can't be! Can it be?" I cried, and tears gushed from my eyes. I couldn't hold them back, and that, I believe, for the first time in my life.

"Yes, unhappy man, she loved you, and I can reveal it to you, because you're a lost man! What's more, even if I tell you that she loves you to this day—why, you'll stay here all the same! Yes, you've ruined yourself. You had certain abilities, a lively character, and were not a bad man; you could even have been of use to your country, which has such need of people, but— you'll stay here, and your life is ended. I'm not blaming you. In my view, all Russians are that way, or are inclined to be that way. If it's not roulette, it's something else like it. The exceptions are all too rare. You're not the first to have no understanding of what work is (I'm not speaking of your peasants). Roulette is for the most part a Russian game. So far you've been honest and would sooner go to work as a lackey than steal... but I'm afraid to think what the future may hold. Enough, and farewell! You, of course, need money? Here are ten louis d'or for you, I won't give you more, because you'll gamble it away anyway. Take it, and farewell! Take it!"

"No, Mr. Astley, after all that's been said now..."

"Ta-a-ake it!" he cried. "I'm convinced that you are still a noble person, and I'm giving it to you as a friend can give to a true friend. If I could be certain that you would give up gambling right now, leave Homburg, and go to your own country—I would be ready to give you a thousand pounds immediately to start a new career. But I precisely do not give you a thousand pounds, but give you only ten louis d'or, because whether it's a thousand pounds or ten louis d'or at the present time is perfectly one and the same to you; all the same—you'll gamble it away. Take it, and farewell."

"I'll take it, if you'll allow me to embrace you in farewell."

"Oh, with pleasure!"

We embraced sincerely, and Mr. Astley left.

No, he's wrong! If I was sharp and stupid about Polina and des Grieux, he is sharp and hasty about Russians. I'm not talking about myself. However... however, meanwhile that's all not it.

It's all words, words, words, and we want deeds! The main thing now is Switzerland! Tomorrow—oh, if only I could set out tomorrow! To be born anew, to resurrect. I must prove to them . . . Let Polina know that I can still be a human being. All it takes . . . now it's late, though—but tomorrow . . . Oh, I have a presentiment, and it cannot be otherwise! I have fifteen louis d'or now, and I began once with only fifteen guldens! If you begin cautiously . . . —and can I possibly, can I possibly be such a little child? Can I possibly not understand myself that I'm a lost man? But—why can't I resurrect? Yes! it only takes being calculating and patient at least once in your life and—that's all! It only takes being steadfast at least once, and in an hour I can change my whole destiny! The main thing is character. Only remember what happened to me of this sort seven months ago in Roulettenburg, before I lost definitively. Oh, it was a remarkable case of determination: I lost everything then, everything . . . I walk out of the vauxhall, I look—one last gulden is stirring in my waistcoat pocket: "Ah, so I'll have money for dinner!" I thought, but after going a hundred steps, I changed my mind and went back. I staked that gulden on *manque* (that time it was *manque*), and, truly, there's something peculiar in the feeling when, alone, in a foreign land, far from your own country and your friends, and not knowing what you're going to eat that day, you stake your last gulden, your very, very last! I won, and twenty minutes later left the vauxhall with a hundred and seventy guldens in my pocket. That's a fact, sirs! There's what your last gulden can sometimes mean! And what if I had lost heart then, what if I hadn't dared to venture? . . .

Tomorrow, tomorrow it will all be over!

NOTES

1. Russian civil service ranks are referred to throughout *The Double*. The following is the table of fourteen ranks established by the emperor Peter the Great in 1722:

Chancellor
Actual Privy Councillor
Privy Councillor
Actual State Councillor
State Councillor
Collegiate Councillor
Court Councillor
Collegiate Assessor
Titular Councillor
Collegiate Secretary
Secretary of Naval Constructions
Government Secretary
Provincial Secretary
Collegiate Registrar

The rank of titular councillor was immortalized in Russian literature in the person of Akaky Akakievich Bashmachkin, hero of "The Overcoat," by Nikolai Gogol (1809–52). Dostoevsky's hero is his direct descendant.

2. Silver roubles and paper roubles (banknotes) circulated simultaneously in Russia at that time, the silver rouble being worth more than the paper.

3. Nevsky Prospect is the central thoroughfare of Petersburg; its mysterious qualities are celebrated in a story of the same name by Gogol.

4. See note 1 above.

5. The Gostiniy Dvor was, and still is, a large shopping arcade on Nevsky Prospect.

6. See note 1 above.

7. A reference to the fable "The Crow and the Fox" by I. A. Krylov (1768–1844): "The crow cawed with all her crow's gullet—/The cheese fell…" Krylov, one of the most beloved Russian poets, is a master of the poetic fable in the manner of La Fontaine.

8. See note 1 above.

9. Balshazzar's feast, described in Chapter 5 of the Old Testament book of Daniel, became the prototype of any sumptuous feast. The house of Clicquot (Veuve Clicquot Ponsardin) in Reims, founded in 1772, produces one of the finest champagnes. Eliseevs' and Miliutin's were actual shops on Nevsky Prospect (Eliseevs' is still flourishing). The "fatted calf" is found in Luke 15:23, the parable of the prodigal son: "And bring hither the fatted calf, and kill it; and let us eat, and be merry." For the table of ranks, see note 1 above.

10. Alexander Pushkin (1799–1837) is the greatest of Russian poets.

11. Demosthenes (384–322 B.C.) was an Athenian political leader, whose powerful oratory awakened the Greek national spirit in the conflict with Macedonia.

12. See note 1 above.

13. Anton Antonovich Setochkin will reappear in Dostoevsky's *Notes from Underground* (1864), where he is the anonymous hero's superior in the civil service.

14. Joseph, comte de Villèle (1773–1854), French statesman, was leader of the ultra-royalists under the Restoration (1814–30) and president of the Council of Ministers from 1821 to 1828. The laws passed under his leadership made him extremely unpopular.

15. *The Story of the English Milord George and Frederike Louise, Margravine of Brandenburg, with the Appended Story of the Former Turkish Vizier Marzimiris,* by Matvei Komarov, was first published in 1782; its ninth edition came out in 1839.

16. *Goliadka* is an endearing diminutive of *goliada* (probably cognate with *goliy,* "naked"), meaning a poor man, a beggar.

17. After the disastrous flood of 1824, the citizens of Petersburg were warned of the danger of flooding by the firing of a cannon from the Peter and Paul fortress.

18. See note 7 above. The line "And the coffer had no trick to it" is from the fable "The Coffer."

19. Field Marshal Alexander V. Suvorov (1729–1800), supreme commander of Russian forces under Catherine the Great, fought successfully against the Turks, put down the Polish uprising in 1794, and fought against the French revolutionary army in Italy until his defeat by Marshal Masséna in 1799. He was known for several eccentricities, one of which was crowing like a rooster.

20. Karl Pavlovich Briullov (1799–1852), leader of the Russian Romantic school of painters, finished his most famous painting, *The Last Day of Pompeii*, in Italy in 1833; in 1834 it was brought to Russia and exhibited at the Academy of Fine Arts in Petersburg, where it met with great public admiration and critical acclaim.

21. A line from the eighteenth-century Russian poet A. P. Sumarokov (1717–77) in the prologue "New Laurels," written for a ballet performed on the occasion of Catherine the Great's birthday in 1759.

22. *The Northern Bee* was a reactionary newspaper edited by Faddey Bulgarin (1789–1859) and Nikolai Grech (1787–1867). Bulgarin was also a bad novelist and a police spy who specialized in denouncing literary figures, Pushkin among them.

23. The pen name of O. I. Senkovsky (1800–58), critic and writer, publisher of the collection "Library for Reading."

24. Grigory ("Grishka") Otrepyev, known as "the False Dmitri," was a defrocked monk who claimed the Russian throne by pretending to be the lawful heir, the prince Dmitri, who had been murdered in childhood. He reigned for less than a year.

25. The words about the serpent are a distorted quotation from the opening monologue of the little tragedy *Mozart and Salieri*, by Alexander Pushkin: "Who will say the proud Salieri was ever .../A crushed serpent, still alive,/Impotently biting the sand and dust..."

26. In Petersburg, owing to its northern latitude, the sun sets in mid-afternoon during the winter.

27. *The Adventures of Faublas*, a novel by the French writer and Girondist Louvet de Couvrai (1760–97), was translated into Russian in 1792–6.

28. A reference to Pushkin's comic poem *Count Nulin*, in which the heroine is said to have been "brought up / Not in the customs of our forefathers, / But in a noble girls' boarding school / By some émigrée Falbala."

29. The name Basavriuk (Dostoevsky added the second "s") belongs to the satanic villain in Gogol's first published story, "St. John's Eve."

30. Jean-Jacques Rousseau (1712–78), one of the most influential writers of the French Enlightenment, favored natural settings and emotions.

THE GAMBLER

1. The original Vauxhall was a seventeenth-century pleasure garden in London. The word entered Russian as a common noun meaning an outdoor space for concerts and entertainment, with tearoom, tables, casino, and so on. The first railway line in Russia was the Petersburg–Pavlovsk line, and the first vauxhall was near the Pavlovsk railway station, so near, in fact, that *vokzal* also became the Russian word for "railway station."

2. Until 1870, the Papal States in central Italy were under the sovereignty of the pope of Rome and maintained their own embassies in other capitals.

3. *L'Opinion nationale* was a liberal French newspaper which condemned the policies of tsarist Russia in Poland.

4. The year of Napoleon's invasion of Russia.

5. V. A. Perovsky (1795–1857), general and aide-de-camp, participated in the war against Napoleon in 1812 and was later made military governor of Orenburg.

6. Hoppe and Co. was a well-known banking firm of Amsterdam and London.

7. The rooster became the symbol of France because of the similarity of the Latin words for rooster (*gallus*) and Gaul (*Gallia*).

8. Germany was made up at that time of independent principalities or states, which were finally united only in 1871, after Bismarck's defeat of the French. Dostoevsky probably drew his Roulettenburg from Wiesbaden, a spa he visited several times. Wiesbaden was a few miles from the border of the grand duchy of Hesse-Darmstadt.

9. Polina's real name is evidently Praskovya, in which case Polina is an affectation (though there is a Russian name Polina).

10. Dostoevsky often refers ironically to this pair of words, which come from the prefatory note to *Confessions*, by Jean-Jacques Rousseau (see note 30 to *The Double*): "Here is the only portrait of a man painted exactly from nature and in all its truth that exists and probably ever will exist."

11. The French writer Paul de Kock (1794–1871) was the author of innumerable novels depicting petit bourgeois life, some of them considered risqué.

12. I. A. Balakirev was the court buffoon of the Russian empress Anna Ivanovna (1693–1740).

13. Sophie Armant Blanchard (1778–1819) was the wife of Jean-Pierre Blanchard (1753–1809), one of the first French aeronauts and inventor of the parachute, and took part in his aerostatic travels. She died in a fire on a hot-air balloon.

14. Blanche and Alexei Ivanovich repeat with one slight modification the opening repartee of Don Diègue and Don Roderigue (father and son) in Act 1, Scene 5 of *Le Cid*, by Pierre Corneille (1606–84). The young Dostoevsky had been an avid reader of Corneille, especially of *Le Cid*.

15. Blanche modifies the famous saying, *Après moi le déluge* ("After me the great flood"), attributed both to Louis XV and to his mistress, Mme de Pompadour.

16. The Château des Fleurs was a dance hall near the Champs-Elysées in Paris, which flourished under the reign of Louis Philippe and closed its doors in 1866.

17. The reference is to an anonymous erotic book, *Thérèse-*

philosophe, ou Mémoire pour servir à l'histoire de D. Dirray et de Mlle Erodice la Haye ("Thérèse the Philosopher, or a Memoir Contributing to the History of D. Dirray and Mlle Erodice la Haye"), published in 1748.

18. The Kalmucks, or Kalmiks, are a Mongolian people settled between the Don and the Volga, and also in Siberia.

19. The Bal Mabille was, in 1813, a drinking spot in the fields around the Champs-Elysées, run by a former dancing master named Mabille. It had great success and grew to great proportions under Mabille's sons. The dancer Rigolboche (Marguerite Badel) created the cancan there in 1845. The Bal disappeared in 1875.

20. The Palais Royal was originally the palace of Cardinal Richelieu (1585–1642). Before his death, he willed it to Louis XIII and his direct descendants, and in 1643 the widowed queen, Anne d'Autriche, moved to it from the Louvre with her two sons, Louis XIV and Philippe d'Orléans, aged five and three, thus making it the royal palace. In 1781–4, the central garden was surrounded on three sides by the present four-story structure, with 180 arcades on the ground floor containing some sixty shops, which were rented out to merchants.

21. The tragic poet Jean Racine (1639–99) is considered to have perfectly realized the ideal of French classical tragedy. In an early letter to his brother Mikhail, Dostoevsky passionately defended Racine against the sort of criticism Alexei Ivanovich offers here.

22. The statue of Apollo in the Vatican Museum, a Roman copy of a Greek original, was once considered the model of male sculptural beauty.

ABOUT THE TRANSLATORS

RICHARD PEVEAR has published translations of Alain, Yves Bonnefoy, Alberto Savinio, Pavel Florensky, and Henri Volohonsky, as well as two books of poetry. He has received fellowships or grants for translation from the National Endowment for the Arts, the Ingram Merrill Foundation, the Guggenheim Foundation, the National Endowment for the Humanities, and the French Ministry of Culture.

LARISSA VOLOKHONSKY was born in Leningrad. She has translated works by the prominent Orthodox theologians Alexander Schmemann and John Meyendorff into Russian.

Together, Pevear and Volokhonsky have translated *The Complete Short Novels* by Anton Chekhov, *Dead Souls* and *The Collected Tales* by Nikolai Gogol, and *The Brothers Karamazov*, *Crime and Punishment*, *Notes from Underground*, *Demons*, *The Idiot*, and *The Adolescent* by Fyodor Dostoevsky. They were awarded the PEN Book-of-the-Month Club Translation Prize for their version of *The Brothers Karamazov*, and more recently *Demons* was one of three nominees for the same prize. They are married and live in France, where Pevear teaches at the American University of Paris.